The State

Essays by

Harry Eckstein
George Armstrong Kelly
Douglas Rae
James Fishkin
John Logue
Clark C. Abt
Michael Howard
Hedley Bull
Richard Haass
Annie Kriegel
David E. Apter

The State

Edited by STEPHEN R. GRAUBARD

W · W · NORTON & COMPANY · INC · New York

Library of Congress Cataloging in Publication Data
Main entry under title:

The State.

First published as the fall 1979 issue (v. 108, no. 4) of Daedalus.
1. State, The—Addresses, essays, lectures. I. Graubard, Stephen
Richards.   II. Series: Daedalus; v. 108, no. 4.
JC325.S72 1980   320.1   80-18966
ISBN 0-393-01387-1
ISBN 0-393-95098-0 (pbk.)

W. W. Norton & Company, Inc. 500 Fifth Avenue, New York, N.Y. 10110
W. W. Norton & Company Ltd. 25 New Street Square, London EC4A 3NT

1 2 3 4 5 6 7 8 9 0

Contents

Preface

CERTAIN FIELDS OF STUDY TODAY AROUSE lively curiosity and controversy among scholars, particularly when these subjects engage the interest of those concerned with the making of public policy. Studies in these fields have never been more illuminating than they are at this moment; there has never been a more imaginative use of new documents and data; there has rarely been a more systematic questioning of established opinions. These fields are flourishing as never before.

Yet other areas of inquiry, scarcely less important, lie fallow in our time, never achieving the level or quality of scholarly treatment they deserve. Perhaps this is merely because of a reluctance to treat subjects that are peculiarly sensitive; perhaps it is owing to a more fundamental incapacity to cope with the too great complexities of a specific matter or the inadequacy of the prevailing paradigms to explain certain new phenomena. In any case, the results are always the same — the subject receives substantially less attention than its intrinsic importance would seem to justify.

Occasionally, the reticence is so substantial that one may speak, without hyperbole, of something like a conspiracy of silence; more frequently, there is enough critical analysis for the subject to figure prominently in the scholarly discourse of a period, but one must ask whether the analysis does justice to the subject. In our own day it seems reasonable to ask this question about the state. Whether one subscribes to the commonplace notion that the state is increasingly burdened, required to cope with issues of unprecedented difficulty and complexity, it is legitimate to ask whether these and other conditions affecting the state are being adequately studied; whether this is a time of excitement and creativity for those who study the state; and whether such a sentiment communicates itself to relevant disciplines and across national frontiers.

Would anyone apply to the state a variant of my encomium for contemporary studies in other fields. Can we say that studies of the state have never been more illuminating than they are at this moment, that there has never been a more imaginative use of new documents and data, that there has rarely been a more systematic questioning of established opinions? Who, indeed, would argue that the field is flourishing as never before? If such enthusiasms seem exaggerated and inappropriate, perhaps inconceivable, is it because the study of the state has a long history, that it has traditionally appealed to scholars of the greatest intellectual distinction in many countries, and that it is difficult to pretend to be breaking new ground. All such questions are legitimate, particularly if they increase our understanding of why the state is studied today in the way that it is, why certain problems have receded from view and others have taken their place, and why the study of states is so often nation-bound, indeed parochial.

An examination of the card catalog on state studies at Harvard's Widener Library tells much about what has happened to the field. Certain of the subject categories speak incontestably of early twentieth-century scholarly concerns; others, important in their day, seem scarcely vital in our own. Still others, clearly added, pencilled in, tell something about how the field has changed since a typist, presumably in the 1930s or 1940s, directed the reader's attention also to the library's holdings under such headings as Administrative Law, Aristocracy, Church and State, Citizenship, Constitutional Law, Democracy, Education and State, Federal Government, Imperialism, Industry, Monarchy, Political Science, Public Utilities, Railroads and State, Representative Government and Representation, Republics, Sovereignty. The category Social Contract is scratched out and replaced by Separation of Powers. Then, interspersed, in pencil, are several new categories: Anomie, Communist State, Law and Politics, Legitimacy of Governments, National State, Public Interest, Welfare State. Why these categories and not others? What other country's librarians would produce subheadings like these? Some would certainly figure almost everywhere; others are quintessentially American. They tell us something about what was significant to those who studied the state in our century. They are a convenient starting point for reflection on what our preoccupations in this area have been, how these have changed over time, and what they appear to be today.

Harry Eckstein's essay serves as an admirable introduction, for his concern is to show how and why American political scientists—once so overwhelmingly committed to what he calls formal-legal studies, with their emphasis on constitutional materials and questions—have more recently demonstrated a decided preference for other kinds of issues, using quite different sorts of data. So long as American political scientists believed that politics could be understood best by knowing the formal organization of states—the legal rules that determined how they operated—the institutional study of these sovereign entities seemed all-important. When in the 1920s and 1930s democratic states found themselves on trial, and particularly when certain of the new "democracies" seemed threatened, this was an additional incentive for looking at constitutional mechanisms, for estimating their utility for coping with the kinds of challenges that had become so common. Hence, the enormous interest, for example, in the way the Weimar constitution in Germany was operating. Earlier, however, outside the American professional political science establishment, argument had begun about whether it was enough to look at formal-legal rules, imagining that such institutional forms governed behavior. These early twentieth-century "muckrakers" pressed for the study of political parties, interest groups, and public opinion more generally—realities, they insisted, that merited close investigation.

Similar demands were being made in Europe for many of the same reasons. It was not until the 1950s, however, that American professional political scientists generally acknowledged the need to go beyond the formal-legal boundaries, to study the state in wholly new dimensions. Eckstein tells us that it has taken a generation to "find new bearings," and that the process, while far from completed even now, appears to have induced a "temporary exhaustion." Each of these facts is important and bears reflecting on.

If the earlier formal-legal study enjoyed such a vogue, it was partly because it coincided with the need to provide civic education in an expanding country to a growing population, substantial segments of which were recent immigrants. The emphasis on institutions—on constitutionalism itself—provided that defense of political consensus that was thought to be so necessary. Behind such parochial national concerns, however, lay a more fundamental commitment to what Eckstein calls "the prevalent mechanistic notion of polities and societies." So long as states were viewed as machines, it was reasonable to dwell on how they were constructed and why they worked as they did. Constitutions were thought of as blueprints; they provided useful information that a "political scientist" would wish to have. So long as the modern mass political party was in its first developmental stages and interest groups were generally amorphous, when the world of political bosses, political clubs, and the like was decidedly off-limits to the academic investigator, it was reasonable to turn to the "dignified" parts of the political process, believing that some coincidence existed between what political institutions were intended to be and what they had become. Political phenomena that deviated from the norm were clearly aberrations, in no sense integral to the political process. All such analysis depended on an idealization of the state, a view of sovereignty that accepted the uniqueness of the state as a corporate body in certain basic respects different from all others. The modern state was seen as a rare and remarkable invention, made by men, presumably for their mutual advantage.

When in the 1920s this overwhelming preoccupation with the machinery of states began to wane, when scholars started to look closely at actual political behavior and political competition, other questions began to be asked and quite other kinds of data consulted. The "decay" of formal-legal studies, already apparent earlier, became a virtual rout by the early 1950s, as one paradigm after another sought to take its place. The "distinctive" science was gone; so, also, was the "distinctive" subject. The state had lost something of its uniqueness and also something of its dignity. It was no longer possible, particularly with the creation of numerous new states, to take at face value various kinds of constitutional camouflage and to imagine that a significant relation existed between what was contained in a legal document and what actually happened in practice. The Western state—once universally admired and thought worthy of emulation, intrinsic to civilization itself—was no longer accepted as providing the paradigm that others would wish to adopt. Eckstein says that "memories" were suddenly recognized to be more important than legal documents.

Where, then, are we today in our study of states? We need to acknowledge that we are in fact thrashing about, trying to understand where the formal-legal mode of analysis can still be useful and where alternative modes of analysis are required. Eckstein sees the modern state arising in "the anomic, godless, unnatural world of modernity in the making." In such a world, the "pathetic fiction" of the state was needed; its uniqueness, dignity, and purpose needed to be believed in. Today, Eckstein writes, the need is for something different: ". . . the designing of a workable modern *polis* is probably the most pressing (and widely ignored) task of modern political thought and practice." In a world that lacks all sense of wholeness, where neither God, Empire, nor belief in a natural order provides this, the state is almost the only institution that can provide some sense of purpose. To do this, however, the state must have a distinctive social function. What can that function be? Eckstein argues that the state must become overwhelmingly and overtly concerned with distributive justice, providing the one service that no other modern corporation is capable of giving. In the premodern world where princes ruled, justice, the waging of war, and the providing of security were the principal princely functions. In that age justice presumed a capacity to manage divisive conflicts and to punish deviance. Today, justice remains the principal function of the state, but the obligation is not only juridical; the state, if it is to achieve its high purpose, must be concerned also with social justice. Eckstein regards this as the only "awesome power" that remains to the state, and implies that in a godless, scientific age like our own, a principle for effecting "social justice" is desperately needed. To discover such a "just principle of allocation," and to apply it concretely would justify the claim that a "new" state is in the making.

Such a charge suggests how new is the agenda for the study of the state today, how utterly different it is from any that was thought of as recently as a few decades ago. Wholly new questions are asked; new moral imperatives force new issues to the fore. Even when traditional subjects are treated, they are considered in wholly new ways. Thus, for example, when George Kelly addresses himself to citizenship, and particularly to the problematic nature of citizenship in modern democracies, he starts from the premise that there has been a demise of the concept of the state in the twentieth century even as there has been a vast expansion in the state's concrete powers. Considering why there has been such revulsion against the state, and how the brutalities of two world wars and the barbarous practices of totalitarian states have contributed to this sentiment, Kelly considers also how the growing identification of the state with coercion (with "unfreedom") has contributed, particularly in the United States, to a disenchantment with its powers and its potentialities. American political theory, Kelly argues, found it more congenial to deal with "political systems" or with "groups," emphasizing countervailing political and social forces, than to deal with what so many considered to be a monolithic power, a Leviathan hostile to basic human values. Today, however, there appears to be a new interest in the "theory of the state," reflecting, in Kelly's view, a weariness with what he calls the "trivialities of empiricism" and "a disillusion with the disguised idealism that was supposed to lead beyond the nation-state." For a long time, clearly, given the American scholarly community's sentiments about the state, there was an effort to avoid the subject. Now, for complex reasons, there is a willingness to confront it. This necessarily leads to a new concern with citizenship. For, as Kelly points out, a state achieves legitimacy through its being "confirmed or consented to by its citizens, that is, all who hold rights within it and receive its protection." The question of the state's purpose, then, becomes absolutely central. Shall the state be concerned primarily with "nomocracy," the preservation of the supremacy of law, or ought its purpose to be "telocracy," governmental promotion of so-called social rights and welfare activities? Kelly posits four analytic models, not intended to be mutually exclusive, which express the fundamental features of four different kinds of societies and imply different relations between the state and the citizen. In his "Civil II," which comes close to defining conditions in democratic societies today, access to the political process has been widened, but politics, in Kelly's words, has been "denatured," and is less a vocation than "an overloaded mediating system of demands and satisfactions." The question Kelly asks of this new telocratic order is whether it will create "a more forceful and organized democratic citizenship," or merely "stimulate the powers of bureaucracy and technocracy." Are we, in short, moving toward government by manager and engineer?

The powers of the state have grown enormously, Kelly agrees, but he attributes this growth principally to a public demand for more services and greater protection. If citizens have unwittingly allowed themselves to become the "clients" of a bureaucracy, and if those who constitute that bureaucracy have become the "nonresponsible and sometimes unresponsive" masters of citizens, it is not simply the empirical expansion of the state that has created "the crisis in citizenship." The state, Kelly argues, needs to be rethought in its normative functions. Until there is a new "theory of citizenship," many of our contemporary political dilemmas must persist, for any such theory presumes first a "theory of the state." Political scientists in an earlier period—almost literally, just the day before yesterday—were mistaken to abandon such normative concerns and to dwell wholly on the specific and presumably real mechanisms that caused the state to function as it did. If the "rational-legal" method of inquiry is capable of answering only a limited number of questions about the state, so the empirical mode—with its emphasis on parties, pressure groups, public opinion, and the like—is similarly limited. Kelly, like Eckstein, asks for a quick return to a more fundamental kind of inquiry.

If the first two essays in this volume suggest how the state has been studied in the past and why certain modes of inquiry have been greatly favored over others, particularly in the United States, Douglas Rae's contribution makes us aware of certain new kinds of dilemmas that are created today by the "ostentatiously egalitarian" ambitions of the modern state, with its obvious interest in supporting social justice. If it is no longer common to think, in Tocqueville's terms, of whether liberty will in fact survive equality, it is imperative to think of how one form of equality is set up in opposition to another, and by what principles one can be favored over another. Rae sees the egalitarian state as trying to "neutralize the stratifying effects of nature and culture," making up for the fact that individuals as we actually find them are not equal. The questions, in a time like ours, are how to promote equality, what strategies are useful for such a purpose, and where the state can successfully intervene to compensate for the inequalities of wealth, health, income, bargaining power, dignity, or self-esteem that are generated by all the activities not controlled by the state. If the state's obligation is to "provide a remedy for the losers," how can such an obligation be met? The recent history of state intervention to achieve large egalitarian purposes demonstrates the difficulties of achieving such ends and of not losing certain equalities, even as one proceeds to secure others. Fundamental policy issues are involved, and they touch the most disparate kinds of demands. What principle should guide policy-making? Shall the effort be made to treat all individuals in precisely the same way, so that there is no possibility of envy or recrimination? Is identical treatment a viable solution? Or, ought different people to be treated differently, if they are in fact to be treated equally? Rae considers all the bureaucratic and other complexities of each of these strategies, and suggests that in the end the government most often settles on a middle course that accomplishes neither of the intended equalities fully. The principle of equal opportunity, for example, implies the existence of rules of competition that are utterly impersonal; it does not suggest, however, that all will win, that all will go to the top. If the rules of impartiality suggest that the state give special support to the children of yesterday's losers, this does not mean that all who are given such opportunity will end up in the same place, with the same success. There will be new winners and new losers; in short, new inequalities will result from the state's interventions, and the problem of "equality versus equality" will remain a permanent one. The state will always be vulnerable to criticism in the name of equality; however, it can also always justify itself in the same name. The debate that has been opened in the name of equality is a debate *sine die*.

Given the conditions and tendencies documented in the first three essays in this volume, it is scarcely surprising that there has been an immense resurgence of interest in political philosophy. James Fishkin writes about how this interest has manifested itself in the English-speaking world. Again, he is over-whelmingly concerned with what has happened in the United States, and with how the public traumas of the 1960s contributed to the creation of a new interest in moral principles and public policy. Reflecting on three types of ethical criteria that are now commonly favored by those concerned with public policy, Fishkin believes all fail a very simple test; in his words, "they are unacceptable because they support policies that impose severe deprivations when an alternative policy would have imposed no severe deprivations whatsoever." In short, "they will all support policies that destroy the most essential interests of some portion of the population when an alternative policy would not have had comparable effects on anyone." Grouping certain celebrated contemporary ethical theories under three large rubrics, principles that he defines as *procedural, structural,* and *absolute-rights,* Fishkin shows that none will by itself satisfy his criteria for resolving complex issues in the area of public policy. Fishkin, like Rae, is concerned with nothing less than thinking through how conflicting claims can in fact be adjudicated, how moral principles can be adduced that will serve to make defensible the public policies that are enacted. How, in short, can we construct moral principles that will justify and influence policy decisions?

All such thinking takes for granted that if the modern state's primary concern is social justice, this concern cannot express itself simply in the moral categories of the nineteenth century. More, it implies that new criteria are needed to judge the efficiency of the state, to estimate whether it is accomplishing the egalitarian purposes it purports to support. Critical commentary on the performance of the modern state—the welfare state—starts generally with some analysis of what the state has attempted to do, the resources it has been able to command, and the results achieved. John Logue, looking at the experience of recent years, particularly in the Scandinavian countries—often thought to be the most advanced and venturesome in these matters—starts by analyzing the "revolutionary" measures of forty years ago, now almost universally accepted, that helped so substantially to reduce poverty and sustain the disadvantaged. As Logue explains, the purpose of the welfare state was not so much to redistribute income within the market system, as "to reduce the degree of inequality between those in and those outside the labor market," and to do this in such a way as to even out income over a lifetime. The welfare state, Logue says, "abolished want," but it did little to diminish class differences with respect to consumption. The ideas for welfare policies came less from the triumph of any particular ideology than from the tempestuous political struggles that extended over decades in many countries, and that involved all the political parties in various kinds of compromise. The contribution of the Social Democratic labor movement to this process needs particularly to be acknowledged, but for welfare policies to triumph, it was essential not only for society to be transformed, but for the Social Democrats to be changed as well.

In recent years, criticism of all these policies has become common. Logue considers the various charges leveled against the welfare state and asks whether it may not today be more a victim of its successes than its failures. If it has indeed "succeeded in banishing the specter of material deprivation through illness, loss of employment, disability, and old age," why has the memory of earlier conditions faded? Are the "heroic struggles" of yesterday to achieve greater social equality simply the struggles of the past? Is the present, with its high taxes, oppressive bureaucracy, and general administrative and political complexity the inevitable but unfortunate aftermath of a time that now, by comparison, seems almost legendary? Or, ought one to recognize that the welfare state is in fact doing today what it was always intended to do, guaranteeing security? Is this not a proper (and sufficient) purpose?

The welfare state has contributed, in the United States and elsewhere, to the creation of new research enterprises that plan, monitor, evaluate, and record what the state is doing, and what success it is having in its several major social welfare efforts. Clark Abt, who writes about these vast research enterprises, recognizes that the welfare function alone does not account for these proliferating studies, but from his essay, it is apparent that welfare issues are prominent among the subjects about which the government wants to be better informed. Because such research is commissioned by various parts of the bureaucracy, and because the information thus acquired is not always shared—and for other reasons as well—the findings are not generally incorporated into large new theories of social and economic change. Instead, vast repositories of vital data are accumulated, and the question of whether or not they are ever used tells as much about bureaucracy itself, politics in the larger sense, as it does about the special problems that attach to applied social scientific research undertaken for a client that is the state, or, more generally, a specific governmental department, agency, or bureau. If, as Abt suggests, the quality of government policy research has improved markedly in recent years, this does not mean that the information is available when it is most needed, or even that it is much used when it comes finally to be published and circulated. Since some of the principal clients for such applied research are legislators themselves, the question of timing can be crucial. The legislator whose public responsibility requires that he "know the costs, benefits, and impacts of a proposed program (or a proposed change in a program or policy) *before* voting on it" realizes from long experience that "instant" research is impossible and that the commitment of funds for specific study is often little more than testimony of his concern. Yet, the research continues to be done, and Abt shows how, in particular instances, it has increased governmental and public understanding of a specific issue. The American example, he believes, is already having its influence abroad; states have access to information today of a kind that was almost unthinkable a generation ago. Technological change—by making the information-gathering even easier—will almost certainly increase the amount of applied research undertaken. The task is to put this mass of information to use to improve social decision-making.

Any reader of this first part of the volume cannot fail to recognize how many distinctly American preoccupations have contributed to its contents. The selection of other (or additional) authors would have substantially altered the discussion, taking us into wholly other intellectual and political realms. No one can pretend, for example, that these themes exhaust the range of analytic possibilities or that they do not indicate a tendency to favor certain subjects over others. Other themes might have been introduced, some with a distinctly American flavor; decision-making theory is an obvious example. Or, a more substantial effort might have been made to demonstrate American indebtedness to European scholarship; the growing Marxist concern with the state, for example, might well have figured. The introduction of any number of such subjects would have done little, however, to contradict the implications of Eckstein's argument that American political science is again today seized of certain subjects, that certain modes of analysis seem reasonable and right while others appear outmoded or old-fashioned, and that certain paradigms command attention and others do not. For better or worse, there appears to be no universal science of the study of the state, and it is probably pointless to search for one.

This same argument is relevant to the study of relations between states. Again, one is not arguing that all analysis of international relations is nation-bound, reflecting in some simple and mechanical way the parochial prejudices of a particular society at a particular moment. Still, when Stanley Hoffmann argued that international relations was an American social science, he was saying that the discipline was "born and raised in America," and that without America there would have been no birth at all. He worried that the discipline was "too close to the fire," and asked for a triple distancing: ". . . it should move away from the contemporary, toward the past; from the perspective of a superpower (and a highly conservative one), toward that of the weak and the revolutionary—away from the impossible quest for stability; from the glide into policy science, back to the steep ascent toward the peaks which the questions raised by traditional political philosophy represent."[1] It is impossible to suggest that all (or any) of Hoffmann's recommendations have been wholly realized in this issue, but his suggestions have greatly preoccupied those who have planned it.

In the study of international relations it is impossible to ignore or under-estimate the contributions made by American scholars. The terms of the de-bate, for many who choose to engage in it, generally have been set by Americans. Still, it ought to be possible to involve others who have not simply succumbed to American arguments and who, even when they argue in ways congenial to prevailing American intellectual and political norms, may be ex-pressing views that are significantly different. It is scarcely an accident that many who have written for this part of the volume approach the problems of international relations from the perspective of Europe. A volume with contribu-tions also from Africa, Asia, and Latin America might have come even closer to achieving the distancing that is so vital for anyone wishing to interpret relations between states today.

Because so much of this first part is concerned with questions of the state and social justice, it is appropriate that Michael Howard remind us of the con-tinuing saliency of issues that relate to the state and the conduct of war. The European state system, as it developed in the seventeenth and eighteenth cen-turies, was intimately linked both to its capacity to make war and to provide defense against aggression. When Enlightenment *philosophes* sought to explain war as a policy pursued by princes and the traditional ruling classes to advance their own interests, it was thought that war would end when the people achieved power. Nationalism, in fact, led not to the abolition of war but to its intensification. War became "popular," a phenomenon of the people. Nations were forged through war, and by the end of the nineteenth century, Howard says, most nations of Western European countries were "psychologically at-tuned to war." World War I, with its fevered apotheosis of the nation-state and of war itself, was followed by a time of profound disillusionment. In Great Britain, particularly, "King and Country" seemed suddenly an almost obscene reference, and many among the young adopted causes that denied altogether the primacy of the nation-state. All this came to an end, however, with the Euro-pean war that erupted in 1939, and that came to involve both the Soviet Union and the United States in 1941. As Howard explains, "both British Liberals and Russian Marxists reverted to nationalism of a highly traditional type." The Sec-ond World War, like the First, became a "Great Patriotic War," waged princi-pally to preserve or restore threatened nation-states.

The reactions after 1945, however, were quite different from those that had followed 1918. Because Great Britain, for example, suffered no terrible blood-letting in the Second World War, certainly none comparable to what it had experienced in the First, it had no sacrifices of its own to dwell on; instead, there was considerable interest in the sufferings experienced by others. The moral problems created by strategic bombing, and, even more, the American use of the atom bomb, came to command the attention of many Britons. In the United States, Howard writes, this reaction came somewhat later and was associated with the revelations of what certain U.S. government agencies had been doing for a quarter of a century. Howard writes: "For an entire generation the CIA be-came a symbol of pure evil almost as powerful as the H-Bomb had been for young left-wing Britons a decade earlier." A defense effort that depends on nuclear weapons systems and clandestine operations cannot involve the people in the way that an earlier technology, associated with a quite different ideology, had succeeded in doing. Inevitably, the task of legitimating the state, of justifiying and explaining its actions, becomes incomparably more difficult. Howard explains succinctly what the consequences of these developments have been; he writes: "The result . . . is that the State *apparat* is likely to become isolated from the rest of the body politic, a severed head conducting its intercourse with other severed heads according to its own laws. War, in short, has once more been *denationalized*. It has become, as it was in the eighteenth century, an affair of *states* and no longer of *peoples*. The identification of the community with the State, brought to its highest point in the era of two World Wars, can no longer be assumed as natural or, militarily speaking, necessary. No Third World War is likely to be fought by armies embodying the manpower of the Nation while the rest of the population work to keep them armed and fed."

Howard sees immense significance in the revulsion that so many in the United States and elsewhere felt over Vietnam; it was not a revulsion simply with the specific methods used in the war, but also with "the clandestine activities, the domestic deception, and the oblique morality that the government of the United States believed were justified by that war and the circumstances that surrounded it." It became increasingly difficult to justify what the state had done; inevitably, there was a palpable decline in esteem for the state and for its military and intelligence forces. Howard writes: "Patriotism in Western democracies once more is seen as the last refuge of scoundrels or, at best, as a symptom of the emotional disorders of the Radical Right."

The disintegration of belief in the nation-state, at least in the West, has, however, not generated a new feeling of esteem for communities of greater international dimensions. Nor should the decline be thought universal. Belief in the state remains immensely potent in the Third World, where it is credited with having emancipated whole peoples and with giving new dignity and purpose to their collective lives. Also, in Marxist societies, the state, far from withering away, has steadily acquired new powers as an agency of social control. What has happened in certain parts of the West, then, is in fact highly atypical, and there is little reason to believe that the situation is permanent, that it may not one day soon be dramatically reversed. If we are unlikely to witness anything like the "enthusiasms" of 1914, at least in most democratic societies, the skepticism that is now so common is in no way guaranteed a long life. The international system today, composed of such disparate states, shows characteristics that cannot fail to be significant for the maintenance of peace. Howard reminds us that "wars have arisen at least as often from the disintegration of decadent States as from the aggression of strong ones." He forbears, however, to define decadence.

Hedley Bull, concerned with a related though by no means identical issue involving world order and international stability, recognizes that many of his professional colleagues view the state as an impediment to peace and security and believe it is imperative to get beyond the nation-state. Bull argues that such attacks on the state are misconceived, not least because the state is here to stay; reports of its imminent demise, he implies, are greatly exaggerated. Also, while international organizations and bodies have proliferated wildly, sometimes greatly extending their authority, they generally have not done so at the expense of the state, whose own role has also been growing dramatically. If states are more numerous and more heterogeneous today, and if there has been a "certain debasing of the currency of statehood as a consequence of the growth of mini-states and microstates," it is also true that for the first time in history the state is the common political form for all mankind. The various separatist and national-ist attacks on the state—so frequently advertised as calculated to bring about the disintegration of states—are themselves frequently conceived as strategies for achieving statehood, for making national boundaries and state boundaries coincide.

When, Bull argues, the state is charged with fomenting war, tolerating eco-nomic injustice, mismanaging the environment, and committing other heinous offenses, it is forgotten that these conditions existed before the advent of the state system, and that the present political structure of the world cannot alone be reasonably charged with producing such conditions. The idea that the aboli-tion of the state would bring about the abolition of war, Bull writes, is based on a verbal confusion; for him, the "causes of war lie ultimately in the existence of weapons and armed forces and the will of political groups to use them rather than accept defeat." While he will not say that some form of international organ-ization could not serve to reduce the hazards of war, he believes that it is unrea-sonable to posit against the existing state system a utopian world political order that will operate perfectly.

The role of states in preserving order locally has far too frequently been ignored. Indeed, too little attention has been given to how states, cooperating with one another, have maintained peace internationally and have created what Bull calls the rudiments of an international society. Such facts notwithstanding, some in the West are impatient with what they conceive to be an obsolete nation-state system. Of these, Bull writes: "It is . . . notable that the prescriptions they put forward for restructuring the world, high-minded though they are, derive wholly from the liberal, social-democratic, and internationalist traditions of the West, and take no account of the values entertained in other parts of the world, with which compromises may have to be reached." Agreeing with How-ard, Bull reminds us that the Soviet Union and the other Socialist states do not seem conspicuously concerned with getting beyond the state; on the contrary, their assumption is that the state is in fact the great benefactor. Bull writes: "For the Soviet Union and other Socialist countries the state is not an obstacle to peace but the bulwark of security against the imperialist aggressors; not an ob-stacle to economic justice but the instrument of proletarian dictatorship that has brought such justice about; not a barrier to the solution of environmental prob-lems, for these exist only in capitalist countries." As for Third World attitudes, Bull writes quite simply: "Among the Third World countries the idea that we must all now bend our efforts to get 'beyond the state' is so alien to recent experience as to be almost unintelligible."

In the end, Bull argues, those in the West who disparage the state and refuse to acknowledge its use or necessity, imagine that if states were abolished, our way of doing things would prevail. In an almost primordial sense we go on imagining that our traditions are superior and that they must win out. Bull warns against so sanguine a view. It is not simply the growth of Soviet and Third World power that preoccupies him. Rather, he reminds us that the revolts of this century have not been only against Western power and privilege, but that they have seriously questioned Western values and institutions; those revolts continue. It we are becoming more sensitive to the seriousness of these challenges, then our thinking needs to be directed more deliberately to the search for a *modus vivendi:* to accommodate state systems that are obviously different, that are informed by quite different values, and with which we will necessarily have to co-exist. Such purposes cannot be achieved by imagining that states can be wished away.

Richard Haass, in addressing himself to many of these same questions, shows a wish to distance himself from certain of the principal protagonists, if only to comment on the arguments of all. Haass recognizes the importance of the controversy and sees that it is not simply an argument between those who believe that state power must remain the chief element in the study of international relations and those who prefer to emphasize the role of transnational and international organizations, both public and private. Rather, it is an argument between those who believe that state power is today being belittled, ignored, or branded as immoral, and those who believe that the new international political and economic organizations, so different from any that existed before World War II, are still insufficiently known and that their vital role in the international system is still greatly underestimated.

Haass considers how the development of a new nuclear weapons technology has altered relations between states, and why today, with certain new technological advances, the balance of terror is becoming increasingly delicate. He considers also why the superpower rivalry in certain areas has become somewhat muted even as it has become more intense in certain peripheral areas. The disintegration of alliances necessarily interests him, not least in requiring him to consider whether such developments in fact increase the prospects for peace. Is force being used in new ways, justified by wholly new arguments and rationales, and involving, inevitably, a great many more players?

Concerned with how the growth of nationalism has affected the authority of the state, Haass concludes that such forces, and also others—the human rights movements and various religious sects and parties—have probably had more influence on state authority than any that has come from supranational organizations, whether in Turtle Bay, the Hague, or Brussels. As for multinational corporations, the subject of endless speculation, Haass, without in any way seeking to deny or diminish their influence, insists that there has been "a clear trend toward increased regulation and restriction of multinational corporations by home and host countries alike." MNCs are being increasingly regulated by states, and this, as much as anything else, suggests that states retain the upper hand. So, also, with the international monetary system. If individual states cannot control or regulate it, this is not because other organizations can or do. Haass remains persuaded that if states do not control markets, state policies remain absolutely crucial for explaining their behavior.

Recognizing that certain contemporary theories dealing with problems of international relations provide a valuable corrective in causing us to withdraw from a too exclusive concern with state action—particularly in the military sphere—and that they have served also to make us more conscious of other actors and forces, Haass asks, however, whether the revisionists do not themselves require revision. Have they not greatly exaggerated the role of nonstate actors and underestimated the power of the state to accommodate itself, not least to challenges to its authority?

If Haass concludes his essay with the thought that states have never been stronger, that their "vigor and bite" have never been greater, Annie Kriegel, writing about the Soviet Union, advances an even more heretical proposition: it makes little sense to talk about states in the Soviet context. She insists on the stability of the Communist system, at least in the short-run, and attributes this largely to Lenin's creation, the Communist party. In the Communist world, she writes, the Party absorbs the state, reducing it to a bureaucracy, "a necessary by-product, a valueless residue." Having, in effect, devoured the state, the Party "turns against the masses, against the civil society, serving as the instrument of repression." The Party becomes the only locus of meaningful action. Not only is the state displaced, but civil society itself is reduced to a shadow of its former self.

Yet, there is substantial resistance to any such interpretation of the genesis and evolution of communism and of what it implies for the future. Indeed, there is a persistent belief in the possibilities of communism reforming itself, becoming more liberal, open, and democratic in the process. Asking whether it is still possible to believe "that for the past quarter of a century the Soviet peoples have been on a civilian Long March toward the double goal of abundance and liberty," Kriegel says that such a belief today implies an unwillingness to see that the idea itself is a Party conception, intended to deceive. So long as the Soviet system is seen simply as different from our own, different only in degree but not in kind, there is no possibility of understanding it. Writing with great bluntness, Kriegel says: "The Soviet system is exceptionally balanced because it does not try to settle questions that fall outside its sphere of competence or jurisdiction—for instance, the welfare of the people or the respect for values such as dignity, justice, and freedom. Its equilibrium is based on the principle that it never stray from its one appointed task—to maximize the chances of attaining what it was conceived for, power on the global scale."

The idea that the Soviet Union is committed to change—that it wants to change itself—is in fact the opposite of the truth. Kriegel believes that the Soviet system "is happy to perfect the tried-and-true methods and techniques that aim precisely to permit it *not to change*—in other words, not to lose time and energy, or better yet, not to run the risks that any transformation implies." The whole Western preoccupation with the "new," with the "never-seen-before" is foreign to the Soviet world. The Soviet system seeks stability and "aims only at identical reproduction in all areas save that of power." The Party regulates the system, the state being the administrative arm of the Party. Society, kept as unstructured as possible, is the place from which the Party recruits its cadres, those who will bear the heavy responsibilities (and risks) of office and reap whatever moral and material advantages the society can provide those who are privileged. In such a society, the concept of opposition is meaningless. Kriegel explains why dissidence is totally different from opposition, and why our loose use of language serves only to confuse.

If the Party is at the center of the Soviet system, and if its concern is power, foreign policy, together with its material foundation, military policy, is necessarily the chief concern of the Party. In Kriegel's view the Soviet system is "implacably bent on external conquest, and that by the most classic of methods—force." Insisting that a "quest for expansion" ought not to be confused with a "quest for adventure," Kriegel sees the Soviets as generally acting prudently and indirectly, merely taking advantage of opportunities that present themselves. The Brezhnev record in this regard is not without some distinction.

If Annie Kriegel has provided a forceful and original analysis of why Soviet society has developed as it has, and how the state has fared under the direction of the Party, David Apter, with no less concern for the historical record, is interested in how the democratic state has fared in confronting terrorism and terrorists. Seeking to establish a typology that will distinguish between various kinds of terrorism, and considering the "dialectic" of the terrorists process, Apter's chief concern is to show how the success of terrorism depends on the simultaneous existence of several major crises. If the state is able to survive terrorist attacks, this is generally less a comment on its own power than on the weakness of terrorism as a political method.

Looking at those who become terrorists, and considering also their intellectual forebears, Apter shows how the cell is intended to operate and how the terrorists' violent and clandestine acts are meant "to separate society from state and to redeem the former by destroying the latter." Symbolism is extremely important. As Apter says: "It is not individuals, who might indeed be quite likable fellows, who are destroyed, but roles—father, king, philosopher, scientist—all those who are part of an institutionalized network that controls, dominates, organizes, and mediates." The primary target, however, is the state, which is seen as the rational center of modern life and inevitably hostile to the kinds of creation and redemption that terrorists favor. The cell, Apter explains, uses "military labels to emphasize *class* war against a generalized middle class, and to radicalize the young to prevent their joining its ranks or becoming part of a technocratic elite."

If terrorism is "the use of illegal violence to gain political ends," violent tactics alone do not make an individual a terrorist. Only when the purpose is to discredit the state, and the aim is to make people lose faith in the possibility of democratic solutions, showing panic before the terrorists' ingenuity, can one speak of a terrorism that seems to be succeeding. Distinguishing between terrorism of the Left and of the Right, Apter insists that neither succeeds except where the state appears powerless and incapable of coping, where all crises are made to appear elements of a single massive disorder that cannot be resolved by rational means, and where all sorts of mythic possibilities advanced by terrorists begin to seem both plausible and just. It is the impotence of government, the withdrawal of people from society, the growth of incivility, and the retreat into a senseless self-protective privacy that gives terrorism its chance. The study of terrorism is meaningful only in relation to the modern state, with its very particular ambitions and vulnerabilities.

The modern state is one of man's more conspicuous recent inventions; whether it honors his ingenuity or mocks his purported creativity is only one of many issues on which there is substantial disagreement today. It matters greatly whether the state is seen as an excrescence on society or whether it is viewed as one of the few institutions capable of providing coherence and direction to individuals increasingly beset by problems associated with anomie and despair. It matters also whether the state is viewed as a machine, with changeable parts, responding to an energy source based on information flowing from a single center, or whether the machine metaphor, even in modern dress, is thought to be hopelessly outmoded. How the state relates to society, what protections and authority it is willing to grant to other corporations, how much it concerns itself with distributive justice and defense—and how it defines both—are all matters of great consequence.

Societies will differ, in part, at least, because of the ways in which the state chooses to deal with such matters. Whether disagreements are resolved through public debate—if, in fact, in a world of growing expertise such debate has much meaning any longer—or whether agreements reflect principally the bargains struck by bureaucrats, pressure groups, and other such bodies is obviously significant. It is easy to make elisions and to imagine that all states fundamentally resemble each other; it is just as easy to insist that they are all different. Both views are almost certainly mistaken. Yet, the creation of a useful typology of states—making valid distinctions based on something other than passion or sentiment—appears to be an almost insuperable task.

What, then, are valid criteria for distinguishing between states? A willingness to tolerate and indeed encourage dissent? An understanding that deprivation cannot be defined simply in social or economic terms? A preoccupation with the moral and intellectual qualities of leaders? A control of bureaucrats by agencies that derive their authority from some sort of popular consent? The persistence of the rule of law? Or, are all these simply nineteenth-century liberal shibboleths, still valid for a few isolated islands in the vast modern sea that is the new international community of states, but otherwise of no great moment?

The essays in this volume first appeared as an issue of *Daedalus*. Thanks are due to the Andrew W. Mellon Foundation for making the volume possible. We have been encouraged by their support to raise certain fundamental and important questions about the modern state and the ways in which it is studied, but also about the directions in which it may be tending.

S.R.G

REFERENCES
[1] Stanley Hoffmann, "An American Social Science: International Relations," *Daedalus*, Summer 1977, pp. 41–60.

HARRY ECKSTEIN

On the "Science" of the State

MODES OF STUDY TELL US about subjects of study. They do so directly, in a way that is obvious, and indirectly, in a way that is not. Here I am concerned with what a special mode of political study can tell us about a special subject of study in the second sense. Before specifics, then, some brief general remarks on the inobvious mode-subject relationship. Because they are abstract and abbreviated, these remarks may well puzzle, but the specific arguments that follow should clarify them.

Three general points should be grasped. First, conceptions of how to make sense of a subject almost always express explicit or implicit *preconceptions* of the quintessential nature of the subject. In political study there appears to be only one exception: rational-choice theory, as regarded by those who consider the premises of such theory largely arbitrary, yet capable by some mysterious process of yielding good theories and explanations.[1] Second, these preconceptions inevitably derive from how subjects appear to inquirers when the preconceptions are formulated. And third, how subjects appear to inquirers has much to do with what they actually are when the notions of proper modes of study come into being—though what they then are may disguise rather than expose their nature: an appearance may be only an ephemeral product of peculiar conditions.

It follows that the fate of a mode of inquiry can tell us whether the "appearance" of a subject in fact accurately represented it. If it did not, we should ask whether we should not discard the preconception as historic aberration, or else, what special, if restricted, role to assign to the concrete phenomena to which a mode of study directs attention. If the latter question is properly answered, it will tell us when generally inconsequential phenomena may be important, and thus about their nature as special cases, including their special role in historical processes and present reality.

In this essay I want to relate these abstract points to some reflections about States. The argument being rather circuitous, I will outline my agenda: (1) The mode of political study to be discussed is "formal-legal" study. (2) I consider this mode of study to be the distinctive "science" of the State: literal *Staatswissenschaft*, not to be confused with "political" science.[2] (3) As a general mode of political inquiry, formal-legal study has such manifest flaws that its very existence (let alone long dominance) must reflect highly peculiar conditions.

(4) Since formal-legal study is highly inadequate as a way of making sense of polities, and yet is the distinctive science of the State, prevalent conceptions of what States are all about also are impugned. States are not polities, but a type of polity arising under odd circumstances. (5) Though most people who see the shortcomings of formal-legal study now tend virtually to ignore its special subject matter, and though I see nothing to be said for it as a basis of political inquiry, there are special conditions under which the formal-legal aspects of political life loom large. Dismissing these aspects because they may have import only in odd cases stultifies understanding. (6) When we know about the special conditions that justify stressing what the "science of the State" emphasized, we can make important inferences about the State: what States are as special types of polities; how the confusion between the species (State) and genus (polities) arose; and, most important, what we can learn about both historical and contemporary States from the status of the "science" attached to their study.

Formal-Legal Study as the Science of the State

THE NATURE OF FORMAL-LEGAL STUDY

Since formal-legal study was, over a long period, a sort of consensual paradigm of academic political study — the normal empirical science of the field — and since it still is widely practiced, a description of the mode of inquiry will cover much ground familiar to political scientists. But formal-legal study is our subject, so we should be explicit about what it is. Perhaps even initiates can learn from an exercise in elucidating its nature. For one thing, formal-legal study, in some respects, is deceptively simple; it entails both straightforward and peculiar suppositions. For another, formal-legalists, unlike their recent challengers, are almost entirely silent about all of their suppositions, which leads to missing questions that may have illuminating answers. Such silence also suggests a particularly close relationship between subject and manner of inquiry. And when elucidated, that formal-legal study was long paradigmatic in political science should immediately become exceedingly puzzling.[3]

Formal-legal inquiry involves two emphases. One is on the study of public law: hence the term *legal*. The other involves the study of formal governmental organizations: hence *formal*. These emphases coalesce, of course, in the study of public laws that concern formal governmental organizations — in the study of "constitutional" structure. This includes not just written constitutions but their equivalents: anything that explicitly prescribes rules for processes and organizations of authority. The most common equivalents are codified usages, like Sir Thomas Erskine May's mammoth codification of the usages of the House of Commons,[4] long used by the Speaker, Clerks, and Members as a sort parliamentary constitution. Others are statutes that prescribe structure and procedures for administrative departments, agencies and general civil services; bylaws of legislative and executive committees; and, of course, where constitutional courts operate, judicial interpretations of such materials.

No formal-legalist has ever followed this emphasis exclusively. No one in his senses would. But formal-legalists do attach extraordinary importance to constitutional and quasi-constitutional materials. They operate on the tacit premise that politics can be understood best by knowing the formal organization of States, as the term State came gradually to be understood after the Peace of Westphalia: the organizations that exercise sovereignty in societies.

Formal-legalists are, explicitly, less concerned with what people do in government than with the nature of the legal rules that govern their functioning, and therefore devote much effort to elucidating what the roles mean. That often involves delving into history, into original intentions. Such studies tend to have a highly descriptive cast, and one of the sages of contemporary political science, David Truman, in fact refers to them as "institutional description."[5] But, of course, formal-legalists "theorize," using constitutional rules as basic independent variables.[6]

For the most part, formal-legal theorizing is of the conventional causal variety. An example (among very many) is Ferdinand Hermens's *Democracy or Anarchy?*[7]—an impassioned attack on proportional representation (PR) as an electoral system that fragments and radicalizes party systems and leads ultimately to the demise of representative government. Electoral laws naturally play a large role in the formal-legal literature on democracy; and since representative governments govern as well as represent, the constitutional definition of executive-legislative relations is a second major theoretical theme for formal-legalists.[8] The most salient *explanandum* of their work is, as for Hermens, the functioning and fate of democracies, for manifest reasons the most conspicuous puzzle in politics during the interwar period and immediately after World War II. Many other matters, though, also are causally related to formal-legal rules, even if not as often: for instance, policy, participation (e.g., voting turnout), and the distribution of influence (e.g., among types of interest groups). Formal-legalism thus is a general "theoretical framework."

In some cases, like that of Hermens's attack on PR, the theorizing based on the framework is bold. More typically for political scientists, it is hedged and loose, as in Duverger's discussion of the effects of electoral laws on party systems. Here, natural, or preexisting, propensities are simply reinforced or mitigated by the rules.[9] A more highly modified form of apparently formal-legal theorizing proceeds from the premise that political actors adapt their behavior to procedural rules to maximize their political values, especially their power.[10] That mode of theorizing, however, is better considered a genre of rational-choice theory in politics, particularly since it usually is also held that political actors manipulate formal-legal rules themselves to their advantage.[11]

Much of the theorizing of formal-legalists is not causal in a familiar way, however. It is of an odd kind; either the theoretical relation involved is an exotic, though readily grasped, species of causality, or it is *sui generis*. Whichever, the relationship is critical in formal-legal study—and, incidentally, what gives it a descriptive appearance when something not at all descriptive is going on. Let us call the relationship *prescriptive*. It occurs very frequently, though more in games than in natural behavior.

Two variables are related prescriptively if one is an explicit rule (a directive) and the other a pattern of behavior that occurs as a consequence of the rule. Examples are legion. Rules ordain that motorists drive on the right side of the road; the pattern of driving on the right is thus explained. Similarly, that bishops in chess move on the diagonals is best explained by a prescriptive relation between a "rule" and a "regularity." Most formal-legal work seems merely descriptive because, in general, formal-legalists assume so close a correspondence between rules and regularities that the statement of rules is treated as tantamount to the explanation of behavior. Obviously, this seriously begs questions, and it is central to any appraisal of the formal-legal mode of political study, as we shall see.

BASES OF FORMAL-LEGAL STUDY

The simplest, most basic reason for considering formal-legalism the distinctive science of the State is that formal-legal study, with its complementary baggage of political history and "theory," played the dominant role in political inquiry when, late in the nineteenth century, it became a distinctive academic field—at the outset, chiefly in the United States.[12] Crick has amply documented the pervasive juridical cast of early American political science—the overwhelming role of expositions of the Constitution and its historic basis in "patriotic writings."[13] He has also shown that the political and the State were, early on, considered virtually synonymous. One of the field's aboriginal Greats (if that is the word), Woolsey of Yale, entitled his summa of the new discipline *Political Science, or The State Theoretically and Practically Considered* (1878); his work is for us a queer mix of natural law (theory) and constitutional structure (practice). Woodrow Wilson, too, calls his major work *The State* (1895); it is an equally odd mix of formal rules and, instead of natural law, history treated as evolution—that is, primitive political life, as then misconceived, followed by a large, quick jump to the State as the polity of civilized peoples.

The formal-legal content of works in political science (political philosophy aside) long remained dominant until the early 1950s—though, as a subtheme, a different kind of political study began developing in and after the period of muckraking, initially outside of departmental political science (e.g., Bentley), then, later, through the influence of psychology (for instance, Lippmann) and, most of all, in Merriam's Chicago "school" of the late twenties and thirties.[14] Novel subjects appear in the texts: parties, interest groups, public opinion. But even in the major late syntheses of the (empirical) field by Friedrich and Finer,[15] constitutional matter remains the core; other subjects are penumbras of formal-legal ones.[16] Political science meant state-science, which meant formal-legalism, mitigated by "history" and moral disquisitions. This state of affairs came under major attack only in the fifties.[17]

It has since taken a generation to find new bearings for the study of the political, and the process is anything but finished (although it seems to have induced a temporary exhaustion). Anyone who understands what formal-legal study is, and who also has some feel for the phenomena of political influence and power or for the role of accustomed norms or socioeconomic conditions in conditioning political behavior and functioning, will be puzzled by the persistent paradigmatic status of the formal-legal. How can one explain it? Crick's magisterial, and for the most part incisive, review of American political science treats this phenomenon as somehow peculiar to the American study of politics and thus searches for an explanation also peculiar to the United States. His argument is that formal-legal study was a product of political consensus (because consensus obviates political philosophy), plus the need to provide civic education in an expanding country and to the growing, largely alien citizenry.[18] The argument has both empirical and logical force. The United States no doubt was a country without grave disputes. The teaching of the Constitution and its patriotic bases no doubt also is well-suited to civics—much more so than close analyses of distributions of power or political attitudes, or the consequences of socioeconomic conditions for political life.

Nevertheless, Crick has, at most, only a tangential part of the explanation. For one thing, American political scientists also led the way in undermining formal-legalism. For another, there just is nothing peculiarly American about formal-legal inquiry—except that political science is historically an American field. Formal-legal studies are just as dominant in the political studies of Crick's own country and those of others, especially again in "departmental" studies.[19] Crick's explanation must obviously be augmented.

Formal-legal study seems to be the product of an extraordinary confluence of forces, two of which particularly deserve mention before getting to my thesis proper. One was the prevalent mechanistic notion of polities and societies. In the nineteenth century one talked increasingly about the machinery of politics, not, organismically, about bodies politic, or indeed about constitutions in the earlier sense of the body's general condition. If one thinks of polities as machines, one will almost inevitably stress their structural arrangements over their histories and environments, for machines function as they do chiefly because of how they are constructed. They have no memories (except in the electronic sense, which is a metaphor) and can function independently of their environments, while organisms depend continuously on extrinsic "inputs." The mechanist, moreover, is likely to equate actual structures and designs, and constitutions, of course, are blueprints of a sort.

A second force has to do with traits of political competition, with the world of power and influence, during the period when the departmental study of politics came into being. Structures of political competition had a low degree of organization during that period. The modern mass party with its large popular membership—far less evanescent than the factional, cliquish associations of notables that preceded it, and far more accessible to study—was barely in process of formation. Interest groups were even more amorphous. And the world of bosses, political clubs, and salons was hardly open to academic investigators. One must remember in this connection that early empiricism was of the primitive positivist variety that Dickens lampooned in Mister Gradgrind. For people who wanted only Facts, Facts, Facts, and who wanted them indubitable, constitutional rules were attractive, and the amorphous, ephemeral, largely hidden facts of political competition, repulsive. Political competition in an age of still quite limited participation and minimal government also was not especially consequential: the early political scientist still lived in the world, if a decaying one, of the Palliser novels, with its almost senseless jockeying for prestigious positions. Politics was not yet Easton's world of the general "allocation of values," but rather that of place-hunting. Had more attention been paid to political competition even in that narrow world, the poverty of formal-legalism would surely have been evident, at least for making sense of conflicts, and thus, probably, for making sense of anything political.

For my purposes here, however, I want particularly to stress another, no doubt more fundamental set of (related) points. The argument on which these points converge is this: formal-legal study does not just have an affinity to what States were thought to be like (machines). It has an even closer relation to the conception of the quintessential nature of the State, gradually developed during and after the seventeenth century and dominant in the nineteenth. And that conception, like any persistent and largely unquestioned myth, or idealization, was rooted in the actual nature of early modern polities, or at any rate in aspects of them that were bound to appear especially conspicuous.[20]

The first, most basic point to note was stated earlier: States were (and are) thought of quintessentially as structures exercising sovereignty in societies. The notion of sovereignty entails many subtleties and difficulties that have been meat and drink to modern political philosophers: whether it may be divided, where it should reside, how it should be constrained, whether it may be defied. In regard to meanings, though, sovereignty is a simple, though historically odd, notion.[21] It has two ingredients. (1) It implies the power to make laws: calculated directives binding on members of society at pain of severe sanctions (hence, the connection of the term with justifiable coercion). (2) It refers to the ultimacy of that power in two senses: other social entities are inferior and subject to the sovereign entity (hence, the notion of the State as having a monopoly of justifiable coercion). And sovereign structures are not subordinated to others.

This conceptual, hence idealized, notion of sovereignty reflects historical realities—early on, emergent realities, the end and essence of which were grasped by some political philosophers. "Legislation," though not wholly unprecedented, is certainly a modern notion—at any rate, if represented as an act of will and not palmed off as reaffirmed usage or, in the guise of equity, as a kind of mislaid, uncorrupted usage. In premodern times, also, we find virtually everywhere a bewildering overlapping of princely, economic, ecclesiastic, and educational functions in a maze of quasi-autonomous corporations (churches, monasteries, cities, guilds, universities, merchant companies, manors), all engaged in a constant struggle for autonomy and dominance, that through ineffectuality produced a tenuous symbiosis—better, what Holt and Turner have called a lack of resolution. From that uneasy, complex, disordered world, particularly spurred by the acute disorders of the age of the Reformation, an ordering device gradually emerged: the great prince, the successful entrepreneur in coercive power and the dispensing of justice—that is to say, sovereign authority. (No wonder, then, that the divisibility of sovereignty became so muchdiscussed an issue.)

Even before opponents of people who used to be called pluralists[22] made the matter explicit, a widespread sense of the uniqueness of the sovereign structures existed, indeed, had to exist if the State as a principle of order was to embody at once custom and God. We need not debate this matter. The point here is simply that the sense of uniqueness that surrounded the State when the science of the political became an academic field quite naturally led to striving for a distinctive mode of study. (That, of course, would also help to legitimate an upstart specialty.) And what about the State is distinctive and special if not, by the late nineteenth century, constitutional structure?

The notion of uniqueness surely played a role in making constitutional materials central in the new field. At least as important, though, is that the idea of sovereignty (deliberately?) separated the structures of the States from those of society. It exalted the State both as abstraction and as concrete fact. The separation of State and society surely engendered a tendency to "endogenous" explanation: the explanation of the political by itself. This meant, and could only mean, the explanation of political regularities by political rules.

Here another historical process becomes critical: the modern development of "formalized" organization, especially in the political realm, paralleling that of sovereignty.[23] Social organizations are formal to the extent that they function, at least in principle, under explicitly prescribed rules; they are informal to the extent that they are networks that function through shared norms or inexplicit expectations of behavior. (These, of course, are always mixed in some degree.)[24]

The modern growth of formal organizations was perhaps first noted by Saint-Simon, who considered it a product of modern science.[25] It is also stressed, derisively, by Comte[26]—derisively, because Comte regarded formal organization as a substitute for, and inferior to, spontaneous (or natural) structure. But these are mere intimations. An elaborate treatment of formal organizations does not occur until Weber's analysis of bureaucracies. He equates their early precursors with the "nuclei" of modern States and deems them dependent on clear-cut hierarchy and an impersonal principle of rule; and he considers states as necessarily based on fully developed bureaucracies.[27]

The formalization of government is, of course, most apparent in the appearance of constitutions, as we now conventionally use the term. An early, but historically isolated, exemplar is Cromwell's Instrument of Government—a historical early birth, like Louis XIV's notion of his position. Explicit constitutionalism—basing government on calculated blueprints—begins with the American Constitution and accelerates in the nineteenth century. (Earlier so-called constitutional documents were not blueprints of rule but affirmations of usage or contracts between princely and other corporations.) Weber's special concern with bureaucracy, however, is very much to the point, since formalization, though most conspicuous in constitution-making, occurred even more in the devising of formal-legal rules to regulate governmental departments, civil services, judiciaries, and local governments. In Britain, where the shift to "modern" rule was less abrupt than elsewhere, the year 1782 somehow keeps turning up as the starting point of the process.[28] Along with Weber, I hazard the opinion that the princely corporation—government—led the way in the historic process of formalization (the history of which unfortunately has not been written). Nowadays we have a lesser or vanished sense of the State's uniqueness, in part because we find varieties of constitutional structure in all sorts of social entities. The bureaucratized voluntary association, and the constitutionally governed union or political party, however, are later phenomena than bureaucratized governments (bureaucratized universities later still). The State seems to be the historic model for the resolution and "ruleful" conduct of authoritative relations of virtually all kinds in the modern world.[29]

Why this modern, obviously (in historic terms) exotic process of formalization? The literature teems with offhand propositions or, as in Weber, essentially typological remarks that do not explain at all: namely, that bureaucracy is rational-legal. Initially, as noted, formalization was considered an intrinsic product of modern science, perhaps because it involves calculation. Political writers uniformly stress curbing traditional privilege and modern power, not least the power latent in the conception of sovereignty, though this may well have been more effect than cause. One can also relate constitution-making to mechanistic notions of societies and polities. All of these explanations no doubt contain kernels of truth.

The most powerful explanations, though, often also are the most obvious and the most often overlooked. The most obvious reason for basing any complex social entity on formal-legal rules surely is that it cannot be based on anything else (unless it be sheer force). This is also true for radically new organizations. Something unprecedented can hardly be based on convention, even disguised convention. The sheer novelty of the modern State, no less than the State's functional requirements discussed by Weber, thus helps explain governmental formalization.[30] Keir intimates just that when he points out that, in Britain, the formalization of governmental structures first occurred in new departments and only much later in the more "ancient" structures.[31]

To complete the argument, it remains to add two points. The most manifest necessary cause of formal-legal study is that there be a good many formal-legal rules to study. By the time political study became a specialty, that was the case. But phenomena are not studied only because they exist; after all, there is much more formal-legal structure now than there was in the nineteenth century, and the formal-legal mode of study is in decline. The rules obviously must seem critically important. In the nineteenth century that was also the case. Here, once more, we can find sufficient reasons in mechanistic thinking. Formalization may have been compelled by a lack of pertinent conventions, but it was also, and increasingly, regarded as a condition of efficiency. Certainly that was the outlook of the mechanicians of the State. And surely that outlook helps to explain the peculiar emphases of the "scientists" of the State.

What was stated abstractly at the outset should now begin to make sense: modes of political study reflect preconceptions of the quintessential nature of subjects of study, and these are, and must be, rooted in conspicuous traits of the subject when the preconceptions are formed. That, in essence, is why formal-legal study may be considered the distinctive "science" of the State.

The near-forgotten Willoughby of Johns Hopkins, one of the Greats of early departmental political study whose philosophical disquisition on the State was once widely read and cited, epitomizes that science.[32] At the very outset of his major work he tells us that Government (sic) is the "machinery" of the State, the concrete manifestation of the *Staatsidee*, which is overarching, sovereign authority (pp. 8-17) as a sort of Platonic form. We are also told that a community becomes a (concrete) State through "political machinery" staffed "by a corps of officials" and run on the basis of a "body of rules . . . determining the manner of its exercise" (p. 4). Further, the study of the State involves, in order, the descriptive study of its "organization," the history of its "forms," the "principles" of administration, and the philosophical analysis of the concepts involved in the other divisions of the field (pp. 4-5). Later (pp. 187 ff.) Willoughby asserts, rather dizzyingly, that from the ruins of the Roman Empire to modern times no "civic life" was to be found in Europe; the *Staatsidee* existed only in its eternal latent form. These notions are backed up by references to rather more perceptive, more unconventional writers (Maine, Bluntschli, and Jellinek),[33] and just as most of Western history is erased in a sentence, so are Aristotle, Machiavelli, and Montesquieu, as pertinent only to the craft of politics, not the science ("philosophy") of the State (p. 7).

The Proper Role of the Formal-Legal in Political Inquiry

We can trace the decay of formal-legalism to the 1920s. Decay starts in early studies of political competition and political behavior, as structures of competition became more crystallized (and formalized), as the outcomes of competition became more consequential, and as the process of "civic incorporation" led to unexpected behavior by new citizens. A sort of counterscience started to develop through men like Wallas, Lippmann, Merriam, and Lasswell, though much of their work was long dismissed as merely nasty antidemocratic theory. The fate of that perfectly engineered constitutional machinery, the Weimar Republic, the product of all, long accumulated *Staatslehre*, also played a major role in the process of decay—though formal-legalists in the main rationalized the Weimar experience away as the product, after all, of misguided constitutional engineering.[34]

Incipient decay became precipitous decline only in the fifties. It is then that the search starts for a new paradigmatic framework of inquiry, a process that has by now disintegrated the field, as theoretical approach after approach has been propounded (group theory, functionalism, political-culture theory, and so on). In that process, what once was central and fundamental has virtually vanished from our studies.[35] The formal machinery of the State has become increasingly a sort of "black box," with only inputs and outputs being analyzed.

This, no less than the earlier dominance of formal-legalism, calls for an appraisal of formal-legal study to complement description and our discussion of its origins. By appraisal, too, we can learn about the modern State from the fate and status of its distinctive science, just as one may explain the science via its subject.

THE GENERAL SIGNIFICANCE OF FORMAL-LEGAL RULES

Undoubtedly, there are reasons for not ignoring formal-legal rules altogether. Let me outline them briefly, though with comments that impugn granting any basic paradigmatic status to formal-legal matter:

1. Formal-legal rules exist and thus must be included in *full* descriptions and explanations of polities. But too much exists, and resources of study are not infinite; thus we can only study what is important, not everything that exists. That compels choice, which implies priorities and judgments of significance.
2. Even if formal-legal rules are not highly significant in themselves, they may indicate more significant matters: for instance, the political norms of societies (which some now consider their "real" constitutions) or elites. But using forms as indicators of norms is never easy; there may be better indicators; and, of course, we may be able to get at norms directly.

3. Formal rules may certainly constrain or weaken tendencies to act in certain ways by denying these tendencies a legal base. But that only tells us something about what does not occur (e.g., the absence of certain extremist groups as electoral parties in present German politics, due to provisions of the Basic Law) rather than explaining what does. It implies, in fact, that formal rules in politics perform a proscriptive rather than prescriptive function. Negative explanations do tell us something but not much, and rarely what we want to know. Beyond this—as, for instance, argued by Duverger (Ref. 9)—rules may affect (a word only too suitable for weaseling) tendencies that have other sources. But that again makes them secondary factors, required only for absolute fullness of explanation.

All this implies only that there is no absolute reason not to study formal-legal political rules, but also none for assigning them any special emphasis.

The case to the contrary is much stronger. The most evident flaw of formal-legal study as a general mode of inquiry obviously is that it is highly time-bound and culture-bound. It perhaps made sense when the attention of political scientists was largely confined to the modern West, but that is no longer so and no longer possible. We can hardly now take seriously the formal-legal documents copied from old colonial powers by new "states." More important, we can no longer arrogantly assume that the modern Western State is intrinsic to civilization and the inevitable destiny of all societies, dismissing other polities as somehow "prepolitical" or, à la Willoughby, not "civic."

Even for the modern West the use of constitutional rules as explanatory variables has yielded uniformly bad results. The acid test is to be found in the effects of electoral laws on other matters. Nothing about constitutional structure has been more studied. As a study proceeds, explanations ought to become more specific, precise, and trustworthy. In this case, however, the opposite has occurred. The simple certainties of Hermens have given way to the waffling of Duverger, to the almost unfathomable complexities of Unkelbach,[36] and, at last, to Douglas Rae's argument (grounded on wide evidence) that electoral laws strongly affect electoral outcomes—e.g., in the way parliamentary seats are distributed (who could doubt it?)—but have only very weak effects on "distal" variables, precisely those that are central in Hermens.[37]

This failure in theorizing about the effects of electoral laws belongs to a larger and foreseeable failure: the weakness of formal-legal explanations of political competition, from party competition to the study of elites. Structures of political competition have become quite formalized in recent times, but the divergence of form from practice has only thereby become more apparent. Similarly, the imitation of Western constitutions in non-Western societies has cast doubt on mechanistic conceptions of polities by making unmistakable the greater roles of cultural "memories" as against legal paper and the intimate connections between polities and social environments (or the lack of environments that can sustain polities of the Western kind).

Perhaps most damaging to formal-legalism is the dubiousness of the distinctive "prescriptive" relationship between rules and regularities, which is in a way the crux of formal-legal thought. To be sure, rules and regularities often do coincide: drivers by and large, drive on the prescribed side of the road; bishops move along diagonals; Australians, who are legally compelled to vote, almost all vote. But rules and regularities may differ. Rules without regularities are legion—consider discrimination by race or sex in the United States, or the vanishing of the legal power of dissolution in the Third Republic. So are regularities without rules. No rule, for instance, prescribes that chess players must try to control the center of the board; yet they usually do try. The whole question of how rules affect regularities is fraught with complexity. A mode of study that at its very core presupposes otherwise lacks credibility, *prima facie*.

The decline of formal-legalism, especially as political competition and the non-Western world became increasingly salient, thus is no puzzle. The mystery is that the decline took so long, and even now is incomplete.

THE SPECIAL SIGNIFICANCE OF FORMAL-LEGAL RULES

Although not much of this will be news to academics in political science, it does make largely implicit matters explicit. And it sets the stage for a more novel question, highly important in a world of formalized organizations and to my knowledge not yet raised by anyone: Are there specifiable circumstances under which formal-legal rules tend to have particular significance, special explanatory power? This is a matter for special theorizing, not one of thinking about a general focus for a whole field of study. The problem being novel, I can only grope here toward a solution. A credible solution of the problem should not only have intrinsic interest, but also implications for how one thinks about the State, or, at any rate, about the close connection between modern States and the emphasis on formal rules in thought and practice.

FORMS AND NORMS One answer might be that forms will significantly govern behavior if they largely coincide with social norms. The "real" constitution, culture, will provide weight to any formal constitution. This seems clearly to be the case in Norway, where constitutional materials, public and private, express a sort of national culture of authority. Constitutions, in this unusual case seem to have less to do with law-making than with the primitive practice of "law-speaking."[38] The essentially normative status of the formal-legal emerges dramatically in Thomas Mathiesen's work on Norwegian prisoners, *The Defense of the Weak;*[39] the lawbreaker's chief defense against dubious treatment is, of all things, appealing to legal rules—and the defense seems to work well because it evokes *moral* guilt.

This initial solution, however, gets us nowhere at all. To know whether forms express norms we must know the norms. And if it is really norms that matter, and we know them to begin with, why bother about forms? This point seems incontrovertible. Yet, however vacuous, the point can get us closer to an informative solution. It can do so because there might be circumstances under which one can assume, with some degree of certainty, that forms *will* correspond to norms—for example, in societies where a strongly positive valuation of formal-legal rules as such exists.

THE "NORMATIVENESS OF FORMS" Let us call this condition the "normativeness of forms," the inverse of the formalization of norms as in Norway. Under what special circumstances is that condition likely to arise? I will suggest two hypotheses, which are not discrete but derive from a higher-order hypothesis of very great importance.

The first hypothesis is that forms will be accorded a special normative status where there is wide, genuine valuation of an integrated polity, but a culturally fragmented society, so that there can be no organic relationship between society and polity. Switzerland, with its ethnic (religious, linguistic) and economic cleavages, still explosive in the last century, seems the prototypical case-in-point. In such a case only forms can do what typically is left to norms. And forms may function well as centripetal social forces to the extent that circumstances (such as international forces) compel solidarity, and, even more, through gradual inculcation by civic education—Crick's point about the American melting pot.

The second hypothesis is that the normativeness of forms will occur in what Spiro has called legalistic cultures.[40] His example of such a culture is contemporary Germany. He only illustrates the conception, so we must define it. A society is legalistic if it exhibits a "culture-theme" that codified law has some peculiar, transcendent, in the old sense "sovereign" (superior, "excellent") quality, a quality mostly familiar to us in religion. A culture-theme (a notion widely held among anthropologists, especially Mead and her associates)[41] is some highly general attitude under which many particular attitudes may be subsumed: for instance, the valuation of achievement in the United States. Culture-themes make coherent specific "culture-items," and in a rudimentary sense explain them.

There are many reasons why legalism, as defined, may be considered such a theme of German culture: the notion of legalism does relate much diverse behavior in Germany. Spiro points out, for example, that the pocket edition of the civil law code, compiled rather late, toward the end of the nineteenth century, is a major bestseller in Germany (as law codes also are in some other Continental countries). It can be bought at kiosks, and its contents seem extraordinarily well known to the ordinary public, even by Continental standards; for instance, the German euphemism for homosexuality is "seventeenth of May," because paragraph 175 of the criminal code covers that subject.[42] German political debates tend to invoke law (natural, divine, constitutional), where elsewhere justice or practical prudence would be at issue; somehow German policy-makers seem to care deeply about whether proposed law is "legal." In addition, the incidence of litigation is astonishing: the lawsuit apparently is the modal German means of conflict resolution. Politicians, says Spiro, will sue over remarks that in the Commons might only be considered funny and unparliamentary. Private litigation occurs at a startling rate and requires an extraordinary number of judges practicing numerous judicial specialties. In Hamburg alone there are about five hundred judges.[43] The law codes prescribe in extraordinary detail, leaving little to judgment. Spiro cites an outlandish example:

> Book Three, Law of Goods
> Section III, Property
> Title 3, Property in Mobile Goods
> V. Appropriation

#961

If a swarm of bees departs, then it becomes ownerless, unless the owner pursues it forthwith, or when the owner gives up the pursuit.

#962

The owner of the bee swarm may, in his pursuit, enter the property of others. If the swarm has moved into another unoccupied beehive, then the owner of the swarm may, for the purpose of its capture, open the hive and take out or break out the combs. He must restore the resulting damage.

#963

If the escaped swarms of bees of several owners unite, then those owners who have pursued their swarms become co-owners of the captured united swarm; the shares are determined according to the number of pursued swarms.

#964

If a swarm of bees has moved into another occupied beehive, then property and other rights to the bees, by which the hive was occupied, extend to the swarm newly moved in. Property and other rights to the swarm newly moved in expire.

(American beekeepers observe exactly the same rules; but no one has codified them, and they are not applied through public law.)

Not least, there is a general tendency to provide explicit statutory justifications for the most ordinary regulating of public behavior: the German authorities tell people on public signs why they may not *legally* park on seeded shoulders; the British simply put up signs telling people a shoulder is seeded — not even an American "Keep Off" — assuming they will know how to behave. And, unlike other Continentals, Germans on the whole observe legal prescriptions punctiliously, sometimes ludicrously so. In Germany a STOP sign really means stop — not necessarily look; it does not mean "be very careful," nor, as I think is the case in Italy and Spain, that one is about to encounter a challenge to one's courage. Much more might be added to illustrate the motif. But enough said. There can be no doubt that a "theme" of legalism does exist in Germany.

The second hypothesis about the normativeness of forms, of course, also requires prior knowledge of a culture. It thus only takes us a step closer to the critical question we must answer to solve our problem: Under what conditions is a culture likely to be legalistic? The usual solution is to attribute legalism to the influence of Roman Law. That legal tradition may explain the use of highly detailed codes of law, but surely it does not explain most other aspects of the pattern. In many ways it is not common-law countries like Britain or America that are the antithesis to the German case, but countries influenced by Roman law, like France and Italy. This indicates that the normativeness of forms, thus legalism, remains a puzzle.

FORMS AS SURROGATES FOR NORMS To solve the puzzle, there is a third hypothesis that can relate the first and second. Forms are likely to be accorded special normative (legalistic) status if a society has experienced a deep, comprehensive breakdown of conventional order, so that a condition of normlessness (anomie) is common. That is, *forms matter to the extent they are needed as surrogates for norms in the conduct of social life* —a condition that may also exist if societies are divided by deep cultural cleavages.

The rationale for this hypothesis, the "master hypothesis" of my argument, involves five steps, each by itself an independent testable subhypothesis:

1. Human interactions do not work unless governed by rules of some sort that people mutually observe. This is not likely to be doubted, but skeptics can easily check the matter out by playing a game without rules or by ignoring the rules of traffic. To reinforce the point, individuals seem to need "rulefulness" in their lives no less than do institutions; see Durkheim on anomie and the enormous subsequent literature on the pains of normlessness.[44]

2. Most of the rules needed to regulate social interaction are simply norms: notions of propriety in one's own and others' conduct, internalized through normal learning.

3. Some individual and social experiences are highly "disorienting;" they make norms doubtful or inappropriate or both. And societies may undergo processes of disorientating change that make it inadvisable, if not in extreme cases impossible, to rely on shared norms to regulate social conduct.

4. We can in such cases conceive of three surrogates for normative regulation. One is power, or coercive will: the typical postrevolutionary surrogate. The second is contract: the negotiation of a mutually acceptable relation (from which so-called constitutional documents of medieval times mostly derive). The third is explicit law, procedural and substantive.

5. The choice among these optional surrogates is not accidental but determined by two factors. One is what sociologists call conduciveness: whether a culture, even in disruption, contains elements that favor one solution over the others. The second is experience: whether some initial choice of a norm-surrogate has proved too costly or ineffectual. In this regard, one may suppose that the legal option is generally superior: "cheaper" in its effects than unregulated coercive force and more dependable than negotiated bargains. Thus, even in the absence of cultural conduciveness, but still more in its presence, legal forms are the quintessential surrogates for internalized norms.

Surely, this explanation of the normativeness of forms makes sense of the contemporary German case and makes that case anything but ludicrous. First, since unification, Germany has undergone shockwave upon shockwave of disorientating experiences: rapid industrialization; losing the First World War and much of a male generation; rapid democratization; the nightmarish Great Inflation; deep economic depression; Nazism, which set out, only too effectively, to smash what remained of traditional German society and then annihilated itself; the occupation; the great migration of refugees from East Germany; the Durkheimian effects of the *Wirtschaftswunder*. It is hard to conceive of more relentless, more continuous, deeper, or wider social disruption, and thus of a more widely suffered or deeper normlessness.[45] Second, German culture was undoubtedly "conducive" to the legal remedy for that condition. This conduciveness may be attributed in part to Germany's Roman Law tradition. Perhaps still more important is the peculiar, later German notion of the *Rechtsstaat*, which treats concrete law as a kind of emanation of Ideal Law (much as the *Staatsidee* treated the concrete State) and which is not to be confused with the notion of government *under* law. In part, contemporary legalism was already firmly rooted in earlier German culture, for normlessness is not a new condition in Germany, except in its degree. Third, the tendency toward legalism probably was strongly reinforced by the German lapse into the costly power solution under Nazism; and Nazism itself was surely, in part, a response to the ineffectuality of negotiation and compromise among a myriad of "interests" (often nominal parties) that marked social regulation in the Weimar period, and for which the German term was, not inappropriately, *Kuhhandel*. "Cattle-dealing" goes on in any polity and society, but as a supplement to normative regulation, not in its stead.

Concluding Reflections on the State

At this point, recall the agenda of this essay as sketched at the beginning. I have discussed the nature of formal-legal political study, including some of its inobvious premises, and analyzed both the reasons for its origins as a paradigmatic mode of academic study and for its strangely persistent dominance in political science. On the basis of the points thus made, I justified calling formal-legal studies the science of the State. I then showed that the formal-legal mode of study (no surprise now) is profoundly flawed as a general mode of political inquiry, so that by implication the conception of the subject of such inquiry must also be askew. The issue that seems to arise most urgently concerns the role that may be properly assigned to formal-legal rules in systematic political inquiry. The answer to that problem turned up a general view of the role of calculated legal rules in social life and the (provisional) finding that legal rules should be considered surrogates for social norms, required to the extent that social orders are disintegrated, so that one cannot rely on "spontaneous" normative regulation.

It remains to deal with one more question to finish the agenda. What can these points tell us, inferentially, about the subject of formal-legal inquiry: the State? The arguments I have made, I think, imply a lot—though I must underline the tentativeness of what follows, the question itself being novel.

THE HISTORIC STATE

We saw rather striking historic parallels between early modern conceptions of the State, the actual development of something akin to the awesome idea of sovereign authority, and the process of formalization of the processes and institutions of concrete sovereignty. Now, if formalization is a functional response to normlessness (however much, once it is widespread, it may itself become an ingrained way of doing things), something important surely follows for the concrete modern State, as well as for the Idea of the State, as propagated largely in hazy Germanic metaphysics.

The philosophers of the *Staatsidee* made of the State, as we saw, something in essence supernatural, even godly: an eternal Principle that lay dormant in the "uncivic" life of the West for a millenium and a half. But if my arguments about

the conditions of formalization are correct, this is sheer idolatry and a profoundly mistaken view; the opposite, surely, is more correct. The State was a
functional response to the general disruption of once integral society. It does
have a connection with science, but less with its spirit of calculation than with
its subversion of conventional beliefs. It reflects also the corrosion of development: the growth of modern commerce and industry, above all its effects on the
sociopolitical stratification of "estates"; and in the same vein it reflects the effects
of novel democratization. The general process was prolonged, except in egre-
gious cases like the German. By the late eighteenth century, though, and certainly in the nineteenth, the society of convention had disintegrated. In place of
accustomed norms and princely powers that still were integral in social life,
came pseudotheological, pseudorational metaphysics and the Idea of the sovereign State as the higher principle of society "liberated" from convention. The
notion was philosophical and vested with eternality; the fact was functional and
therapeutic and simply a special phase of history. The sense of uniqueness and
separateness engendered by the State reflects the disintegration and disjunction
of social life and the attendant loss of a sense of divine or natural order. In the
anomic, godless, unnatural world of modernity in the making, the State was
necessary, and its Idea a needed, if somewhat pathetic, fiction.

What is universal is the polity, as a special aspect of society, but connected
with, not elevated above, the rest of social life. The *polis* is its prototype. It
appears in feudalities, principalities, guilds, companies, colleges, and universities. (Surely this point gives added credence to my attempt elsewhere to extend
the notion of the political to all social institutions; see Ref. 2). The exaltation of
the State in its Idea is fraudulent, though under the circumstances a benign and
necessary fraud. It ratified what earlier had been at most ambition and self-
delusion on the part of particular princes, even if delusion rooted in a nascent
reality and philosophy.[46]

Constitutionalism as restraint on power, not merely formalization, also assumes a special sense in this interpretation. The exaltation of the State, however
useful, obviously was dangerous. Already to Louis XIV it was suggested that
God was a copy of the sovereign, not the reverse. Anything both exalted and
worldly must be restrained, or one risks the extermination camp. In this way
the standard view of constitutionalism intersects with mine.

Similarly, the pervasive sense of malaise we find in current work on the
State, most of all in the present fad-problem of "governability," ceases to surprise. I will try to show momentarily that governability is not really a problem
at all, at least not in the sense it has been discerned. The malaise it expresses
probably has more to do with a sense of the disjunction of social and political
life, and a search for a reintegration that is still incomplete, than with political
paralysis: it is absurd to diagnose paralysis amid the contemporary mass of "outputs." But sociopolitical reintegration—the designing of a workable modern
polis—is probably the most pressing (and widely ignored) task of modern political thought and practice.[47]

THE CONTEMPORARY STATE

For the sake of space, let us leave aside so-called nation-building in the non-
Western world, though a great deal could be inferred about its pangs and pros-

pects from my argument. I wish to comment now on the fulfilled State of developed societies. To what has the disjunction of the political and social at its roots led? And how envisage their reunion?

One may see totalitarianism as a grotesque response to disjunction, for its essence is the absorption of social life by political authority.[48] A more benign response (even if much bemoaned) is what has been called the "new corporatism," whose essential nature is a set of special relationships, based on functions or occupations, among divisions of government and their specialized clients in society. These fragmented entities[49] do, in a special way, reunite the social and the governmental. We find the new sociopolitical corporations in just about all phases of contemporary life: farmers have them, as do unions, business corporations, professional societies, and so on. Each corporation is a special world within an increasingly hollow framework of national States, archaic in the West and nascent elsewhere. Why should we be disquieted by that fragmentation? It does once again unite the social and political, though in a way for which as yet we have neither a sociology nor a philosophy. And within its own compartments, it does "work." In any case, it "governs."

Of course, something *is* wrong; and surely it is the lack of a sense of wholeness in contemporary developed States. In the premodern polity that sense was supplied by God, by the idea of Empire, by a belief in natural order. All of these can be considered majestic words for convention—for normative society. Now we have nothing left that is majestic but the State. But States (except in special cases, like the German) have been overtaken by history—being creatures of historical transition, that was inevitable.

For want of divinity and nature, the State as a principle of wholeness still is needed. And to sustain it, the State needs, like the aboriginal prince, a distinctive societal function—and a "high" function—if it is to express the integration of neo-corporatistic polity. Let me suggest such a function. It is based on Lowi's distinction among three types of political "issues": distributive, regulative, and redistributive.[50] The first two are "narrow"; the third is "broad." The notion of broadness denotes that many people are activated and that issues are deemed widely consequential. Above all, their outcomes are perceived in zero-sum terms. But the great majority of policies in the hugely multifunctional governments of contemporary developed societies are, in fact, perceived as narrow. In the distributive category they may involve subsidies to particular groups, commercial protection, contracts to carry out governmental tasks, and the like. Issues of this sort may escalate to the level of contention entailed by "redistribution," but they rarely do. Regulatory issues, which prescribe modes of conduct for citizens, industries, and associations, tend to be even more safely narrow, and thus may be left to the specialized world of the new sociopolitical corporations. In view of the loads on governments, of experience and expertise, and of the need for cooperative activity by regulators and the regulated, that, it seems to me, is just as it should be. In any case, it cannot be otherwise. The State as a "unit" is simply a mythical source of resolutions of distributive and regulatory issues, but, as a "unit," it has in those realms been surpassed by its f. agments.

If the State has a proper realm, then, it surely is the redistributive: the most conflict-laden realm, the realm of winners and losers, of haves and have-nots. Lowi himself calls it, rather emotively, the realm not of behavior but of "being."[51] What is redistributive is in the eyes of the beholders; in the main, though, the policies so beheld are general fiscal and monetary policies, social welfare policy, and issues of equality and discrimination. Here the new corporations are powerless and themselves in conflict. And their internally negotiated, fragmentary policies either do the work of redistribution blindly (which is dangerous) or are molded by its larger framework.

The moral involves a certain twist of history. The aboriginal worldly function of princes, long before States existed, was (aside from war and security) that of seeing to "justice." Justice then involved the management of divisive conflicts and punishing deviance. It was an integrative, not a moral, function. In the contemporary world, justice remains the essential princely power. But in our fragmented, interdependent world, the justice of the princely sector must not be merely juridical; it must be largely *social* justice. The realm of social justice has always been the awesome and sacred realm of social life. But it has always been left to myth and abstraction. In the *polis* it was (ideally) the realm of philosophic wisdom: thus of true citizens. In the "uncivic" society that preceded the modern State it belonged to the divine and natural order: the "chain of being." In a godless and scientific (not natural) world, a principle for that function still is needed, even if it is not needed as the surrogate for the norms of everyday life. What but the State can be that principle when illusions and enchantment have been corroded? It is the only awesome power we still have.

Of course, the *Staatslehrer*, in their wilder flights of fancy did see the State as somehow sacred. But they missed the main implication. They did not equate sacred principles with social justice: forces that decide the just allocation of fundamental "values" to society's ranks and conditions.

Just as all societies need regulation of conduct, so all need a just principle of allocation. The first, in our world, belongs properly to the "new corporations"; the other, to what one ought perhaps to call the "new State."

REFERENCES
    [1]Anthony Downs, *An Economic Theory of Democracy* (New York: Harper & Row, 1957), pp. 7 and 21; Ronald Rogowski, *Rational Legitimacy* (Princeton: Princeton University Press, 1974), esp. pp. 31-33.
    [2]For my reasons, see my article "Authority Patterns: A Structural Basis for Political Inquiry," *American Political Science Review* 67(4) (December 1973). The main reason: there is an overwhelming case for including all authority relations in political study, not just governmental ones. The equation of formal-legal study with "state-science" does not presuppose this point, which holds even if one uses a much narrower notion of the political.
    [3]Formal-legal study played a predominant role mainly in macropolitics, where the units of analysis are polities or other large organizations (e.g., parties), because it specially pertains to organizations, especially large, complex ones.
    [4]*Treatise on the Law, Privileges, Proceedings and Usages of Parliament*, 16th ed. (London: Butterworth & Co., 1957). Sir Thomas first published his "Parliamentary Practice," as it is commonly called, in 1844; many editions (the first eight his own) followed. His codification was anticipated by John Hatsell in 1781 in *Precedents of Proceedings in the House of Commons*. Students of British history will realize that a handbook of "precedents" is nothing quite new in that country, where tradition and modernity long blended (perhaps still do), whereas a "treatise" on law and practice is much more innovative.
    [5]David Truman, *Research Frontiers in Political Science* (Washington: Brookings Institution, 1955).
    [6]They also, needless to say, write "prudence": what constitutional rules ought to be. An early sage of the academic field of political study, Henry Sidgwick, in fact considered that to be the field's *raison d'être*, and wrote a mammoth primer on the subject: *The Elements of Politics* (New York: Macmillan, 1891).

[7]Ferdinand Hermens, *Democracy or Anarchy?* (South Bend: Notre Dame University Press, 1941).

[8]Particularly emphasized are modes of choosing heads of states, and Prime Ministers and Cabinets; the dismissal of ministries and powers of dissolution over parliaments; and rules concerning executive emergency powers. A counterpart to Hermens is F. M. Wakins, *The Failure of Constitutional Emergency Powers under the German Republic* (Cambridge, Mass.: Harvard University Press, 1939).

[9]Maurice Duverger, *Political Parties* (New York: Wiley, 1954), pp. 204-205. Duverger uses "encourages" (conversely, hinders). Surely that means "causes," in a blander way.

[10]An exquisite example is Robin Farquharson, *Theory of Voting* (New Haven, Conn.: Yale University Press, 1969).

[11]See Rogowski, Ref. 1 above.

[12]The standard historical study of American political science is Bernard Crick, *The American Science of Politics* (London: Routledge & Kegan Paul, 1959).

[13]Ibid., pp. 8-11.

[14]For good summaries, see ibid., ch. 4, section 3 and ch. 8, section 2.

[15]C. J. Friedrich, *Constitutional Government and Democracy* (Boston: Little, Brown, 1937). Herman Finer, *The Theory and Practice of Modern Government* (New York: Holt, 1949).

[16]Of course, scholars like Pareto, Michels, Durkheim, Weber, and Simmel wrote in a quite different vein, but they were not "departmental" political scientists. Their impact on the departments is recent. One of my own teachers referred to Weber, in 1948, as "an obscure German philosopher."

[17]The early fifties were a period of unparalleled soul-searching in the field. See, among a plethora of similar efforts, the UNESCO Survey, *Contemporary Political Science* (Paris, 1950); The American Political Science Association's *Goals for Political Science* (New York, 1951); and the Brookings Institution lectures, published as *Research Frontiers in Politics and Government*. The pervasive note is one of things gone awry, of a need for new objectives and methods, but without any precise notions of proper reform. At the same time, pronouncements on the state of the field became the conventional, dismal subject of presidential addresses to the profession; Pendleton Herring started the custom in 1953.

[18]Crick, *The American Science of Politics*, esp. ch. 2.

[19]The long-lived standard work on British politics, Sir John A. R. Marriott's *English Political Institutions* (Oxford: Clarendon)—originally published in 1910, four times revised, and last printed in 1955—contains, as Introduction, a long discussion of the varieties of constitutions. To put that of the British into perspective: there follow discussions of the Crown, the Cabinet, the Civil Service, both Houses of Parliament, and so on—and not a word about parties, groups, opinions, or power. Moreover, the content is overwhelmingly formal-legal; there is little about what really goes on. Even J. E. C. Bodley's *France* (London: Macmillan, 1907) deals mainly with the "constitution" (with a historical introduction and a conclusion on parties); we only now think of it as a precocious work in a different vein because it expounds the notion of "two French political traditions." Germany, home of *Staatswissenschaft* as a kind of jurisprudence, hardly need be mentioned, but Theodor Eschenburg's post-World War II book *Staat und Gesellschaft in Deutschland* (Stuttgart: Schwab, 1956), the standard departmental work, is almost entirely about the first subject in its title; the other enters through discussion of how rules relate the German State to German society.

[20]A brief etymological note is in order here. The term "State" comes, circuitously, from *status*: a condition of something. In the late Middle Ages the word appears as estate: an economic condition and, also, a set of people sharing rank and function. Here is, I think, the first political, or authoritative, connotation of the word. (The French *état* also had intermixed economic, functional, stratificatory, and political meanings.) Not until the eighteenth century did the term take on the notion of the polity. One could infer much from this, as one always can from etymology; changes in meaning and matter are related. But note only that a distinction between State and society (as in Eschenburg, Ref. 19) would have been conceptually senseless until modern times. I will come back to this crucial point later, in a different way.

[21]Before being fully politicalized, the term "sovereign" generally stood for higher rank or for excellence. It was more often applied to God than men. Inferences are left to readers, and to my conclusion.

[22]Younger readers should not confuse "pluralists" with Dahl or Polsby. I refer to earlier writers like Figgis, Laski, or Cole, who attacked the special normative status attributed to the State.

[23]A certain time-lag was involved; that is, the development of sovereign structures seems to precede their formalization. See the continuation of the argument in the text.

[24]See, among innumerable sources, John Madge, *The Origins of Scientific Sociology* (London: Tavistock, 1963), p. 203. Also, Talcott Parsons and Edward A. Shils, eds., *Toward A General Theory of Action* (Cambridge, Mass.: Harvard University Press, 1954), p. 40.

[25]See Emile Durkheim, *Socialism and Saint-Simon* (Antioch: Antioch Press, 1958).

[26]August Comte, *Early Essays on Social Philosophy* (London: Routledge, n.d.), esp. p. 325.

[27]See, for instance, *From Max Weber: Essays in Sociology*, Hans Girth and C. Wright Mills (eds.) (Glencoe, Ill.: The Free Press, 1946), pp. 210–211.

[28]An excellent source for this point is D. L. Keir, *The Constitutional History of Modern Britain* (London: Black, 1955), pp. 373-394.

[29]Earlier organizations like guilds, colleges of physicians and surgeons, and the like, to be sure, were chartered. Their charters, though, were mostly grants of monopolistic privilege or internal autonomy or both. Their organization was, to use Comte's term of highest praise, spontaneous.

[30]Obviously, this point also explains, by extension, the formalization of the economic, professional, and voluntary associations that appear later than sovereign States.

[31]Keir, *Constitutional History*, p. 373. We may infer from this that the devising of constraints hardly is a sufficient, or even an important, part of the explanation of the process of formalization.

[32]W. W. Willoughby, *The Nature of the State* (New York: Macmillan, 1896, fourth printing, 1911).

[33]Bluntschli's famous *Theory of the State* would, however, also serve my purpose; e.g., his very definition of States as "organized national persons" (sic).

[34]See, for instance, Refs. 7 and 8.

[35]When we now read, say, Richard Rose's standard test on British politics, *Politics in England* (Boston: Little, Brown, 1965), in comparison with Marriott's (Ref. 19), we wonder what has become of about 95 percent of Marriott's subjects: Crown, Cabinet, parliament, etc. The answer: they have been relegated to a part of one chapter on policy-making, with little space devoted to formal-legal matters.

[36]Helmut Unkelbach, *Grundlagen der Wahlsystematik* (Goettingen: Vandenhoeck & Ruprecht, 1956).

[37]Douglas W. Rae, *The Political Consequences of Electoral Laws* (New Haven, Conn.: Yale University Press, 1967).

[38]Harry Eckstein, *Division and Cohesion in Democracy* (Princeton, N.J.: Princeton University

[39]Thomas Mathiesen, *The Defense of the Weak* (London: Routledge & Kegan Paul, 1965).

[40]Herbert J. Spiro, *Government by Constitution* (New York: Random House, 1959), ch. 15.

[41]Margaret Mead and Rhoda Metraux, *Themes in French Culture* (Stanford: Stanford University Press, 1954).

[42]Spiro, *Government by Constitution*, p. 216.

[43]Arnold J. Heidenheimer, *The Governments of Germany* (New York: Crowell, 1961), p. 138.

[44]A fine summary may be found in S. DeGrazia, *The Political Community* (Chicago: Chicago University Press, 1948).

[45]One concrete indicator of this is the unusually high incidence of "don't knows" and "no opinions" in postwar public opinion polls. We know that these categories should usually be larger than they are, because people tend to provide answers where answers are expected. When about 30 percent provide no response to questions that raise normative issues, something highly out of the ordinary is occurring. See, for example, Karl W. Deutsch and Lewis J. Edinger, *Germany Rejoins the Powers* (Stanford, Calif.: Stanford University Press, 1959), p. 15 and *passim;* and, more generally, the *Jahrbuecher der oeffentlichen Meinung*, I and II.

[46]Even for Louis XIV, *Dieudonné*, the idea of sovereignty is still embryonic, though already associated with social disruption and congenial philosophizing. For Louis, divine right involved chiefly the personalization of impersonal and corporate power—not so much true absoluteness as the rejection of priestly principles and the notion that the political function lodges in a social "estate" (for which the French also is *état*). Sovereign power and megalomania are not the same.

[47]Reintegration is not to be confused with the wide use of socioeconomic variables to explain political ones. That, too, involves separation, which is not overcome by equal-signs. The social variables remain extrinsic.

[48]See my introduction to the section on totalitarianism and autocracy in *Comparative Politics*, Harry Eckstein and David E. Apter (eds.) (New York: Free Press, 1963).

[49]In 1958, before the problem of governability had been invented, I called their existence in larger polities "polycentricity," in an essay in *Patterns of Government*, S. Beer and A. Ulam (eds.) (New York: Random House, 1958, 1963).

[50]For an overview of the distinctions among them, see Theodor Lowi, "American Business, Public Policy, Case Studies, and Political Theory," *World Politics*, July 1964.

[51]Theodor Lowi, "Distribution, Regulation, Redistribution," in *Public Policies and Their Politics*, R. Ripley (ed.) (New York: W. W. Norton, 1966).

GEORGE ARMSTRONG KELLY

Who Needs a Theory of Citizenship?

A SHORT WHILE AGO C. B. Macpherson wrote a crisp and lively paper entitled "Do We Need a Theory of the State?" By theory he intended "great theory" in the style of Bodin, Hobbes, Hegel, Green, and Bosanquet (i.e., connecting human nature with the state's ideal values), and not simply a coherent account of empirical political processes, further qualified as "pluralist-elitist-equilibrium theory."[1] His answer was that liberals of both the normative (e.g., Nozick and Rawls) and empirical (e.g., Lasswell or Dahl) schools either do not need such a theory or cannot obtain it from essentially economistic premises about man, but that social democrats and Marxists do, and that the former may be able to develop one by paying close attention to the contemporary debates of Marxist theoreticians.[2]

Since I do not share certain of Professor Macpherson's presuppositions regarding the actual or ideal political orders, I shall not pursue his rationale in exploring "citizenship." But I am indebted to him and to others for reopening the question of the state, because I doubt whether a reasoned analysis of the concept of citizenship can make very much sense without it, even though we must realistically allow that the citizen's activity is pluralistic and not exclusively state-oriented.

Today's problematic nature of citizenship (in the democracies, and especially the United States) is in part linked to the demise of the concept of the state in the twentieth century, the very time when the powers of the empirical state were growing inordinately. That demise was related to a sequence of factors that are in no sense joined propositionally: (1) A revulsion against the notion of "state" emerged from the brutalization of peoples by state action in World Wars I and II and in the demonic practices of totalitarianism. (2) "State" was further stigmatized by linkage with a superannuated idealism of the nation's corporate will, which now either passed into the equally mystical notion of "society"—sometimes an idealized world order—or was dispelled by empirical analysis and the decompositional method. (3) Marxist theory, increasingly influential, tended to reduce the state to an epiphenomenon of economic domination and class struggle. (4) Liberal theory, which had traditionally preached a minimal and consensual state with formal-legal anchorage, tended more and more to identify the state with the coercive power of regimes and to confuse it with the realm of unfreedom. (5) In the United States, whose new modes of political science would achieve hegemony by midcentury, the national experience had stressed a

21

diffused notion of political community overweighed by the activity of voluntary associations and private profit-making corporations. (6) That political science, as it abandoned institutional analysis for behavioral analysis in the presumed interest of greater realism and empirical specificity, strove to eliminate the notion of state altogether, substituting such concepts as "group," "political system," and "political process," and allying its manner of analysis with parallel developments in psychology and sociology.[3] (7) That same political science also tended to see the functions and jurisdictions of the state (or whatever other term was used) as the arena of countervailing social and economic forces—at most, as a regulator of pluralism without independent majesty; at the minimum, as a "black box" where they resolved their periodically shifting claims.[4]

Two chief impulses were at work: one was to attack the state as inhospitable to human values, whether these were of a higher or an ordinary sort; the other was to render it analytically innocuous for political science. In both cases there was an attempt to achieve "demythification" in the service of a curious rationality by which free men could be conceived and studied as objects of science.

Many of the same influences that produced the banishment of the state both as a source of veneration and as an object of inquiry remain potent today. Even within political philosophy itself, welfare liberals like Rawls, minimalists like Hayek and Nozick, conservatives like Oakeshott, and communitarians like Nisbet are all either vocally or tacitly skeptical of the state's right or capacity to inaugurate justice, embody the common interest, or promote freedom.

But it is no clearer today than it was a generation ago whether Leviathan is (or ought to be) analytically null or whether it is the *bête infernale*. A paradox of its continuing existence and extension of function is well expressed by Giovanni Sartori:

> Though the state expands, political processes can no longer be contained within, or brought under, its institutions. Consequently, the concept of state gives way to the broader and more flexible idea of the political system. . . . This leads to a dilution of the concept of politics which comes very close to vaporizing it [i.e., politics] out of existence.[5]

Can it be possible that the expansion of the state—an entity declared nugatory as early as Bentley—destroys its own concept and comes close to "vaporizing" the concept of politics itself? If we do without the concept, how are we to judge the realities? The relentlessly behavioralist concept of politics—*who gets what, when, how*—does not of course need any corresponding notion of the state, for it might as easily apply to a family, a faction, a firm, or a farm. But our conventional concept of politics—the public business—unless totally unmasked and deprived of substance, does require the regulative notion of a state, not just because it is there, but because men must be guided in how they use it. There was surely a concept as well as a structure of the state at a time when political involvement was reserved to ascriptive minorities. This may be true as well in an age when the empirical state, incredibly distended and entangled in its social jurisdictions, discourages unflinching qualities of political vision as well as the analyst's ability to account for its precise boundaries and accepted criteria of legitimation. Indeed, the so-called legitimation crisis and the postliberal intensification of the "administration of things" also seem to combine in blurring our conception of the proper sphere of the citizen.

No one can doubt that the empirical state persists today and is perceived as such by its indwellers. "Modernized" Westerners deplore the state's cost, waste, and corruption; seek security beneath its umbrella; and scramble for its uneven distributions. State expenditures in the modern Western democracies now approach or exceed 40 percent of the gross national product.[6] The inhabitants of "people's republics" know all too well what a state is and what it can do. Four score of Third World countries are more or less precariously trying to build and maintain states, which are sometimes the only integrating factor of their elusive commonality. "Welfare state" is a term embedded in ordinary language. Despite the relative military or economic impotence of certain countries, neither world opinion nor international organizations nor multinational corporations have rendered the state's armature a fiction or caused any basic collapse of the state's value as a vehicle of common law. Instances of violence superficially perceived as revolutionary (i.e., directed toward the overthrow of the state and its powers) often turn out, on closer examination, to be representational conflicts (i.e., directed toward the regime) over the distribution of material or moral goods that the state is in a position to grant, but not without the pain of change.[7] Western Marxists are suddenly discovered debating the issue of the "relative autonomy of the state."[8] And I would judge that a return to the "theory of the state," however tentative, betokens not just a weariness with the trivialities of empiricism but also a disillusion with the disguised idealism that was supposed to lead beyond the nation-state.

What, then, would be a satisfactory normative description of the state? My cursory remarks will be vulnerable to criticisms on all flanks. Nevertheless, they must be hazarded. I begin with Georges Burdeau's observation that "the state is . . . the form by which the group finds its unity in submission to law."[9] This means, in brief, that the state is not a nation; neither is it an express form of regime, nor "the people," nor a gestalt of the agents of government. It also means that the state is the embodiment, although not necessarily the source, of law (the mysterious word *sovereignty* is often shipwrecked on this issue). At its core, the state is a juridical ensemble that enables men—especially strangers—to live together in relative peace, intelligible concord, and with reasonable expectations of one another's performances. This necessarily implies coercion and punishment, but it implies much more. In Avineri's brilliant gloss on Hegel, the state is both *instrumental* and *immanent*.[10] It is instrumental because it secures the peace that permits persons a higher vision as expressed through their talents and particularity. It is immanent because it is the general form by which man's aspiration is reconciled with his actuality in the secular sphere.

Thus the state is not merely juridical, nor is it simply an alien apparatus correcting man's social vices, although it must sometimes be called on to protect some from others or even from themselves. As I have written elsewhere:

> The state is a network of exchanged benefits and beliefs, a reciprocity between rulers and citizens based on laws and procedures amenable to the maintenance of community. These procedures are expressive of the widest range of mutual initiative and compliance that the members can regularly practice, and they depend on a consensus that asserts individual freedoms while accepting such constraints [or sacrifices] as are necessary to the cohesion and self-respect of the whole. . . . Self-defense, self-determination, welfare, public virtue, and the advancement of culture comprise some of its major values, to the degree that these reflect a common

interest. The organization of the state's powers is directed toward these ends. Obviously, "welfare," "virtue," and "culture" will often collide in collective life. The state must buffer and temporarily settle these collisions.[11]

It must also renew itself for new bufferings during the quasi-eternity that politics may be expected to last.

In brief, the normative state has pacification, adjudication, and guidance functions. Its purpose is not to fulfill instantly the wants and needs of its citizenry (however organized in tribes, "estates," groups, or parties) but rather best to express the values that are its own in a lawful way. This entails, historically and globally, that the parliamentary or democratic regime is not the only legitimate form of state, although it denies the legitimacy of countless regimes (modern states would seem to have to be constitutional, i.e., with the distinguishing features of garantism, pluralism, and the division of powers). It implies that the state requires the capacity for wisdom, arbitration, and authority. *Wisdom* is a function of the talent and integrity of the state's agents, the propriety of its institutions, and the gathered strength of its political traditions. *Arbitration* depends on a sensitive balancing of values, rights, and interests by the appropriate parts of the state machinery (especially judicial and administrative). *Authority*, whose failure in the modern world was so eloquently dissected by Hannah Arendt,[12] "depends on an acquiescence in certain forms and uses of power; but it does not inhere totally in persons or even in role-playing persons as a general rule. It is an intersubjective sensing of patterns of conformity built on social and public confidence."[13] The task of state-building and state-maintenance is to act so as to approach these conditions. Conversely, it will be the task of citizens to contribute to the enterprise by debating their interests and values in order to cultivate a common viewpoint, by judgment and surveillance of the state's agents, by adaptation to consensual rules and procedures, by forming reservoirs of new capacities, and by practicing a reciprocity of respect. A state's *dignity* is articulated through its agents and magistrates; its *legitimacy* is confirmed or consented to by its citizens, that is, all those who hold rights within it and receive its protection.

Several points are to be noted about this vignette. First, it is not metaphysical. Second, it is suitable to a number of constitutional arrangements that will undoubtedly vary according to a state's territorial or demographic size, social structure, culture, technology, and other factors. Third, it makes no privileged assumptions about human nature: although it enjoins virtue and public-spiritedness and connects these with knowledge, it does not claim these must be achieved by the manipulation of some fixed set of moral propensities, only that they are encouraged by the regular practice of trust and reciprocity. Fourth, it assigns a special role to the art of politics, refusing to reduce this sphere either to a psychology of power or to a reflection of the prevailing economic order. Finally, it exposes the practical failing of most empirical states—either because their personnel are corrupt, or they are excessively partisan, or their reactions are guided by short-sighted expediency.

I fully recognize that my description is not compatible with a minimalist state; but I feel that historical reality itself has prejudiced the credibility and effectiveness of such a state, however seductively it may be reborn in philosophy. I recognize, too, that in my normative discourse I have sidestepped the nasty actualities of the power state—both the Machiavellian assumption that it is the brute truth of politics and the apocalyptic diagnosis that it can be overcome through a social-structural revolution guided by science. My belief here is that my own scheme—which I have described elsewhere as the neutral state (meaning *positively* neutral, not merely permissive)—is regulatively logical and possible, neither mired in the *libido dominandi* nor dissolved by some quantum leap in brotherhood and equality born from the terrible triumph of the "wretched of the earth." It is, above all, the kind of state in which citizenship is rendered possible.

Is this state, in the language of a continuously fertile discussion, *nomocratic* or *telocratic* (i.e., rule-governed or purpose-governed)? These distinctions, as we shall see ahead, are important to the rationale of the democratic state in the twentieth century. "Nomocracy," writes de Jouvenel,

> is the supremacy of law; telocracy is the supremacy of purpose. Modern institutions [i.e., Western] were developed around the central concept of law. Individual security is assured if the citizens are not exposed to arbitrary acts of the government, but only to the application of the law, which they know. . . . The guarantees of such a regime are precious. But institutions of a judicial type are not [designed] for action.[14]

By contrast,

> What distinguishes contemporary government is its vocation for rapid social and economic progress. . . . Once government activity has a relatively precise goal, the regime's inspiration is *telocratic* and political forms necessarily reflect this.[15]

The tenor of these remarks discloses de Jouvenel's distaste for telocracy, that is, for governmental promotion of so-called social rights and welfare activities. In slightly different language we can find similar reproofs in the writings of Lippmann, Hayek, Nozick, and Oakeshott.[16] Yet it is abundantly clear that in practice, if not always in rhetoric, most contemporary Western governments have operated with telocratic assumptions. And it is certain that explicit telocracy has had its share of defenders. For example, as Andrew Shonfield writes: "The efficient and humane modern state is 'telocratic,' taking an increasingly long view of its purposes."[17] Surely this is also asserted by François Mitterrand when he sees human freedom depending on "the reform of economic structures and relations of production" as determined by "the science or scientific approach to existing economic and social facts, at a given moment and in a given place."[18]

It is important to notice a certain slippage in the levels of analysis in this debate. De Jouvenel would appear to refer his dichotomy to the actions of a government or a regime and not, as I have defined it, the state. Hayek, who finds the notion of a state inadmissible (except in international relations),[19] bases his defense of the "Great Society" on the nomocratic "conception of the common welfare or of the public good," further defined as a "catallaxy."[20] Oakeshott denies all telocratic license to the general-purpose or sovereign organization of a political community, while granting it to subordinate special-purpose associations, using the medieval distinction of *societas* and *universitas*.[21] However, as we have seen, Shonfield writes "state" explicitly. And Georges Burdeau argues likewise, implicitly, when he speaks approvingly of "law [having] an active function in the arrangement of social relations . . . [being] no longer a reflection or an echo, but a creative power. . . . "[22] This is of course what Lippmann, like Hayek, condemns: "When legislatures and electorates are asked to settle not more or less specific issues of justice, but the purposes, plans, and management of a social order in the future, they have no rational criteria for their opinions."[23]

The position taken here, which follows from my normative definition of the state, is that the state cannot, in any ordinary sense, be telocratic, although it has the responsibility of managing telocratic initiatives that are (and frequently were, if we brush away ideology) the periodic practice of liberal governments or regimes.[24] The state cannot be telocratic and remain neutral: this is the price that eternal justice must pay to mundane order. What the state must do (and the reference here is not only to its pacificatory and adjudicative functions, but to its guidance function as well) is to cushion and resolve telocratic thrusts that collide, threatening the integrity of the unit or the legitimate rights and well-being of its parts, and confusing the reasonable expectations of the members of the body politic. Historically, when public morale and political restraint were defective in achieving this result, the burden was best borne by an independent judiciary. Yet an intelligent citizenry can also play a role in not pushing hostile claims to the breaking point or endowing special interests with the halo of presumptive rights. And we should acknowledge that substantial telocratic projects inaugurated by a government may thwart the alternance of power that is held to be a *sine qua non* of the practice of Western democracy.

We are above all concerned with the species of state that arose in parts of modern Western Europe, the United States, and certain former British dominions, usually described as "the democratic state." This kind of state has been in evolutionary process along different national lines since the turn of the nineteenth century, with yet deeper roots in a more distant past. Applauded by many progressive thinkers prior to World War I as the consummation of political wisdom, liberty, and "civility," both in practice and as goal, it received some rather harsh buffetings in the twentieth century. The prophesied polity of nineteenth-century liberals was transformed: from a state of political rights to a state of social intervention; from a state of individualist to pluralist (or even corporatist) conception; from a formal-legal to a quasi-administrative state. Questions of leadership, organization, participation, and welfare became highly problematic. Competitive markets ceded partially to oligopolies or to the discontinuous planning of the mixed economy. Still, the credo of the democratic state remained cherished in the core countries, even though there were increasing doubts about exporting the system. That credo and those doubts, from which we can take our point of departure, are well expressed in three propositions by A. D. Lindsay:

> Government strictly understood is necessarily confined to the few. The people cannot govern but they may control. . . . The democratic problem is the control of the organization of power by the ordinary person. . . . Modern conditions have made this problem much more difficult than it has ever been.[25]

Or, put another way, the problem has been to achieve the desired consequences of an "arbitral view of state function," including these important conditions:

The state must not be allowed to fall into the hands of men concerned only for the interest of a limited group. It must be sensitive to all, without succumbing to any one or to any limited coalition of interests. . . . [Moreover], the problem is not only that of preserving the state from selfish domination. Because "the public interest" is not a matter of fact but of moral valuation, there may well be two opinions about the rightness of any given decision. The state will remain at peace only if the government's policy is morally intelligible at least to the more powerful interests that it affects.[26]

If the foregoing is valid, it then becomes a part of the task of citizenship (however its rights and responsibilities are directly exercised or delegated) to control if not govern; to control somehow through the exertions and in the interest of the ordinary man; to control against selfish or partial domination of the state; and to contribute to the moral intelligibility of state action. These conditions modify and restrict, but do not contradict, what I have previously said about the normative state. Moreover, it is quite obvious that they are not being effectively achieved by the empirical states of the Western countries, especially the United States.

Some linguistic research will be useful in grasping the concept of citizenship. In English at least, *citizenship* (derived, of course, from *city* and *civitas*) has a number of interesting cognates, among which are *civic* and *civil* and their substantives *civism* and *civility*. Sparing the reader the tedium of the dictionary (in this case, Webster's *Second International*), I shall attempt to summarize the results of my exploration:

1. *Civic* and *civil*, responding to particular resonances, both make reference to citizenship, the relations of citizens, and the common public life. In the case of *civic*, we may say that the tone is more affirmative, even patriotic, as when we refer to "civic virtue" or "civic duty." *Civil* is more passive and, conceivably, less political: "civil rights" or "civil life," but also "civil behavior" or "a civil answer."

2. *Civic* and *civil* are both connected to life in cities, to the *citadin* as well as the *citoyen*. The latter term implies culture and refinement ("civilization"), as opposed to rusticity and barbarism.

3. *Civil* has the additional meanings of "civilian," "polite," "orderly," and "legally entitled to obtain private justice." Its derivative *civility* carries all these same connotations, with special emphasis on the attainment of a decent level of culture and social behavior.

4. *Citizenship* applies to a free city-dweller (a *bourgeois*) or to the member of a state who exchanges political allegiance for the right to certain privileges and protections (the dictionary's "right to a privilege" as opposed to "right," *tout court*, is a notion fraught with some ambiguity). Some modern writers would cut this short by saying that citizenship is "the right to act in the public realm." But this leaves us with the burning question: What precisely is the public realm?

Adepts in political theory and ideology will recognize that the identification between *civic* and *city* (i.e., city-state), as in the academic locution "civic humanism," originally an aristocratic ideal, deserves further stress.[27] They will also know that, in the wake of the Scottish political economists, Hegel, and Marx, the term *civil* has been used specifically to indicate the commercial or bourgeois society that launched the Industrial Revolution—a society of "contract," or economic connections, embedded in, or perhaps dominating, but in some significant way exclusive from, the state. Indeed, the word *civil*, first used as emphatically distinct from *ecclesiastical* in the seventeenth century, became a kind of counterpoint to *political* in the nineteenth, until relieved of this burden by an extension of the word *social* (connected with the rise of sociology). Impacted in these attempts to cope with new phenomena or to reorder the received wisdom in new ways lies some of the cryptography of the notion of modern citizenship.

There is a basic cleavage between civic and civil. In our common terms of today, the civil is more oriented toward private individualism and the civic toward public solidarity. Cato is civic; Henry Ford is civil. Of course these simple symbols scarcely exhaust the issue. Granted some license of metaphor, I submit that we can profitably use the dualism to explore some of the quandaries of citizenship. I must stipulate that I understand the concepts civic and civil in two ways: (1) They are expressive of more or less historical situations in which certain social and political imperatives have occurred; and (2) they dwell, with more or less vitality, within the complex concept of citizenship itself, externally as a means of defining it, internally as a level of consciousness or principle of action in the life-world of the modern citizen.

Requirements of space compel me to abbreviate my descriptions of these models enormously.[28] The task is further complicated because both civic and civil are apparently divisible in two: I call them Civic I and Civic II, Civil I and Civil II. Although these neutral-sounding labels pack no adjectival wallop and are unfortunately reminiscent of the well-interred categories of Charles Reich, I prefer them to terms that might resonate more, for two reasons. First, I would like to maintain the ambivalence between their phenomenological and historical properties. Second, I feel that more concrete terms would mostly ring hollow or skew the descriptions ideologically, for example, "solidaristic," "messianic," "constitutionalist," "welfarist," and the like. I intend something more and something less than such notions, but I must apologize in advance for this poverty of imagination. Each model does have an extensive set of descriptive variables; each will recur disproportionately in the notion of citizenship, depending on person, role, situation, perceptions, and ideological milieu. The civic dimensions are more aggressive and participatory, stressing obligations; the civil are more passive and *zweckrational*, stressing security and rights. Some of this same sense is conveyed in Isaiah Berlin's famous dichotomy of positive liberty (freedom as self-realization) and negative liberty (freedom as absence of coercion).[29] We live today in an overwhelmingly "civil" condition of political consciousness, although aspects of the "civic" are latent within it: Almond and Verba's "civic culture" is more accurately a "civil culture."

Civic I is best introduced by the phrase *dulce et decorum est pro patria mori*. It is the attitude of the small and solidary polis-type unit, the self-aware citizenry where politics and faith are mobilized in a common task and members feel conscientiously responsible for the destiny of the community.[30] Institutions such as education and the family subserve or at least do not conflict with the civic enterprise. The community is confident in its foundations, defensive in its posture: the roles of the captaincy and the magistracy are virtually interchangeable.

Civic II stands to Civic I somewhat in the same way as romantic stands to classic. Most specifically, the consciousness may be attached to the rise of nationalism in the nineteenth century.[31] As opposed to Civic I, the ethos is more creative than protective, stressing liberation rather than defense. Prophetic leadership is more in evidence; the canvas of *Gemeinschaft* is far broader;[32] political arousal is more hierarchically achieved. The militancy of Leipzig or Budapest (or the Sierra Madre) is not the militancy of Marathon. In cases of success, patriotic self-awareness is often linked to the nation (a heightened notion of kindred and culture) and deceived by the day-to-day platitudes of state politics.

Civil I is a condition of mind where the heroic is exchanged for the secure; where the political is exploited to free men not from the enemy, but from the arbitrary ruler or from each other, and where "rights" are formalized and institutions constructed to guarantee this outcome. This impulse creates a "civil society," commercially competitive and detached from the most stringent demands of citizenship; a tolerant society of plural religious truths; a formal-legal society aspiring, in view of the above, to the rule of laws and not of men; and, finally, a society of "civility" where, as in a great city, bonds can be forged with strangers across social distances through settled rules of conduct and with hardly a whiff of *Gemeinschaft* —a vast agora where strangers meet.[33] In Civil I, "politics" is basically a protection for the "social"; but though the two are distinct, the social forces manage to weigh on politics in both direct and deviant ways. This ethos is fundamentally the nomocracy of de Jouvenel and Hayek. Paradoxically, it reinvents citizenship—up to a point—through the granting and exercise (over time) of civil and political rights and by the representative electoral process. In Civil I, politics is legitimized not only by the dogmas of the economic system, but also by the conviction that the constitutional state is expanding.

Civil II, many of whose features have affected citizenship in the last generation, is both an extension of Civil I and a break from it: it is an extension because in many essentials it carries forward the goal of democracy and attempts, willy-nilly, to preserve certain features of Civil I like representation and the rule of law; it is a break because it has also been a response to crisis conditions endemic in war, economic depression, and a later prosperity that the nomocratic order could not manage, and also because it has involved a basic redefinition of the relations between public and private and among state, society, and economy.[34] Moreover, the state now actually structures conditions necessary to the reproduction of private capital. Generally speaking, Civil II has widened access to the political process, but it has also tended to denature politics into less of a vocation or species of vision and into more of an overloaded mediating system of demands and satisfactions. Could the advance toward a telocratic order inaugurate a more forceful and organized democratic citizenship, a *démocratie gouvernante* in Burdeau's phrase, or would it stimulate the powers of bureaucracy and technocracy?[35] The complete returns are not yet in, but they would not appear to favor a highly meaningful civism or even much civility. They would not appear to control against the selfish or partial domination of the state or enhance the moral intelligibility of state action. As a voluntarily retiring U.S. Congressman has put it: "I think the American public has been right all along in their bemusement, indifference, and downright animus. We haven't done our job in educating people. The country has no goal, no sense of direction, no vision. Congress is a bureaucracy. We have government by manager and engineer."[36]

A great deal has been left out of these encapsulations. Moreover, I have made no attempt to discuss specific national experiences, which vary considerably, from Sweden to New Zealand. But it now comes time to ask, What is the impact of this on the bewildered notion of citizenship? I should recall here that the citizen (especially as he self-consciously examines his role) does not dwell pristinely in the world of Civil II or, more accurately, with a foot planted there and another in Civil I. Obviously, he is in part allegiant to the nation, to which he has given a part of his *amour-propre*.[37] He knows that his country is precious to him, and that some have been called on to die for it; he may also love his city with a passion that is far from just "civil"; he may harbor notions of national greatness in his heart. He may, conversely, practice his version of citizenship through active, even criminal, opposition to state institutions that he considers unjust. Further, citizenship may signify passive entitlement, security, and the enjoyment of "rights," whether or not exercised. Or it may mean participation in altruistic but essentially nonpolitical associations like playgrounds or hospitals. It may vanish bleakly in the death of the public soul. Is the contemporary citizen confident of his status or bearing? One of our ablest political theorists thinks not: "The state has simply outgrown the human reach and understanding of its citizens. It is not necessarily monstrous, divided, or subjugated, but its citizens are alienated and powerless. They experience a kind of moral uneasiness."[38] That the state has grown and become obscure is undeniable. Yet it has, to a considerable degree, grown in support of public demand—that is, the demands of citizens. If they bear the weight of anxiety, they must also bear a part of the blame, for citizens have allowed themselves to become clients of a bureaucracy and have, probably unwittingly, allowed nonresponsible and sometimes unresponsive officials to become their masters. Moreover, although it is an important one, the expansion of the empirical state has not been the sole factor in the crisis of citizenship.

It is not possible in this essay to canvass all the current problems, but I would like to mention a few that seem to have particular bearing in the so-called welfare era:

1. As the state expands there is, at the same time, an unbalanced expansion of some of the most uncivic features of "civil" society. In the ideological space of Civil I—however much it has been despised as elitist and bourgeois—a more or less flexible and shifting balance was maintained between the guidance and adjudication mechanisms of the state. This contributed to the persistence of nomocratic legitimacy. It is not specifically Civil I that caused the catastrophes of the twentieth century (although its technology certainly did), but the evil confluence of Civil I and Civic II, when the robust economic ideology and political cosmopolitanism of the former inspired the cultural, often messianic explosions of the latter. However, a value that Civil I brought forward abundantly was what Benjamin Constant called "modern liberty," akin to our notion of negative liberty. Modern liberty was not, in the first instance, participatory, for politics was being superseded by commerce in promoting the renown of the city. It was an instrument of protecting man's free enjoyment of his lawful private activity against the invasion of others, including the state. Constant saw

that the danger of modern liberty lay in the fact that it could too easily lead to an excessive preoccupation with private well-being and too great a renunciation of the burdens of citizenship,[39] for citizenship tended to become mobilized only when enough people believed their rights, security, and property were threatened. Response depended on a sort of utilitarian calculus and protected "civility," that is, the semiautonomous activities of civil society.[40] In Civil II this same ethos remains to a very great degree: citizenship is mobilized at the point of threat (at least in time of peace) around interests or issues that remain in some sense private, or at least restricted to special groups (rarely extensive to fundamental rights). The irony is, of course, that many of our adepts in modern liberty are now petitioners to a state that allocates hard goods and not just judicial remedies, to a politics that penetrates society with distributions. In such circumstances the practice of modern liberty becomes an aspect of consumerism.

2. In Civil II, where the complexities of social corporatism have revised the content of individualism, previous definitions of *public* and *private* have changed, and this in a number of senses. Of course, in its original meaning public referred to what went on in the street, open to public view, outside the intimacy of the family. Later, our vocabulary appropriated an ambiguous notion of "public affairs," sometimes seen as relating to the affairs of state, but sometimes to other matters of wide interest; correspondingly, one spoke of a "private sphere" that included large sections of the (free enterprise) economy and, at the very least, the activity of voluntary associations. The notion of public and private sectors is still with us. But the terms are again in flux, as we perceive in the moral sphere. In effect, Civil II appears to present us with at least four frames of reference: the strictly private, where what we do is our own business (now considerably retracted in the economy but extended in moral affairs); the social, where people commune or participate, but the state has little or no influence; the socio-public, including a vast range of institutions—industries, universities, foundations, etc.—where the partnership, stewardship, or penetration of the state is prominent; and the official or strictly public, which comprises matters or functions distinctly assigned to government. Citizenship has been conceptually disoriented because of its problematic extension in the third of these milieux. Often, the citizen operates there without obvious guidelines, with divided loyalties, with unexpected consequences, and with, as Walzer puts it, "moral uneasiness." Confusions of the public, the social, and the private bewilder the goals of the citizen, just as they obscure his rights and duties. The dynamic of the state is to expand the public realm; the propensity of the citizen is to get lost in it.

3. In a well-known formulation made a generation ago by T. H. Marshall, the concept of citizenship was analytically divided into three parts:

> The civil element is composed of the rights necessary for individual freedom— liberty of the person, freedom of speech, thought, and faith, the right to own property and to conclude valid contracts, and the right to justice. . . . By the political element I mean the right to participate in the exercise of political power, as a member of a body invested with political authority or as an elector of the members of such a body. . . . By the social element I mean the whole range from the right to a modicum of economic welfare and security to the right to share to the

full in the social heritage and to live the life of a civilized being according to the standards prevailing in the society.[41]

Broadly speaking, Marshall assigns civil rights to the eighteenth century, political rights to the nineteenth, and social rights to the twentieth. This seems to follow a certain logic of democratization issuing from the Enlightenment and undauntedly approaching fulfillment despite the terrible tempests of the past seventy years, a movement from what John Dewey once called the "Great Society" toward the "Great Community."[42] For our purposes, we can say that the first two stages belong to Civil I and the last chiefly to Civil II.

Marshall's thesis is open to certain doubts, not simply because "conspiratorial elites" endemic in Civil I have delayed the consummation of a full and satisfying citizenship, but also because of its own ambiguities. Marshall seems too readily to associate citizenship, at all levels, with the acquisition of rights. No one will question that rights are an enablement to the practice of citizenship. But it is far from clear (especially under the rubric of modern liberty) what responsibilities are to be associated with those rights. This is especially difficult to judge when, as opposed to the earlier rights that were clearly connected with the state in respect to control and moral intelligibility, the social rights of Civil II appear to be indefinitely expansible. In the words of a recent writer, "Some Americans . . . hold as *rights* what only the luckiest human beings in history have managed to attain, usually in struggle, suffering, and defeat."[43] Does the receipt of a right—especially in the redistributive welfare sense—actually activate or redefine the scope of citizenship? For Marshall, "the right to share to the full in the social heritage" evidently assumes that the rights-holder will make a contribution to that heritage. But is this necessarily true? Marshall speaks of "a direct sense of community membership based on a loyalty to a civilization which is a common possession . . . a loyalty of free men endowed with rights and protected by a common law."[44] If this is so, what is that sense of civilization? Or is it instead possible that the acquisition of social rights can promote what Habermas calls "civil privatism,"[45] accentuating divisions between the social and the political and "massifying" the phenomena observed in Civil I? With the swelling of bureaucracies, might this not encourage a new category of "negative citizenship," that is, persons tied to the state for their livelihood and protection, in the manner of clients, but basically uninvolved in public issues and public business? And might this not debase the civil gains (given the increased importance of administrative as opposed to judicial procedures) or the political gains (insofar as "government" and "opposition" become less coherent and lose the power of public interest-aggregation to the closed politics of a self-perpetuating administration)?

4. Some mention must be made of the capacities and energies of the citizen. His capacities are clearly hindered when traditional modes of access to government are blocked not only by the size and unfamiliarity of the public space, but also by the breakdown of the representative process and the party system and by his increasing inability to fathom the rationale of public policy or understand the law. In Europe at the end of World War II it was widely believed (especially by a resurgent Left and a democratized Catholicism) that mass parties, possessing the technical means and the functional virtuosity for assembling the frag-

mented parts of the general will and bringing them constantly to bear on government action, could manage the adversary social claims of Civil II. This hope has been pretty well dashed by corporate bargaining and "partitocrazia." Just as in the malfunctioning system of Weimar Germany, the parties had aggregated interests within the regime, out of sight of the public, rather than as a prelude to public choice, they now also began to sacrifice this opaque initiative to the bureaucracy. In the United States and certain other countries whose parties were scarcely "massified," the evolution has been different, but no less baneful to citizenship. The personalization of politics (partly through the media clichés) has produced the idiocies of image-making. Potential party cadres have often been assimilated to the bureaucracy. And despite the vast increase of employees in the public sector, it cannot be said that any heightened consciousness of citizenship accompanied the phenomenon.

As for energies, it must be remembered that not only is a person's public time and commitment limited, but that the small portion of it bestowed on the contemporary commonwealth can be reallocated to other enterprises: intensely private group relations, salvationary religions, aestheticism, physical culture, barbarism, and so on. Politics is no exclusive passion that cannot be replaced. The technological sterility and bureaucracy—and the unintelligibility—of modern government seem unlikely to discourage these other options,[46] but their callousness may also promote the abrupt and spasmodic reentry of smoldering energy to the political process.

5. The citizen also faces a theoretical problem. In contemporary life he is what Walzer correctly identifies as a "pluralist citizen."[47] This not only means that he is confused by his ventures into what I earlier called the socio-public realm, but a number of other things as well. It refers to the condition that Almond and Verba praise in *The Civic Culture*, that multiple memberships in nonofficial, voluntary groups encourage civic interest and are reservoirs of citizenship.[48] A century and a half ago Hegel theorized the "corporations of civil society" in this fashion.[49] And for Tocqueville, "those associations that are formed in civil life without reference to political objects" substituted for aristocratic leadership in a democratic country; without them, "civilization itself would be endangered."[50] This reservoir theory is both attractive and plausible.[51] But there is a darker side to pluralist citizenship. The groups *may* be explicitly political. Their members may "actually [be] making claims against the state, and then they *may be* obligated to disobey its laws . . . [becoming] disobedient citizens and, in critical cases, traitors."[52] The poignant questions of private judgment and loyalty infest pluralist citizenship. Can a citizen also be a traitor? Probably not, in any normal way, although we should not infer from this that moral claims can never supersede the state's commands. But there are two strategies for coping with this problem. One is Walzer's neo-Lockean argument that separates *society* ("pact of association") from the *state* ("trust of government") and further submits that there are cases where men owe a higher allegiance to society, being *alien* from obligations to the state.[53] I cannot do justice here to Walzer's sophisticated reasoning, but it seems to me that his assessment of loyalty moves precariously between such focuses as one's individual conscience (or the promises one has made), a primary group of stated purpose to which one is joined, the best interest of the national society, and society

understood as humanity. At one extreme, subjectivism; at the other, a hyposta-
tization of will and interest at least as mysterious as that of the state. Other
writers in the liberal tradition have even avoided Walzer's careful reference to
the state. For example, John Dewey, who wrote, "The moment we utter the
words 'the State,' a score of intellectual ghosts rise to obscure our vision,"[54]
appears to have believed intensely in the value of citizenship, in a citizenry
publicly active and alert to scientific problem-solving, without much respect for
its focus, at least until he endorsed New Deal interventionism in *Liberalism and
State Action* (1936).

I think Walzer and many other liberals or radical liberals confuse the state
with the regime. Above all, we should not take a Donatist view of the administration of the public sacraments. My own position is that the citizen (fully granting his plural activities) is bound in loyalty to the state, although it is the
normative, rather than the empirical, state to which he owes his allegiance in the
last resort. That state will be highly cognizant of the implications of plural
loyalties (despite the damage that, as we have seen, can be wrought by mobilized single-issue pressure groups).[55] But it cannot tolerate the formalized principle of disobedience, for the appeal may be to a solipsistic, capricious, or
destructive source. Since the gravest injustices of the empirical state are usually
attributable to the regime, the citizen's appeal will, in effect, be from the regime
to the state. Walzer's citizens can be protected—and even the right to rebellion
can be asserted—by a more intelligible process than the liberal myth of how
men choose to enter or leave political life: by pooling their "rights" or picking
them back out of the bundle.

6. It is nevertheless indisputable that in Civil II the notion of citizenship has
been buffeted by a crisis of allegiance, in both theory and practice. Whether or
not one agrees with Habermas's specific analysis of the "legitimation crisis,"
many of his observations are acute. As he writes: "The ultimate motive for
readiness to follow is the citizen's conviction that he could be discursively convinced in case of doubt," and "Traditions important for legitimation cannot be
regenerated administratively."[56] This is surely correct. I am not so convinced
that the replacement of "administered capitalism" by true socialism would solve
the issue, for I know of no socialism that would axiomatically transform the
"structurally depoliticized public realm" in a benign way. Yet the questions of
control and moral intelligibility must be answered.

Questions of legitimation were also raised in Civil I (not least in the strong-
holds of the "social movement"), but, not fortuitously, the liberal-constitutional
system handled them quite skillfully on two grounds: the procedural ground
that laws made to be obeyed could nevertheless be changed by the political
process; and the idealistic ground that democracy was being progressively implemented. Civil II has a deeper problem with legitimacy. First, it is not so easy
to give an uncontested description of the system that is held to be legitimate: it is
overburdened with transactions, and its structures and functions, not to mention its institutions, are less coherent. Second, in a period when the acquisition
of social rights is paramount, these rights may be multiple or preferential; any
derogation of a supposed social right may be conceived as a reason for with-
holding loyalty. Political "communicative competence" can only be restored
when the state and its "notion" are intelligible to those in its jurisdiction, when

its laws and the expectation of justice are clarified, and when its values are rebalanced.

No attempt has been made here to construct a theory of citizenship, for it cannot be done under present conditions. I have instead tried to assort and clarify the principal confusions of citizenship in the empirical context of the modern democratic state. I have also endorsed the need to rethink the state in its normative proportions and have given my views about how we might start. That contemporary states are far from the norm I have little doubt. Nor do I doubt that citizenship lacks both true civility and civic commitment. My own guess is that citizenship will be frozen in these dilemmas until or unless the empirical state changes its ways. If it should be asked, "Who needs a theory of citizenship?" my answer would be, "The state." But there must first be a theory of the state to inform the citizen.

REFERENCES

[1]C. B. Macpherson, "Do We Need a Theory of the State?" *Archives européennes de Sociologie*, 18 (2) (1977): 223-224.

[2]Ibid., 226–230.

[3]See Alexander Passerin d'Entrèves, *The Notion of the State* (New York: Oxford University Press, 1967), pp. 59-65.

[4]See especially Theodore J. Lowi, *The End of Liberalism* (New York: W. W. Norton, 1969), pp. 310-313, for a concise indictment of pluralism and interest-group liberalism.

[5]Giovanni Sartori, "What is Politics?" *Political Theory* (February 1973): 20.

[6]See Bob Rowthorn, "Late Capitalism," *New Left Review*, 98 (July-August 1976): 71-73.

[7]I borrowed the term "representational violence" from Martin Needler, *Political Development in Latin America: Instability, Violence, and Evolutionary Change* (New York: Random House, 1968), p. 47, and used it in a somewhat different fashion in my *Hegel's Retreat from Eleusis: Studies in Political Thought* (Princeton: Princeton University Press, 1978), pp. 207-208.

[8]See Claus Offe, "Political Authority and Class Structures—An Analysis of Late Capitalist Societies," *International Journal of Sociology*, 2 (1) (1972): 70ff; and Ralph Miliband, *Marxism and Politics* (New York: Oxford University Press, 1977), pp. 66ff, especially p. 83: "Different forms of state have different degrees of autonomy or independence (the terms are used interchangeably here) from all classes, including the dominant class."

[9]Georges Burdeau, *Traité de Science politique*, vol. 2: *L'État* (Paris: Librairie Générale de Droit et de Jurisprudence, 1949), p. 145.

[10]Shlomo Avineri, *Hegel's Theory of the Modern State* (New York: Cambridge University Press, 1972), p. 101.

[11]Kelly, *Hegel's Retreat*, pp. 100-101.

[12]Hannah Arendt, "What Is Authority?" in *Between Past and Future* (New York: Viking Press, 1954), pp. 91-141.

[13]G. A. Kelly, "Politics, Violence, and Human Nature," *NOMOS XVII: Human Nature in Politics* (New York: New York University Press, 1977), p. 132.

[14]Bertrand de Jouvenel, "Sur l'évolution des formes du gouvernement," *Du Principat* (Paris: Hachette, 1972), pp. 77-78.

[15]Ibid., p. 79.

[16]Walter Lippmann, *An Inquiry into the Principles of a Good Society* (Boston: Little, Brown, 1937); F. A. Hayek, *Law, Legislation and Liberty*, vol. 1: *Rules and Order* (London: Routledge and Kegan Paul, 1973), vol. 2: *The Mirage of Social Justice* (London: Routledge and Kegan Paul, 1976); Robert Nozick, *Anarchy, State, and Utopia* (New York: Basic Books, 1974); Michael Oakeshott, *On Human Conduct* (New York: Oxford University Press, 1975).

[17]Andrew Shonfield, *Modern Capitalism* (New York: Oxford University Press, 1965), p. 419.

[18]François Mitterrand, *Politique* (Paris: Fayard, 1977), pp. 516, 524.

[19]Hayek, *Rules and Order*, p. 48.

[20]F. A. Hayek, "The Principles of a Liberal Social Order," in *Studies in Philosophy, Politics and Economics* (Chicago: Chicago University Press, 1967), p. 164.

[21]Oakeshott, *On Human Conduct*, especially pp. 199-206.

[22]Georges Burdeau, *Traité*, vol. 6: *La démocratie gouvernante: son assise sociale et sa philosophie politique* (Paris: Librairie Générale de Droit et de Jurisprudence, 1956), p. 358.

[23]Lippmann, *Good Society*, p. 294.

[24]The state is of course telocratic in the sense that it promotes the values mentioned earlier (which are clearly separable from procedural justice). But it promotes these values negatively through adjudication and the maintenance of concord.

[25]A. D. Lindsay, *The Modern Democratic State* (New York: Oxford University Press, 1962, 1943), pp. 25-26.

[26]S. I. Benn and R. S. Peters, *The Principles of Political Thought: Social Foundations of the Democratic State* (New York: Collier Books, 1964), p. 324.

[27]Cf. J. G. A. Pocock, *The Machiavellian Moment* (Princeton University Press, Princeton: 1976).

[28]More detailed descriptions of these models are given in my unpublished paper, "The Civic and Civil Models of Public Behavior," from which certain parts of this essay are adapted.

[29]Isaiah Berlin, "Two Concepts of Liberty," in *Four Essays on Liberty* (New York: Oxford University Press, 1969), pp. 118-172.

[30]There is a complexity of the relationship between politics and faith in Civic I that cannot be encompassed by the notion that they are undifferentiated; see on this, Roland Robertson, *The Sociological Interpretation of Religion* (New York: Schocken Books, 1972), p. 84. My definition of Civic I is drawn wide enough to accommodate instances of Judaism and Christianity as well as "Olympian religion." Rousseau's "civil religion" (*Social Contract*, IV, viii) is intended as an artificial support for the waning of the relationship.

[31]But not limited to the nineteenth century: the *prise de conscience* of Islam or of the Muscovite Empire, as well as developments in the Third World of today, could fit the picture.

[32]See Ferdinand Tönnies, *Community and Society* (New York: Harper & Row, 1963), pp. 43-44, for the spiritual "leap" to conditions of ideal community transcending the criteria of neighborhood and immediate familiarity.

[33]See on this, Richard Sennett, *The Fall of Public Man* (New York: Cambridge University Press, 1974), p. 264.

[34]A classic treatment is Karl Polanyi's *The Great Transformation* (Boston: Beacon Press, 1957).

[35]There is a tendency to confuse "bureaucracy" and "technocracy." Conceivably, a truly glacial technocratic administration might (at what cost?) avoid having to deal with the time-consuming interest-group politics of Civil II that encourages the growth of bureaucracy.

[36]Rep. Michael Harrington (D-Mass.), quoted in *The Boston Globe*, 5 November 1978.

[37]See J.-J. Rousseau. *Economie politique*, in *The Political Writings*, ed. C. E. Vaughan, 2 vols., (New York: John Wiley, 1962), i, p. 256.

[38]Michael Walzer, *Obligations: Essays on Disobedience, War, and Citizenship* (New York: Simon and Schuster, 1971), p. 204.

[39]Benjamin Constant, "De la liberté des anciens comparée avec celle des modernes," in *Oeuvres politiques*, ed. C. Louandre (Paris: 1874), p. 283.

[40]For a theory denying even a minimal spontaneity of common response, see Mancur Olson, Jr., *The Logic of Collective Action* (Cambridge, Mass: Harvard University Press, 1971), especially pp. 125-131 and *pass*.

[41]T. H. Marshall, "Citizenship and Social Class," in *Class, Citizenship and Social Development* (New York: Harper & Row, 1965), pp. 78ff.

[42]John Dewey, *The Public and Its Problems* (Chicago: Swallow Press, 1954), pp. 154-157.

[43]Michael Novak, *Choosing Our King* (New York: Macmillan, 1974), p. 280.

[44]Marshall, "Citizenship," p. 101.

[45]Jürgen Habermas, *Legitimation Crisis* (London: Heinemann, 1976), p. 75.

[46]Indeed, the moral pluralism and individual life-styles of Civil II legitimize them as safety valves.

[47]Walzer, *Obligations*, p. 227f.

[48]Gabriel Almond and Sidney E. Verba, *The Civic Culture* (Princeton: Princeton University Press, 1963), pp. 323ff.

[49]G. W. F. Hegel, *The Philosophy of Right*, tr. T. M. Knox (Oxford: Oxford University Press, 1967), paras, 250, 253, pp. 152-153.

[50]Alexis de Tocqueville, *Democracy in America*, tr. Henry Reeve, 2 vols. (New York: Vintage Books, 1945), 2, pp. 114-115.

[51]Being trained for politics in this fashion obviously does not mean the education of the young in school: cf. Arendt, *Between Past and Future*, p. 177.

[52]Walzer, *Obligations*, p. 227.

[53]See especially Walzer's thoughtful essay "The Obligation to Disobey," *ibid.*, pp. 3-23.

[54]Dewey, *The Public and Its Problems*, p. 8. There is an interesting parallel in Dewey's assertion of the validity of the religious in the absence of religion: see *A Common Faith* (New Haven: Yale University Press, 1934), especially, p. 28.

[55]This worry is expressed in the article "Disarray and Inefficiencies in American Government Generate Wide Concern," *The New York Times*, 12 November 1978.

[56]Habermas, *Legitimation Crisis*, pp. 43, 47.

DOUGLAS RAE

The Egalitarian State: Notes on a System of Contradictory Ideals*

SUCCESS OFTEN PUNISHES PEOPLE, and usually punishes ideas: with success come practice and notoriety, and from these emerge public knowledge of incapacity, incompetence, and contradiction. If Richard Nixon had lost one more election, his half-decent mediocrity would perhaps have survived; if Lenin had been promptly shot at the Finland station, romantic admiration for him and for Marxism might have flourished and endured; if equality had remained a radical ideal, many more of us could remain innocently committed to it. It is not of course imagined that equality has succeeded in actual practice, but we have come to an era in which we can hardly discuss government and the state without thinking about equality and the prospect of its application to practice.

The modern state seems everywhere ostentatiously egalitarian and almost everywhere promises to become more so. Indeed, a casual survey of governments that face obvious crises of legitimacy—South Africa, Rhodesia, Uganda, and the like—suggests that an open disregard for equality is the surest ideological poison in the world at large. Our own government is engaged in the promotion of more equalities than one can readily recount: affirmative action for blacks and women; equal employment rights for victims of cancer; Sysiphean tax reform; redistribution of health care and its cost; transfer systems of many sorts; even the downward redistribution of monies from the National Endowments. Perhaps none have a profound effect on a capitalist economy, but they are certainly numerous and symbolically salient. For these reasons, the "egalitarian state" seems sufficiently familiar and plausible to bear discussion.

If anything is to be learned about this phenomenon, it is necessary to recognize that equality plays an important implicit role in government and even in everyday life. For example, it has been a good century since anyone seriously advertised capitalist markets as egalitarian institutions. Yet in the pricing of goods, for example, they are. A shopper in a supermarket understands the price marked on an item to be an equal price for all and would rebel at being asked to pay more than someone else. Or to take the example of poker, a game whose main object is certainly *not* the promotion of equality: the value of a given full house is the same for every player, and a dollar bet is a dollar bet from any chair at the table. We don't stop to think of these features as egalitarian, but they are in truth just that. Similarly, some important features of the modern state—liberty, for instance—are predicated on some form of equality without being

37

explicitly advertised as such. If a court of law ruled that liberty does not extend to persons of class X or that liberty of expression is denied to proponents of doctrine Y, the judge's understanding of the very notion of liberty would be in question. Unlike "privilege" or "license," notions like "liberty" and "right" tacitly entail a certain equality of distribution.[1] These implicit commitments are important, and any analysis that left them out would miss too much.

In cumulative effect, these implied and explicit commitments to equality are more than sufficient to justify the notion of an egalitarian state. But, more important, they lead to a host of contradictions and confusions in which *equality is set against equality*. The most famous recent example is Bakke v. University of California at Davis. The University under its affirmative action program was attempting to provide equal access to medical training for blacks, Hispanics, and women; Bakke claimed denial of equal consideration for himself and other white males; and all six separate Supreme Court opinions were, in the end, confused or confusing attempts to apply the notion of "equal protection under the law." This case reveals, with almost comic hyperbole, that governments now are required less to decide *whether* equality than to choose *which* equality. This promises to remain a characteristic predicament of the state for some time to come. It therefore behooves us to sort out some main kinds of egalitarianism to which government may or may not commit itself, and to begin anticipating the ways they are apt to contradict one another. That, at any rate, is the aim of this essay.[2]

How to Cut Cake Equally

The abstract idea of equality is possibly the most versatile of human constructions. It is, of course, an essential constituent of mathematics and of logic. It is the principle by which sorting processes (whether of machine parts or of books or of computer "bits" or even of people) must proceed, namely, by putting relevantly equal items together. It is logically essential to the notion of literal truth itself, since this amounts to an equation between an assertion and relevant aspects of its object. It is even, in the most elementary way, constitutive of personal identity; for example, "I'm me." It has virtually unlimited application to experience and imagination, a versatility that derives from the extreme austerity of the concept: saying "X equals Y" does not in itself commit us to *any* further beliefs about X and Y, which may turn out to be numbers or persons or objects. Small wonder, then, that its political uses should have a certain variety.

Perhaps the least revealing use of equality in politics is associated most closely with its broader uses. This is the doctrine that people *are*, somehow, equal. For Hobbes this meant that we are rough equals in egoism and in our capacity for violence; for the Church Fathers it meant that we are all children of God; for eighteenth century radicals it meant that we are all creatures of reason.[3] In recent years, these philosophical assertions have at times become confused with the flatly false empirical assertion that human individuals are equal in biological vigor or intelligence or in their capacity for work. While there is no doubt a statistical equality among large blocs of people (notably races), nothing could be more absurd than to imagine this kind of individual-by-individual equality. Indeed, the very purpose of concepts like vigor, intelligence, and diligence is precisely to point up *in*equalities among people. As Rousseau keenly observed two centuries ago, a main point of our ideas and customs is to locate and promote inequalities. The egalitarian state, as it attempts to neutralize the stratifying effects of nature and culture, finds itself confronted with substantial problems, because people both as we find them and as society shapes them are *not* equal.

Our concern here is to sketch the main sorts of things that the innocent contention that government *should*, somehow, treat its subjects as equals may suggest, and to consider some of the ways these may contradict one another. To begin, let us take something much smaller and much less complex than the state. Consider the banal (and pejoratively "philosophical") problem of cutting a cake equally. We may plausibly begin, as does Isaiah Berlin,[4] by supposing that there is a single egalitarian solution, that is, slicing the cake into as many identical pieces as there are guests. But as we shall see, there are alternative routes to equality, even for so simple an occasion as this notional tea party. By looking at these in a simple context, we can point out some main difficulties that most certainly will arise in the livelier and more intricate world of politics and the state. If these alternatives seem strained in relation to a philosopher's cake, please forgive that much and rejoice in their clarity: momentarily, politics will complicate them. Here are five types of complications to the cutting of a hypothetical cake.

1. The cake, cut in equal slices, is served at a party to which our host has invited ten persons—but *only* ten. What, we may wonder, do the equal slices for this inner circle mean to those left out altogether? Perhaps the most basic inequality has been inflicted *before* the cake is sliced or served.

2. Imagine that the guests belong to different castes or classes. Three of the ten are, perhaps, black, and our party occurs in Cape Town. Or, they are English dons, four of whom speak with "high" Oxford accents, the others, with accents different and "lower." It would be one thing to divide the cake (or, more interesting, conversational deference) equally among persons; it would be another to divide these equally among the blocs formed by race or class. It is one thing to ask: Did our host listen to Smith the same way he listened to Jones? It is another to ask: Did our host listen to blacks the same way he listened to whites? At our imaginary banquet, the difference between these questions is perhaps second-rate; in life itself, the difference is first-rate.

3. The cake in question turns out to be the last of seven courses. Two of our guests have distinguished themselves over the first six courses. Herr Grobrian has eaten nearly all of the shrimp, consumed the best pieces of the duck, and helped himself to the tip of each asparagus shoot as the dish was passed, leaving the stalks for others. He has more than held his own in every dish save the parsnips, which he modestly urged on the others. Frau Magrian, seated beside our gluttonous friend, has been governed by an over-polite denial of appetite. She is the sort of person who never quite manages her share of good things, and she finishes six courses with hunger gnawing at her stomach. It would be one thing for our host to cut the cake in equal slices for Grobrian and Magrian

(forgetting, in effect, about the other courses). It would be another to cut the cake to bring about overall equal meals for these two diners. These two views lead to equalities that are very different from one another indeed.

4. Our guests are again alike in caste and class, and the cake is the only course to be served. But imagine a chocolate cake served in equal measure to a guest who loathes the taste of it; or an angelfood cake served to a woman who is violently allergic to eggwhite; or a boysenberry fudge cake palatable only to our host, served in equal and generous slices to all. Slices of equal size will accomplish equality in one sense: no guest who despises the cake will wish he had gotten somebody else's slice. But those who like the cake, or at least have no allergy to it, will be getting more value from their slices than the others; equal slices, unequal value. The difference between the underlying notions of equality here is important.

5. We have so far assumed a divisible, homogeneous cake, implying that equality (at least of a literal sort) is possible. But suppose, like Solomon's baby, the cake became worthless when cut into pieces. Or suppose the cake to be so small as to contain fewer than ten worthwhile bites. Under these circumstances, and many such others, the host might issue equal forks, not equal slices of the actual cake, and let his guests fight it out with these equal implements. Or, quite differently, he might draw names from a hat so that each guest has the same chance of winning a slice. The forks correspond to one view of "equal opportunity," and the names in a hat correspond to a radically different conception. Which, if either, corresponds to the form of equality best pursued by the state when actual equality is impossible or undesirable?

It is clear that these alternatives would be quite silly if we really meant to think about private entertaining. Yet, in the case that actually concerns us—the egalitarian state—every one of the objections made to each alternative is important and has important consequences for practice. This essay will therefore be organized around the five kinds of differences implied in these objections.

Who Are the Equals?

Equality is quite obviously a relational idea. To establish one agent as an equal in isolation from others is like one hand clapping: there must be a class of equals or none at all. In our cake-cutting metaphor, the host defines this class to correspond with his guest list, and our first objection is that he has failed to include a properly extensive class of equals. An analogous question has from the beginning nagged governments that have sought to establish equality among their subjects.

A nineteenth century vision of equality, at least of political equality, gives a misleadingly simple idea about this issue. Suffrage and civil liberties were once mainly confined to (white) Christian men of property. Then, nearly everywhere in the West, and, fitfully, even in Russia, this narrow class of equals was expanded to include dissenters and Jews, racial minorities, women, and the unpropertied. In a later era (beginning, oddly enough, with Bismarck's Germany) broader economic assurances were granted to all citizens, and the formal right to unemployment insurance, minimal doctoring, and the like, has in most Western states become a universal perquisite of citizenship. These last are, of course, more relevant to proletarian and marginal citizens, but the guarantees are universal. Thus it seems natural to suppose that equalities must correspond to the (full) jurisdictions of governments—neither more nor less.

But the moral and ideological bases of egalitarianism do not naturally fit the borders of governments. Moral argument is universal in form; governments are not. A high moral equality recognizes no obvious difference between an American citizen and a citizen of Mexico, or between a citizen of Switzerland and a citizen of Chad. A government, in contrast, knows no practicable similarity between its own citizens and the rest of the world. Equalities that appear radically inclusive in nineteenth century terms—extending to *all* of a government's subjects—may appear very narrow indeed by universal morals. If we are arguing on a high moral footing, and the subject of equality is mankind, then it sounds rather silly to say, "All bona fide citizens of state X have a God-given right to life, liberty, and the pursuit of happiness." Yet, given the existing arrangement of governments, very little can be practicably asserted for any larger group in the name of equality, a point admirably dramatized by David Singer[5] when he asks how many European or American proponents of equality, or even of weaker but universal moral positions, would be anxious to bear the cost of economic redistribution on a world scale.

We can see this perhaps more clearly by comparing equality with some less purely relational notion such as minimal welfare. Suppose we had several states and some general idea of minimal welfare, or even, simply, the idea of an annual income of at least $1,000. We could apply this notion separately within each government's jurisdiction, and when all had managed this for their subjects, we could properly conclude that minimal welfare had been achieved for everyone without regard to nationality. The idea is "additive" and can be achieved by attending separately to national communities. There will, of course, be a certain relativity to what counts as minimal welfare in Iran and Sweden, but that is not our immediate concern. But equality is a purely relational concept. It is not additive and *cannot* be accomplished by separate attention to national communities or any other subdivisions of the world. If we established some rough equality in relatively wealthy European states—Denmark, Germany, or France—and in states less well-off—Greece or Spain—it would not follow that we had accomplished equality for Europe considered as a whole. This "nonadditive" property of equality implies that, once we have chosen a large class of proper equals, then only equally large governments can effect the transformation in question.[6] In the United States this has, since the New Deal, brought about a concentration of some distributive powers in Washington, since equality in Mississippi and (separately) in Connecticut implies nothing by way of equalization in the country at large. Even within single states there is a powerful movement to detach some important distributive activities from local government (notably school finance) and concentrate them in larger units to achieve a larger equality. It very often happens, in short, that governments are too small to achieve equality once it is founded on universal morality.

But there are other ways in which governments may seem too big rather than too small. In distributing the right to political participation, it sometimes appears that even quite small governmental units are too large to be the basis for the (equal) distribution of these rights. School bond referenda in American towns are one such case. Consider two families, one with school-age children, the other without; or two families, one with a tax liability for the bond, the other, again, without. While the case for equality of voting rights remains a strong one, the case for equal votes among these families on a particular school bond referendum seems perhaps too broad. The intuitively appealing ground for inclusion is, in Robert Dahl's term, the criterion of "affected interest."[7] When decisions affect only part of a community, as do such referenda, one may think that the properly egalitarian suffrage is *less* extensive than the whole. One must of course look with some skepticism on arguments of this sort, since nearly everyone has at least an indirect interest in any substantial issue such as the education of youth. But there is enough here to suggest that no simple conclusion should be reached about an association between the ideal of equality and an unlimited extension of governments.

There are still further issues in which setting up too large a "class of equals" may mask important inequalities. Suppose I were to argue that university faculties give a more than equal share of places to Chinese-American scholars, or that the National Basketball Association obviously plays favorites with respect to black players. By looking merely at large categories, I could no doubt vindicate this view; yet this would wrongly hide the fact that within smaller categories— based on levels of quality in scholars and in basketball players—it may well be that these groupings receive less than their equal share of places. It is true, for example, that blacks in major league baseball earn higher salaries on average than whites. But if we subdivide players by position and by quality of perform- ance (e.g., batting averages and the like), we find that blacks receive lower sala- ries than whites at every level of performance in each position on the field.[8] Large categories of people and a morally defensible view of equality do not go together in all instances.

Public school integration provides yet another important illustration of the same point. Suppose we have a school district with equal numbers of white and black children. In calculating some index of integration for the district at large, we are perhaps well satisfied by the result. But in looking at the actual schools within the district, we might discover that no single school served blacks and whites at the same time. Or, having integrated individual schools, we might fail to note a pattern of segregation in individual classrooms. The hypothetical ex- ample is, of course, artificially tidy, but it corresponds to a phenomenon alive in Los Angeles, New York, Boston, and other major American cities. Valid conceptions of equality drive us toward both larger and smaller classes of persons, and these will not in general correspond neatly with the boundaries of government.

Emancipatory Assignment versus Equal Allocation

If we think about a political economy like the antebellum South, or a colo- nial plantation system, in which blacks are the unfailing victims of massive inequality, and assume that this scheme of inequality is sustained by the coercive powers of the state when necessary, we will see that such a system is doubly inegalitarian. First, it sustains and perpetuates a highly unequal allocation of resources, rights, and statutes. Second, the beneficiaries of this inequality are all (or nearly all) drawn from one racial bloc, while the victims are all (or nearly all) drawn from another racial bloc. This permits two basic lines of reform—one aimed at the system of allocation itself, the other, at its racial incidence—that spawn two very different species of egalitarianism. Since Americans—including jurists, politicians, journalists, and intellectuals—have very often confused the two, it's worth taking a moment to elucidate the distinction.

Let's distinguish three elements in a politico-economic system: (1) people, distinguished from one another by markers like race (or sex or religion or even sexual preference); (2) some roles in political and economic life; and (3) some resources, rights, privileges, or powers. The operation of such a system can be divided into two parts: *allocation* concerns the division of resources, rights, privileges, and the like, among roles; *assignment* concerns the selection of persons to occupy these roles. Schematically:

(1) people   ASSIGNMENT   (2) roles   ALLOCATION   (3) resources
              ——————————→   ←——————————

One form of egalitarianism, which we can term "simple" or "direct," moves toward allocation, while a second form, which we can term "emancipatory," centers exclusively upon the assignment of persons to roles. Emancipatory equality leads *not* to a reduction or eradication of simple or direct inequalities in allocation but to an equalized incidence of these inequalities over races (or sexes, ethnic groups, and the like). It is a logical and empirical possibility that the state may successfully pursue emancipatory equality without any commitment to simple or direct equality. And the pursuit of simple or direct equality need not be associated with any progress toward emancipatory equality, except insofar as it reduces the importance of the struggle for privileged roles.

Consider, for example, two racial blocs distributed on an income scale ranging from $0 to $500,000 per annum:

```
      B  B  B  B    W   W   W   W   W   W   W   W
  $0                                              $500,000
```

A simple egalitarianism would compress these incomes toward some single level—say, $10,000—so that all have equal incomes. An emancipatory egalitarianism would retain the wide variation in incomes but reassign appropriate proportions of racial blocs upward (and downward) to bring about, for example,

```
      W   W   B   W   W   B   W   W   B   W   W   B
  $0                                              $500,000
```

While simple egalitarianism attacks unequal allocation itself, emancipatory equality alters the assignment of persons to redistribute the incidence of inequality over racial (or other) blocs. It need not reduce the extent of simple inequality in the allocation of basic resources at all.

Given the history of our black citizenry, it is easy to see why an emancipatory view of equality should be especially prevalent in the United States. In *Up from Slavery* and his infamous speech at the Atlanta Exposition of 1896, Booker T. Washington stressed the emancipatory view as the *only* conceivable approach. Washington thought blacks could only lose by attacking basic inequalities through the union movement or radical politics; better, said he, for blacks to accumulate those skills that will permit them to creep up through the class structure in order to mix with whites. White activists—and jurists—generally found little difficulty in sympathizing with this conception and were led eventually to the present doctrine(s) of "affirmative action." Even in its most draconian form—with firm racial quotas—affirmative action is a supremely emancipatory doctrine that passes over simple inequality without comment. As long as an equal per capita share of blacks is found at the top—in medicine, law, the universities, business, and government itself—we are not required to concern ourselves with the distance between these fortunates and the majority left below. Emancipationism merely rearranges the incidence of simple inequality, and those who mistake it for simple equality are tragically wrong.

Emancipatory equality has so far been described as if race alone divided society and as if race alone might stand as a basis for equalizing the incidence of inequalities. There is some justification for this because of the special role of racism directed against blacks throughout our history. But why not equalize between Anglo and Hispanic; women and men; gay and heterosexual; Catholic, Protestant, and Jew; Appalachian and lowlander? In a pluralistic society, with its rich array of "markers," there are very many possible emancipations. The trouble, of course, is that equalizing the incidence of inequality over one such cleavage will not in general equalize its incidence across another. And how is the juridical apparatus of government to set priorities among competing emancipationist demands? Can it say (with a straight face) that such demands for equality are *unequal*? If not, an intractable tangle of emancipatory demands will ensue. And we may thus considerably diminish the efficiency of our economy while at the same time we fail to diminish the simple inequalities that are as much neglected by ten emancipatory efforts as by one such undertaking.

Finally, life has many aspects to it, and these are interconnected. To emancipate in one aspect of life gives no guarantee of emancipation in another. It is one thing to rule out discrimination in hiring practices, and a radically different thing to require that equal proportions of each race and sex be hired. That is indeed one of the most familiar domestic difficulties in American politics today. And the so-called reverse discrimination that may be required to resolve the contradiction will be an issue for some time to come. We will not dwell on this at length because it is so familiar; Table 1, however, shows a somewhat less familiar shard from the same pot.

A naive reading of these macabre data would suggest that some odd reverse discrimination has taken hold in the courts in Florida, for black murderers are *less* apt to receive the death sentence than white ones. A more careful reading, of course, leads to the explanation: killing whites is evidently a more "serious" crime (than killing blacks), whites do more of it, and whites therefore are more apt to find themselves on death row. Now here is the catch: a policy that sought to give blacks greater protection as victims of murder (e.g., making the death

Table 1. Rate of Capital Sentencing, Given Convictions for Murder, by Race of Killer and Victim, Florida, 1973-77[10]

Race of Killer

		Black	White		
Race of Victim	Black	$\dfrac{11}{2320} = .005$	$\dfrac{0}{111} = .000$	$\dfrac{11}{2431} = .005$	
	White	$\dfrac{48}{248} = .168$	$\dfrac{72}{2146} = .034$	$\dfrac{120}{2392} = .050$	
		$\dfrac{59}{2566} = .023$	$\dfrac{72}{2257} = .032$		

sentence stick to black and white corpses equally) would given them greater risks as killers.

When the state confronts a whole series of emancipatory equalities, each touching on several aspects of life at once, an impossibly overdetermined puzzle must be the eventual result. And one might be tempted to say that simple equality, however costly, may come to seem more attractive even to its affluent "victims."

Marginal Versus Global Equalities

A government or agency, which controls only part of social and economic life, has two quite different ways of promoting equality. It may seek to achieve equality within the sectors it touches, or it may attempt to promote equality in social and economic life as a whole. The first is what I will call *marginal*, the second what I will call *global*, equality. If, as one must expect, the unregulated side of society and its economy produces inequalities, these two views will lead to systematically different courses of action. In our cake-cutting metaphor, the marginal view will lead to equal portions, while the global view will lead to unequal portions designed to make up for unequal consumption of earlier courses in the meal. In the life of the state, more dramatic differences are to be expected.

Suppose, for momentary simplicity, that two members of society sought just one sort of thing, say, grapefruit, and that their acquisitions could come either from a private or public process of allocation. Smith gathers one hundred grapefruit privately, while Jones gathers only fifty, also privately. The state then sets out to promote equality between them by dividing a public pile of fifty grapefruit. In the view of marginal egalitarianism, Smith and Jones are each entitled to twenty-five of these public fruits. But this will, of course, leave

Smith's initial advantage intact. A global view would have the state (in the limiting case) award all fifty public fruits to Jones to make up for Smith's private advantage. The example is all too simple, but it helps to establish the poles of the complex continuum that lies between these two egalitarianisms, and clarifies the velocity with which the two may collide.

Marginalist egalitarianism supports a state that limits its agenda but dispatches those relatively few issues in an even-handed way. The laissez faire state, and its more recent "libertarian" analogue,[11] are not ostentatiously egalitarian. Yet they do entail important equalities: an equal right to whatever property one may acquire, an equal right to impartial justice, an equal liberty of thought and expression, formally symmetrical rights to vote and to participate in politics, and so on. Even the very capitalist institutions around which these ideologies of the state revolve were *once* assertively egalitarian, laying claim to (potentially) universal rights of property, production, and exchange against the explicitly inegalitarian fetters of feudalism. By the nineteenth century it had become common to treat this array of institutions—the liberal state with capitalist markets—as an embodiment of liberty, where liberty is seen in opposition to equality. But from the beginning, the real issue has not been liberty versus equality but a conflict between marginal and global views of equality. Here, for example, is Locke advocating a marginal conception of equality:

> I cannot be supposed to understand *all* sorts of equality. Age and virtue may give men a just precedency; excellence of parts and merit place others above the common level . . . and yet all this consists with the equality which all men are in, in respect of jurisdiction or dominion one over another which was the equality I . . . spoke of as being proper to the business at hand, being that equal right that every man hath to his natural freedom, without being subjected to the will or authority of another man. (Italics added)[12]

Locke, like Smith and even Nozick after him, is not arguing for liberty *against* equality, but equality of liberty as this may be embodied in the relatively narrow purview of the state and its system of property.

The polar opposition, therefore, is not so much more egalitarian as it is more *broadly* egalitarian. Here, the state is expected to promote equality in society understood globally. If ungoverned activities generate inequalities—of wealth or health, income or bargaining power, dignity or self-esteem—it becomes the state's job to provide a remedy for the losers. If recent political history has a lesson to teach, it is that the institutions of marginal equality described above are not ideally suited to the tasks of global equality. Such a state may be nearly useless in combating the most vulgar racism and the most extravagant exploitation, as long as the direct action of government is not required to sustain these evils. The thought, embraced by a million American liberals, that narrowly understood civil rights would emancipate the blacks is a tragic example of this. And countless smaller difficulties almost daily suggest that we are stuck with an awkward balancing act that protects the marginal equalities—the equalities of right—and at the same time promotes a more global conception of equality in social life.

Once we are committed to the general notion of global equality in society and also to the proposition that the state's agenda should be limited, then we must reach for compensatorily inegalitarian policies. These must be aimed to "make up for" inequalities generated in ungoverned activities (or in the past— e.g., Does the United States owe contemporary blacks compensation for slavery?). And once this occurs, the state will surely be charged with failure to maintain equality in its policies seen marginally. School busing becomes a plausible egalitarian policy, not because all children alike are bused (they aren't), or because each child receives the same net gain or loss from this policy (some lose, others gain), or because busing treats children, or anyone else, equally (it doesn't). Busing arises because equality in schools is a responsibility of the state, and is deeply affected by the *de facto* segregation of real estate markets, and because these markets are beyond the agency of the state. It is not that the proponents of busing are stupid or malicious, but that they must resort to marginal means to accomplish the work of global ideas. This cannot, in the end, be done without busing or some similarly inegalitarian remedy. The problem with busing is not, in short, busing, but rather that there is a mismatch between the globally egalitarian responsibilities of the state and the limited means of action available to it.

Equality and Value

We come now to two further ways of conceiving equality, best introduced by way of military example. An army quartermaster receives a memo requiring that every soldier be given "equal" footwear. In one view, he will issue boots with similar leather and construction, but cut to fit each man's feet, an allocation based on a comparison of individual needs, for example, the lengths and widths of feet. The aim will be to provide boots of equal value to each (relevantly different) soldier. A second view will lead to a simpler solution: identical boots for all, perhaps size $8^1/_2$D. In this view, boots are so equal as to rule out all envy, all incentive to switch boots. For surely, even a soldier with size 12E feet can gain nothing by trading in his $8^1/_2$Ds for another's $8^1/_2$Ds. These two ways of providing equal footwear rest on profoundly different conceptions of equality, both important to an understanding of the egalitarian state. Here are some additional "equalities" that further substantiate the two conceptions:

1A An equal right for every American to speak his native language

1B An equal right for every American to speak English

2A An education equally suited to the talents and interests of every child

2B An equal scientific education for every child

3A A tax amounting to an equal sacrifice at each income level

3B A tax of X dollars for everyone, rich and poor alike

The "A" solutions follow the conception that leads our quartermaster to find shoes to fit each soldier; the "B," the conception that leads him to issue everyone boots of the same size. Each conception turns on its own test of equality, namely:

Test A: Is X as well off with what X gets as Y is with what Y gets?[13]

Test B: Is X as well off with what X gets as X would be with what Y gets? (Likewise, is Y as well off with what Y gets as he would be with what X gets?)[14]

Test A leads us to find language rights or an education or tax rates or boots that will be of the same value for each subject. We will find ourselves treating different people *differently in order to treat them equally*. Test B leads us to insist on the same language rights, the same education, the same taxes, the same boots for all. Here, we will be making sure that no subject has a reason to switch places with another. And if all are treated identically, nobody can rationally entertain a sense of envy. We will, in this view, treat people, who may or may not be different, *identically in order to treat them equally*. There is, as anyone knows even from inarticulate experience with these two conceptions, every difference between them.

We are, in general, as attracted by Test A as we are repelled by Test B. Indeed, many of the most vehement antiegalitarian arguments are predicated on the second of these views and leave out the first. And the greatest of modern egalitarians was quite careful to place himself on the better side of this divide:

> equality of provision is not identity of provision. It is to be achieved, not by treating different needs in the same way, but by devoting equal care to ensuring that they are met in the different ways most appropriate to them, as is done by a doctor who prescribes different regimens for different constitutions, or a teacher who develops different types of intelligence by different curricula. The more anxiously, indeed, a society endeavours to secure equality of consideration for all its members, the greater will be the differentiation of treatment which, when once their common human needs have been met, it accords to the special needs of different groups and individuals among them.[15]

Only in a society where everyone has the same needs, tastes, and vulnerabilities—only, that is, in a society of denatured clones—will these two conceptions sustain common solutions to the issues confronted by governments. For, if any two of us have different needs, treatments of equal value to us will be different; and once government responds to these differences, full equality of the second sort will have been breached. It is as crisp as that.

The equality of full comparisons among distinct individuals (Test A) may appeal to intuition, but it does not generally appeal to the given needs of the state and its bureaucracy. First, such equality requires vast information about the public—its needs, tastes, and vulnerabilities. This information must be continually updated and continually applied to the fresh nuances of every allocative decision faced by government and its separate agencies. Second, once the appropriate "treatments"—educational policies, say—have been devised, the field administration required to apply the relevant distinctions to actual persons must itself become a source of cost and complexity. In bureaucratic terms, "uniform" solutions corresponding to Test B are just incomparably easier to manage and enforce. A third difficulty is epistemological and has a long history in economic theory. How are we to know that X is as well off with what he gets as Y is with what Y gets; that, for instance, two kids derive equal value from their educations, or that two taxpayers sacrifice the same net utility from paying up to the IRS? All such inferences require "interpersonal comparisons of utility," which must rest in turn on some quantitative integration of knowledge about separate minds (and sometimes bodies). While every decent person can, and must, make approximate comparisons of this sort in daily life, making them in a precise way is very difficult indeed. And, more relevant here, making them in a way that will stand up to the crude inference procedures available to the state, in courts or bureaucratic tribunals and the like, is a forbidding task indeed. How are bureaucrats to show the difference between treating different people differently in order to treat them equally, and treating different people differently to favor some over others? When we begin to ponder these questions, we find little difficulty in guessing why Test B and its relatively rigid conception will frequently win out over its more flexible rival in the halls of government.

Nor is it always and utterly clear that the more sensitive approach *should* prevail. This second thought turns on two desiderata. First, uniform treatment may have substantial utilitarian benefits in many cases. Consider, for instance, the matter of language rights. The flexible view (1A) can and does lead to duplication of communications, while the more rigid view (1B) removes these by coercing linguistic minorities to speak the common language. Second, the full comparisons implied by Test A may promote and foster paternalism in the state and its bureaucracy. The full implementation of this form of equality requires direct, extensive, and continuous consultation of mass publics. This exceedingly costly democratization may be short-circuited by the construction of working dogmas about what is beneficial and in what degree for particular groups. Sometimes these will be entirely benign, as is the current working principle that ramps are better than stairs for people in wheelchairs. Others, founded perhaps on racial and sexual stereotyping, may be vastly less benign.

Yet, very often the state must muddle through in such a way as to somehow balance these two opposing conceptions. The energy crisis is one such instance. If hardships are to be imposed, they should be imposed equally on all of us. One view is that prices should be encouraged to rise to a point at which demand declines to appropriate levels. These prices would be more or less uniform for all consumers, embodying equality as prescribed by Test B. But *is* that equality between rich and poor, between commuter and urbanite, between Northerner and Sunbelter? Yes, in the sense that none would envy the price at which others buy fuel oil or gasoline, but not in the sense that a lower-middle-class commuter in Burlington, Vermont, would quickly grasp. Yet, if policy responds to his view of fuller comparison, so that energy has lower unit cost in Vermont than in Virginia, this may appear blatantly unequal to those who pay the higher costs; and both will be right, according to one conception of equality or the other, and the government will be somehow wrong *however* it proceeds. Most likely, most of the time government will proceed on some middle course that accomplishes neither equality fully.

Equal Opportunities

The distinction between equal opportunity and equal results is known and recognized everywhere. A main difficulty, however, stems from our shared idea of equal opportunity, an idea that combines two deeply antagonistic conceptions.

The doctrine of equal opportunity has two utterly different interpretations. One is that of "impersonal competition": values (typically jobs, places in school, and the like) must and should be *un*equally distributed. Generally, this is so because these values are "lumpy" or "indivisible":[17] there can only be so many "good" jobs in a firm, and there can only be a single "best" one. These prizes should, we are told, be unequally distributed, whether necessity requires it or not, for two further reasons. First, they provide incentives for hard work, investment in "human capital," and other behaviors that generally promote the common good. Second, and more cynically, these inequalities provide a stable basis for class relations: one is always able to co-opt the most able "misfits" from the underclass, and one has a handy way to blame losers for their losses. The essential *method* is that the rules of competition be utterly impersonal. The competitors are not equal in their talents and will soon enough be unequal in their successes and failures. But the rules by which they are sorted out give equal terms of judgment to all. This impartiality is necessary if we are to "bring up" the most able children of yesterday's losers, if we are to provide an efficient scheme of incentives, and if we are rightly to blame losers for losing. Note what is most important about this doctrine: its aims are *not* mainly egalitarian, but utilitarian in nature.[18] It is, indeed, a doctrine aimed at promoting and protecting the interests of the strong.

Only by historical relativity has this doctrine of impersonal competition come to appear mainly as a species of egalitarianism. If we begin with a system of racist (or anti-Semitic, or anti-X) assignment, and if we suppose that the victims of these barbarities are able to win under impartial rules, we then have an egalitarian interpretation of impersonal competition that makes practical sense. A system that promotes the ascendance of the strong and gifted is not mainly egalitarian; it becomes egalitarian when this happy class of winners happens to include some of those who had been victims of more vulgar arrangements. This is why nondiscrimination, as entailed by impersonal competition, also comes to play a main role in emancipatory doctrines of equality for women, blacks, Hispanics, and others. But this same scheme must promote and foster inequality between gifted and ungifted blacks, between strong and weak women, between more and less talented Hispanics. Only because of its egalitarian *method* (impersonal rules), and because of its relation to these emancipatory issues, is this view to be counted as an egalitarian one.

A second doctrine of equal opportunity proposes that all should enjoy *equal prospects of success*. If the first doctrine (impersonal competition) suggests the model of a chess match, this one suggests the model of a *lottery*. In the former, every person may, and indeed *must*, live by the same rules; in the latter, every ticket has an equal chance of being drawn first. In the former, players of unequal skill have predictably *un*equal prospects; in the latter, all players, however talented or oafish, have equal odds for holding the winning ticket. This second conception of equal opportunity is egalitarian in its intent and enjoys none of the utilitarian advantages associated with impersonal competition. It provides no incentive structure; it gives no reason to expect that talented members of an underclass will move up; it gives no argument better than hard luck to blame

failure on failures. The doctrine of equal prospects does not promise equal results, but it does offer an a priori equality among individuals, and it will, with
great likelihood, dispatch the emancipatory functions just discussed better than
the doctrine of impersonal competition.

This second conception has two advantages in a society like our own. First,
it is consistent with a whole host of practical tactics designed to promote
emancipatory equalities for blacks, women, Hispanics, and other minorities. If
quotas are set for university admissions or hiring, and they are properly apportioned, equality of prospects within *and* between blocs is maintained. Or, as in
the famous University of California at Davis case, if separate pools are set up for
each bloc of applicants, this is consistent with the doctrine of equal prospects
between racial blocs (though competition within each pool may advantage the
more able black over the less able black, and so on). A second advantage is
simple clarity. While a doctrine of equal prospects must eventually prove unac-
ceptably costly to society—even to its "winners"—it is at least free of confusion.
In this particular it differs decisively from the main conceptions abroad in our
land.

This notion combines and conflates impersonal competition with equal prospects. It seems often to be thought that the former leads to the latter, and that
whatever violates the latter provides evidence for violation of the former. But
note that any relevant variation in personal gifts between two individuals must
upset this doctrine. Impersonal competition is, by design, *meant* to produce
unequal prospects, that is, to bestow advantages upon those who enjoy advantages. But let us put this aside momentarily and suppose that no relevant inequalities of given talent come into play. Imagine, even, that we begin with an
utterly egalitarian society where full simple equality prevails. Then for the first
time we set up some simple inequalities by creating some roles with special
privileges. These are to be assigned by an impersonal competition. A first difficulty is that the first generation of winners will give their offspring head starts in
the second generation of competition for these privileged roles. They will give
them better nutrition, better training, and better cultural coaching than can be
provided by losers of their generation. The second-generation system will remain an impersonal competition, but will no longer entail equal prospects, even
for a genetically matched set of competitors. This hybrid system is in this sense
self-cancelling in the span of two generations even under the most favorable
imaginary conditions.[19]

A second difficulty has so far been hidden by my inattention to the standards on which an impersonal competition is to be run. An impersonal competition must avoid rules that discriminate directly such as: "All white
candidates get a 10 percent bonus in scoring this test," or "Karl Smith and his
friends are ineligible to compete," or "Women must start half an hour late and
finish an hour early." By naming names and naming arbitrary categories, these
rules fail the test of impersonality. But impersonality is not the same as *neutrality*, for rules can bias prospects without naming beneficiaries and victims. It is
impersonal enough to require that candidates be judged for their physical bulk,
but this is not neutral in regard to sex; it is impersonal to say that command of a
European language is a prerequisite to success, but this is not neutral toward
Native Americans; it is impersonal to require prestigious university degrees for

elite jobs, but this is (at present) far from neutral with respect to race. This is no novel discovery and has been forcefully argued over the past decade. My concern is merely to point out that the American idea of equal opportunity is based on the conflation of two ultimately incompatible systems. One system, impersonal competition, is meant to promote unequal prospects, and the other is defined by the absence of such inequalities. Even the most powerful of states will not in the end manage to combine these two doctrines in a stable way, and will not do so for the same reasons that it cannot square a circle.

There, in outline, are five main ways in which the road to equality branches before the state. There is, of course, much more to say about the roads between these intersections and about the smaller lanes farther down the roads we choose. I shall content myself here with a quick synopsis and a small speculation. By way of synopsis, suppose that the government has set forth some program of equality, E, and that we wish to complain against it neither in the name of liberty nor in the name of efficiency, but in the name of equality itself. No matter what content, we can be assured that a critique is available to us under each of these headings:

1. The subject of equality:
    - E grants equality to too few people
    - E grants equality to too many people
    - E grants equality to the *wrong* people

2. The structure of equality's subject:
    - E doesn't grant equality, but merely equalizes its incidence over (perhaps racial) blocs in society
    - E wrongly tries to eliminate simple inequality itself; it should merely have evened out its incidence upon, say, blacks or women

3. The domain of equality:
    - E is equal so far as it goes, but it fails to diminish the (vast?) inequalities generated by processes it neglects to govern
    - By aiming to make up for (rightful) inequality in the rest of life, E (wrongly) treats its subjects unequally

4. The value comparisons on which equality is based:
    - E treats different people identically and thus treats them equally (as if it had given everyone shoes of the same size)
    - E treats people differently, which is not what we mean by equality

5. Procedure, prospect, and result of equality:
    - By treating people impersonally, E biases itself toward the strong and against the weak
    - By granting equal prospects of success to all, E (wrongly) negates the advantages of the strong

> - By attending merely to opportunities, not to results, E makes people equal only in their struggle to excel

The formula "Equality versus Liberty," or "Equality versus X," may of course still make sense, but it must share attention with the simpler formula "Equality versus Equality," and many of the fundamental decisions faced by government must fit this latter description. As our little menu suggests, the state can always be criticized in the name of equality; but, equally, the state can quite generally apologize for itself on the same ground.

Let me finish by turning to Tawney's wonderful little allegory, meant to ridicule the old and occasionally true formula "Equality versus Efficiency," namely, the view that equality leads to our having less and less to allocate equally:

> Given five fat sheep and ninety-five thin, how induce the ninety-five to resign to the five [the] richest pastures and shadiest corners? By [somehow] convincing them, obviously, that, if they do not, they will die of rot, be eaten by wolves, and be deprived in the meantime of such pastures as they have. . . . for there is nothing which frightens thin sheep like the fear of being thinner.[20]

The intervening half century has perhaps left these sheep a trifle less emaciated than they once were. But it has also brought a fresh battery of persuasions beyond this simple intimidation. For we may now find fat sheep telling thin ones that all the fields and pastures *are* equal if only you think about them, and about being equal, in *just* the right way.

REFERENCES

*This paper draws liberally on my collaborative work with Douglas Yates and Joseph Morone of Yale and Jennifer Hochschild of Duke, intended for publication as a book, "Equalities," in 1980.

[1] This equality in the distribution of rights was evidently once obscure enough to require explicit language. Thus, for instance, the Virginia Declaration of Rights (1776) uses the locution "equally free," while modern usage generally leaves the "equality" implicit.

[2] This essay aims merely to identify the main "first-order" contradictions in the form equality versus equality; in actuality, these are often combined to form second- or third-order difficulties. These are explored in my collaborative work with Douglas Yates, Joseph Morone, and Jennifer Hochschild. See Note 1.

[3] These and other quasi-empirical premises of political equality are explored in Sanford Lakoff, *Equality in Political Philosophy* (Cambridge: Harvard University Press, 1964). Toqueville in *Democracy in America* provides an amazingly rich analysis of such beliefs and their relationships to social history.

[4] Isaiah Berlin, "Equality," *Proceedings of the Aristotelian Society*, New Series, vol. 16, 1956.

[5] David Singer, "Famine, Affluence, and Society," in *Philosophy, Politics, and Society*, Peter Laslett and James Fishkin (eds.), 5th Series, (Oxford: Basil Blackwell, 1979), pp. 21-35.

[6] This becomes a critical point where invidious distinctions, corresponding to race, caste, or class, are at issue. A somewhat fuller exploration is to be found in my "A Principle of Simple Justice," in *Philosophy, Politics, and Society*, Peter Laslett and James Fishkin, (eds.) 5th Series (Oxford: Basil Blackwell, 1979), pp. 134-154.

[7] Robert Dahl, *After the Revolution* (New Haven: Yale Univeristy Press, 1970).

[8] *Government and the Sports Business* (Washington, D.C.: The Brookings Institution, 1974).

[9] An elegant critical assessment of this view in its contemporary forms is offered by Edwin Dorn in *Rules and Racial Equality* (New Haven: Yale University Press, 1979).

[10] These data are from William Bowens and Glenn Pierce, as summarized by Peter Ross Range in "Will He Be First?" *New York Times Magazine*, March 11, 1979, p. 78.

[11] For instance, Robert Nozick, *Anarchy, State and Utopia* (New York: Basic Books, 1973).

[12] John Locke, *Second Treatise of Government*, Part 6, Sec. 54.

[13]More precisely, suppose "V_{ii}" reads "the value Mr. I obtains from his own lot and "V_{jj}" reads "the value Mr. J obtains from his own lot." Test A is then met if, and only if, it is the case that

$$V_{ii} = V_{jj}, \text{ for all persons i or j}$$

[14]Suppose (extending the notation from the previous footnote) that "V_{ji}" reads "the value Mr. J would obtain from having Mr. I's lot," and "V_{ij}" denotes the value Mr. I would get from having Mr. J's lot. Test B, then, requires that

$$V_{jj} = V_{ji} \text{ and } V_{ii} = V_{ij}$$

This is equivalent to a conception that Hal Varian calls "equity." (f. "Equity, Envy and Efficiency," *Journal of Economic Theory*, 9: 63-91.

[15]R. H. Tawney, *Equality*, 4th Ed. (London: George Allen and Unwin Ltd., 1952), pp. 49-50.

[16]This difficulty is, indeed, made a foundation of neoclassical economic theory in Vilfredo Pareto, *Manual of Political Economy*, tr. Ann S. Schwier, (New York: Augustus M. Kelley, Publishers, 1971). See in particular p. 47ff.

[17]See on this and subsequent points, Bernard Williams, "The Idea of Equality," in *Philosophy, Politics, and Society*, Peter Laslett and W. G. Runciman (eds.), 2nd Series (Oxford: Basil Blackwell, 1962) pp. 110-131.

[18]See, for instance, the discussion of "population" in Pareto, *Manual*, p. 281ff. for a cold-bloodedly utilitarian account of impersonal competition in economic production.

[19]See Williams, *The Idea of Equality*, for his "warrior class" illumination of this point.

[20]Tawney, *Equality*, pp. 150-151.

JAMES FISHKIN

Moral Principles and Public Policy[1]

MORALITY HAS ALWAYS PLAYED A MAJOR ROLE in our most intensely debated problems of public policy—from slavery, Prohibition, and civil rights to more recent issues such as abortion, the environment, affirmative action, reverse discrimination, and the employment rights of homosexuals. Yet for most of the last half century professional moral and political philosophers have thought it inappropriate to enter this arena of policy debate. Preoccupied with issues of language, and hamstrung by the sharp division between facts and values, they felt their professional role required a kind of neutrality on substantive moral issues.

This neutrality left the subject in a moribund state, so much so that in 1956 Peter Laslett could plausibly declare, "For the moment anyway, political philosophy is dead."[2] While there had been philosophers writing in English about political questions of the broadest importance for over 300 years, by the mid-1950s, this tradition appeared to have been broken. Even though the subject experienced a modest revival in the years following, in 1962 Isaiah Berlin could still write an essay entitled "Does Political Theory Still Exist?"[3] and no one could regard an answer to that question as beyond controversy.

By now, however, it should be evident that political philosophy in the English-speaking world has undergone an enormous resurgence. Futher, this resurgence has been sparked by a direct engagement with the moral issues of the day. In the pages of *Philosophy and Public Affairs, Ethics,* and in many other journals in philosophy, political science, and law, the morality of particular public policy problems is now being debated: income distribution, equal opportunity, triage situations, abortion, famine relief, the role of morality in war, sexual harassment, problems of population and futurity, and the value of human life are only the most obvious examples.

This change has come about, in part, as a legacy from the sixties. The civil rights struggle and the Vietnam War both placed substantive issues on the agenda of moral and political theory: civil disobedience, the doctrine of the just war, equal opportunity, and criteria for legitimate political authority. It is not surprising that those who became engaged by these issues in their personal lives might come to consider them in their professional lives as well.

There are other factors in this revival. The fact/value distinction is no longer taken quite so seriously, nor is it applied so sharply. The analysis of "ordinary language," a preoccupation once so fashionable, has now largely faded from the scene.

Whatever the reasons, moral issues of direct relevance to public policy now receive an enormous amount of scholarly attention. This phenomenon is certainly a fortunate one for the health of political theory, but there is one deeply troubling aspect of this revival. Moral and political philosophers have reentered the arena of policy debate with the same general kinds of principles as those that already dominate mass public discussion. Philosophers have, of course, refined many particulars, but in certain fundamental respects their proposals are the same as those found in public debate. These principles, if taken at face value, are too simple for the actual complexities of policy choice. A government that adhered strictly to these prescriptions would find itself committed to policies that are, I will argue, morally indefensible. Perhaps contemporary theorists do not really intend their principles to be taken at face value. Perhaps they have in mind the addition of exceptions or qualifications that would rule out nasty counterexamples. If so, then this essay can be interpreted as a recommendation about the spirit in which these proposals must be taken. For unless these principles are explicitly modified for the cases to be proposed, they stand vulnerable to obvious objections.

My argument is a systematic version of the "mental experiment" that Joseph Schumpeter proposed in 1942 for evaluating the principle of democracy. He asked us to "transport ourselves into a hypothetical country that, in a democratic way, practices the persecution of Christians, the burning of witches, the slaughtering of Jews." Even if every procedural nicety proposed by the reader were satisfied, Schumpeter argues that "we should certainly not approve of these practices on the ground that they had been decided on according to the rules of democratic procedure." Schumpeter concluded that "there are ultimate ideals and interests which the most ardent democrat will put above democracy." Given any specification of procedures, it is possible to imagine those procedures applied so as to legitimate unacceptable results for some portion of the population. While democracy has great value as a political method, it is insufficient as an ethical "end in itself." Even when fully implemented, it is not a criterion that, by itself, can settle the question of the moral legitimacy of public policies.[4]

I want to apply a test analogous to Schumpeter's mental experiment to the full range of ethical criteria that are now being seriously applied to public policy. Virtually all of the principles currently prominent in contemporary moral and political theory fail this simple test: they are unacceptable because they support policies that impose severe deprivations when an alternative policy would have imposed no severe deprivations whatsoever. That is, they will all support policies that destroy the most essential interests of some portion of the population when an alternative policy would not have had comparable effects on anyone.

This criticism applies to three broad categories of principles that together cover virtually all the ethical criteria now being seriously applied to public policy. First, there are principles such as majority rule, unanimity, and theories of consent. We can call these criteria, defined in terms of a decision rule, *procedural* principles.[5] Second, there are principles such as equality, utilitarianism, and Rawls's general conception of justice. These principles offer us a theory of something that has value (money, utility, or even rights and liberties) and then specify some structure according to which it should be distributed. Should we prefer more equal distributions? Or distributions with a higher total? Or distributions with a higher minimum? We can call these criteria, defined in terms of a structure of distribution, *structural* principles.[6] Third, there are principles that offer guarantees that a person will never experience consequences of a certain kind. Robert Nozick's recent work offers the most prominent example of this position. We can call these criteria, defined in terms of inviolable guarantees, *absolute-rights* principles.[7]

All principles of these three kinds violate our minimum test—they would all support policies imposing severe deprivations when an alternative policy would have imposed no severe deprivations on anyone—for if we are to take their proposals seriously, and apply them consistently, without exceptions or further qualifications, we will find ourselves legitimating consequences as dreadful as those in Schumpeter's mental experiment. Let us apply our minimum test to each of these three kinds of principles.

Procedural Principles

Consider Idi Amin's infamous expulsion of Asians from Uganda. Approximately 50,000 Asians, who had built up positions of hard-won prosperity over several generations, were forced to leave virtually penniless. Many were Ugandan citizens who became stateless persons when their papers were confiscated. There were strange disappearances, robberies, and murders. Those who survived cruel treatment at the hands of the Ugandan authorities eventually found refuge in some fifteen countries, principally Great Britain.

In the spirit of Schumpeter's mental experiment, we can ask: Would it change our evaluation of Amin's treatment of the Asians if he had first held a procedurally fair plebiscite on the issue? The policy was, in fact, resoundingly popular among black Ugandans. It should be clear, however, that majority rule should not be invoked as a moral principle to legitimate these results. Even though a majority might support it, we still feel on firm ground in condemning such a policy. This difficulty applies not only to majority rule, but to all procedural principles. We will first consider nonunanimous procedural principles (i.e., those that require less than unanimity) and then turn to the unanimity rule itself.

Any procedural principle requiring less than unanimous agreement from some portion of the population (e.g., majority rule, two-thirds, or some general consensus specified by the principle of consent) can obviously legitimate severe deprivations on those whose support is *not* required by the principle. The Ugandan Asians are symbolic of the theoretical vulnerability of any minority that finds itself in a losing coalition.

But there appears to be one procedural principle that avoids this difficulty. Unanimity, after all, requires the agreement of everyone for any new policy.[8] Whatever its other impracticalities, it seems to pass our simple test. For unanimity endows everyone, including the Asians, with a veto.

However, these merits of the unanimity rule fade quickly when we account for policy omissions as well as commissions. A *commission* is a change in existing policies; an *omission* is a continuation of existing policies.[9] Severe deprivations may result from policy omissions as easily as from commissions. And once this possibility is realized, the unanimity rule fits within our general argument.

It is true that under unanimity even one person can always avoid losing by policy commission. But, of course, *everyone* except one person can, therefore, lose by policy omission. Anyone has a veto. Anyone can, by himself, produce a policy omission that affects everyone else.

How can deprivations be imposed by omission? Imagine only that some group requires food to avoid starvation (perhaps because of a famine) or emergency assistance or medical care (perhaps because of a flood or other natural disaster), and that such events pose a new policy problem. If there is not already a policy, the veto of any new policy could have consequences as dreadful (for all not part of the blocking coalition) as any acts of commission discussed above. Or, suppose the issue is not a new one but merely an old one about which agreement has never been reached. Perhaps there is mass poverty and a small, wealthy elite just sufficiently numerous to block any redistribution. The continuing absence of any redistributive measures (unemployment compensation, medical care, food assistance) could deny fulfillment of the most basic human needs to the bulk of the population.

When omissions are taken into account, it is obvious that unanimity is no more successful than any other decision rule in preventing a regime from imposing (avoidable) severe deprivations. The severe deprivations that a regime fails to prevent can be as terrible as those that it decides to impose.

Hence any purely *procedural* principle fails our minimum test, for any such principle would legitimate policies imposing severe deprivations (through commission or omission) on some portion of the population, even when these deprivations are entirely avoidable. Nonunanimous principles can obviously do this through policy commission. And once the effects of omissions are reckoned in, the unanimity rule becomes vulnerable to the same objection. For this reason, procedural principles are by themselves insufficient to resolve ethical questions about public policy. If there are to be adequate moral principles for public policy, they cannot be purely procedural in form.

Structural Principles

The Ugandan government attempted to justify the expulsion of the Asians as a measure that would redistribute the economy into the hands of black Africans. Although it was not successful as a redistributive policy, let us imagine our reaction to it *if* it had been. Suppose that redistributing the goods of the Asians—their wealth, business, jobs, homes, or other entitlements—improved the overall *structure* of distribution of those goods. If our structural criterion is equality, let us assume that the resulting distribution is more equal. Or, if we are utilitarians, let us assume that a greater aggregate utility results. Or, if (following John Rawls's general conception of justice)[10] we are interested in the level of goods at the bottom, let us assume that this redistribution increases the minimum share. Whatever our structural criterion, we can imagine that the redistribution of goods from the Asians improves the overall structure. We can then imagine that, as a result, the Asians are either expelled or forced into the lowest positions or into the countryside, as Amin at one point, threatened.

Would we approve such treatment of the Asians merely because it improved the overall structure of distribution? Surely we are compelled to ask: If a change in the distributional structure is desired, is there not some other way of attaining it, some way that does not impose such severe deprivations on the Asian minority, or on anyone else, some way that, perhaps may demand sacrifice but does not impose such severe consequences on any particular group?

Let us suppose that the structural principle at issue is equality.[11] My objection to the principle of equality here is that even if there were a route to greater equality that did not impose severe deprivations, the principle of equality would be entirely insensitive to it. It would have us be indifferent (in the technical sense of rating alternatives precisely equal) between two policies: (a) The Ugandan strategy of equalization, and (b) a route to the same end that imposes no severe deprivations on anyone. If these two policies lead to the same degree of equality, on that principle there is no moral issue in choosing (a) rather than (b). We *could not be wrong* in choosing the Ugandan strategy. The fact that one policy would impose such severe deprivations on the Asians counts for nothing in comparing them. As long as the final result is a more equal distribution, equality would legitimate this kind of outcome.

The general point can be seen from an abstract example. Put simply, imagine that we have a society of six persons, and that under a status quo, situation X, we can rank them in terms of their shares of goods. Person A has the most, so he is in position 1; person B has the next most, so he is in position 2; and so on. Now let us imagine an alternative situation, Y, that is *structurally identical* to X in that the share of goods in each position under Y is exactly the same as under X. The top position has precisely the same share under Y as under X, the second position has precisely the same share, and so on. Hence any structural principle, such as equality, utilitarianism, or Rawls's general conception of justice (that the minimum share should be maximized), must view X and Y as identical. There could be no moral issue of a structural kind if we chose to move from X to Y, for they have identical structures.

X		Y	
Positions	Persons	Positions	Persons
1	A	1	B
2	B	2	C
3	C	3	D
4	D	4	E
5	E	5	F
6	F	6	A

However, there is one crucial difference between X and Y in this example. Under Y, person A has been moved from the top position to the lowest one while everyone else has been moved up one notch. I will assume in this example that the differences between *adjacent* positions are minimal while the differences, of course, between positions that are not adjacent may be substantial. Thus each individual who is moved up only a single position under Y is not significantly benefited. However, A, who has moved from the top position to the bottom one, has experienced a very substantial change in his position. In moving from X to Y we have played a kind of musical chairs in the assignment of persons or positions. While no one has gained much by the change, A has lost badly.

Let us apply any structural principle to the problem of choosing between two alternative policies: (a) retention of X as a status quo, and (b) shift to Y from X. The essential point here is that *any* structural principle must be indifferent between these two alternatives. Because X and Y are structurally identical, any such principle—whether equality, utilitarianism, Rawls's "maximin" criterion (requiring that we maximize the minimum), or something else—must be indifferent between them. They have precisely the same degree of equality, the same total, the same minimum. Because there are no structural considerations at issue in the choice between X and Y, they must be rated equal by any structural principle.

But because they are rated equal by any such principle, such a structural principle would legitimate the choice of (b), the shift to Y as an alternative, rather than (a), the retention of X. It would legitimate such a choice because there would be, by hypothesis, no grounds for a moral objection to the change. According to such a principle, one alternative must be fully as good as the other.

But the alternative that is rated equally good (b) would move A from position 1 to position 6. Assuming that this change in fortunes is sufficiently drastic, this would involve the imposition of a severe deprivation upon A. We can, in other words, consider this a destruction of A's essential interests. Further, this deprivation is accompanied by no substantial benefits to anyone else (since the differences between adjacent positions were assumed to be insignificant) and no improvement on structural grounds—no improvement, that is, in the overall degree of equality, the total goods or welfare, the level at the bottom, and so on.

It should be added that there is nothing special about this particular example. Innumerable instances could be adduced where structural principles would fail our minimum test because of their unique focus on the abstract structure of distribution without any sensitivity to the way persons are assigned to positions in that structure. A in this example could as easily be a large group as an individual. Any number of similar examples could obviously be devised where severe deprivations result from changes in assignment to structurally identical positions.

This is the special property of structural principles: they are entirely indifferent to such effects on persons independent of effects on positions. Structural principles have no place for the information in the second columns under X and Y, that the persons in particular positions under Y are different from the persons in those positions under X. Yet it is persons and not positions who would experience these moves, and it is the life history of particular individuals that would be affected, positively or negatively. Ranked positions by themselves are only abstractions from those life histories. Thus structural principles are insufficient by themselves to resolve ethical questions about public policy, for they have the crucial defect that, by their logic, they cannot take into account ethical questions about the assignment of persons to positions. An adequate principle for public policy cannot be purely structural in form. Yet, it is fair to say that most of the ethical criteria commonly applied to discussions of public policy fall unambiguously within this category.

A few words should be added about how this argument applies to John Rawls's important book *A Theory of Justice*. A principle must be structural in form to fall within this critique. The complexity in Rawls's case is that he offers two quite different formulations of his principles, and only one version is clearly structural in form. That version is his "general conception of justice" that requires all social "primary goods," namely, "liberty and opportunity, income and wealth, and the bases of self-respect," to be distributed in "maximin" fashion (to maximize the minimum share).[13] This general conception is clearly a structural principle because it offers an account of something that has value ("primary goods"), and then requires that situations be preferred according to whether they improve the structure of distribution of that value (by raising the minimum share).

However, Rawls also offers another, more complex set of principles that he calls the "special conception" of justice. This special conception requires that liberties be equal, and first in order of priority; that equal opportunity be next in priority; and that income and wealth be distributed in "maximin" fashion. His priority rules require that no amount of liberty, however small, should be sacrificed for any amount of opportunity, however great. Further, no amount of equal opportunity, however small, should be sacrificed for any amount of income and wealth, however great.[14]

The relation between this special conception and the overall maximum notion of the general conception is controversial.[15] I only need say this about it. If Rawls is correct in believing that his special conception merely constitutes a special case of the general conception (a more detailed specification of what it would mean to maximize the minimum share of primary goods), by the logic of structural principles that version of the theory should fall within this argument. My own suspicion, however, is that Rawls's special conception is not that kind of principle. It is, in fact, the kind of more complex principle that does not clearly fit any of our three categories. In this respect, it is a principle of a different kind from those that have dominated public discussion and thus the kind of principle that does not fall within the limits of this argument.

However, its complexity does not save it from other difficulties. There are serious questions to be raised about both its derivation and its substantive implications. But these issues are too complex to be dealt with here.[16] For present purposes, my argument here should be interpreted as applying only to one of Rawls's two formulations of his principles. It is the "general conception"—because it is clearly structural in form—that must share the defects of equality, utilitarianism, and the other structural principles discussed here.

Absolute Rights

Let us modify our original Ugandan example. Suppose that the Asians are not the richest but the poorest minority, and that there is a temporary food shortage that threatens the poorest sections of the country with starvation. And even though food has been stockpiled for just such an emergency, the government—perhaps in realizing it is *only* the Asians who are threatened with starvation—does nothing.

Robert Nozick's theory of absolute rights could be invoked by the government to legitimate such a policy of inaction, for Nozick's theory provides only one basis for evaluating a policy: Does it violate rights? And rights in Nozick's sense can be violated only when certain "side-constraints" are crossed—when actions of force, theft, or fraud interfere with someone's "entitlements" or cross someone's "boundaries." In this case, if the government chose *inaction*, no side-constraints would be violated. Everyone's rights would remain intact and everyone's boundaries would remain uncrossed if the government were to do nothing at all.[17]

The crucial fact about an absolute-rights theory such as Nozick's is that prescriptions follow only from rights violations. It is this simplicity that apparently provides such a theory with much of its appeal. But it is also this simplicity that renders it indifferent between alternatives that all avoid violating rights. According to this kind of theory, all such alternatives must be equally good.

Compare two alternatives in this case: (a) the policy of saving the Asians from starvation, and (b) the policy of doing nothing. Neither of these policies violates rights in Nozick's sense. There would be no moral issue—in terms of the absolute-rights theory—in choosing (b) rather than (a)—even though the Asians would starve needlessly if (b) were chosen. On Nozick's theory, we could not be wrong if we chose (b) rather than (a). One must be fully as good as the other. The starvation of the Asians, as long as it does not result from a rights violation, counts for nothing.

This difficulty is not merely the result of Nozick's particular formulation of absolute rights. It is an instance of a more general problem that applies to all absolute-rights theories, that is, all theories that require that the state *never* violate the rights of anyone; for depending on the precise formulation, all theories of this kind will either fail our minimum test or they will produce logically inconsistent injunctions. They will either (a) justify imposing severe deprivations when an alternative policy would not have imposed any severe deprivations whatsoever, or (b) they will yield inconsistent prescriptions by absolutely ruling out every alternative policy in a blind-alley situation where, no matter what the state does, someone's rights will be violated. My general claim about absolute-rights theories is that those formulations that maintain logical consistency are all subject to the objection that they fail our minimum test.

The general form of an absolute-rights theory is that their prescriptions can all be captured by the injunction: Never violate the rights of anyone. We can divide formulations of this basic absolute-rights injunction into those that are (i) complete or (ii) incomplete in the protection they offer against the imposition of severe deprivations.

In other words, there is a kind of absolute-rights theory that would completely and absolutely prohibit policies imposing what we have been calling here "severe deprivations," consequences that destroy a person's most essential interests. Let us imagine that we arrived at a reasonable specification of all of the extreme harms that we wished to count as severe deprivations and that we then formulated a rights theory of the absolute kind intended to rule out all such deprivations. Such a theory would represent alternative (i) just mentioned; it would be *complete* in the protection it offered against severe deprivations. I will argue that any such complete absolute-rights theory must be subject to inconsistency. On the other hand, any absolute-rights theory of the incomplete kind must fail our minimum test.

Any formulation of absolute rights offering complete protection will result in inconsistency for any problem in which every alternative open to the regime violates someone's rights. The absolute-rights injunction, recall, is never violate the rights of anyone. One case of rights violations contravenes this injunction as much as numerous cases would. An absolute-rights theory does not simply require minimizing rights violations. Rather, it requires that they be avoided entirely.[18]

There are cases in which any absolute-rights theory that offers complete protection will produce inconsistent results. We have only to consider the general case in which, corresponding to each alternative policy (including the policy of inaction), there is a group of one or more persons who will suffer severe deprivations under that policy.

Given the enormous variety of consequences that can count as severe deprivations connected to government omissions and commissions, there is no shortage of such cases. We need only imagine a triage situation or some other "tragic choice" in which someone will die no matter which policy is chosen.

To make the point as simply as possible, let me propose a hypothetical example. Imagine a medieval city that attempts to deal with the plague by setting up a kind of quarantine. Every house whose inhabitants show signs of the disease is sealed off completely so that nothing can escape. As a consequence, the occupants all die of starvation (or perhaps suffocation). But the policy saves the bulk of the town. A large proportion of the inhabitants who would surely have perished otherwise are saved.

Let us assume that, owing to ignorance of how the disease is spread, this was the only known strategy that offered reasonable prospects of saving a large portion of the population. Thus the available policy alternatives can be distinguished as:

1. Letting the disease run its course (or adopting only remedies known to be ineffectual)
2. Quarantine

The second option can be presumed to impose severe deprivation on some persons who might not otherwise die from the disease, as any house that showed signs of the plague among any of its occupants would have to be quarantined. Ignorance about who has the disease or about how it is spread has cruel consequences here.

It should be evident that if (1) and (2) are the only alternatives, they *both* impose severe deprivations. Any government that attempted to live up to the injunction never to impose severe deprivations would find itself in a blind alley.

If every alternative (every possible action or inaction) violates someone's rights, then the absolute-rights injunction leads to the prohibition of every alternative. But to say of each alternative that it is wrong is to say that it would be right to adopt some other alternative (or combination of alternatives) instead.[19] However, every other alternative is also wrong in this kind of case. Hence this self-contradictory set of prescriptions—a moral blind alley—results from any complete absolute-rights formulation applied to such cases.

Now this kind of blind alley may be avoided by an incomplete, rather than a complete, formulation of absolute rights. By omitting some severe deprivations from the protection afforded by absolute rights, it is possible to avoid such inconsistent injunctions.

Nozick deals explicitly with the problem in this way. He protects against all actual "boundary crossings" (committed without consent) by proposing a side-constraint notion of rights. However, objectionable consequences that do not involve such boundary crossings (that is, that do not violate side-constraints) are not prohibited in any way by the theory.

Of course, distinguishing positive boundary crossings from failures to act is not the only way in which an absolute-rights theory may be incomplete in the protection it offers against severe deprivations. For example, other interesting absolute-rights theories have been developed that distinguish from all other consequences those consequences directly *intended* by an action.[20]

Whatever the strategy of incompleteness, the difficulty is that if a severe deprivation is not ruled out absolutely, it becomes a matter of utter indifference for such theories. Absolute-rights theories offer no mechanism, apart from the absolute prohibition, for taking account of such deprivations.

Consider the case in which the bringing about of severe deprivations is not covered by absolute rights. The deprivations might not be covered because they would be brought about by a failure to act rather than an action. Perhaps if food is not provided, people will starve, or if medical care is not provided, people will die of disease. Using Nozick's strategy of incomplete protection, such severe deprivations that result from failures to act would not count as violations of rights. Or, perhaps the severe deprivations do not count as rights violations because they are not deliberately intended. Thomas Nagel has proposed an absolute-rights theory of this kind.[21]

Consider any such policy, A, that imposes severe deprivations that are not covered by the absolute-rights prohibitions. Because these deprivations do not violate rights, an absolute-rights theory must be entirely insensitive to them. Within an absolute-rights theory there is only room for two judgments: either a policy is prohibited (because it violates rights), or it is not prohibited (because it does not violate rights). If a policy (A) imposing severe deprivations falls into the latter category because it violates none of the proposed rights, it must be considered to be as good as any other policy that violates no rights.

Now consider an alternative policy, B, that violates no rights and also imposes no severe deprivations on anyone. Perhaps B is the policy of organizing a voluntary project to provide the food or medical assistance denied by A. Or perhaps B involves a government project to provide the assistance.

Any absolute-rights theory must be entirely indifferent between a policy B that imposes no severe deprivations on anyone and a policy A of the kind described above, which does impose severe deprivations, but not by actions covered by the absolute-rights prohibitions. For if neither A nor B violates rights, they must both be equally legitimate policies. The only value posited is non-violation of absolute rights, and both policies satisfy it equally.

It is in this way that absolute-rights theories that avoid inconsistency by removing some deprivations entirely from any prohibition by absolute rights must also violate our minimum condition. By ignoring entirely the imposition of such deprivations, such theories must be indifferent between (that is, they must rate as equally good) an alternative (A) that imposes such deprivations and an alternative (B) that does not. My objection is that within such a theory, we *could not be wrong* if we chose the policy that needlessly imposes the severe deprivations. Such severe deprivations, if they do not fall under the absolute prohibition, must count for nothing in comparing the alternative policies.

It is the very simplicity of such theories—a simplicity that results from their utter dependence on a single injunction—that renders them too clumsy and insensitive for complex cases involving conflicting claims, conflicting rights, or conflicting efforts to avoid severe deprivations. It is for this reason, I believe, that absolute-rights theories are defective. No adequate principle for public policy should fall unambiguously within this category.

*   *   *

Moral and political theorists must set about the task of inventing new principles that are not purely procedural, structural, or absolute rights in form. Perhaps these various kinds of principles need to be combined in new and complex ways. Or perhaps principles of an entirely different kind must be devised. In any case, I believe that principles of the kinds just discussed cannot by themselves be relied on to deal adequately with the ethics of public policy.

It should be emphasized that our minimum condition for acceptable moral principles is not, in itself, adequate as a guide to policy, for it offers only an intentionally *incomplete* prescription: that we not impose severe deprivations when they are entirely avoidable. However, this principle leaves two kinds of cases entirely undecided: cases where every alternative policy would impose severe deprivations on someone, and cases where no alternative policy would impose severe deprivations on anyone. Our minimum condition does not presume to resolve these more controversial cases. Rather, I proposed it only as a way of singling out certain horrendous and entirely avoidable wrongs that an adequate principle should not legitimate. It is merely a general way of formulating a class of counterexamples.

If some readers find this minimum condition obvious and unsurprising, so much the better, for they will have granted me the basis for my argument. What I do believe to be surprising is that so many of the principles that are currently prominent are vulnerable to so obvious an objection. We have arrived at this juncture, I believe, because theorists have reentered the moral arena with principles of the same general kinds as those that already dominate public debate. Principles of these three kinds, if taken at face value, are simply inadequate to the complexities of policy choice. Different theories that do not clearly fit any of our three categories will be required if more defensible principles for public policy are to be developed.

REFERENCES

[1]In this essay I rely on arguments I develop more systematically in *Tyranny and Legitimacy: A Critqiue of Political Theories* (Baltimore: Johns Hopkins University Press, forthcoming). For an extended discussion of the "simple test" employed here, see Part I.

[2]Peter Laslett, *Philosophy, Politics and Society*, First Series, (Oxford: Basil Blackwell, 1956) p. vii.

[3]Isaiah Berlin, "Does Political Theory Still Exist?" in Peter Laslett and W. G. Runciman (eds.) *Philosophy, Politics and Society*, Second Series, (Oxford: Basil Blackwell, 1962), pp. 1-33.

[4]Joseph Schumpeter, *Capitalism, Socialism and Democracy* (New York: Harper & Row, 1942), pp. 240-43.

[5]This group of principles can be described more precisely. By a procedural principle I mean one that specifies a rule of decision but specifies nothing about the content of those decisions, apart from possible requirements that the rule of decision not be altered in the future. By a rule of decision I mean a specification that support (i.e., agreement, concurrence, or actions of assent) from certain combinations of persons (i.e., certain numbers, proportions, or particular named persons, perhaps in some specified order) is necessary and sufficient to produce authoritative (i.e., legitimate) actions by the regime.

[6]This group of principles can be specified more precisely. By a structural principle I mean a principle that will determine any state of affairs, X, to be better, equal, or worse than any other state of affairs, Y, based entirely on the information available from an account of payoffs to positions under X and under Y. By payoffs I mean goods or welfare in a sense specified by the principle. By positions I mean groupings of individuals, each group consisting of 1/nth of the population listed in order of their shares of goods or welfare. In other words, given a matrix of payoffs to positions for any two situations X and Y, a structural principle will choose between the two situations (or rank them precisely equal).

[7]An absolute-rights principle is one that evaluates policies according to whether they conform to the injunction: Never violate the rights of anyone. Observance of this injunction is taken to be necessary and sufficient for a policy's legitimacy; violation is sufficient for its illegitimacy. By a right I mean an unconditional guarantee that a person, A, will not experience certain consequences (specified by the theory) as the result of the actions of others (or as the result of certain kinds of actions). If, in ways specified by the theory, other persons harm him or interfere with his actions, they violate his rights. For an absolute-rights theory it is important that the guarantee be defined in an *unconditional* way. By this I mean that A's claim to be protected from certain consequences (as the result of the action of others) cannot be dependent upon the enforceability of protection for anyone else. In other words, we would be able to determine in any particular case whether A has a right not to experience consequences of type X (as a result of the actions of others) without our also having to know whether protecting A requires our not protecting someone else. Absolute rights offer protection regardless of such considerations pertaining to the protection of others. In this way they are unconditional.

[8]There are, of course, important issues about what we mean by "everyone." Would the unanimity rule include children, criminals, the insane? For an illuminating discussion of who should be included as members in the polity, see Robert Dahl's "Procedural Democracy" in Peter Laslett and James Fishkin (eds.) *Philosophy, Politics and Society*, Fifth Series (Oxford: Basil Blackwell/New Haven: Yale University Press, 1979).

[9]Hence some "commissions" will actually be changes in policy that result in a failure to act, e.g., a cancellation of programs previously adopted, while some "omissions" will actually be retentions in policy that continue action, e.g., the noncancellation of programs previously adopted.

[10]John Rawls, *A Theory of Justice* (Cambridge, Mass.: Harvard University Press, 1971), p. 303.

[11]By the principle of "equality" here I mean that Douglas Rae (in this volume) calls "simple" or "direct" equality—the principle, in other words, applied to allocation. His other, "emancipatory" usage of the term, which he applies to problems of assignment, falls outside of the "structural" category as I define it here. For a discussion of various measures of equality in the "structural" sense, see A. K. Sen, *On Economic Inequality* (New York: W. W. Norton, 1973), ch. 2.

[12]These examples might suggest that our minimum test has a status quo bias. However, there are cases where maintaining a status quo can impose severe deprivations, even when some change from the status quo would not. For a discussion of these complexities, see my "*Tyranny and Legitimacy*," ch. 10.

[13]Rawls, *A Theory of Justice*, p. 303.

[14]Ibid., pp. 301-302.

[15]See, for example, Brian Barry, *The Liberal Theory of Justice* (Oxford: Oxford University Press, 1973) ch. 6-11. See also my "Justice and Rationality: Some Objections to the Central Argument in Rawls's Theory," in the *American Political Science Review*, 69(2) (June 1975): 615-629. I also explore this problem in some detail in Part III of *Tyranny and Legitimacy*.

[16]See, James Fishkin, "Justice and Rationality," and *Tyranny and Legitimacy*, Part III.

[17]Robert Nozick, *Anarchy, State and Utopia* (New York: Basic Books, 1974), pp. 28-32.

[18]The kind of theory that would simply minimize rights violation is not an absolute-rights theory at all. It is the kind of theory Nozick labels—and rejects—as a "utilitarianism of rights." Ibid., pp. 28-32.

[19]Throughout this essay I assume that *ought* implies *can*.

[20]See, for example, Thomas Nagel, "War and Massacre," in *War and Moral Responsibility*, Marshall Cohen, Thomas Nagel, and Thomas Scanlon (eds.) (Princeton: Princeton University Press, 1974).

[21]Ibid.

JOHN LOGUE

The Welfare State: Victim of Its Success

THE "WELFARE STATE" IS A TERM constantly used but rarely defined. It is positively value laden everywhere except in the United States, where it has had a bad press. As generally used, it implies the provision of economic security for the overwhelming majority of the population through a large public sector and a considerable sense of social solidarity. It is a state democratic in form, interventionist by inclination, and eager to manage the capitalist economy to achieve steady economic growth and maintain full employment. It is identified politically with European Social Democrats and with liberalism in America, although the success of the former has far exceeded that of the latter.

This essay will examine the nature and origin of the welfare state and some of its problems, both real and those perceived as real. Its point of departure is the Scandinavian experience, for Denmark, Norway, and Sweden are welfare states par excellence. The homogeneity of their populations and the manageable size of their societies give their problems and policies a degree of clarity absent in the United States or Britain. Because they have not been plagued by separatist movements, urban terrorists, racial divisions, or ethnic and linguistic strife, their politics have been able to focus on the central issues of the welfare state— economic production, distribution, and security. The Scandinavian countries seem to be a more advanced form of a general developmental pattern common to Western European industrial nations, though not, perhaps, to the United States and Japan, which may well be *sui generis*. Since Marquis Childs popularized the notion in the mid-1930s, Scandinavia has been seen as a kind of laboratory of social change.[1] With regard to the welfare state, at least, this is a valid view: the forms developed there are purer, and the problems faced are not those of failure but of success.

In Praise of the Welfare State

> By a double re-distribution of income through social in-
> surance and children's allowances, want, as defined in
> the social surveys, could have been abolished in Britain
> before the present war.
>
> —*Social Insurance and Allied Services*,
> Report of the Beveridge Committee, 1942

The addition of the adjective "welfare" has broadened the concept of the state. Previously the state's domestic role was that of policeman and arbiter, a provider of roads, limited education, and, in countries with state churches, religious solace. But former practitioners of the art of statecraft would have difficulty recognizing their charge today. The bulk of the modern state's budget and manpower are devoted to new obligations in the field of social welfare.[2] Its precepts, derived from the norms of the popular movements—particularly labor—of the end of the nineteenth century, also provided the political basis for its development. Where they were weak, as in the United States, the construction of the welfare state remains incomplete. Where they were strong, as in Scandinavia and Britain, a fundamentally new state form developed that is defined not by the number involved in government nor by its ideology but by its policies: the provision of economic security and an adequate standard of living for all its citizens.

This was a concept foreign to the nineteenth century liberal state, which was as mean as Scrooge. It took care of the poor after a fashion derived from the late medieval period, but with all the moral outrage of the self-made middle class. Poverty was evidence of immorality—of failure to apply oneself, to work hard, to save, if not worse—or ignorance. The poor law was the last refuge for those whose resources were exhausted and whose self-respect would soon follow; its purpose was as much to keep the poor out of sight and under discipline as to keep them from starving.

The origins of the modern welfare state lie in the reactions to this practice. To the socialists, the poor law was one more proof of the inhumanity of capitalism, and the Social Democratic press was filled with accounts of the scandalous mistreatment of its "beneficiaries" and the profiteering of its administrators. Paternalistic conservatives saw it as a threat to social and political stability, and their response is epitomized by Bismarck's coupling of innovative social insurance—health and disability insurance and old-age pensions—with the Anti-socialist Laws in the 1880s. Social liberals made it a prime target for reform, and the decade before the First World War saw their initiation of what would become governmental systems of sick pay, disability compensation, and unemployment insurance in Britain, the United States, and Denmark, among others. It was the extension of these faltering first steps, their integration with nongovernmental (principally trade union) benefit plans, and the codification of piecemeal reforms that gave birth to what can properly be called the welfare state in the 1930s and 1940s.

Empirical studies immediately before and after the First World War in-dicated that the principal cause of poverty was loss of employment income. The primary focus of the welfare state has been the provision of income security measures to protect the living standards of those forced out of employment temporarily by sickness or unemployment, or permanently by age or disability. A major secondary cause of poverty was found to be the poor "fit" between employment income and family size, and steps were taken to improve the posi-tion of those with large families and small incomes through family allowances, housing subsidies, subsidized day care, and similar measures. Some services, most notably medical care and education, are provided outside the market on the basis of need to the particular benefit of the economically worst off. The weakest members of society—the elderly, the handicapped, and children—are the beneficiaries of a range of special measures; in fact, the level of aid to the weak has become a new norm for evaluating the conduct of the state. The level of support provided in the best developed welfare states—unemployment com-pensation and sick pay at 90 percent of normal industrial wages, old age and disability pensions at adequate, though hardly munificent levels, free medical and dental care, free education with living stipends, six months of paid preg-nancy leave divided between the parents, and the like—raises the living stan-dards of those outside the labor force and those worst off inside it to levels not too unlike those of the middle class. Together these constitute a dramatic expan-sion of the role of the state, with far-reaching consequences for political devel-opment. And, remarkably enough, what was thought revolutionary forty years ago is thoroughly accepted as the natural order of society today.

It is important to underline what the welfare state is not. It is not insurance in the normal sense of the term. Some of its transfer payments—particularly sickness, disability, and unemployment compensation—are frequently de-scribed as "social insurance" against insurable risks,[3] an accurate description of their historical origins. Typically, state schemes in these areas replaced or sup-plemented benefits previously provided by unions or benefit societies, and were funded by special social insurance contributions. Today the label is misleading. Social insurance contributions are distinguishable from other taxes only in name; much of the financing is provided by general state revenues. Nor are the schemes actuarially sound as private insurance plans must be. The costs are often shifted generationally; current beneficiaries are supported not by past pay-ments but by current payments of future beneficiaries. The aim of insurance remains: eliminate the risk of income loss and the psychological insecurity that stems from it. But the schemes ultimately rest on social solidarity, for many people could undoubtedly find other, more rational means of insurance.

Nor is the welfare state an attempt to tamper with the distribution of income *inside* the market: it is *after* the market distribution of income that an effort is made to reduce the degree of inequality between those in and those outside the labor market and, to a lesser extent, among those employed. The matter of inequality of income in the market fundamentally has been left to private organ-izations—trade unions and employers—though in some countries where unions are particularly weak, as in the United States, wage-and-hours legislation sets minimum standards for the unorganized. Where unions are particularly strong, as in the Scandinavian countries, they have reduced market wage inequality by raising the wages of the most poorly paid, particularly the unskilled and women, relative to the well paid. It is only in the last decade that some Western European governments have sought to intervene directly in the formation of wages through various incomes policies, such as Labour's Social Contract in Britain, and this intervention has, to a limited extent, narrowed wage differentials. Some of the consequences of this policy will be examined later.

The welfare state does not attempt to redistribute income among classes as much as even out income throughout life. The economically active pay for increases in the goods and services provided to children, to all those in school, during periods when an "economically active" individual has been forced out of paid employment, and after retirement. Income is redistributed between age groups, the healthy and the sick, the employed and the unemployed, smokers and nonsmokers, the single and those with large families—*within* social classes. Redistribution among social classes is slight because the tax system that supports it is fundamentally proportional, not progressive. While it looks progressive on the surface because of the high income tax rates on large incomes, the proportion of the theoretical income tax rate actually paid falls as income rises. Moreover, a large portion of the revenue needed to support welfare measures is generated by regressive taxes on consumption (the value-added tax [VAT], a kind of general sales tax, reaches 20 percent in Denmark and Sweden) and by "social insurance contributions" that affect only wage and salary, but not property, income. A mild redistribution among social classes occurs because sickness, accidents, and unemployment are class related, and the ceilings on payments tend to reduce income differentials among individuals from different occupational groups when they are sick or unemployed. The welfare state has abolished want, not class differences in consumption.

Finally, the welfare state is not the realization of a particular ideology but the fruit of political struggle and hard-fought compromise. It is informative to look at its origins.

If the groundwork for social insurance was laid by conservatives and liberals in half a dozen countries before World War I, it was between the wars that the welfare state took form. The Austrian Social Democrats, unable to take power nationally, constructed the model welfare city-state in Vienna. The Social Democrats in Scandinavia, depending on social liberal and agrarian parties for support, postponed socialization and made social welfare a right; Sweden was converted in a generation from what Zeth Höglund trenchantly characterized as "the fortified poorhouse" into what Per Albin Hansson called "the people's home," Franklin Roosevelt, running scared before Townsend's old folks' clubs and Huey Long's share-the-wealth demagogy, pushed through social security and unemployment compensation—the Keynesian response to the Depression of eliminating the worst misery and restoring purchasing power.

World War II gave the drive for the welfare state new impetus, for wartime sacrifices demanded recompense. As one British soldier on his way to Normandy put it to Ernest Bevin, then minister of labor and former head of the Transport and General Workers' Union, "Ernie, when we've done this job for you, are we coming back to the dole?"[4] Roosevelt and Churchill enshrined freedom from want in the pantheon of Allied values. The report of the British government's Committee on Social Insurance and Allied Services, chaired by William Beveridge, turned the welfare state into a war goal and became a best seller.[5] After the war, the development of the welfare state in the West became general.

Though the welfare state drew support from a variety of sources, its key source of strength was the Social Democratic labor movement. Yet it violated socialist ideological concepts in a variety of ways. Orthodox socialists argued that a redistribution of the ownership of property from the few to the masses was the necessary prerequisite for the abolition of poverty and insecurity amid plenty; that without it, the growth of productive forces and the immiserization of the mass of the working population went hand-in-hand; and that a reconciliation between capitalist production and the welfare of the working people was an obvious impossibility.

Constructing the welfare state thus required a transformation of the Social Democrats as well as transformation of society. How that happened is reasonably clear in Scandinavia, *the* Social Democratic success story between the wars. It was here that the Social Democrats succeeded in taking power (Denmark in 1929, Sweden in 1932, and Norway in 1935) and holding it without absolute majorities while their fellows failed elsewhere in Europe. Of peripheral interest before, they now took center stage. Others—once their models, most notably the German Social Democrats—were to tread in their footsteps after the war. What has happened in Scandinavia reveals a good bit about the dynamics of the welfare state.

Despite similar historical roots and nominal Marxism, the Scandinavian Social Democratic parties were quite different. The Danes were notoriously moderate, while the semisyndicalist Norwegians achieved the distinction of being the only major European Social Democratic party outside of Russia to adhere to the Communist International en masse and persisted in describing themselves as "revolutionary communists" after their break with the Comintern in 1923. Once in power during the Depression, however, they pursued the same welfare state policy.

The explanation rests in part on their trade union base, solid and reformist, and on the fact that splits sapped the strength of the Left. But a major factor was the crisis of confidence in orthodox socialist doctrine. The worst capitalist crisis brought anything but the anticipated socialist victory. In quick succession the Social Democratic bastions fell. Hermann Müller's Social Democratic government in Berlin was replaced by a conservative government under Brüning in 1930. The second Labour government in Britain collapsed in total disarray over the question of reducing unemployment payments to meet the terms necessary for international bank loans; its leaders MacDonald and Snowden supported the cuts and were swallowed by a national coalition with the Tories in 1931. In July 1932 the Social Democrats failed to resist the *coup d'état* that von Papen's right-wing government carried out against the Social Democratic state administration in Prussia, clearing the way for the peaceful transition of power from the conservatives to Hitler in January 1933. The courageous but tardy armed resistance of the Austrian Socialists proved futile in February 1934 as Dollfuss completed his *coup* and the army turned its artillery on the housing projects that had been the pride of Social Democratic Vienna.

Drawing the obvious lesson, the Scandinavian Social Democrats became partners in a compromise that was neither negotiated nor announced but that nonetheless formed the basis for the construction of the Social Democratic welfare state. The socialization of the means of production was postponed indefinitely. There would be no expropriation of wealth or property. The government, however, would take an active role in aiding those worst off; the wolves of want would be driven from the door. Few would lose absolutely, and a great many would gain. Here was a Social Democratic program that did not force conservatives into the ranks of incipient fascist movements and that could be supported by liberals who abhorred socialization. At crucial junctures in the 1930s, alliances with the liberal and agrarian parties guaranteed Social Democratic governmental survival.

If this policy violated socialist doctrine, it was in keeping with trade union practice. The model for this new state in the womb of the old was the trade union benefit society. The union funds that provided sickness, death, travel, and unemployment benefits in the skilled trades were often direct descendants of the benefit funds of the guilds. These benefit societies grew out of the long tradition of group solidarity inherent in close-knit, traditional communities, a norm writ large in the welfare state. Social Democratic governmental personnel were steeped in their practices. A variety of programs of the welfare state, including unemployment and disability compensation, sick pay and health insurance, and pensions, trace their origins directly or indirectly to unions' collective provision of benefits. The welfare state did not assume obligations in the individual sphere; rather, it made collective benefits already in existence universal.

The expansion of welfare programs to meet the needs created by the Depression coincided chronologically with Keynesian economic theory. Welfare measures were justified not only in terms of human need but also as part of a Keynesian policy of reviving consumer demand. The Social Democratic goal of full employment, too, fit Keynesian theory. If it took more planning—and it did—the Social Democrats were more than willing to replace the anarchy of capitalist production with limited economic planning. The triumph of Keynesian theory occurred in conjunction with the construction of the welfare state, and one suspects that it is of considerable historical importance that the Keynesian revolution took place under the aegis of the Left. The superior economic performance of Social Democratic governments reinforced their popular support at this crucial juncture, and the fashion in which they tied together economic growth and the improved material welfare of all segments of the community deflated the social bases of the extreme Right and Left alike.

The combination of Social Democratic welfare measures and Keynesian economic theory has been markedly successful. The expansion of the public sector introduced an element of stability into the economic cycle by ensuring predictable demand in that area. The expansion of social services plays an important role in absorbing workers made redundant by automation and rationalization in production. The expansion of countercyclical welfare benefits— higher unemployment compensation, income-related housing subsidies, and the like—automatically reduces swings in demand. Astute use of a countercyclical fiscal policy plus special countercyclical measures to stimulate investment and production in the private sector—such as the Swedish schemes of freezing a portion of profit during booms and releasing it for investment during recessions, and of producing for stock during economic downturns—tends to reduce the severity and length of recessions. The continual push for full employment through selective employment measures and general fiscal policy is an important welfare goal itself: it also holds down the cost of liberal unemployment benefits.

Were the pioneers of the welfare state to tour modern Stockholm or Frankfurt, or Viennese working class districts or Welsh mining villages, they would be stunned by what they saw, though more by the results of rapid economic growth and far-reaching technological changes than by the realization of their egalitarian hopes. Eugene Debs would find modern America equally surprising.

But economic growth by itself does not abolish poverty nor ensure welfare International comparisons of living standards are always problematic, and although OECD figures suggest that American and Scandinavian averages, for example, are very much alike, the process of averaging conceals the striking difference in living standards between the lower quarter or so of their populations. The cumulative impact of taxes, transfer payments, and social services in Denmark, for instance, is to triple the ability to consume of the bottom fifth of the population and to increase the income of the next fifth by one-half.[6] A simple visual comparison of Scandinavian towns with American equivalents provides strong evidence that reasonably efficient welfare measures can abolish poverty as it was known in the past; economic growth alone, as the American case indicates, does not.

One should not exaggerate the degree of economic equality achieved in the welfare state. The inequality in the market distribution of income is reduced, not eliminated. Some are still less well off than others. Class lines in consumption are clear. But the hopeless poverty of the past has succumbed to the combination of rapid economic growth and the redistributive programs of the public sector.

The consequences are impressive. At the individual level, abject material poverty—among its many aspects, unhealthful housing and the inadequate heating, winter clothing, and nutrition that guaranteed sick children and the constant cough of the elderly in working class districts—is gone. *How* it has been banished has brought a sense of material security, perhaps as important psychologically on an everyday level as it is materially in the crunch. It is very hard to fall through the fine mesh of the income security net, unless one consciously cuts a hole and jumps through to choose the life of the hermit, the prophet, or the aging hippie.

Beyond its ministry to material needs, the welfare state's emphasis on general health, life-long education (most obvious to the tourist because of overtly educational television programming, but more astonishingly evident in the annual enrollment of a fifth of the adult population in Sweden in adult education courses), increased vacations (four to six weeks for manual workers), the welfare of children, and culture in the broadest sense have had some effect (though not an easily quantifiable one) on nonmaterial standards of living.

On the societal level the results are equally impressive. High levels of unemployment compensation have made unemployment of little use in regulating demand. Retirees are guaranteed a share in the economic growth whose foundations they helped lay during their working life, an element of intergenerational justice important in times of rapid economic growth and increasing life expectancy. The social solidarity that helped bring about the elimination of the most pressing domestic material problems now provides the basis for popular support for extensive aid to underdeveloped countries. Finally, a greater degree of equality in ability to consume should make the market function more efficiently in distributing goods to satisfy needs; and the elimination of those forms of economic dependence resulting from high unemployment and the lack of economic security should increase labor mobility and make the labor market more efficient in matching jobs and employee desires.

Despite the bitterness of initial conservative opposition, welfare measures proved quite compatible with governments of the center and Right. Programs once enacted quickly ceased to be subjects of partisan conflict.[7] When the Tories returned to power in 1951 they acted to return some nationalized industries to private hands but did not tamper with the National Health Service. By the late 1950s the welfare state seemed as much a part of the common political heritage of the West as the espousal of democratic government.

The Death of the Work Ethic, Taxes, and Other Problems

> Historical accident and national idiosyncrasies have pushed Sweden ahead on the road to *Brave New World*. . . . All that stands between ourselves and Sweden is a certain protective shell granted by the Western European heritage. But it is fragile, and it is being eroded from within and without. To watch present Swedes may be to watch our future selves.
>
> —Roland Huntford, *The New Totalitarians*

For all its success, the welfare state has increasingly become an object of criticism. A resurgent Right, in which some commentators profess to find something new, has launched a sustained attack on the public sector and the level of taxation necessary to support it. The Social Democrats and liberals, on the defensive, have become advocates of replacing direct, visible, and sometimes progressive taxes with indirect, invisible, and invariably regressive ones. Aging New Leftists, entrenched in the universities and social services, find themselves in the uncomfortable position of being the foremost defenders of the very institutions they had criticized with such vigor at the beginning of the current decade.

Admittedly, political and academic fashions, while more durable than those of Paris, often seem equally quaint in retrospect. Yet like clichés, they reflect an element of truth. It would be well to take stock of the most prominent criticisms.

> The growth of the public sector has hamstrung the private sector. Investment that should go into creating new manufacturing jobs goes to nursery schools instead. The economic decline of some Western nations, like Britain, is related to the growth of a fundamentally nonproductive public sector that encourages inefficiency—for example, by pumping government money into bankrupt industries to save jobs—at the expense of the dynamic private sector.

The development of the welfare state has meant a steady increase in the size of the public sector. Its growth has not come at the direct expense of the private sector, for both have grown during rapid economic expansion. But the public sector has clearly grown more quickly. Government revenues now amount to more than half the gross domestic product (GDP) in the Netherlands, Norway, and Sweden, and nearly half in Denmark. In Austria, Belgium, Finland, France, Germany, and Britain, government revenues amount to between 40 and 43.5 percent of the GDP; in the United States, government revenues amount to just under a third of the GDP. There is no clear correlation between the size of public sector and rate of growth in the advanced industrial economies. Between 1972 and 1977 Norway fell in the upper range on both; Holland and Sweden, in the upper range on size of public sector and in the middle and lower range, respectively, on growth; Britain, in the middle range on size and in the low range on growth; and the United States, in the low range on both.[8] A variety of other factors are involved.

The growth of the public sector has been motivated not only by welfare goals but also by the requirements of the private sector, and it has absorbed a substantial portion of the costs of private production. A speed-up in production tempo and the use of untested chemicals add to the numbers of disability pensioners and early retirees. New production techniques require more education. Increasing the number of married women with small children in the labor force requires expanded day care. The public sector has also assumed the burden of retraining workers displaced through automation. Far from being a conservative factor, the welfare state has *allowed* the acceleration of technological development.

The expansion of the public sector since 1974 has not been the cause of recession and stagnation but the result of it; the costs of unemployment compensation and other anticyclical payments and measures have risen while employment in the private sector has fallen. It has been highly conducive to political stability.

> The welfare state has undermined the need for personal savings. Individuals save less and consume more in the certainty that the state guarantees their material security. The result is a shortage of investment capital.

Individuals save, but they do not buy stock or put their money in the bank. Their savings go into owner-occupied homes that, given the performance of the American stock market over the past decade, have been more profitable than investments of most money managers have been. Furthermore, the major source of new capital formation in a number of countries, including both the United States and Sweden, are pension funds that represent deferred (i.e., saved) wages. American pension funds are currently estimated to be on the order of $500 billion, or four times the size of individual private savings, and own about a quarter of the equity of corporations listed on the stock exchanges.[9]

> Welfare benefits are so high, they reduce the desire to work. There must be an incentive to work since people (except you and me) are fundamentally lazy. No one in his right mind will choose to stand on an assembly line eight hours a day if he/she can collect almost as much for doing nothing. Cutting benefits would reduce the number of unemployed.

While there are problems of disincentive for individuals caught in a few categories, in general there is a notable gap between welfare benefits and employment income. Since the war, the dramatic increase in the number of women in the labor market has caused the proportion of the population employed to rise, despite a fall in male participation rates (a result of longer education and earlier pension ages). Part of this increase can be attributed to the effects of the women's movement, but the overwhelming portion is purely economic: given high tax rates (necessary to finance social benefits) and rising patterns of consumption, two salaries are increasingly necessary. The rise in unemployment is simply the result of economic crisis.

But the welfare state has brought changes in popular attitudes toward work. Economic security reduces all phenomena of dependence. Full employment leads to increases in labor mobility and, hence, job turnover. Employers are forced to devote time and resources to training new workers, and money to improving working conditions to hold the old ones. Absenteeism seems to be related to job security and sick pay. There is the not entirely apocryphal story about the Volvo plant in Gothenburg, where absenteeism is a notable problem. When rumors of layoffs began to circulate, the number calling in sick dropped so drastically that Volvo ended up with more workers than were needed to man the production line and was therefore forced to undertake the very layoffs that had been rumored. It is harder to get people to do work they do not like. *"But who will collect the garbage?"* The answer has been both to import foreign laborers to do the dirtiest, most dangerous, and most unpleasant work, and to reduce the level of dirt, danger, and unpleasantness while raising the pay. The garbage still gets collected. Except, of course, during strikes.

> Taxes are just too high.

The alleged destruction of the work ethic, the fall in the savings rate, and the erosion of work incentives are matters of widespread public disinterest. The question of taxation is another matter. If few want to dismantle the welfare state, a great many would like to undo its economic underpinnings by holding on to their share of the tax bill.

Running a welfare state is an expensive business, cheap only in comparison to war. The tax levels necessary to support it are unprecedented. In the last

twenty years, the proportion of the GDP collected by various levels of government has risen from between 30 to 35 percent in Western Europe to between 40
and 50 percent; in a few countries, including Sweden, government revenues are
approaching 60 percent. Everything is taxed: income and expenditures, luxuries
and necessities, virtues and vices. Marginal income tax rates easily top 50 percent for Scandinavian production line workers—in the 1930s the income tax did
not affect them at all—while the VAT adds 20 percent to the prices they pay.
Additional excise taxes on smoking and drinking take the pleasure out of vice.
By comparison, the United States seems a low-tax paradise; direct income and
social security taxes rarely exceed a quarter of income, and sales taxes typically
run about 5 percent.

The 1970s have seen a tax revolt of unprecedented breadth. It is so widespread that it is almost *de rigueur* for serious politicians to pledge both to cut
taxes and to maintain governmental programs. The implausibility of this combination must grate on their consciences, but political competition leaves little
leeway for logical consistency. There have been times in the past when citizens
demanded to know how a tax cut would affect government spending, but that
is, as the recent election in England attests, hardly a cardinal issue currently.

The most dramatic example of tax protest occurred in Denmark in 1973
when voters swept a Social Democratic government out of office in an election
that completely disrupted the long-standing stable pattern of Danish party politics. One voter in four cast his ballot for one of two new antitax parties, the
larger of which was led by an iconoclastic tax lawyer, Mogens Glistrup. A
former university instructor in tax law, Glistrup became an overnight TV personality by proclaiming in a prime-time interview on the eve of the tax deadline
in 1971 that he paid no income tax. Nor did other reasonably intelligent Danes,
he said. His appeal to the dissatisfied was ecumenical and endures despite his 3½-
year trial for income tax evasion and ultimate conviction, now under appeal.
His attraction seemed to stem from a combination of (1) the rapid rise in highly
visible direct income taxes under a nonsocialist coalition government between
1968 and 1971 when many nonsocialist voters expected tax cuts, (2) the high
level of affluence after fifteen years of economic expansion that undermined the
appeal of social welfare and income security programs, and (3) the revelations of
tax avoidance by the rich, dramatized by Glistrup himself, which destroyed the
illusion that the system of taxes was fundamentally just and that, in the Danish
phrase, "the strongest shoulders bore the heaviest burdens." Voters who believed they were paying their fair share of taxes were overcome by a sense of
having been swindled, compounded by envy: the rich did not pay and the lazy
long-haired young made off with the spoils. Both feelings contributed to the
moral outrage expressed in the 1973 election. Ironically, Glistrup, the self-
proclaimed tax evader, became the political beneficiary.

Sweden's taxes, however, have not occasioned much protest, although they
are notably higher than Denmark's. The reasons are instructive. The Swedes
have been careful to avoid sharp increases in direct taxation. While the overall
level of taxation has risen sharply during the last decade, the proportion of
revenues generated by income taxes has remained constant. Most of the new
revenues necessary to cover social welfare benefits have been raised by a tax on
the wage sum paid out by employers, an indirect income tax that does not

immediately appear to come out of wages. Further, the embarrassing persecution of several internationally prominent Swedish cultural figures undertaken by the Swedish Social Democrats in 1975-76 served as a public
demonstration that all Swedes would pay their fair share of taxes, regardless of
position. The nonsocialist parties in Sweden were cautious in their pledges of
tax cuts, in the hope that they would not arouse expectations they could not fill.
This policy seems to have paid off; there is no sign of a tax protest party in
Sweden.

The welfare state is inimical to individual freedom.

The quick answer to this classic argument used by conservatives since the
inception of the welfare state is that poverty, hunger, disease, and economic
dependence are more so. But perhaps the argument is more valid when material
needs are less pressing. In any case, it forms the basis of a most comprehensive
critique of the Swedish welfare state and, by extension, of others as well. Roland
Huntford argues that Sweden is well on its way toward an amateurish brave
new world, a utopia of welfare and conformity in which a variety of aspects
of life, including education, housing, work, sex, and leisure, have all become
transmuted into tools of social control.[10] What Huntford saw was a negative mirror image of what others praised, and his attack carried some weight
because it pointed at things that were real—the element of corporatism in
Swedish politics, for example—and that were then generally ignored. Unlike
many Anglo-American critics of the Scandinavian welfare system, Huntford
did not argue that there was a correlation between welfare and unhappiness.
Swedes were happy, said Huntford: that was precisely the problem.
     Huntford's view was irritating to Swedes who ill-temperedly denied they
had sunk into a stolid contentment in which material equality and mental conformity went hand in hand. His interpretation contains an element of faith not
easily subject to empirical disproof. Yet the question that he raises is terribly
important: Now that the welfare state has been constructed, what is its
purpose?

Where Do We Go from Here?

The welfare state has become the new point of political departure. Its success in abolishing material deprivation has changed the political agenda. Some
of the consequences for the individual—greater economic security and independence, new attitudes toward work, less willingness to pay taxes—have been
sketched above. Their consequences for the political system are notable. The
very success of the welfare state has undermined social solidarity to the point
that the appeal to egoism of a "cut our taxes and the devil take the hindmost"
position cuts across class lines.
     Yet despite the success of tax-cut rhetoric, it seems doubtful that the con-
servative drive against the public sector will lead to more than minor retrench-
ment in the welfare state. Reversal of central policies—pensions, sick pay,
national health insurances, or the like—is out of the question. It is the fact that

this security net is in place that emboldens the attack. The question is one of marginal adjustments; the basic policies are irreversible.

It seems likely that the various protests are signs that the welfare state is approaching its limits. It is close to satisfying the material needs that are its *raison d'être* in Scandinavia, although that point is still far distant in the United States. Many benefits cannot be raised without creating serious problems of disincentives. A conceivable interpretation of the tax protest is that a balance has been reached between demand for benefits and willingness to pay for them, at least through direct, visible taxes. That this point occurs earlier in the United States and, perhaps, Britain than in Denmark or Sweden stems from the varying levels of social solidarity and the ease with which welfare beneficiaries are stigmatized.

In other areas, however, the internal dynamics of the welfare state suggest it is moving out of equilibrium. Both the integration of interest organizations in state economic policy and the compromise that left the distribution of power and wealth untouched become increasingly problematic when redistribution of income via the public sector approaches its maximum. The process is particularly advanced in Scandinavia, but some of the same features are evident in Britain, Germany, and, occasionally, the United States.

The welfare state differs from its liberal predecessor in the extent to which society is organized. Not only are labor and employers organized, tenants' organizations bargain with landlords, homeowners' associations negotiate with the government, and viewers' committees demand a voice in radio-TV programming, creating political power where none existed before. Conscious choice intrudes into a realm once thought to be beyond human control. Wages are set by bargaining, not by natural law. Unemployment is a result of conscious decision, generally by the government, not of market forces.

The implications of the extent of organization in the labor market are clear. Take, for example, Scandinavia, where between two-thirds and three-quarters of all blue- and white-collar employees are organized (as compared to one-third to one-half in Britain, Germany, and Holland, and one-quarter in the United States) and where bargaining is centralized at the national level. The combination of centralized bargaining—employers and unions hammering out a single national contract that sets the general national wage pattern for the next biennium—with full employment offers the frightening prospects of wage inflation that would price Scandinavian goods out of the world market or a series of catastrophic general strikes/lockouts that would destroy the economy. The situation in industrial conflict becomes comparable to the stalemate between the nuclear powers: the only effective weapon in your arsenal is the one that cannot be used. Under such circumstances, the state becomes a permanent third party in contract negotiations.

The state's role in the past in wage negotiations was that of mediator, a role still enshrined in the labor legislation of a number of countries, including the United States. But to an increasing degree, the role of the state has become that of enforcing limits in wage bargaining consistent with national economic policy. Wage formation has become a matter for political decision.

Where the union-government nexus is strong, the political decision can be imposed with union cooperation, as in Sweden and during the early years of

Labour's Social Contract in Great Britain. Where it is weak, as during the Heath government, or where the unions are so democratic that members can defeat a contract, as in Denmark, the state turns increasingly to coercion. Thus in Denmark, the last three national contracts have been imposed by parliamentary action, and wage negotiations have become a crucial element in political calculations on governmental coalitions and on calling elections. And the last three British elections have been fought, in large measure, over the question of which party is capable of integrating the unions in national economic policy: Labour through persuasion, or the Tories through coercion.

Running the welfare state requires effective management of the economy and that, in turn, requires state coordination of the activities of economic interest organizations, whose very power precludes their independence. The informal consultation of the 1930s and 1940s between government and interest organizations has grown into the latter's formal integration into the structure of political decision-making, epitomized by the Harpsund meetings in the 1950s at which the Swedish government's economic policy for the following year was worked out in conjunction with representatives of the economic organizations. Interest organizations had to some degree assumed the representative functions of parliament. There was considerable justice in the charge that this represented a new form of corporatism.[11]

The extension of state activity into directing what had previously been autonomous spheres of behavior has increased the power of those who wield the levers of central authority while it has politicized new aspects of social and economic life. Its long-term implications are disturbing. Consider state-union ties. The link between government and unions in the welfare state stems historically from ties between the unions and Social Democrats that predate the Social Democratic assumption of power and that were, in part, responsible for it. Social Democratic government changed the antagonistic relationship between state and unions. The unions were assured that economic gains won at the bargaining table would not be lost in parliament and that, conversely, political gains would be won in parliament and need not be sought through political strikes. Close party-union collaboration gradually brought the integration of unions and state. Union counsel helped to shape policy at every level: within the Social Democratic party, in its parliamentary group, in the cabinet. Social Democratic cabinet members were often recruited directly from trade union office. That the unions eventually were integrated into the administration of state economic policy as well did not imply their subordination: the policy had been shaped collectively and was based on shared union and party goals.

The overt aim of Social Democratic governmental-trade union collaboration was to achieve a more equitable distribution of goods and services through improving the position of the weakest members of society by giving them an increased share in the *growth* in national income, while leaving the existing distribution of income, wealth, and power unchanged. This was, as discussed above, the basis for consensus support for the welfare state.

From the union point of view, the bargain was eminently rational. The maintenance of full employment and the redistributive aims of the government required a steady and high rate of economic growth. If the existing distribution of wealth and income was not to be altered, the change in the relative distribution of income must come entirely out of the increment in the national income and, to a substantial degree, via governmental expenditures. A policy of cooperation to increase the rate of economic growth was a reasonable one for the unions under these circumstances.

The partnership of state and unions in Scandinavia seemed to ensure economic growth, labor peace, and rising standards of living. Legislative action and union bargaining supplemented each other. Wages and hours set by contract meshed with the social benefits and taxation legislated by parliament. Union wage demands were fitted into the general framework of Social Democratic economic policy. To take a single example, the "solidaristic wage policy" called for highly paid skilled workers to forego wage increases they might have won to improve the relative position of the poorly paid unskilled and women workers.[12] Wage restraint by the best paid did not benefit the least well off directly, for their wages typically do not come out of the same pocket. Instead, the policy increased wage equality between the high- and low-wage sectors of the economy by holding down wage increases and pushing up profits in the most efficient firms and raising wages and lowering profits in the least efficient. This was important in channeling investment into, and holding down prices in, the efficient high-wage, but inflation-sensitive, export sector. The higher wage bill for unskilled workers hastened the death of inefficient firms, and their work force— after state-supported retraining—could be redeployed in more efficient, higher wage industries. The state and unions together carried out a policy of industrial renewal.

Union leaders argue that influence achieved through cooperation with Social Democratic government produces more for their members than would the dubious gains from industrial militance, which often backfires politically—wage gains are eaten up by inflation, and what is won at the bargaining table is lost in parliament. Union-state cooperation eliminates these problems. Indeed, because Social Democratic governments are relatively permanent, unions can take a longer view in calculating what is rational—in terms of weighing wage demands relative to employment policy, tax rates, and the like—as opposed to the short-run concept of rationality of the past, where gains deferred meant gains likely to be lost to layoffs, unemployment, disability, plant closures, inflation, or taxes before they were in hand.

The long-term viability of this view is open to question. The alternation between Social Democratic and nonsocialist governments undercuts any calculation of future government policy. Also, as the unions in imposing industrial discipline have come to appear an arm of the state, members have become increasingly restive. It is relatively easy for dissidents to capture local power, which increases the problems of maintaining discipline. Thus, internal union politics becomes a matter of considerable significance to the broader political system.

As long as union-state cooperation was demonstrably linked to income redistribution, maintaining support for it in the unions was simple. But as suggested, income redistribution by the public sector seems to be approaching its political limit. The effort of the state to run an incomes policy neutral in its effect on distribution of income increases the problem. Wages are easily controlled, since it is in the employers' interest; prices are harder to manage. Interest rates have to be raised for the same reason that wages have to be held down. And the policy becomes positively unpalatable when its goal is to increase investment by raising profits, for the direct benefits to those who exercise wage restraint are few and long deferred. In time their patience wears thin, as during the last years of Labour's Social Contract, especially when real wages fall. The combination of full employment, adequate social benefits, and well-organized unions *does* create a predisposition for inflation in welfare state. But if wage restraint is a necessity, something has to be offered to compensate directly those who practice it.

The success of the welfare state has been built on increased organization and coordination, on increased complexity, and on the increased importance of the expert. To provide adequate social services, local governments have to be of substantial size; hence the consolidation of municipalities and the disappearance of local governments that had existed for centuries. Managing an economy where unions are highly organized requires collective bargaining kept within the limits of an incomes policy. Successful planning also demands coordination, centralization, and expertise. Without it, income security measures are far too expensive to be maintained. But the process of achieving it diminishes democracy, even when it is carried out in the interests of the overwhelming majority.

The drive by the Left for participatory democracy in the 1960s had more impact on its own organizations than on the society at large. It converted European parties of the Left—with some notable exceptions—from enthusiastic advocates of state power into skeptics. A revival of the demand for participation is not unlikely as the welfare state no longer focuses on increasing equality in the ability to consume through the public sector. Let me sketch some of the reasons why.

The end of the threat of material deprivation as a factor in everyday life has far-reaching consequences. Those whose childhoods were shaped by the Depression will continue to be grateful for the security the welfare state provides, but the younger generation, as always, is ahistorical. Past achievements are preludes to new demands.

An obvious consequence of welfare policies is the declining value above a certain threshold of wage increases: basic needs are guaranteed, and the tax collector gets most of the wage gain. One needs to keep pace with inflation, of course, and wage increases continue to be of substantial interest, but the single-minded focus of the past is gone. Indeed, Swedish studies show that job satisfaction is less related to wage levels than to the degree of control over one's own work.[13]

The youth rebellion of the 1960s left its mark. Though students and workers made common cause only in France, the spirit of rebellion infected the generation of manual workers who had grown up during the boom of the 1950s and 1960s elsewhere. Automation, rationalization, and plant closures brought a wave of strikes in Britain, France, and Italy in which the demand for worker control of decisions on these issues played a major role. There were major wildcat strikes in the German coal-and-steel industry and in the state-owned iron mines in Northern Sweden in 1969 that were symbolic because they were directed against firms in which wages were good and in which the union leadership was incorporated into managerial decisions. Unions had some influence, yet their members felt they had none.

The European countries are in the midst of a drive to democratize the economy that will, in time, transform economic relationships. In the 1960s the Left expected the change to occur with revolutionary speed; the process is perhaps the surer for the reason that it did not. The 1970s have seen the expansion of the powers of works councils and employee plant committees in most Western European countries; the addition, or increase in the number, of worker representatives on company boards in France, Sweden, Denmark, Luxembourg, Norway, and Germany; massive job redesign experiments such as the abolition of the assembly line in the newest Swedish auto factories; increase in job security through legislation; expansion of the scope of collective bargaining to include organizing production, investment policy, and other managerial prerogatives; and proposals for the redistribution of stock ownership. When carried out it will add up to a fundamental realignment of authority patterns in the economy, as revolutionary as the imposition of the factory system in the early part of the nineteenth century. But this time it will be a democratic realignment.

Democracy on the job will also help to induce wage restraint without income redistribution and without increasing coercion. It is a nonwage benefit that can be traded for wage restraint, has no negative impact on the balance of payments, is not demonstrably inflationary, and cannot be taxed. The Swedish and Danish "wage earner fund" proposals also provide the prospects of increasing equality by redistributing wealth as the welfare state redistributed income: existing wealth will be left untouched, but the ownership of new capital will be apportioned more equally, with a substantial share going to those who have generated it through their labor and their willingness to forego wage increases.

A Victim of Success

The welfare state is a victim of its success, not of its failures. It has succeeded in banishing the specter of material deprivation through illness, loss of employment, disability, and old age that has haunted past generations. But the abolition of the threat has also abolished the fear it engendered. The collective memory of the population is short; political allegiance is often based on past wrongs, rarely on past achievements. For the present generation, the welfare system is the status quo, not a monument to the courage, ingenuity, luck, compromises, and (perhaps) brilliance of its pioneers. Its reforms seem to be of declining marginal utility. What is the addition of dental care to the national health service compared to the creation of the national health service itself? Its moments of drama and heroism are past.

Yet the costs of maintaining it have not declined. To the contrary, they have become an important part of the average family budget. The wage-tax squeeze is real, as the ratchet effect of inflation increases income taxes on the same real income. So is the sense of being cheated by the rich who dodge their taxes and the lazy young and unemployed who live off the system. Its institutions have become more centralized, more expert, more complex, and less democratic. The increasing incorporation of interest groups in state administration is a new form of political participation, but one that makes many uneasy. Management of the economy requires coordination. When consensus fails, coercion is tempting. Organized discontent is promptly incorporated into the same neo-corporatist structure,[14] a dubious channel of expression. Problems of inflation and labor discipline seem to be built in. Affluence has undercut the sense of solidarity that was the basis for its political support. In some ways it seems to have moved into political disequilibrium.

I am, perhaps, too optimistic in suggesting that democracy extended into the economic realm is a likely approach to dealing with disequilibrium. Coercion may be a simpler alternative to induce organizations to pull together rather than in different directions. The very complexity and scope of state activity may have reached the point where no one but the professional is capable of making informed decisions, and where the informed layman is on his way to becoming a figure of interest to historians only. When the complexity of politics reaches the point where it no longer *can* be made comprehensible, the demagogue's task is easy.

The current period of economic stagnation has meant a reduction in real income for many. Only the inflation in money wages has kept this point from becoming obvious, for after having run to stay in place, one is left with the same warm glow of accomplishment as if one had covered a great distance. The growth dividend to be shared by the public sector and private consumption has been small and, in some cases, when the GNP has gone down, there has been none.

One can conceive of a situation in which a real decline in private ability to consume becomes so obvious, that it becomes politically difficult to defend high levels of support for identifiable minorities. This is less a problem in Northern Europe, where the beneficiaries of welfare measures are virtually indistinguishable from the remainder of the population, than it is in the United States and, increasingly, Britain, where they are distinguishable by race, ethnicity, religion, language, and culture. In Northern Europe, unlike Britain, foreign workers have been temporary residents, not immigrants. They are in the economically active ages, cannot get in without having a job (hence lower unemployment rates), leave their families in their home country (hence no family allowances or education costs, and much lower medical payments), live in poor housing by choice because they want to send money home, and go home themselves before they reach the pensionable age and the high health care costs that go with it. However, they pay their full share of taxes. The existence of this rotating pool of young, economically active males who cost little and pay much has helped balance the inflow and outflow of funds in the social welfare sphere. It is, however, drying up because of the recession.

Demographic trends also seem ominous. An increasing portion of the population in the future will be made up of retirees who will live longer and make heavier demands on the medical system. There are some who cultivate a dark vision of a revolt by the middle-aged against supporting the old. Yet, surely the fact that they too will be old in time will restrain them. And an older age for retirement would benefit healthy retirees as it eases the tax burden of middle-aged.

The welfare state as it is today is enjoying a modest resurgence because it is doing what it does best: guaranteeing security. Economic crisis and the sense of economic insecurity it engenders have reinforced the sense of social solidarity. The success of the welfare state rests, after all, not on altruism, but on the certainty that you, too, will someday need the help of others. There is nothing like a little economic insecurity to make citizens appreciate the fundamental security the welfare state provides.

REFERENCES

[1]Marquis Childs, *Sweden: The Middle Way* (New Haven: Yale University Press, 1936).

[2]To cite a fairly typical example of the dimensions of state reorientation, in 1977 the Danish military, judiciary, police, central administration, and church—traditional government—employed 15% of 573,000 public employees. The social sector broadly defined (health, education, income security, and other programs pertaining to public welfare) employed 60%. In 1974-75 public expenditures were divided as follows: administration, military, church, courts, police, foreign ministry, and debt service, 20%; social sector, 68%; economic support—roads, transportation, agricultural, various economic subsidies—12% (Danmarks Statistik, Statistisk *Årbog 1978* [Copenhagen: 1978], Tables 322 and 324). In 1890, the division between these three sectors was 65%, 28% and 6% respectively (Danmarks Statistik, *Statistiske Sammendrag 1913* [Copenhagen: 1913], Tables 86 and 90).

[3]Even conservatives often approved such measures. Cf. F. A. von Hayek, *The Road to Serfdom* (London: George Routledge & Sons, 1944), p. 90.

[4]William Harrington and Peter Young, *The 1945 Revolution* (London: Davis Poynter, 1978), p. 21.

[5]*Social Insurance and Allied Services* (The Beveridge Report) (London: HMSO, 1942). Beveridge was a former head of the London School of Economics and later a Liberal peer.

[6]Det økonomiske Råd, *Den personlige indkomstfordeling og indkomstudjævningen over de offentlige finanser* (Statens Trykningskontor, Copenhagen: 1967), pp. 52-56.

[7]In the United States, for example, the resurgent Republicans attacked a variety of New Deal measures after the war; Social Security was not among them.

[8]OECD figures for 1977.

[9]Jeremy Rifkin and Randy Barber, *The North Will Rise Again—Pensions, Politics and Power in the 1980's* (Boston: Beacon Press, 1978), pp. 10, 81, 84.

[10]Roland Huntford, *The New Totalitarians* (London: Penguin Press, 1971).

[11]Since the timely appearance of Philippe Schmitter's article "Still the Century of Corporatism?" in 1974 (in Fredrick B. Pike and Thomas Stritch, [eds.], *The New Corporatism: Social-Political Structures in the Iberian World* [University of Notre Dame Press, London: 1974], pp. 85-131) focused attention on the subject, a considerable body of theoretical and empirical material has been developed on corporatist structures in a number of Western European countries. Cf. the special issue of *Comparative Political Studies*, 10(1) (April 1977), devoted to corporatism in Western Europe, and Gerhard Lehmbruch and Philippe Schmitter, (eds.), *Corporatist Policy Formation in Comparative Perspective* (Sage, forthcoming).

[12]The solidaristic wage policy has been remarkably successful. Internationally, average wages for women in manufacturing come closest to matching average male rates in Norway and Sweden, according to ILO figures (ILO, *Women at Work*, 1/1978, p. 18). Danish wage statistics indicate that between 1958 and 1978 the average unskilled worker's wage rose from 83% of the skilled average to 88%, and that the average woman's wage rose from 61% to 80%.

[13]Cf. Bertil Gardell, *Arbetsinnehåll och livskvalitet* (Prisma, Stockholm: 1976).

[14]Olof Ruin reports the paradox that the wave of demands for individual participation in Sweden in the 1960s, that arose in part out of opposition to corporatist structures, led in turn to corporate participation, "Participatory Democracy and Corporatism: The Case of Sweden," *Scandinavian Political Studies*, 9 (1974): 171-184.

CLARK C. ABT

Social Science Research and the Modern State

THE MODERN STATE IS DISTINGUISHED by the extent and number of its activities, most of which are planned, monitored, evaluated, and recorded—however imprecisely. It uses thousands of book-length reports and computer tapes containing economic, demographic, sociological, and technological data to assess its policies and programs. In the United States, government agencies and research contractors share equally in producing this information; a good deal of it, however, remains concentrated as raw data and first-level analysis, without the government necessarily following through to develop and test integrated theories of the social impacts of its policies. This is so because government works within too limited a time frame to permit protracted theoretical work that may prove useful in determining policy, and because governments tend to worry that ideological considerations will contaminate theoretical work, leading to other difficulties.

But if the map of social policy knowledge has been expanded greatly, it is still massively incomplete, and in many places distorted, resembling perhaps Renaissance maps of the New World. New territories of impacts have been identified and measured, sometimes more quickly than the rate at which the forces of social change erode coastlines and the convulsions of social upheavals throw up new landscapes.

New frontiers are constantly being defined in the interrelationships among education, work, poverty, and economic growth. The Negative Income Tax experiment conducted by the U.S. Department of Health, Education, and Welfare in North Carolina shows some of the powerful educational effects of labor force participation changes. Its Seattle-Denver Income Maintenance experiments link welfare, family change, income, and employment behavior in wholly new ways. Its National Day Care experiments show certain of the powerful child development impacts of employment training and school changes. And its Co-insurance Payments, Hospital Cost Containment, Second Surgical Opinion, and Catastrophic Illness experiments relate health care costs, income, and health impacts. The Labor Department's Youth Incentives demonstration shows the impact of employment and education on the most underemployed teenagers, and its Work Equity experiment on work-conditioned welfare reform shows how jobs, family status, and welfare systems interact. The Experimental Housing Allowance Program of the U.S. Department of Housing and Urban Development relates income, age, and residential patterns to welfare programs.

Despite the addition of such realms of information to our societal maps, we have not yet been able to integrate them into a unified theory of social and economic change, to put together disparate microdata and findings into macro-theories and policies. This is so partly because researchers work for different political kingdoms that do not effectively share their maps and, indeed, often compete. Also, transnational communication in the use of such research is very underdeveloped. Knowledge of public opinion changes developed in voting studies by American political scientists and survey sociologists, for example, are not well known in Germany, Scandinavia, and Canada. Many American economists and engineers concerned with environmental impact and energy resources scarcely communicate with their colleagues abroad.

New Information about the State

The new information from program evaluations and social experiments is much more comprehensive than earlier case studies and research reports. Data are based on representative time-series samples and can be generalized to specific population subgroups and conditions. The new information is also more detailed and exact. Using rigorous scientific methods of data collection and analysis, government social researchers are now better able to make causal inferences about how government policies and programs affect particular population subgroups and the costs to different income classes of an entire country. Paradoxically, the information may seem to tell governments less about society and the modern state than did earlier research findings. Government (and other) decision-makers in the past were surer of the consequences of their policies and programs, not because they knew *more*, but because they knew *less* about what they did not know. Until the 1960s, census data, national income accounts, nationally standardized and administered test scores, public health data on communicable diseases, social security statistics, voting records, and military and trade intelligence represented the peaks of social research on the state. Impressive as these data bases were (and still are), they often offered less scope, depth, precision, and reliability of information than the additional kinds of data produced today.

Interdisciplinary application of economics, sociology, psychology, statistics, and electronic computing in social pilot programs, social experiments, program evaluations, and computer models makes analysis of the new information easily available to the state. Without these new intellectual and hardware technologies, the high cost of obtaining information would make its collection unfeasible.

But if governments now know so much, why are they not able to institute more effective social programs? What use is made of all this new information? Are the data being collected in an almost totemistic way, as if to ward off the evils of ignorance simply by collecting and relating social facts? Or is this new information being used to increase the equity and efficiency of government? If so, why do government policies and programs not improve society more rapidly (or at all)?

In the United States about $500 million is spent annually by federal and state governments for program evaluation, roughly half going to government researchers, half to private research firms and universities. Perhaps 20 percent of the current $500 billion worth of government programs are evaluated, so that the government spends about one thousand times more on programs than on obtaining information about them. If program evaluations can improve efficiency or equity more than one-tenth of one percent, they will more than pay for themselves. With this and the hope of economies in mind, Congress in the early 1970s passed legislation calling for one percent of all new program budgets to be reserved for evaluation research.

If such a small percentage of government programs is evaluated, one would expect that an increased demand for information would include an increased demand for evaluation. But increased demand for evaluation does not in itself lead to fuller information utilization because of several obstacles. Information collection is not always synchronized with the peaks of policy interest. Policy and program questions are usually asked when budgets are tight or when particular constituencies express themselves politically. By the time such questions can be answered scientifically—two to ten years later—other urgent policy issues have superseded the ones that provoked the original questions. The answers inevitably receive scant attention. This unsynchronized information flow may be somewhat mitigated by the fact that the most difficult social problems tend to persist, but there is no question that much of the analysis is neglected.

Program administrators, interested in evaluations of the costs and effects of program components, have the formal intent of improving programs, but the unstated intent of justifying and protecting what they do. Program comparisons are not of great interest because government officials are committed to their own programs and cannot act on any others. A quite different kind of information is needed at the level of such government program sponsors as the Congress and other elected officials, who are more interested in securing information about program equity (who gets what and who pays) than about program efficiency; they are more interested in norm-referenced program comparisons (such as the costs incurred per job created) than in goal- or criterion-referenced tests of programs (such as the achievement of local full employment). Unfortunately, the heterogeneous forms of information produced for program operators are difficult to use in making comparisons of equity, not least because different things tend to be measured in different programs. As for the program equity comparisons called for by sponsors, they are of little use to administrators whose chief concern is improving the internal efficiency of their programs. Also, information from program evaluations and related policy research will often be viewed by program sponsors or administrators as threatening the survival of a program, or at least as providing ammunition to critics. Whether the threat is actual or perceived, it will generally work against full use of the information-gathering research or the active dissemination of its findings.

Dysfunctional information standards provide yet another obstacle to the policy application of the new information. Evaluations based on academic standards will often yield results that come in too late for utilization by government; where timely, the information is too often theoretical and its practical applications are not perceived. At the other extreme, excessively pragmatic standards will often result in biased, incomplete, erroneous, and ungeneralizable information.

Information standards will generally vary across the professions. Sponsors trained in one profession may disdain the information gathered according to the standards of another. Government decision-makers trained in law, impatient for quick results and accustomed to relying on precedents and their own judgments, may consult experts, review the literature (which is often obsolete if it exists at all), or send out a small team of generalists to conduct a superficial survey. A more accurate and objective statistical analysis of program impacts may be rejected by the legally trained as a costly academic exercise in abstractions.

The proliferation of government programs and related literature and the constantly changing context in which programs operate may force information seekers to choose between narrow specialization and comprehensive superficiality, a task that is itself time-consuming in terms of organization and selection. Many potential government users find it easier to resort instead to partially informed judgments and generalization based on limited personal experience.

A final obstacle to utilization of information is the specialized language or jargon of most reports. The typical technical report is largely inaccessible to anyone not technically trained. Government policy leaders, often generalists who get their information from newspapers, television, magazines, and knowledgeable cronies, cannot fathom the research results that are only infrequently (and then often inaccurately) reported in the media, and that rarely circulate through political friendship networks. Thus the knowledge generated for policy purposes very often fails to reach those who need it *when* they need it. Research findings not written in plain language are unlikely to be publicized. And studies from academic or private social science research, with their caveats and hermetic professional terminology, are unreadable and unusable and probably unwanted by those who originally sought the information, many of whom perhaps are no longer in policy-making positions. At the other extreme are low-grade superficial advocacy reports. Compared to the more abstract, condensed language of the physical sciences, where cosmic phenomena can be expressed in terse equations, social science communications are still limited to language that uses verbal and mathematical expressions in making distinctions, giving the impression that social science, if science, is also, in part, advocacy and opinion too.

Information-Producing Institutions

Government policy research was initially conducted by academic scholars. Independent, nonprofit policy research institutions were rare before the end of World War II; Brookings, one of the earliest, dates from the 1920s. Until the early 1960s, most government social policy research was conducted within government and by a small number of university spin-offs such as the Institute for Social Research at the University of Michigan, the Bureau of Social Science Research at Columbia University, the National Opinion Research Center at the University of Chicago, and the Stanford Research Institute.

Since the mid-1960s the trend has been toward a diversified mix of private nonprofit and profit-making research institutions or "think tanks," many with loose university affiliations. Two, the Stanford Research Institute and the Research Triangle Institute, have severed most of their university ties. Others, such as the Institute for Research on Poverty, University of Wisconsin, and the National Opinion Research Center, University of Chicago, retain their university affiliations. Today more than half the federal government social policy research is conducted by private research organizations; among these, half of the largest are nonprofit.

The "War on Poverty" generated a great number of new social programs in the mid-1960s. University staffs, asked to manage large programs such as the Job Corps and also to provide research, were for the most part unsuccessful. Universities were not organized to support interdisciplinary efforts of this kind, and professors did not care to work in hierarchically organized projects; also, academic staffs were unaccustomed to complying with stringent applied research schedules and budgets. Aerospace and electronics industry firms brought in to remedy these defects also failed, primarily because of their inexperience in social science research and their insensitivity to behavioral issues. Finally, interested social scientists from all three sectors—government, universities, and industry—together with the few "think tanks" that existed at this time— Brookings, Rand, and SRI—created new policy research organizations to provide the government with information on social policies. SDC and the Urban Institute "spun off" from Rand; RTI, from the University of North Carolina and Duke University; SRI, from Stanford University; Abt Associates, Inc., from Raytheon Company, Harvard, and MIT; Mathematica, Inc., from Princeton University; and Westat, Inc., from the University of Colorado and the Census Bureau.

Quality of the New Information

Quality of information is judged according to several kinds of standards; these include its *relevance to policy*, *timeliness*, the *economy* of obtaining it, and the net benefit or expected *payoff* from its use. Because these are of particular concern to government policy researchers, the priorities of policy research differ from those of academic basic research.[1] Policy researchers attempt to provide the most valid, reliable, and accurate information possible within the constraints of schedule and budget. Basic research is intended to create new knowledge, however long it takes and whatever its cost. It is this disjunction between applied and basic research that causes the gap between social experimentation and program evaluation, and theories of social change.

Massive amounts of both kinds of information—basic and applied—are supplied to the modern state, but most of the recent growth has been in information produced by applied social research. The rates of growth for basic research are about the same as the national economy growth rates in the last two decades, but applied research information has grown much faster. In the last ten years particularly, social policy research information has been funded at about $1 billion a year, compared to one-tenth of that amount in previous decades.

The quality of information produced by applied social research has been mixed, but it is thought to be much better than it was ten years ago and is still improving. We can, for example, determine more precisely and reliably how many people are likely to reduce their demand for medical services as a function of co-payments, or what percentage of unemployed workers will seek subsidized jobs, or what incentives will keep particular youths in school, and we can shape policies accordingly. It is possible even to estimate with a fair amount of accuracy the percentage of a population subgroup that is likely to participate voluntarily in a particular government program, together with the benefits and costs of participation for both the beneficiaries and the taxpayers.

Yet the standard for timeliness, so important in policy research, is still met only infrequently, and then only because the most difficult policy problems tend to persist or recur, even where information intended to address one crisis is finally delivered long after a new crisis has replaced it. This is so because improvements in the scientific quality of information relating to social change have been attained chiefly by experimental methods and evaluations applied to several successive data cross-sections in time, and these generally require years to collect.

Much of the information currently produced by policy researchers may also not meet the policy research community's own standards of validity. In fact, until recently only a small percentage of the information was based on the ideal of a carefully controlled experimental design using statistically equivalent treatment and control groups. Thus, both the validity of attribution and the validity of generalization were often (and still are) subject to unknown degrees of bias and error. Yet this does not mean that the results of imperfect policy research are mere noise. Information on current population status, needs, and processes can still be considered useful, even if such flawed research cannot determine conclusively the net benefits of government policies and programs.

Fortunately, governments increasingly insist on the use of adequate experimental designs and approximations of the biomedical double-blind field tests to obtain more valid and generalizable information. This new intellectual technology involving social experiments has been developed to meet the government's need for more accurate and reliable information about what works, what does not, and why. Many government-sponsored social experiments now use randomized field trials with statistically equivalent treatment and control groups to achieve a much more satisfactory internal and external validity than was possible with the previous uncontrolled or nonequivalent comparison designs. Large samples assure high levels of statistical confidence (usually at least 0.95) for findings of test program impacts and benefits and their costs and distributions. Multiple locations in addition to large national probability samples are used to obtain geographic and demographic replicability and generalizability. Successive measurements of impacts on program participation and target populations create time-series data spanning several years (generally at least three and sometimes as many as ten) to assure stability of research findings, and provide essential data for the sequential process analyses used to determine *why* and *whether* government programs work.

In 1974 J. P. Gilbert, R. J. Light, and F. Mosteller estimated that as much as 80 percent of their admittedly nonrandom, but probably representative, sample of projects producing information for the government was based on flawed research designs of uncertain validity.[2] Policy research practices have improved since then, with the diffusion of experimental techniques to social research and greater use of randomized, controlled field experiments. Today much of the information produced appears to meet scientific standards of validity, accuracy, and reliability. Just how much, however, awaits investigation, but most "meta-evaluators" agree that government policy research has improved over the 20 percent estimate of five years ago.[3]

Unfortunately, improvement in quality has been achieved at some cost to timeliness; hence, the immediate utility of information is thereby reduced. Most social experiments that are large enough and long enough to produce valid and reliable information on social program results take five to ten years to complete. The first year (sometimes two) is devoted to conceptualizing the research program, organizing procurement, soliciting competent competitive bidders, and selecting a research contractor. The second year is spent on research design, instrument development and testing, and critical regulatory review by government. It is generally not before the third or fourth year that a major social experiment can be operated in the field and baseline survey data generated. Then, at least two and often three or four years are needed to gather the time-series data on the impacts on participants. Another year for data reduction and analysis brings the total to at least five years, and perhaps as many as nine. It can easily take another year to disseminate the results.

How Information-Gathering and Analysis Are Sponsored

Information produced for the modern state is rarely sponsored as described. The ideal model for the most developed nations with some parliamentary form of democratic government is a sequence something like the following: The *legislators* ask whether a social policy or program works, and why. The *administrative agency* undertakes to evaluate the program and to report back the following year; it then delineates research tasks, requests and obtains proposals or grant applications, and selects a research contractor or grantee. The *contractor* completes the research and delivers a conclusive report to the agency within a year. The *agency* then provides the legislators with a decisive summary and a briefing. The *legislators* consider the best interest of the nation and decide whether to expand, maintain, modify, contract, or terminate the policy or program.

This model is violated most of the time and all along the line. More often than not it is the executive agency's appointed research, planning, and evaluation "shops" that propose the funding of information collection, not legislative committees (although there is a modest trend toward passing legislation that mandates program evaluation). The legislature is generally interested in who gets what—a type of equity concern—and how much it costs. Its concern is the budget even more than efficiency.

Little direct information is promised within a year, or even scheduled so ambitiously, because it is known that reliable research requires a much longer time to accomplish. A game is sometimes played between budget-granting legislators and budget-seeking administrators, in which each knows what the other wants, cannot give it, and so substitutes something that *can* be given, even if it falls somewhat short.

The legislators want to know the costs, benefits, and impacts of a proposed program (or a proposed change in a program or policy) *before* voting on it. If they have some favorite theories they want them confirmed, not challenged, by facts. They know the information will not be in hand in time for the voting decision (unless the issue is one of the many unresolved, recurring ones for which re-search was initiated earlier). Often they will not have the information before the next election, when it might be useful for taking a position on a specific cam-paign issue. Most legislators understand this; the old hands who control policy and funds through the committees know it from repeated experience. Yet they continue to ask policy questions, and for more than rhetorical reasons. They ask because it would be unintelligent and irresponsible not to ask, and because by asking, they are signaling their concerns to the policy-implementing executives, thereby possibly stimulating some responsive information-gathering actions. They are saying, in effect, "Show us that you, too, are worried about these concerns of ours and will respond by gathering information, even if it cannot be produced in time to be of much use in making decisions. At least try to act as if the information has already been gathered, that you have studied it, and that it indicates what we suspect. Then we need not be in quite such a hurry to hear from you; we can fund some of your requests and feel we have done our duty."

The executive agency administrators respond conscientiously to such requests for information—which they often had planned to gather anyway—but know they cannot produce anything in time for the particular issue-and-decision cycle. They know it is part of the price for obtaining funds for gather-ing other kinds of information, and that it will help them administer their programs better and defend their budgets. It seems a reasonable price to pay. Everyone wants to know all about everything in time to make intelligent deci-sions, but few believe this to be possible.

How New Information Is Disseminated

Legally, much of the information produced in the United States is within the public domain, but this does not automatically guarantee its wide dissemi-nation. It can be, and often is, delayed, filtered, allowed to become stale from protracted nonuse, or selectively distributed. This gate-keeping function is usu-ally exercised formally and informally by the sponsoring agency. The simile applies less to dissemination practices in the United States than elsewhere, where the gate may not always be open, even legally. In the United States, with its disclosure laws, a better analogy might be corporate annual reports, which call attention to the good news but merely report the bad.

In most nations, if research findings support the sponsoring agency's policies or programs—and particularly when their survival or growth is being debated—the information tends to be promptly and widely disseminated. In the United States particularly, findings inconclusive or unsupportive of policy will general-ly not be censored, but the information may languish in small editions of un-distributed reports that are essentially inaccessible to all but those who know something about the information already. This is not to say that information "unpopular" to its government sponsors is forever inaccessible. Modern demo-cratic governments rarely lie in reporting on social policy matters; they simply refrain from telling the whole truth promptly and aggressively if they consider it unhelpful. If the information is insufficiently supportive of the agency's poli-cies and programs, it may still be disseminated a few months later; in the United States, it usually is. In either case, in the United States the information reaches its target audiences—elected and appointed officials, researchers, journalists, and the general public—within months. Elsewhere it may take longer, but complete suppression in democratic societies is uncommon.

How Information Is Used

How does all this new information affect policy decisions in the modern state? No conclusive answer is possible, for we can never be sure that a change in government policy or public behavior occurs because of the new information. At the national level, we can only make informed guesses about the relationship. However, at a less aggregated level, some point between the individual organization and the nation, we see that the policies and programs of administering agencies that have produced and used large amounts of the new information are demonstrably different from those that have made little use of the new information. If we assume that government agencies on the same level are more like each other in the ways they use information than they are like other kinds of organizations with similar missions, but that these agencies vary in the way they use *new* information, we have the crude makings of a natural control group. This cross-sectional comparison can be augmented by a comparison of one agency's behavior before and after receiving the new information, if we assume that the agency's mission and methods have not changed substantially over time in other respects.

A comparison of the U.S. Department of Labor with the Department of Energy, for example, reveals significant differences in the ways they use policy and program information. The Labor Department has spent over $1 billion in the last decade to test and evaluate the impact of its employment programs on the behavior of its clients; the Energy Department has spent less than $100 million to collect information on the impact of its programs on energy consumers. The difference is one of kind more than magnitude, however, because the Energy Department spends much more than the Labor Department to obtain research and development information. Differences cannot be attributed to the newness of the Energy Department because most of its component organizations have existed in one form or another for thirty years.

Both departments have had their share of disappointing programs. Labor Department programs have attempted to reduce structural and seasonal unemployment, with only partial success thus far (e.g., the Youth Employment and Training and Supported Work Programs and certain aspects of the Job Corps). Energy Department programs have tried to increase the availability of national energy resources and to decrease dependence on foreign sources through substitution and conservation, with almost no success. The Labor Department has surveyed its clients extensively and periodically through the Bureau of Labor Statistics and other information-gathering organizations. It knows the number of its clients, their status (employed or unemployed, worker or employer), and their typical labor-market behavior. It knows program participation rates (actual and potential) and unit costs well enough to forecast, at least roughly, program costs and benefits. The Energy Department knows much less about energy consumers and producers. What is worse, it has managed to alienate both groups. Because it has neglected collecting pertinent behavioral information, opting instead for engineering and macroeconomic research, it does not know why its programs for expanded nuclear power, coal gasification, gas price deregulation, solar energy, and energy conservation are widely opposed.

At least some of the Labor Department's programs work, and there is some understanding of why others do not work, so that obvious errors are less frequently repeated. None of the Energy Department's major programs appear to work well, and there is little evidence to suggest that the Department understands why. It is repeating the mistake it made with nuclear power and conservation in failing to secure consumer acceptance of expanded applications of coal and solar energy.

Partial decentralization of policy and program decision-making in the Labor Department permits participation of expert administrators who have access to good information sources. In the Energy Department, decision-making is centralized, and there is little participation by lower-level or local administrators with specialized knowledge; thus potentially available information is underutilized. The Labor Department, led by an experienced policy economist, bases its decisions on well-researched, empirically derived information and on knowledge of who uses the program, and its successes and failures. The Energy Department, also led by an experienced policy economist until recently, bases its decisions on economic theory and on unresearched demand estimates of how its programs *should* work and how its clients *should* respond (if only they were more patriotic, if only they understood their own interests better!).

Consider a before-and-after comparison within a single government agency. Like the Department of Energy, the attention of the Department of Housing and Urban Development (HUD) was originally riveted on matters physical and economic, rather than social and political. The Department launched a series of massive research projects in the late 1960s to determine how better building technology could improve housing for the poor at lower cost; it was already clear that, in the United States, at least, low-income housing was definitely not low-*cost* housing. Project Breakthrough, the In-Cities Housing Experiment, and related efforts consistently showed that costs could not be significantly reduced using hardware technology if other obstacles to the organization of housing production remained (multiple tiering of contractors, building codes, and the tangled web of union contracts). Nor could the housing needs of the poor, including the *social* need for residential desegregation, be met by continuing to construct low-income, high-rise housing developments segregated by income and, usually, also by race.

In the late 1960s HUD became aware of social policy research and the information it could provide about the behaviors of housing producers, consumers, and markets. It was receptive to the idea of sponsoring and using the new information, probably in part because its recent leadership had included experienced social scientists. Also, HUD had a mandate to deal with inner-city problems, which in the late 1960s meant economic deprivation and racial conflict—clearly "people problems" that could not be solved through the use of improved hardware technology.

HUD instituted a series of major social experiments at this time, some still in progress. The Model Cities Program explored many of the urban reform opportunities, admittedly without much clear success. Its goals were so many and diffuse that it became difficult to determine exactly what treatments had actually been specified and tried, and what their results (if any) were. Having learned from this first series of relatively uncontrolled social experiments, and from the failure of Project Breakthrough's physical technology experiments, HUD in the early 1970s initiated the Experimental Housing Allowance Program, with its scientifically more rigorous Housing Allowance Demand Experiment, Housing Allowance Supply Experiment, and Administrative Agency Experiment.

These social experiments have produced unprecedented quantities of high-quality information on the housing needs, demand, mobility, consumption, and other behaviors of thousands of poor and near-poor households in twelve major urban areas. Before such consumer response information was available, either national housing programs were launched at great risk and cost, only to fail, or little was done to address the poor's housing needs precisely for fear of failure. With new information available, HUD will be able to design its programs more cost-effectively and with less risk, while also avoiding expensive panaceas such as the earliest Project Breakthrough and supply subsidies. Although the best solutions have not been found yet, what *has* been found is that some modest programs such as Section 8 housing allowances have socially desirable effects.

A Brief Look at the Probable Future

Technological breakthroughs in interdisciplinary social research, computer hardware, and audiovisual communication will have increasing impacts on the modern state in the next twenty years. The American example will certainly be followed by the other developed nations; this trend, in fact, is already evident. Germany, Scandinavia, France, and England and the Commonwealth are ten to fifteen years behind the United States in applied social research. As with other aspects of technology, it is reasonable to assume that the comparative American advantage will be eliminated in areas where capital investment requirements do not exceed funding capacities and where appropriate expertise is available.

The rapid five-year generational changes in computing and communications technology should help accelerate the use of social research technology to produce information for government. Computers will become sufficiently cheap and compact for application in most social research operations. The netting together of cheap, interactive TV sets, computers, desk consoles, and pocket terminals into enormous, decentralized data banks and high-speed central processors is probably only a decade away. Social scientists then will no longer be able to excuse themselves from doing quantitative empirical work by complaining of the costs of large data samples and statistical analyses.

The 20 million books, or 70 billion bits, now stored in the Library of Congress can already be stored in 20 IBM 3850 computers.[4] In a decade many researchers are likely to have instant access to this kind and size of data base. The average 35 percent-per-year growth in computer storage capacity over the last two decades, together with the miniaturization made possible by silicon chip technology, will make computing a standard tool of social research and will enormously increase its use in information production, analysis, and consumption. Indeed, the effective translation of this increasing mass of information into better social decision-making will be one of the next major tasks of social science research.

REFERENCES

[1] James S. Coleman, "Policy Research and Academic Research."

[2] J. P. Gilbert, R. J. Light, and F. Mosteller, "Assessing Social Innovations: An Empirical Base for Policy," *Evaluation and Experiment*, Carl A. Bennett and Arthur A. Lumsdaine (eds.) (Chicago: Academic Press, 1975).

[3] Personal communications, Professors Henry Aaron, Kenneth Arrow, Robert Boruch, Donald Campbell, James Coleman, Richard Light, and Peter Rossi.

[4] Lewis Branscomb, "Information: The Ultimate Frontier," *Science*, 203, 12 January 1979.

MICHAEL HOWARD

War and the Nation-state[1]

THE RELATIONSHIP BETWEEN THE STATE as an institution and the conduct of war has always been close. States normally identify themselves by their relationship with one another. In most cases—at least before 1945—they came into existence and defined their boundaries by the use, or the threatened use, of force. This assertion and maintenance of independent identity was both logically and historically prior to other, more continuous and evident functions of the State, such as the management of distributive justice or the legitimization of internal force. Unless the State *existed*, independent of external authority, these functions could not be fulfilled. It is for this reason that the military capability of a State is assumed to be so major an element in its effectiveness as an actor in the international system. Conversely, domestic attitudes toward military activity will affect the institution of the State itself. Sentiments of loyalty and commitment to the State are ultimately tested by the degree of readiness on the part of its citizens to engage in military service, or accept comparable hardships, on its behalf; and states that can command such readiness, whether through voluntary commitment or effective social control, are likely to be treated with greater respect internationally than those that do not.

The story of the development of the European States-system in the seventeenth and eighteenth centuries is thus very largely a military one. During this period, conflicts between princely landowners over property rights were slowly transformed into interstate conflicts over commercial and security interests. Hereditary rulers acquired ever greater fiscal, military, and administrative control over the communities subordinated to them, and those communities became, reciprocally, increasingly involved in the military and foreign concerns traditionally regarded as *arcana regni*, the private concern of the Crown. Military activity led to growing demands on communal resources of money and, sometimes, of manpower. These demands by the Prince led to counterpressures from the representatives of the community for participation; the cry "no taxation without representation" was heard in Europe, before it crossed the Atlantic, as early as the sixteenth century. In Britain, the United Provinces, and North America the consequent internal conflicts led to the emergence of polities in which the newly emerging state apparatus of professional armed forces and civil bureaucracies was effectively brought under communal control. Elsewhere in Europe, where aspirations to communal participation were effectively stifled by triumphant monarchies, a dichotomy continued to exist between a state apparatus responsible to the monarch alone, and the communities he governed and that contributed to his wars. It was a dichotomy that led the French *philosophes* of the eighteenth century, and their disciples in Germany, Britain, and North America, to believe wars occurred only because they served the interests of the princes and the traditional ruling classes that supported them. Once "the people," or "the Nation," took power, it was assumed by liberal ideologues, wars would automatically cease.

The dichotomy between princes and peoples, between the state apparatus and the community, was violently resolved in the series of great revolutions, foreshadowed by the American Declaration of Independence, that swept Europe between 1789 and 1918, when in one country after another the representatives of "the people," or "the Nation" (the terms were initially interchangeable), assumed control of the State. But so far from inaugurating the expected reign of peace, this "nationalization" of the State meant simply the nationalization of war; and the new *international* conflicts were fought with an intensity inconceivable under *l'ancien régime*. Loyalty to the Crown was always to some extent contractual: an evil prince could be disowned; allegiance could be renounced or limited. But how could this be done with a Nation that was simply an extension of oneself, the embodiment of the communal General Will? What the Nation willed was its own justification: there were no limits to the demands it might make on its members.

Inevitably, nationalism was characterized almost everywhere by some degree of militarism. Self-consciousness as a Nation implies, by definition, a sense of differentiation from other communities, and the most memorable incidents in the group memory usually are of conflict with, and triumph over, other communities. It is in fact very difficult to create national self-consciousness *without* a war. The French nation became identified with its military triumphs: Marengo, Austerlitz, and Jena set the seal on the newfound national consciousness. Trafalgar and Waterloo added a substantial increment to a British national sentiment that reached back four hundred years to Crécy and Agincourt and was to be enhanced even in our own times by the Battle of Britain and El Alamein. Russian national self-consciousness began to stir in 1812, German in the following three years; and when Germany eventually became a nation in 1871, it was in consequence of comparable military cataclysms—Königgrätz, Gravelotte, and Sedan. And had the citizens of the United States really thought of themselves as a Nation until they had proved themselves to be one on the battlefields of the Civil War?

It could indeed be asserted in the nineteenth century that no Nation, in the true sense of the word, could be born *without* war; that no self-conscious community could establish itself as a new and independent actor on the world scene without an armed conflict or the threat of one. In the writings of nineteenth-century theorists of nationalism—Mazzini in Italy and Fichte, Hegel, and Treitschke in Germany—war was explicitly identified as a positive value, part of a natural process of struggle whereby mankind evolved to ever higher forms of political organization. This was the dialectic that Marx, by substituting the class struggle for the struggle of Nations, turned on its side rather than its head. And in the latter part of the century this politico-philosophical doctrine was reinforced by the natural sciences, using Darwinian concepts of the survival of the fittest as the natural process of evolution. The purely historical concept of the Nation merged into the biological one of the Race.

All this filtered down into the national educational systems, for which the State everywhere in Europe was taking over responsibility from private charitable or ecclesiastical bodies. Whether as a result of deliberate policy or not, the schools of Western Europe in the last quarter of the nineteenth century produced a generation psychologically attuned to war. National history was depicted by writers both of school textbooks and of popular works as the history of the Nation's military triumphs. Other Nations were defined by these authors in terms of military relations. Foreigners were people with whom one went to war and usually defeated, and if one had not done so last time, one certainly would the next. Service to the Nation was seen in terms of military service; one found personal fulfillment in making "the supreme sacrifice" so that the national cause might triumph. The Nation, with all its symbolism, was made the object of a quasi-religious veneration, usually sanctified by all the ritual and liturgy of the Christian churches. As a result, when the young men of Europe went out in 1914 to die in their millions, they did so for an ideal epitomized in the three words: God, King, and Country—*Gott, König, und Vaterland*. Feudal, religious, and national loyalties were blended in an image of intense emotional power. Even for those who recognized neither God nor King, *La Patrie* provided an adequate substitute for both. In Britain, France, and Germany in 1914, the Nation, almost in its entirety, was fused with the State.

This emotional fusion was institutionalized and strengthened as the war progressed by the demands the war effort made on the belligerent populations, without whose total participation, in field and factory as well as in the armed forces, the struggle could not be carried on at all. The power of the State was extended into entirely new areas of social and economic life; while, reciprocally, the process of political consultation and representation developed to an unprecedented degree. In Britain, concessions were made to trade-union power and female suffrage that before 1914 had been resisted to the last ditch. The war transformed Britain from an oligarchy into a democracy. In Germany the last relics of monarchical power were effectively destroyed even before 1918 by forces of militant populism largely channeled by the Army; forces that, reluctantly quiescent during the subsequent decade of defeat, reemerged with redoubled strength in the form of National Socialism. It is still unfashionable to say so, but Nazi Germany was a nation in arms comparable to France during the revolutionary and Napoleonic eras; and therein lay the cause of her astonishing military prowess that it took the combined power of every other major industrial power in the world (except Japan) to overcome.

The interwar years saw a reaction in Western Europe against this apotheosis of the Nation-state and the glorification of war that had accompanied it. In Britain, in particular, some of the finest minds among the younger generation came to regard "King and Country" as dirty words, and committed themselves to causes, not the least that of communism, that denied the validity of the Nation-state altogether. But this reaction was moderated by the experience of the Second World War when it was discovered that, if one was to counter the grotesque exaggerations of militaristic nationalism that survived in Germany and elsewhere, traditional national values as well as traditional military skills had a great deal to be said for them. When the very survival of their communities appeared to be threatened, both British Liberals and Russian Marxists reverted to nationalism of a highly traditional type, and were grateful for such moral strength as they could draw from it. For the peoples of Europe, the Second World War no less than the First was a "Great Patriotic War," fought for the preservation or restoration of their Nation-states; and if during the course of the war communism received an enhanced respectability in Western Europe, that was because in such countries as Yugoslavia, Italy, and France the Communists proved to be among the most effective fighters for national independence.

In the case of Britain this enhanced sense of national pride and achievement, the memories of the Battle of Britain and El Alamein, survived for a decade after the war and had an unfortunate effect. It made it difficult for the country as a whole to appreciate, and come to terms with, the underlying weakness of its position. Few at the time understood the extent to which Britain's survival and ultimate victories had been made possible not by her own strenghth but by that of the Soviet Union and the United States. This self-image as a great power made the British reject all opportunities to link their destinies with those continental European peoples they had defeated or liberated and obstinately continued to regard *de haut en bas*. It was also a self-image that accounted for the massive popular support enjoyed by the Suez expedition, whatever doubt and opposition may have been expressed by the elites. The appalling blow to national pride administered by the disastrous outcome of that affair, the realization of the gap that existed between Britain's pretensions and her effective power, created a deep trauma in the national consciousness. Once more, as after 1918, the sense of national pride and unity began to disintegrate; and the events of 1939-1945, already part of the national myth, began to be examined with a more cold and critical eye.

This time the reaction against the glorification of national achievement took a different form. The Second World War, like the First, had called forth a massive degree of popular participation in the war effort. But in Britain and the United States—unlike the Soviet Union—this had not taken the form of a mass slaughter, of an *effort du sang*. Although in Britain virtually every adult member of the population was involved in some kind of war service, only a small number of names had to be added to the war memorials that still testify, in every parish church in the country, to the depth of the wounds inflicted on British society between 1914 and 1918. So when a new generation in Britain began critically to scrutinize the conduct of the second war, it focused less on the sacrifices suffered by its own society than on the destruction inflicted on others; especially on the moral problems involved in strategic bombing, in general, and the use of nuclear weapons, in particular.

Few argued that the Second World War had not been necessary or that those who had died in it had "given their lives in vain." But the overkill resulting from the strategic bombing of Germany, most of it inflicted during the last six months of the war, and the unnerving scale of the destruction of Hiroshima and Nagasaki raised questions of a different kind. The victorious peoples in the Second World War, like their enemies, certainly drew their main strength from the ideology of nationalism; but as the war progressed, their leaders proclaimed with increasing emphasis that they were fighting also for the vindication of international public law and the creation of a new international order in which no transgressor nation would go unpunished. The Second World War may have ended with the destruction of Dresden and Hiroshima, but it ended also with the Nuremberg Trials and the Declaration on Human Rights. In the postwar world it was difficult to maintain that national loyalties absolved the citizen from the obligation of individual moral choice or that he could legitimately seek salvation in the kind of total commitment to his country's service that, however respectable in 1914, had now been effectively discredited by the excesses of National Socialism.

When nearly ten years after the destruction of Hiroshima by nuclear weapons the Western nations declared that in future they proposed to rely primarily on the use of such measures, on an even more horrific scale, for the preservation of their own liberties, these doubts grew. They appear to have been most strongly felt in Britain; nowhere in the United States did protests reach the intensity generated by the British Campaign for Nuclear Disarmament between 1958 and 1964. But the United States was not to be presented for another decade with the problem that confronted the British at the end of the 1950s, where the State admitted that it could protect the community from total annihilation only by posing a threat to inflict comparable destruction on the civil society of its adversary. It was a threat as open to question on political and military grounds as it was on moral. Under such circumstances, the alienation of a large number of idealistic young people from a state apparatus that proposed to do such things, and that could offer no convincing prospect of protection in return, was not altogether surprising. It was a situation in which patriotism was quite evidently not enough.

In the United States such massive protests were to come later and over a different issue. The belligerents during the Second World War had not only learned how to inflict massive destruction on distant civilian targets; they had also developed, to an equally unprecedented extent, methods of stratagem, subversion, and psychological warfare. Side by side with the conventional operations of the armed forces there had been waged a covert war of intelligence, espionage, deception, and propaganda, the full details of which are only now being revealed and that involved some of the most intellectually gifted members of the community in activities of a deeply clandestine nature. The countering of enemy intelligence activities by all means available, the penetration of his espionage services, the dissemination of deceptive information, "black" propaganda, and the organization of insurgency within his territories were only some of the activities legitimized by wartime necessity and brought, by those involved in them, to a very high level of expertise. These weapons remained in the arsenals of the belligerent powers after the war and were revived when, after 1948, the Soviet Union and the Western democracies faced each other in a confrontation that was war in all but name. Reluctance to prosecute this conflict by armed force gave both sides an additional *rationale* for the use of such covert operations; and honorable men of great ability served their countries by engaging in activities of a kind unjustifiable by any criteria other than the most brutal kind of *raison d'état*, and the knowledge that their adversaries were doing the same. The revelation in the early 1970s that U.S. agencies were engaged in such occupations, and had been so engaged for the past quarter of a century, came as a deep shock to American liberal opinion. For an entire generation the CIA became a symbol of pure evil almost as powerful as the H-Bomb had been for young left-wing Britons a decade earlier.

It may be that clandestine activities of this kind arise as inevitably from the nature of the contemporary international system as do nuclear and other advanced weapons systems from the development of scientific knowledge. But whether justified or not, nuclear weapons systems and clandestine operations between them have the effect of reversing that progressive nationalization of the State that every war fought since the French Revolution incrementally enhanced. For even the most open and democratic of governments have to keep their preparations for nuclear warfare and their covert intelligence operations as secret from their own peoples as from their putative enemies. There can be no sense of mass participation by citizen-soldiers in nuclear or clandestine warfare as there was in the great military acts of the two World Wars. It was not easy, for example, for even the most loyal citizens of the United States to identify themselves with such activities as the CIA's successful intervention in Iran in 1953 or its less effective operations in Chile. Nor do nuclear missiles arouse the same emotions of national pride and possessiveness as did the battleships of pre-1914 Europe or even the aircraft carriers of the Second World War. The almost insoluble problems of command and control that are posed by the use of nuclear weapons, or those, equally intractable, of constitutional responsibility for the operation of clandestine services, only pinpoint the difficulty of legitimizing such activities of the State in the eyes of the community through the normal operation of the constitutional process.

The result of this development is that the State *apparat* is likely to become isolated from the rest of the body politic, a severed head conducting its intercourse with other severed heads according to its own laws. War, in short, has once more been *denationalized*. It has become, as it was in the eighteenth century, an affair of *states* and no longer of *peoples*. The identification of the community with the State, brought to its highest point in the era of the two World Wars, can no longer be assumed as natural or, militarily speaking, necessary. No Third World War is likely to be fought by armies embodying the manpower of the Nation while the rest of the population work to keep them armed and fed.

The effect of these developments has also been alienation in a deeper sense. On the one hand we have a new generation less inclined than their fathers of the World War era to acquiesce passively from patriotic motives in the activities of the State *apparat*. On the other hand the functionaries of that *apparat* may become increasingly impatient of measures of popular control no longer justified by a requirement for popular participation and that can only impede the efficient functioning of the machine in their charge. Sometimes they may be tempted to cut constitutional corners. It was not simply the initiation and conduct of the war in Vietnam that aroused such disquiet in the United States and elsewhere; it was the revelation of the clandestine activities, the domestic deception, and the oblique morality that the government of the United States believed were justified by that war and the circumstances that surrounded it. So grave did this situation become under President Nixon that, for a terrible period, the executive arm of the United States felt itself to be almost a beleaguered garrison surrounded by a hostile population, against which any means were legitimate in order to ensure its own survival. The apparatus of the State seemed not only severed from the body of the nation on whose behalf it was supposed to function; at times, indeed, its activities appeared to be directed *against* that nation.

Although it was in the United States that these tensions were most dramatically and dangerously displayed, they exist in other democratic countries as well; everywhere, that is, where people can freely express their views. The armed forces are no longer seen as the school and embodiment of the Nation. They are once more widely regarded in Western societies, as they were by Anglo-Saxon liberals in the nineteenth century, as a suspect professional group with atypical values and a vested interest in conflict, perverting national resources to unproductive or counterproductive ends; while the intelligence services are shunned like lepers by those academic communities that, a generation ago, did so much to create them. Patriotism in Western democracies once more is seen as the last refuge of scoundrels or, at best, as a symptom of the emotional disorders of the Radical Right.

It can be argued that this trend is symptomatic of no more than that robust Whiggery that is the life blood of any free society and the strongest guarantee against the creeping advance of totalitarianism, and that during the last sixty years has run far too thinly in our veins. Mistrust of the State and its activities has for liberals always been the beginning of political wisdom. It is certainly difficult to look back on that apotheosis of the Nation-state many of us have experienced in our own lifetime without amazement that such absurdities should have been proclaimed and such crimes committed in its name. It is natural enough that people of independent spirit and intellect should now scrutinize all traditional claims on their loyalties with a measure of skepticism. It is not only natural, but positively desirable that all concerned with political studies should seek for new patterns of world politics that would make possible wider loyalties—international, transnational, supranational—loyalties that would dissolve the old system of States that has apparently produced no more than an endless series of increasingly destructive wars. What the conservative pessimist sees as the disintegration of the only system that made orderly government and political intercourse possible is for the radical optimist the first stage in the reintegration of mankind in new political patterns that will transcend the old "war" system and make possible perpetual peace.

There are, however, a number of difficulties with this approach. In the first place, the Nation-state may have been a myth, but it was a socially valuable one, and one that has by no means outlived its usefulness. By breaking down the frontiers of the small inward-looking communities that preceded it, it released human and economic resources that have hugely increased the total welfare of mankind, and created mechanisms, admittedly and always imperfect, by which peoples can control their own destinies in a manner impossible for pre-nationalistic communities. Control and participation on a local communal level was always possible; but it was only after the French Revolution, to take one example, that the hundreds of little French communities could participate in the control of the affairs of the larger unit where ultimately their fate, especially in questions of war and peace, was decided. The Nation-state was based sometimes on a real community of culture and sometimes on a cultural concept that had to be deliberately created or re-created. Usually its basis of cohesion lay somewhere between the two; but the Nation was normally the largest cultural unit with which people found it possible to identify themselves; and that identification was, as we have seen, powerfully assisted by national wars.

The disintegration of the Nation-state as a consequence of the erosion of the loyalties built up during the era of the World Wars does not, unfortunately, show any signs of leading to the emergence of higher loyalties to broader communities. Englishmen, Germans, French, and Italians, for example, show no signs of turning into "Europeans." Rather, the contrary is happening. Antagonisms between constituent groups that had been mediated, if not totally dissolved, by the national myth, and were in consequence susceptible to control by the national state system, have reappeared, often with redoubled violence. These may take the form of the reemergence of such submerged cultures as the Basques, the Bretons, the French Canadians, the Flemish, the Scots, the Irish, or the Welsh. They may take the form of class antagonisms, as in Britain, France, and Italy, or racial antagonisms, as in the United States. The symptoms are sometimes mild, sometimes acute, and Europeans are probably more troubled by them than are Americans. But in every case the new focus of loyalty is set not higher, but lower. The disintegration of the Nation-state has been regressive. As a result, it is increasingly difficult for the State to fulfill those functions, not simply of defense, but also of the maintenance of acceptable order, the administration of communally agreed justice, and the management of economic resources, that are its *raison d'être*. Too many of its citizens see it not as an instrument of communal action, but as a tyrannical adversary. The young idealist finds self-fulfillment in fighting rather than in serving it.

This is the more disquieting in that the State is a body that has, by definition, a legitimate monopoly of the use of violence or, as it is usually termed under such conditions, armed force. That use is legitimate insofar as the State *apparat* represents, or is generally held to represent, the entire community; and when it does resort to force it does so as the agent of the community expressing its will through agreed constitutional processes. Force can be legitimately used only on the authorization of responsible political leaders by trained men acting under strict discipline in accordance with the provisions of both military and constitutional law. This politically legitimized monopoly of force is the primary characteristic of any State worthy of the name. It is a monopoly that has often been abused: there can be few countries where responsible citizens have not at one time or another been appalled at the use to which their armed forces have been put. But the erosion of that monopoly can lead only to chaos. It is undeniable that political groups using violence to achieve their objectives may eventually, by their very success, achieve legitimacy and create new states, or new regimes in old ones. Their struggles form the basis for a new myth to sanctify their activities and mobilize communal support for their power. But general acceptance of the view that violence may be used by small groups within wider communities, recognizing no legitimacy save that created by their own aspirations, can only bring about a situation of such disorder, resentment, fear, and vindictiveness that all political consensus disintegrates and the classic formula takes effect: anarchy followed, cyclically, by tyranny. Indeed, that is not infrequently the intention.

In practice, very few militant activists are in principle anarchist, willing the end that is likely to follow from the means used. For the most part, they are concerned not with abolishing the State but with remodeling it; whether by changing the political elites or by the formation of new states that give fuller representaton to the indigenous communities. Where they have succeeded in doing so, the power of the State over the community is usually imposed more strictly than ever before. There may be almost insoluble difficulties in adjusting or constructing states to make them truly responsible to the wills of the communities for which they claim to speak, or in creating new states to speak for communities at present voiceless. But that does not mean that the Nation-state itself no longer serves an essential purpose in the ordering of the affairs of mankind, and it must therefore continue to make large claims on the loyalty of its citizens.

Nowhere is this more clearly recognized than among the peoples of the Third World, where the achievement of effective statehood, based on some communal myth of struggle against oppressors, is rightly seen as an essential condition for making their voices heard and their interests respected within the international community. And how indeed can a people become, or remain, part of the international system until they have achieved recognition as a Nation-state? In spite of the development of transnational pressure groups of various kinds, national governments remain the only effective mechanism by which the ordinary man and woman achieve some sense, however slight, of participation in, and responsibility for, not only the ordering of their own societies, but also the conduct of the affairs of the world as a whole.

We are today, indeed, witnessing a new and astounding phenomenon in the revival of Islam as a vehicle through which many Third World peoples express their resentment against the Western cultures that for so long dominated them, and seek to create, or re-create, a community overriding existing State barriers. Yet even this is not likely to reverse existing trends. For either new and enlarged political units will evolve, giving institutional expression, as did the new States of Italy and Germany in the nineteenth century, to the new found sense of cultural unity of their peoples; or else State differences based on cultural diversity will persist as stubbornly within Islam as they have within Christendom. In either event, States, in smaller or greater number, will persist, and that persistence is only too likely to be strengthened and sanctified by war.

Finally, in no part of the world does the power of the State *apparat* show fewer signs of diminishing than in that controlled by the ideology that predicted its inevitable withering away. In Marxist societies the myth of the Nation has been not so much transcended as reinforced by the myths of Marxism-Leninism. No historic Nation-state has yet been destroyed by Marxist revolutions; normally Marxists have taken over the existing State *apparat* and operate it far more effectively than their predecessors as an instrument of social control. In the Third World, Marxism has flourished only where it has either reinforced, or gained reinforcement from, popular nationalism. And the myth of popular control, as in the French Revolution, justifies all measures of State power. Those who object to the activities of the State identify themselves automatically as enemies of the people.

In Communist states there can be no alienation between the State *apparat* and the community it serves. The armed forces and the activities associated with them are not starved for lack of government appropriations and popular support. The academic community does not consider relations with the intelligence or the security services to be reprehensible, or if they do, they do not say so out loud. There exists, in the shape of the Party, a highly effective instrument for ensuring social control of the community by the State and the elites who operate it. One does not have to assume nefarious or aggressive intentions on the part of the Soviet leadership to recognize that the immense military power of the Soviet Union, a society where there is little evidence of any serious attempt to question the loyalty owed by citizens to the State, presents a phenomenon we cannot ignore when we come to assess what developments we see as desirable and what we see as undesirable in our own societies in the West.

The erosion of national cohesion evident in some Western societies, connected, at least in part, with the denationalization of war, is thus not typical of the world as a whole. In the West this cohesion was built up through the development of certain habits of behavior now being widely abandoned. Elsewhere, and particularly in socialist countries, it is the result of mechanisms of social control that are constantly being improved. One would wish as little to restore the historical conditions that made possible the former process as to imitate the latter. The remarkable recovery of France, for example, and the continued cohesion of both West German and Japanese societies, in spite of all internal pressures, shows that the process of disintegration is neither necessary nor irreversible, and the malaise of the sixties and seventies may eventually be seen as a transitory phase. But the fact remains that societies lacking the cohesion created by a strong national myth, or that imposed and maintained by political elites using mechanisms of social control, are likely to be patients rather than agents in the international system: at best ignored, certainly exploited, and not improbably eliminated altogether. In any event, their weakness will be a source of continuing international instability. Wars have arisen at least as often from the disintegration of decadent States as from the aggression of strong ones. The decline of national loyalties, in spite of all the hopes placed on it by generations of liberal thinkers, will thus not necessarily enhance the prospects of world peace.

REFERENCES

[1]This article is based on a lecture given at Oxford in November 1977 and printed by the Clarendon Press in 1978. The author is grateful to the Oxford University Press for permission to make use of it.

HEDLEY BULL

The State's Positive Role in World Affairs

We are constantly being told, at least in the Western world, that the state (and along with it, the system of states) is an obstacle to the achievement of a viable world order. First, the state is said to be an obstacle to peace and security: while the world continues to be organized politically as a system of states, war will remain endemic—a condition of affairs that could be tolerated before the advent of nuclear weapons but can be no longer. Second, the state is said to stand in the way of the promotion of economic and social justice in world society. It is the sovereign state that enables the rich peoples of the world to consume their greedy, mammoth portions of the world's resources, while refusing transfers to poor countries; and it is the sovereign state, again, that makes it possible for the squalid and corrupt governments of many poor (and some not so poor) countries to ignore the basic needs of their own citizens and to violate their human rights. Third, the state is held to be a barrier to man's grappling effectively with the problem of living in harmony with his environment. The connected issues of the control of the world's population, the production and distribution of food, the utilization of the world's resources, and the conservation of the natural environment, it is said, have to be tackled on a global basis, and this is prevented by the division of mankind into states.

Those who see the problem of world order as one of getting "beyond the state" (or the sovereign state or the nation-state) are not necessarily agreed as to what form of universal political organization should replace the system of states, or what combination of suprastate, substate, or transstate actors should deprive the state of its role. But they all feel that there is some basic contradiction between, on the one hand, the unity or interconnectedness of the global economy, the global society, the global polity, and, on the other, the system under which each state claims exclusive jurisdiction over a particular area of the earth's surface and of the human population. Thus political economists tell us that we must transcend the state in order to manage "the economics of interdependence," lawyers sound the clarion call of an advance "from international law to world law," and political scientists speak of the need to disavow the "states-centric paradigm."[1] The term "statist" is applied in a new, pejorative sense to describe those unable to free themselves from the bad old ways.

No doubt the system of sovereign states, when compared with other forms of universal political organization that have existed in the past or might come to exist in the future (e.g., a world government, a neo-medieval order in which there is no central authority but in which states are not "sovereign," or an order composed of geographically isolated or autarchic communities) does have its own particular disadvantages. But the attack on the state is misconceived.

In the first place it seems likely that the state, whether we approve of it or not, is here to stay. If this is so, the argument that we can advance the cause of world order only by getting "beyond the state" is a counsel of despair, at all events if it means that we have to begin by abolishing or subverting the state, rather than that there is a need to build upon it. Of course, the state is not the only important actor on the stage of world politics: nonstate groups and movements of various kinds play a role, as do individual persons. There never was a time in the history of the modern international system when this was otherwise: in eighteenth and nineteenth century Europe, too, states shared the stage with chartered companies, revolutionary and counterrevolutionary political parties, and national liberation movements. Indeed, it is difficult to believe that anyone ever asserted the "states-centric" view of international politics that is today so knowingly rejected by those who seek to emphasize the role of "the new international actors."[2] What was widely asserted about European international relations from the time of Vattel in the mid-eighteenth century until the end of the First World War was the *legal fiction* of a political universe that consisted of states alone, the doctrine that only states had rights and duties in international law. But assertion of such a doctrine does not imply that the actual course of international political events can be understood in terms of this fiction rather than in terms of the actions of actual persons and groups of persons, such as are set out in any history of the period.

It is sometimes suggested that in recent decades "other actors" have increased their role in world politics at the expense of that of the state, but even this—although it may be so—is difficult to establish conclusively because of the impossibility of reducing the question to quantitative terms.[3] It is true that international governmental and nongovernmental organizations have multiplied visibly, that multinational corporations have had a dramatic impact on the world economy, and that vast new networks of contact and intercourse have grown up at the transnational level. But the state's role in world politics has been growing dramatically also.

There has been a geographical spreading of the state, from Europe outward. Two centuries ago most of the non-European world lay beyond the boundaries of any sovereign state, in the sphere of the Islamic system or of Oriental empires or of tribal societies. Today the sovereign state is established throughout the world. No doubt the multiplication of states—the United Nations began with 51 member states and now has 151—has been accompanied by an increase in heterogeneity among them. There has been a certain debasing of the currency of statehood as a consequence of the growth of ministates and microstates, and many of the non-European ones—to which Michael Oakeshott contemptuously refers as "imitation states"—are imperfectly established and unlike the originals in important respects.[4] But for the first time the sovereign state is the common political form experienced by the whole of mankind.

At the same time the role of the state in world affairs has expanded functionally. Whereas a few decades ago states in their dealings with one another confined themselves to diplomatic and strategic issues and allowed economic, social, and ideological relations among peoples to be determined for the most part by the private sector, today the state has extended its tentacles in such a way as to deprive businessmen and bankers, labor organizations and sporting teams, churches and political parties of the standing as international actors independent of state control that they once enjoyed. It has been said that the growth of transnational relations has deprived traditional interstate politics of its previous autonomy.[5] But what is rather the case is that the growth of state involvement in trade, in exchange and payments, in the control of migration, and in science and culture and international sporting events has brought an end to the autonomy of transnational relations.

It is difficult to see evidence of the decline of the sovereign state in the various movements for the regional integration of states that have developed in the post-1945 world, such as the European Economic Community, the Organization of African Unity, the Organization of American States, or the Association of South East Asian Nations. It is not merely that the EEC, which provides the most impressive example of progress toward a goal of regional integration, has not in fact undermined the sovereignty of its member states in the sense of their legal independence of external control. Nor is it merely that the very considerable achievements of the Community in promoting peace, reconciliation, prosperity, and cooperation in Western Europe have depended more upon intergovernmental cooperation than on Community institutions bypassing the constituent states. It is that the movement for European integration has been led from the beginning by the conception that the end goal of the process is the creation of a European superstate, a continental United States of Europe—a conception that only confirms the continuing vitality of "statist" premises.

Nor is there much evidence of any threat to the state as an institution in the attempts—sometimes successful, sometimes not—of nationalist separatist groups to bring about the disintegration of existing states, as in Nigeria, Pakistan, Yugoslavia, Canada, the United Kingdom, or Iraq, to name only a few. For if we ask what have been the goals of the separatist Biafrans, East Bengalis, Croats, Quebecois, Scots, or Kurds, the answer is that they have been trying to create new states. While the regional integrationists seek to reduce the number of states in the world, and the nationalist separatists seek to increase it, both are as committed as the defendants of existing states to the continuation of the state as an institution. It might be thought that a serious challenge to the position of the state lies in the tendency of Socialist and Third World states to accord rights and duties in international law to nations that are not states; and that, in particular, national liberation movements—most notably, the Palestine Liberation Organization—have achieved a degree of recognition in the United Nations and elsewhere that in some way sounds the death knell of the state, or at all events brings to an end its claims to a privileged position among political groups in the world today. But again, what we have to notice is that the thinking both of the national liberation groups and of the states that lend support to them is confined within statist logic. What national liberation movements seek to do is to capture control of existing states (as in the case of the PLO or the FLN in Algeria), to create new states (as in Eritrea or Nagaland), or to change the boundaries of states (as in Ireland). In seeking recognition of their claims in international society, the starting point of their argument is the principle that nations ought to be states, and the strongest card they have to play is that they represent nations that seek to be states.

It is not a matter for celebration that regional integrationists and nationalist disintegrationists are as unable as they appear to be to think beyond the old confines of the states-system. There are other ways in which their aspirations might be satisfied than by seeking to control sovereign states.

One may imagine, for example, that a regional integration movement, like that in the countries of the European Community, might seek to undermine the sovereignty of its member states, yet at the same time stop short of transferring this sovereignty to any regional authority. If they were to bring about a situation in which authorities existed both at the national and at the European level, but no one such authority claimed supremacy over the others in terms of superior jurisdiction or its claims on the loyalties of individual persons, the sovereign state would have been transcended. Similarly, one may imagine that if nationalist separatist groups were content to reject the sovereignty of the states to which they are at present subject, but at the same time refrained from advancing any claims to sovereign statehood themselves, some genuine innovation in the structure of the world political system might take place.

We may envisage a situation in which, say, a Scottish authority in Edinburgh, a British authority in London, and a European authority in Brussels were all actors in world politics and all enjoyed representation in world political organizations, together with rights and duties of various kinds in world law, but in which no one of them claimed sovereignty or supremacy over the others, and a person living in Glasgow had no exclusive or overriding loyalty to any one of them. Such an outcome would take us truly "beyond the sovereign state" and is by no means implausible, but it is striking how little interest has been displayed in it by either the regional integrationists or the subnationalist "disintegrationists."

In the second place, those who say that what we have to do is get "beyond the states-system" forget that war, economic injustice, and ecological mismanagement have deeper causes than those embodied in any particular form of universal political organization. The states-system we have today is indeed associated with violent conflict and insecurity, with economic and social inequality and misery on a vast scale, and with failures of every kind to live in harmony with our environment. But this is no reason to assume that a world government, a neo-medieval order of overlapping sovereignties and jurisdictions, a system of isolated or semi-isolated communities, or any other alternative global order we might imagine would not be associated with these things also. Violence, economic injustice, and disharmony between man and nature have a longer history than the modern states-system. The causes that lead to them will be operative, and our need to work against them imperative, whatever the political structure of the world.

Let us take, for example, the central "world order goal" of peace. It is true that the states-system gives rise to its own peculiar dangers of war, such as those that have been stressed by exponents of "the international anarchy" (C. Lowes Dickinson), "the great illusion" (Norman Angell), "the arms race" (Philip Noel-Baker), or "the old game, now forever discredited, of the balance of power"

(Woodrow Wilson). It is true that war is endemic in the present states-system, not in the sense that it is made "inevitable" (particular wars are avoidable, and even war in general is inevitable only in the sense of being statistically probable), but in the sense that it is institutionalized, that it is a built-in feature of our arrangements and expectations. We may agree also that nuclear weapons and other advanced military technology have made this state of affairs intolerable, if it was not so before.

But the idea that if states are abolished, war will be abolished, rests simply on the verbal confusion between war in the broad sense of armed conflict between political groups and war in the narrow sense of armed conflict between sovereign states. Armed conflicts, including nuclear ones, will not be less terrible because they are conducted among groups other than states, or called police actions or civil uprisings. The causes of war lie ultimately in the existence of weapons and armed forces and the will of political groups to use them rather than accept defeat. Some forms of universal political organization may offer better prospects than others that these causes can be controlled, but none is exempt from their operation.

Of course, it is possible to imagine a world government or other alternative form of universal political organization from which war, economic injustice, and ecological mismanagement have been banished. But so is it possible to imagine a states-system so reformed that it has these utopian features: a world of separate states disciplined by the arts of peace, cooperating in the implementation of an agreed universal standard of human welfare and respectful of a globally agreed environmental code. It is a perfectly legitimate exercise to compare these different utopias and to consider whether some are more feasible than others. What is not acceptable—but what critics of the states-system commonly do—is to compare a utopian vision of a world central authority, or of whatever other alternative universal political order they favor, with the states-system, not in a utopian form but as it exists now.

In the third place, the critics neglect to take account of the positive functions that the state and the states-system have fulfilled in relation to world order in the past. The modern state—as a government supreme over a particular territory and population—has provided order on a local scale. To the extent that Europe, and at a later stage other continents, were covered by states that actually maintained their authority and were not constantly breaking down as a result of internal or external conflicts, local areas of order have been sustained by states over vast areas of the world. Most of our experience of order in modern times derives from these local areas of order established by the authority of states; and the chief meaning that we have been able to give to the concept of world order before very recent times is that it has been simply the sum of the local areas of order provided collectively by states.

States, moreover, have cooperated with one another in maintaining a structure of interstate, or international, order in which they confirm one another's domestic authority and preserve a framework of coexistence. For all the conflict and violence that have arisen out of their contact and intercourse with one another, they have formed not only an international system, but also a rudimentary international society. They have sensed common interests in preserving the framework of coexistence that limits and restrains the rivalry among them; they have evolved rules of the road that translate these common interests into specific guides to conduct; and they have cooperated in working common institutions such as international law, the diplomatic system, and the conventions of war that facilitate observance of the rules. Experts on "the international anarchy" will tell us, and rightly so, how precarious and imperfect this inherited structure of international order is, and exponents of "spaceship earth" will show how inadequate it is to meet the needs of the present time. But it does represent the form of universal political order that has actually existed in modern history, and if we are to talk of extending the scope of order in world affairs, we need first to understand the conditions under which there is any order at all. The critics of the states-system contrast it with the more perfect world order they would like to see; but the historical alternative to it was more ubiquitous violence and disorder.

We associate states with war: they have claimed, and still claim, a legal right to resort to it and to require individual citizens to wage it in their name. They dispose of most of the arms and armed forces with which it is waged, and notwithstanding the large role played in modern war by civil factions of one kind or another and by so-called barbarian powers beyond the confines of European international society, states have been the principal political groups actually engaged in war. But if we compare war among modern states with other historical violence or with future violence that we can readily enough imagine, we have to note that, with all its horrors, it has embodied a certain normative regime, without which violence has been and might be more horrible still.

Thus states when they go to war have recognized a need to provide one another and international society at large with an explanation in terms of a common doctrine of just causes of war, at the heart of which there has always been the notion that a war is just if it is fought in self-defense. No doubt there is great ambiguity and much disagreement about the meaning of this rule; other causes have been thought to be just in addition to that of self-defense. It is only in this century that limitations on the right of a state to go to war have been clearly expressed in legal terms, and the limitations are in any case observed more in the breach than in observance. Yet the conception that resort to war requires an explanation in terms of rules acknowledged on both sides is a mark of the existence at least of a rudimentary society; it imparts some element of stability to the expectations independent political communities can have about one another's behavior. Where—as in the encounter between political communities that do not belong to a common states-system or international society— war can be begun without any feeling of a need for an explanation, or the explanation felt to be necessary derives from rules accepted on one side only and not on the other—as in Europe's belief in its civilizing mission, or the Mongols' belief in the Mandate of Heaven, or in the conception of a crusade or holy war— no such element of stability can be achieved.

Modern states, moreover, wage war under the discipline of the belief that some means are legitimate in war and some are not, a belief expressed sometimes in a doctrine of morally just means in war, sometimes in a body of laws of war, sometimes simply in an unthinking acceptance of what Michael Walzer calls "the war convention."[6] At the heart of this is the notion that the soldiers or military agents of the enemy state are legitimate objects of the use of force and that others are not. On the one hand, this notion sanctifies a particular kind of killing and maiming, breaking down the ordinary civil prohibition of taking life and causing physical injury; on the other hand, it establishes boundaries between the kinds of killing and injury that are part of war and the kinds that are not. On the basis of these boundaries, states have built up rules to limit the force they employ against one another, to distinguish belligerents and neutrals and thus contain the spread of conflict, and to uphold standards of humanity and protect the innocent. Of course, it is not only in the special case of war in the strict sense, war between states, that war takes place in a normative framework: such a framework sometimes surrounded the armed conflicts of primitive, feudal, and oriental societies also. But in modern times there has been a sophisticated body of rules that are held to apply to war between states but not to armed conflicts in which one or both parties is a nonstate group, such as a civil faction or a "barbarian" power. These rules for the conduct of war are notoriously prone to be disregarded, and in the twentieth century they have been subject to special strain, but they are part of the heritage that has been bequeathed to us by the states-system.

More important even than the conceptions of legitimate ends and of legitimate means in war has been the notion that war to be legitimate must be begun, as Aquinas put it, on the proper authority. Cardinal to the distinction between war and mere brigandage or private killing is the idea that the former is waged by the agents of a public authority, which is recognized to be entitled to resort to force against its adversaries, and signifies that it has done so by issuing a declaration of war or in some other way. In the modern states-system it has been held that states alone have this authority: deeply divided though they have been, states have usually been united in maintaining that they are entitled to a monopoly of the legitimate use of force, both domestically and across state frontiers. Of course, they have not always been successful in preserving their monopoly, which has been broken from time to time by civil factions, by "barbarian" powers, and by pirates. States also experience difficulty in maintaining a united front, on the issue: the Socialist and Third World countries at present, for example, uphold the right of national liberation groups to resort to force internationally, and in the Second World War both the Western powers and the Soviet Union supported partisan groups in their struggle against Germany. Nevertheless, the idea that the right to engage in war should be confined to certain public authorities and should not be generally available to self-appointed political groups of all kinds is one of the most vital barriers we have against anarchy, and the modern states-system has passed on to us a rule embodying this idea that has proved workable.

At present, of course, the state's monopoly of the legitimate use of force is under some challenge, especially from national liberation groups. This is not new or unusual, and the challenge is mitigated to the extent that these groups are themselves would-be states whose claims to legitimacy and recognition rest in large measure upon the belief of their supporters that they should be states. Neither national liberation groups themselves nor their supporters in the Socialist countries and the Third World (they enjoy in some cases considerable support in the West also) put forward any general attack upon the state's monopoly position or advocate a wide or indiscriminate license to resort to force. We do, however, find that some Western critics of the states-system put forward a general attack on the state's monopoly position, as if the attempt of states to confine to themselves the right to use force were some unwarranted attempt to cling to an unfair privilege, to be opposed in the same spirit in which men opposed the Big Trusts or the propertied franchise. We are told that the "elite claims" of states are inappropriate now that there is "a rich diversity of authorized participants in the processes on international law."[7] The suggestion seems to be that "a rich diversity" of actors in world politics should be entitled to maintain "private armies" and go to war to support their demands, so long as these demands measure up to certain policy criteria ("world order with human dignity") drawn up in New Haven or elsewhere.

This kind of talk is not only dangerous in an era of frequent resort to force by small armed groups with no claims to representative status of any kind, and widespread availability of destructive weapons; it is also shallow in overlooking the difference between a modern state, endowed with authority as well as mere power and exercising rights to the use of force recognized by the domestic and the international legal order, and a mere political cabal or party that has chosen to turn itself into an armed band. No doubt there are illegitimate governments and insurgent or vigilante groups with just causes. But in the absence of authority to resort to force across international boundaries, possession of a just cause should be regarded as totally irrelevant. International society does not maintain that groups within a state have no right of revolution against an illegitimate government. It does, however, seek to protect itself against the use of force by civil factions across state boundaries. The convention we have restricting the use of force across international boundaries to states accomplishes this. The rule confining the right to the international use of force to states is readily recognizable and widely accepted, even if it is sometimes violated. A rule that confers this right upon any political group with a cause we regard as just is one that imposes no barrier at all.

We associate states not only with war but also with sovereignty—which in internal affairs connotes supremacy, the supreme jurisdiction of the state over citizens and territory, and in external affairs connotes independence, freedom from external control. The claims of the state to a right of external sovereignty or independence are sometimes taken to imply rejection of all moral or legal authority other than that of the state, and indeed such claims have sometimes been put forward in its name. When they are (as by Hegel or Treitschke), they are a menace to international order. A state's rights to sovereignty, however, are not asserted against the international legal order but conferred by it (from which it follows that they can be qualified by it, and even taken away). A state's right to sovereignty or independence is not a "natural right," analogous to the rights of individuals in Locke's state of nature: it is a right enjoyed to the extent that it is recognized to exist by other states. So far from it being the case that the sovereignty of the state is something antithetical to international order, it is the foundation of the whole edifice.

The order provided by the states-system, founded upon the exchange of recognition of sovereignty, is rightly said to be inferior to that provided within a properly functioning modern state. Within the states-system there is still no authoritative legislature, empowered to make laws, amend and rescind them in accordance with the will of the community; no independent judicial authority to which the impartial interpretation and application of the laws is entrusted; no central authority commanding a monopoly of force to ensure that the law will prevail. It is this perception of the contrast between the more perfect order enjoyed by individual persons in domestic political systems and the less perfect order enjoyed by states in international society that provides the impulse behind the desire to create a central world authority that will reproduce the conditions of domestic society on a universal scale. The states-system does, however, provide an imperfect and rudimentary form of order that holds anarchy at bay. It provides external support to the internal order created by states in areas where their writs run. And it maintains among states a regime of mutual tolerance and forbearance that limits conflict, sustains intercourse, and provides the conditions in which cooperation can grow.

The case for the states-system as it has operated in the past is that it is the form of universal political organization most able to provide minimum order in a political society in which there is not a consensus broad enough to sustain acceptance of a common government, but in which there is a consensus that can sustain the coexistence of a plurality of separate governments. When independent political communities have little or no intercourse with one another—as between European communities and pre-Columbian American communities, or between the former and China before the nineteenth century—a states-system is not necessary. Where such intercourse exists but consists of almost unmitigated hostility, as between Europe and Islam during much of the history of their encounter, a states-system is not possible. But in relation to European political society from, say, the sixteenth to the early twentieth centuries, a strong argument was put forward to the effect that the attempt to create strong central authorities, or to restore and develop the central authorities that had existed in the past, would lead only to division and disorder; whereas there could be fashioned—out of the surviving rules and practices inherited from Christendom and the new body of precedent emerging from the experience of secular Europe—a decentralized form of interstate society. The question now is how far this argument is still valid in relation to the decentralized interstate society of today, now expanded to encompass the whole globe and inevitably diluted and modified in the process.

Today, order in world affairs still depends vitally upon the positive role of the state. It is true that the framework of mere coexistence, of what is sometimes called "minimum world order," inherited from the European states-system, is no longer by itself adequate. The involvement of states in economic, social, cultural, and communications matters has led us to judge the international political system by standards which it would not have occurred to a nineteenth century European to apply. We now expect the states-system not only to enable independent political communities to coexist, but also to facilitate the management of the world economy, the eradication of poverty, the promotion of racial equality and women's rights, the raising of literacy and labor standards, and so on. All of this points to a universal political system that can promote "optimum world order," a system that can sustain not only coexistence but cooperation in the pursuit of a vast array of shared goals.

If one believed that states were inherently incapable of cooperation with one another and were condemned—as on the Hobbesian theory—to exist permanently in a state of war, there would be no escape from the conclusion that

the requirements of world order in our time and the continued existence of
states are in contradiction of one another. In fact, states can and do cooperate
with one another both on a regional and on a global basis. So far is it from being
the case that states are antithetical to the need that we recognize to inculcate a
greater sense of unity in human society, that it is upon the states-system that
our hopes for the latter, at least in the short run, must principally depend. It is
the system of states that is at present the only political expression of the unity of
mankind, and it is to cooperation among states, in the United Nations and
elsewhere, that we have chiefly to look if we are to preserve such sense of common human interests as there may be, to extend it, and to translate it into
concrete actions. We do not live in a world in which states are prepared to act as
agents of the international community, taking their instructions from the UN or
some such body; but we do have to restore the element of consensus among
states, without which appeals for a sense of "spaceship earth" are voices crying
in the wilderness.

   In the fourth place, there is no consensus in the world behind the program
of Western solidarists or global centralists for "transcending the states-system."
In the Socialist countries and among the countries of the Third World there is
no echo of these views. From the perspective of the two weaker sections of the
world political system, the globalist doctrine is the ideology of the dominant
Western powers. The barriers of state sovereignty that are to be swept away,
they suspect, are the barriers that they, the weaker countries, have set up
against Western penetration: the barriers that protect Socialist countries from
capitalism and Third World countries from imperialism. The outlook of the
Western globalist does indeed express, among other things, an exuberant desire
to reshape the world that is born of confidence that the economic and technological power to accomplish it lies at hand. One senses in it a feeling of impa-
tience that the political and legal obstacles ("ethnocentric nationalism," "the
absurd political architecture of the world," "the obsolete doctrine of state sovereignty") cannot be brushed aside. It is also notable that the prescriptions they
put forward for restructuring the world, high-minded though they are, derive
wholly from the liberal, social-democratic, and internationalist traditions of the
West, and take no account of the values entertained in other parts of the world,
with which compromises may have to be reached.

   For the Soviet Union and other Socialist countries the state is not an obstacle to peace but the bulwark of security against the imperialist aggressors; not
an obstacle to economic justice but the instrument of proletarian dictatorship
that has brought such justice about; not a barrier to the solution of environmental problems, for these exist only in capitalist countries. It is true that the Socialist countries are heirs to a profoundly antistatist ideology. Classical Marxism
looks forward to the withering away of the state and hence of the states-system,
while also (although the point is less clear) treating the nation as a transitory
phenomenon; it is neither interstate nor international but class struggle that
provides the main theme of world history. But the outlook of the Socialist countries is shaped less by ideology than by practical interest: finding themselves a
minority bloc of states in a world dominated by the military power, the industrial, commercial, and managerial enterprise, and the scientific and technological excellence of the capitalist countries, they have had a greater need than
the West to avail themselves of the rights of states to sovereignty, equality, and

noninterference. In a period when Western leaders have talked of expanding the role of the United Nations, of accepting the implications of increased international "interdependence," or of the need for a unified, global approach to the environment, the Soviet Union has seemed to stand for a dogged defense of the entrenched legal rights of sovereign states. Of course, where the entrenched legal rights in question have been those of colonialist or white supremacist states, the Soviet Union had been willing enough to attack them. So also the Soviet Union was willing enough to proclaim the subordination of the sovereignty of Socialist states to the higher law of "proletarian internationalism" in intervening against Czechoslovakia in 1968. But in responding to the aggressive challenge of American globalism—as in rejecting the Baruch Plan in the 1940s or the UN's Korean action in the 1950s or the Congo action in the 1960s, the Soviet Union and its Socialist allies have adopted a conservatively statist position.

Among the Third World countries the idea that we must all now bend our efforts to get "beyond the state" is so alien to recent experience as to be almost unintelligible. Because they did not have states that were strong enough to withstand European or Western aggression, the African, Asian, and Oceanic peoples, as they see it, were subject to domination, exploration, and humiliation. It is by gaining control of states that they have been able to take charge of their own destiny. It is by the use of state power, by claiming the rights due to them as states, that they have been able to resist foreign military interference, to protect their economic interests by excluding or controlling multinational corporations, expropriating foreign assets, planning the development of their economies, and bargaining to improve the terms of trade. It is by insisting upon their privileges of sovereignty that they are able to defend their newly won independence against the foreign tutelage implicit in such phrases as "basic human needs," "the international protection of human rights," or (more sinister still) "humanitarian intervention."

Of course Third World countries have not displayed the same solicitude about the sovereign rights of Western countries with which they have been in conflict that they have shown for their own. Like the Socialist countries, they have been strong champions of interference in the domestic affairs of colonialist and white supremacist states, which they have seen not as interference but as assistance to peoples who are victims of aggression. While they insist on the right of developing states to have wealth and resources transferred to them, it is the *duty* of the advanced countries to transfer these resources that they are insistent upon, rather than any corresponding rights—as emerges from the Charter of Economic Rights and Duties of States, which the UN General Assembly endorsed in 1974.

In the controversy over establishment of an International Seabed Authority controlled by the developing countries—where it is the advanced countries whose deepsea mining operations will be subject to the Authority's control, and the developing countries that will gain from distribution of the rewards—the Third World countries are the champions of subordinating sovereignty to a common effort to preserve "the common heritage of mankind."

Finally, those in the West who disparage the states-system underestimate the special interests the Western countries themselves have in its preservation and development. We have noted that distrust of the state and the states-system appears to flourish especially in Western societies. A number of factors account for this. The liberal or individualist political tradition, so much more deeply rooted in the West than elsewhere, has always insisted that the rights of states are subordinate to those of the human beings that compose them. Loyalties that compete with loyalty to the state—allegiances to class or ethnic group or race or religious sect—can be openly proclaimed and cultivated in Western societies and often cannot be elsewhere. Moreover, it is only in the West that it has been possible to assume that if the barriers separating states were abolished, it would be our way of life and not some other that would be universally enthroned.

It is the last point that is the crucial one. We in the West have not had—to the same degree as the Socialist countries and the Third World—a sense of dependence on the structure of the states-system. We assume that if the division of the world into separate states were to come to an end, and a global economy, society, and polity were allowed to grow up, it would be our economies, our ways of doing things, our social customs and ideas and conceptions of human rights, the forces of modernization that we represent, that would prevail. On the one hand, we have not had the feeling of vulnerability to "nonstate actors" shaping us from outside that Socialist countries have about Western libertarian ideas, or that developing countries have about Western-based multinational corporations, or that Islamic countries have about atheistic materialism. On the other hand, we have believed that our impact on the rest of the world does not depend merely on the exercise of state power. Our ways of doing things attract the peoples of Socialist countries even without efforts by our governments to promote them, and the withdrawal of Western governors, garrisons, and gunboats from the Third World countries has not brought the processes of Westernization at work in these countries to an end. Socialist and Third World states have sought to combat our influence—by withdrawing from the international economy, by excluding or controlling foreign investment, by building walls around their frontiers, by suppressing the flow of ideas—and the designs of Western globalists or "one-worlders," as we have noted, are designs to remove these obstacles. But Socialist and Third World states are in part in league with us. For while Socialist states seek to remain untainted by capitalism, Third World states to be free of imperialism, and both to diminish the West's dominant power, both are also seeking to become more modern; and because they cannot fail to recognize in the societies of North America, Western Europe, and Japan specimens of modernity more perfect than themselves, are compelled to imitate and to borrow. In Western attitudes toward the rest of the world there is still the belief, more deep-seated perhaps than that of the heirs of Marx and Lenin who rule the Soviet Union today, that the triumph of our own ways is historically inevitable.

There is some question whether this belief is well-founded. In the 1970s there has occurred a shift of power against the West and toward the Soviet Union and certain of the Third World countries. It has become more apparent that the revolt against Western tutelage that has played so large a part in the history of this century is a revolt not only against Western power and privilege, but also in large measure against Western values and institutions. Although the evidence is contradictory (consider, for example, the contrary cases at the present time of China and Iran) and we cannot now foresee what the outcome of the process will be, there are many signs in the extra-Western world of a conscious rejection of Western ways, not merely of capitalism and liberal democracy but even of modernity itself. In many parts of the world there is under way an attempt to revert to indigenous traditions, to restore institutions to the condition in which they were before they became contaminated by contact with the West, or at least to create the illusion that they have been restored. Just as the Western powers for more than a decade have found themselves a beleaguered minority in the United Nations, so they are coming to see themselves as forming a redoubt in a hostile world. There is a new attitude of defensiveness, even of belligerence, in Western attitudes toward the Soviet Union; and the countries of the Third World, until recently regarded as weak and dependent states in need of our help, are increasingly viewed as alien, hostile, and in some cases powerful and competitive states against which we need to defend ourselves.

At all events, the preservation of world order is not a matter of removing state barriers to the triumph of our own preferred values and institutions, but rather a matter of finding some *modus vivendi* as between these and the very different values and institutions in other parts of the world with which they will have to coexist. In thinking about world order it is wrong to begin, as the critics of the states-system do, by elaborating "goals" or "relevant Utopias" and drawing up plans for reaching them. This is how the "policy-scientist's" mind works but it is not what happens in world politics. It is better to begin with the elements of world order that actually exist, and consider how they might be cultivated. This must lead us to the state and the states-system, without which there would not be any order at all.

REFERENCES

[1]See, for example, Miciam Camps, *"First World Relationships": The Role of the OECD* (Paris: Atlantic Institute for International Affairs; New York: Council on Foreign Relations, 1975) and Joseph Nye and Robert Keohane, *Transnational Relations and World Politics* (Cambridge, Mass.: Harvard University Press, 1972). Also Richard A. Falk, *This Endangered Planet* (New York: Random House, 1971), and *A Study of Future Worlds* (New York: Free Press, 1975).

[2]See especially Nye and Keohane, *Transnational Relations*.

[3]See, for example, Richard W. Mansbach, Yale H. Ferguson, and Donald E. Lamport, *The Web of World Politics. Non-state Actors in the Global System* (Englewood Cliffs, N.J.: Prentice-Hall Inc., 1976).

[4]Michael Oakeshott, *On Human Conduct* (New York: Oxford University Press, 1975).

[5]Nye and Keohane, *Transnational Relations*, Introduction.

[6]Michael Walzer, *Just and Unjust Wars. An Argument with Historical Illustrations* (New York: Basic Books, 1977).

[7]Michael Reisman, "Private Armies in a Global War System," in *Law and Civil War in the Modern World*, John Norton Moore (ed.), (Baltimore: Johns Hopkins University Press, 1974), p. 257.

RICHARD HAASS

The Primacy of the State . . . or Revising the Revisionists

To what extent do relations between states still hold the key to security and stability in today's world? In the study of contemporary international relations this is a fundamental question under which we can subsume questions like the following: How important is military force and armed conflict to the protection of interests? What will be the impact of a revival of ideology, especially nationalism, but alternatively of an overwhelming concern with human rights or religion? What trends can we observe in the distribution of political and economic power?

Until recently the primacy, if not the monopoly, of the nation-state has been taken for granted. As Arnold Wolfers states:

> The "billiard ball" model of the multi-state system which forms the basis for the states-as-actors theory leaves room for no corporate actors other than the nation state. By definition, the stage is pre-empted by a set of states each in full control of all territory, men, and resources within its boundaries.[1]

This emphasis on the politics of power is found also in the works of Raymond Aron, Hans Morgenthau, Kenneth Waltz, Hedley Bull, and other members of the "traditionalist," or "realist," school, the dominant voices in the study of international relations since the Second World War.[2] It is a perspective, in the words of one of its mild critics, that tends to see the process of international relations as a "tournament of distinctive knights."[3]

Paradoxically, this statist perspective gained currency at a time when it seemed the opposite had become the case. War, the foremost expression of state power, had been rendered counterproductive by the atom bomb, or at least less likely on a grand scale. Politically, internationalism seemed on the rise. A new Europe was beginning to emerge, and the success of the United Nations seemed probable, if not certain. Decolonization would bring about a large number of new states, but the nationalism that was inherent in their formation promised to be but a way-station on the road to greater international cooperation. Most important, a new era of economic transnationalism based on public institutions, private corporations, and freer movement of goods, capital, and labor was expected to lessen, if not remove, barriers between states.

Given this context, it is no wonder that the state-centric view of the world has its share of dissenters.[4] The traditional approach is inadequate, they say, and to see the world as little more than the interaction of sovereign states tells more about the prejudices of the observer than about the nature of reality. Their alternative vision coined a new vocabulary—interdependence, multinational, intergovernmental, transnational—and now presses the claim for the validity of the concept of "world relations" rather than the more biased one of "international relations." They portray the nation-state as becoming increasingly weak, unable to perform the functions demanded of contemporary authority. As Stanley Hoffmann writes, "The form of the nation-state, including its traditional apparatus of legal rights, is preserved, even universalized, yet its substance is transformed. The old boy is still there, but he has lost much of his vigor and bite."[5] But not merely has the old boy lost his power, he is no longer the *only* boy on the block. In any contemporary analysis of world relations greater consideration is due the roles of international organizations, multinational or transnational corporations, and the proliferating groupings and forces that now assume many of the functions once held by the nation-state. Thus it is proposed that the focus of world relations should be on transnational relations, on the "contacts, coalitions, and interactions across state boundaries that are not controlled by the central foreign policy organs of governments."[6]

To the charge that there is nothing new in the existence of nonstate actors on the world scene, the antitraditionalists, or "modernists," are right to respond that what is relevant is not their "newness" but their importance. Yet the relative importance of General Motors and the United Nations in our world as compared to the medieval Church or the Dutch East India Company in theirs is not the only issue. As pertinent is the question of the independence, or autonomy, of these nonstate actors. How much "power [do they have] over resources essential to the state" and how successfully can they "bargain directly with the legitimate wielders of political power"?[7] Perhaps more than anything else, the mythology surrounding the multinational corporation needs to be examined in detail.

The answers to such questions are basic to how we view and study the world and, ultimately, to how we try to shape it. Although traditionalists recognize the existence of international actors other than states, and modernists concede that the nation-state remains dominant in certain areas, the difference between the two remains large and significant. Shall the model or paradigm have as its basis relations among states or transnational forces and institutions? Which is to be the exception? Which is to be the rule? The intent of this essay is not to choose between them but to use them both; as is often the case, debates may be as important for what they reveal as for what they settle.

I

A fundamental attribute of statehood is the ability of a government to manage the use of force. Internally, this ability is basic to the maintenance of order; without it, a government jeopardizes its claim to international recognition, and, in fact, its very existence. Externally, the inability to marshal sufficient force against an adversary will result in a diminution of influence, territory, or sovereignty. Both traditionalists and modernists recognize that the management of force remains the exclusive or near-exclusive prerogative of the state, but view the importance of this function differently. We can see this clearly by setting up alternatives: if force remains critical in affecting events, the state will continue to be the preeminent actor in the international scene; if force decreases in importance in world affairs, the claim of the state to preeminence is weakened. The latter formulation is the modernist one, and this school goes on to point out that not only is force per se less important than previously, but also that force has become less important relative to other forms of influence in which the nation-state does not possess a monopolistic or even dominant position.

The importance of force divides in turn into separate considerations. Is it likely either that conflict will become less frequent or that constraints against resorting to aggression will become stronger? And what can be discerned regarding the utility of force—can it be translated into influence and assets for the state that wields it most effectively?

Any prediction that armed conflict will be less a feature of the international system than in the past is most certainly premature and most probably incorrect. The old agenda of *casus belli* continues to exist. Rivalries over territory, ideology, and security can be found in every region of the world. Besides these and other familiar reasons why states go to war is a new or at least more prominent agenda: national and tribal boundaries that do not correspond to state jurisdictions, massive refugee problems, and a growing competition for resources on land and in and under the sea. These potential sources of conflict must be seen in the larger context of the quantitative and qualitative enhancement of military capabilities by virtually every state in the world, an increase that reflects both indigenous efforts and military transfers, conventional and nuclear. Without arguing the unsophisticated theme that "arms cause wars," it is still possible to suggest that the rapid rate of increase in military capabilities by many countries has engendered new uncertainties and instabilities that in particular circumstances could intensify existing pressures to resort to war. Moreover, and contrary to some reports, the technological impact of many new weapons systems is not yet clear. Although recent generations of relatively inexpensive and high-performance systems may serve as an "equalizer" by strengthening a weak defender, in other conditions, or with different tactics, these or other weapons can be deployed to the benefit of the state that takes the initiative. Neither the tank nor the surface ship is ready for the museum; nor is the offensive on the wane.

The likelihood of conflict varies also with the states being considered. Obviously, the United States and the Soviet Union present unique questions. Although any discussion of the possibility of nuclear war involves matters highly theoretical, if not theological, it is clear that existing arms control institutions are not adequate to maintain stability in an era of rapid and fundamental innovation. Technological advances have begun to erode the foundations of strategic stability and deterrence.[8] The balance of terror is becoming more delicate.

For the time being, however, mutual fear of nuclear war continues to mute superpower competition, directly and in areas of common high interest. But it has not been able to prevent competition in peripheral areas, especially through means that lessen the chance of direct military confrontation. Attempts to establish rules of the game to regulate this competition have met with limited success; despite the lofty rhetoric of the 1972 "Basic Principles of Relations," it has been difficult to extend détente beyond Europe to somewhat more than crisis management (as opposed to prevention). Similarly, attempts to moderate Soviet behavior through the manipulation of incentives and penalties have not worked, nor are prospects auspicious. With the improvement of its navy, the development of efficient air- and sea-lift capabilities, and the use of proxy forces and advisers, the Soviet Union shows an increased willingness and capacity to project military force into distant regions. That the USSR, besieged with economic and political problems at home, most probably will be compelled to rely on this dimension of power to assert its superpower status abroad does not augur well for international stability.

The general fragmentation of the international system also has eroded constraints against states going to war. In part, this stems from the nuclear might of the superpowers, who have distanced themselves from confrontation that could escalate to nuclear war. As a result, fewer events fit into a context of confrontation between the two rivals. This general fragmentation also reflects the increased dynamism of other states, a number of which have refused to adhere to either bloc, further decreasing the universality of the East-West axis. The blocs themselves have become less integrated. The Soviet camp has been weakened over the years by the defections of China, Yugoslavia, and Albania, and by other factors that have brought about greater differentiation among the communist countries. In the West, the postwar political and economic recovery of the major alliance states and the emergence of a number of relatively strong states such as Israel, South Korea, Taiwan, and Brazil have posed new challenges to American hegemony. Finally, the bloc leaders themselves have lost some of their will to lead. Not every event fits into an East-West perspective, and of those that do, not every one is important enough to evoke the full alliance commitment. New centers of political, economic, and military autonomy have evolved; the resulting uncoupling and fragmentation are both a cause and a consequence of conventional and, potentially, nuclear military proliferation. A world of diffused technology, widespread military capacity, reduced bipolarity, and uncertain alliance guarantees is not likely to be one of less conflict.

Clearly, force will continue to play a decisive role in the contemporary world. The nuclear capabilities of the two superpowers and others have not rendered force per se less useful; to the contrary, in certain circumstances they promise to enhance the impact of discrete applications.[9] At the same time, outstanding political differences inhibit the proscription of force by sanctions and other cooperative actions. The inadequacy of U.S. policy in Southeast Asia should not yield the conclusion that force is obsolete, only that to be effective it must be tailored to local environments and placed within the context of a larger policy. A large number of cases in the Middle East, South and East Asia, and Africa indicate that force can be the key factor in determining the resolution of disagreements. Moreover, although force is but one ingredient affecting prospects for the long-term stability and viability of states, it can be the most critical in creating a government or state and in defending either, once established. Indeed, the very sanctity of the nation-state, and the widespread support of the principle that wars are fought for limited objectives rather than for total conquest and for territory as in times past, have made the resort to force more likely and its usefulness in realizing finite aims more apparent; as in poker, reduced stakes permit more to play the game.

II

At first glance, the present era would seem to be the age of the nation-state as never before. Membership in the United Nations has reached 151 and no doubt will continue to rise as new "islands" claim independence. As James Mayall has written of the new world's embrace of the old world's concept of the state,

> Whether or not it lacks indigenous historical roots in some parts of the non-European world, it has been successfully exported everywhere. And this success is now firmly rooted. It stems from the universal and enthusiastic acceptance of the Western theory of sovereignty.[10]

Few colonies, trusts, or other nonstate entities remain. Those organizations or movements with special status, such as the PLO or SWAPO, do not challenge the state system but rather the present political authorities ruling Israel/Palestine and Southwest Africa/Namibia, respectively. As such, they are at most transitional entities, for failure or success will terminate their special status.

Ironically, one of the driving forces of the decolonization movement—nationalism—itself threatens many of the states it helped bring into being, as had been predicted by some observers. Writing over a decade ago, Michael Howard noted that

> dynamic nationalism is likely to increase rather than diminish in the foreseeable future. . . . the increase in education will bring about an increase in political self-consciousness on the part of hitherto dormant minorities, even within the recently independent states, and to this inherently fissiparous process there is no logical end.[11]

Logical or not, even an incomplete list of current nationalist revivals would be quite substantial: Catholics and Protestants in Northern Ireland, Welsh and Scottish, Basques, Bretons, Croats, the Flemish, the Timurs, the Eritreans, the Baluchis, and French-speaking Canadians.[12] This apparent divergence between nationalism and the state should not be surprising. In part, it is a result of the latent tension between nation and state.

> Boundaries between nations are generally blurred, giving rise to complications with the institution of the territorial state. Existing political state boundaries often do not coincide with historical, economic or strategic boundaries. They never fully coincide with national boundaries: no state encompasses only one nation and no nation is wholly encompassed in one single state.[13]

n addition, the tension between nationalism and the state reflects changes in the nature of each. Initially, nationalism was primarily an anticolonial movement for political independence, while the modern state, owing to advances in agriculture, industry, transportation, and communications, achieved a degree of centralization and integration that distinguished it sharply from its precursors. But the very emergence of cohesive independent states has contributed to a new nationalism, one concerned with the disposition of social, cultural, economic, and political power within the state. Given the luxury of the modern state's relative security from threats to its existence, groups and individuals have come to challenge central, often majority control of resources, language, education, and media. Having firmly established its existence, the state has become a victim of its own success. But does the emergence of powerful nationalist forces create a threat to the state? In one sense it does not. If some movement is successful, what emerges is either a new state or one that is transformed, in which special rights are granted or degrees of autonomy permitted within a federal structure. The status quo either remains or is rearranged, not replaced; a challenge to any single nation-state is not a challenge to the institution itself.

Yet if the institution survives, it does so in altered form. The survival of states depends increasingly on an accommodation with the new nationalism. Within the territorial unit there is now a greater differentiation and independence of parts. Although in the eyes of international law the state remains as it was, in reality a change has taken place. To retain its primacy externally the state has been forced to cede some of its control domestically.

Nationalism is not the only political force with which the state must contend. The traditional right of the state to govern its citizens as it pleases has been challenged by the human rights movement. Support for standards of treatment of citizens—in part an outcome of the Nuremburg trials and the 1948 Universal Declaration of Human Rights and its associated covenants and protocols—and the basic responsibilities of governments to provide for the welfare of its people have come from Amnesty International, other governments, and a variety of groups and persons around the world. [14] The often strong reactions by governments to allegations of human rights violations testify to their sensitivity in this area. In some instances, external pressure has done more than simply embarrass. Emigration controls have been relaxed in a number of countries, and repression moderated or the number of political prisoners reduced in others. [15]

Such pressures from the outside are, however, limited. There is no supranational enforcement mechanism, and human rights decisions are left to individual governments or to some form of dialogue between governments or between a particular government and its citizens. In most cases, the key factor is one of governmental and state vulnerability, whether to its own people or to the dictates of another state. In the end, support for human rights is less a challenge to the rule of states than to how states rule.

There are as well a variety of ideas and beliefs that attempt to influence not so much the state system as the behavior and loyalties of people within states. Difficult to collect and categorize, these consist of forces and movements, ideas and activities, the secular and the religious, the organized and the diffuse, calls for revolution and calls for restraint. Some are intended to affect states; some, individuals. The Church possesses significant ability to affect the behavior of its members in certain domains (such as contraception) and can serve as a focal point for many forms of political and social opposition to a regime or a particular policy. The revival of Islamic fervor is having a major impact on both the social development and political orientations of the predominantly Muslim countries. Other ideologies, from cosmopolitanism to ethnicity and modernization, to the antimaterialist countercultures, continue to influence people throughout the world. As history has shown, ideologies may or may not be consistent with the interests of the government or state; in the case of communism it would seem that the ideology has been adapted to serve the state. As recent debates in UNESCO reveal, there appears to be growing support for increased state regulation of the means and content of communication and information in whatever direction the boundaries of states are crossed.[16] Already states possess some ability to limit their vulnerability to the movement of ideas and information. Television and radio signals can be jammed, reading matter censored, individuals and groups suppressed, and passports and visas denied. It is impossible in the modern world to insulate a society totally from foreign or unwanted ideas, but the degree of openness and permeability can to some extent be managed.

States have much less to fear from the encroachment of supranational institutions. The United Nations remains at the mercy of its members, and especially the five permanent members of the Security Council. Similarly, neither international law nor courts can compel states to adopt their norms or accept their verdicts.[17] Nor does regionalism constitute a serious threat to the sovereignty of states. To the degree that any autonomy is awarded to the regional authority, it tends to be minimal; nevertheless, as Hedley Bull has pointed out, should complete political unification or economic integration evolve among a group of states, so that a common government can claim a degree of authority parallel to the federal government in the United States, the regional body would not be an alternative to the nation-state as much as a new and larger one.[18] To the extent the state has competitors for political power, the forces of nationalism, human rights, and religion are far more to reckon with than the bureaucrats of Turtle Bay, the Hague, and Brussels.

III

It is in the spheres of economic power and decision-making that the traditional role of the state appears most seriously threatened. Even without fully endorsing Charles Kindleberger's claim that "the state is about through as an economic unit,"[19] the modernist would argue that not only is the monopoly of the state in this area obsolete, but so is its primacy or even dominance. The modernist critique of the state's economic role is tied closely to the theme of interdependence—we live in a world in which no state can adopt a policy of autarchy, or even self-sufficiency, by necessity being dependent on the exchange of resources, goods, technology, markets, and so on. While such a web of mutual dependencies is nothing new, the modernist claims that the degree of interdependence is now greater and more complex.[20]

Yet, interdependence is not automatically inconsistent with the notion of the primacy of the state as an institution. It becomes so only if the processes of interdependence involve independent actors other than states to a significant degree. Thus, the basic questions of the importance and autonomy of nonstate actors remain. In the sphere of economics three areas are central to any answers: the role of transnational organizations such as multinational corporations and banks; international institutions, including the International Bank for Reconstruction and Development, or World Bank, and the International Monetary Fund (IMF); and the various "systemic" processes affecting money supply, exchange rates, and trade that are intrinsic to the operation of the international economic order.

If economics is the key to the modernist perspective, the role of multi-national corporations, or MNCs, is the key to the key. As characterized by Raymond Vernon, "They sprawl across national boundaries, linking the assets and activities of different national jurisdictions with an intimacy that seems to threaten the concept of the nation as an integral unit."[21] At first glance statistics appear to support this assertion: regardless of the criteria used, figures indicate the major importance of multinational corporations to the world economy.[22] But importance does not imply independence. Multinational corporations rely on the ability of states to maintain political, economic, and military environments conducive to their operations. More specifically, MNCs increasingly operate in environments of controls, restrictions, and conditions established by nation-states, whether these are the "home" state of the parent company or the "host" state of the affiliate or subsidiary.[23]

Home states, and in particular the United States—which remains the most important—have a range of means to oversee and regulate the activities of their multinationals. Antitrust measures can be enforced and pursued with determination; disclosure (through the Securities and Exchange Commission, for example) demanded; the payment of exorbitant "agent fees" made illegal; and virtually all company practices investigated, as has been done in the United States by both the Justice Department and the Congress. Controls on exports prevent the dissemination of key technologies for political, economic, or security considerations, either comprehensively or to selected countries. In recent years the United States has restricted the export of computers, advanced oil drilling equipment, and nuclear enrichment and reprocessing technologies, among others. Exports of military goods and services are regularly controlled. Embargoes, partial or complete, continue in force against certain countries. For economic reasons, home states can apply restrictions on the outflow of capital and other dealings with foreign exchanges. In relations with other states, home states have the option of entering into reciprocal arrangements to allow companies to avoid double taxation, for example, and can refuse to protect subsidiaries against the actions of host countries, thereby leaving all investment risk in the hands of the parent company. Inducements for investing abroad, including tax benefits and subsidies, can be withheld.

The means available to host countries to control the multinationals operating within their borders are also considerable. Host countries can demand a percentage of state ownership of foreign MNCs and, over time, shift the relationship between host government and foreign company—from foreign ownership to participation and nationalization. Alternatively, joint ventures can be made mandatory from the outset, with provisions for "fading out" foreign equity included. A more simple arrangement might require that a share of key industries or sectors be reserved for state enterprises. Requirements can be set for the training of local inhabitants, transfers of technology, procurement of goods and capital in local markets, and a local role in management. Many host countries now have laws that prevent takeovers of domestic industries by foreign corporations, and are closing off certain sectors and industries—defense, banking, transport, communications, aerospace, electricity, computers, retail trade— from foreign involvement. Finally, host governments, like home governments, can manipulate taxes, exchange requirements, repatriation of capital, subsidies, and other factors to make the investment environment either more or less favor-able for foreign firms.

There is thus a clear trend toward increased regulation and restriction of multinational corporations by home and host countries alike. Still, the MNC is not helpless. Capital can be shifted into currencies that appear stronger; money raised in markets (such as the Euromarkets) outside the jurisdiction of states; and "transfer-pricing," or the manipulation of prices between parent and subsidiary or two subsidiaries, engaged in to minimize liability where taxes are highest. Multinationals also represent unique sources of wealth and expertise. Should the Law of the Sea Conference produce agreement among states regarding the development of the "common heritage of mankind," it will be to a few MNCs that states will turn for the actual mining of the seabed. Similarly, many of the world's extractive and manufacturing endeavors would be impossible without MNC cooperation, and thus many small and weak states can ill afford to alienate key multinationals. Perhaps the most basic power of the multinational corporation, one that reflects its capacity to benefit both home and host countries, is its continued ability to choose where, when, and how much to invest. As a recent UN study has noted,

> A developing host country can always succeed in excluding transnational corporations from its territories, but it is powerless to force them to come in, or to stay, if there is little prospect for profit. . . . Any enterprise that faces stringent demands or conditions in regard to its activities will consider whether it should slow down future expansion, cut back its producing activities, reduce its financial exposure in the national economy, or even close down a facility altogether.[24]

Yet the options of noninvestment and disinvestment need to be weighed against the availability of alternative investments and will reflect the capacity of a particular MNC either to forego an investment or shift existing ones. Manufacturing companies, for example, normally possess greater mobility than do those in extractive industries, especially when some resource is in short supply. In the end, investment decisions between host country and corporation will reflect their financial strengths and how easily each could replace or do without the other. What emerges is a classic bargaining situation, one in which both company and state can benefit.

> As transnational organizations become larger and more numerous, the demands for access to territory of nation-states will also multiply. The value of that access, consequently, will go up. The national governments who control access will thus be strengthened. In this sense, the growth of transnational operations does not challenge the nation-state but reinforces it. It increases the demand for the resource which the nation-state alone controls: territorial access.[25]

Even if such a balance is not always the case, a clear trend can be discerned; to borrow Huntington's phrase, a "new equilibrium" has evolved after the great initial impact of MNCs and the strong wave of reaction this provoked in nation-states.[26] The two will co-exist, but more often than not on terms set by states, which have regained the upper hand if it can be said they ever lost it.

In the context of the primacy of the state, international economic institutions such as the World Bank and the IMF are similar to international political institutions. Their capacity to act is controlled in large part by the participating states. They are unlike the United Nations in that, in the World Bank, for instance, no single state has a veto power, nor can any single state dictate the terms or recipient of a loan. Attempts by the Congress of the United States, for example, to stipulate such conditions were successfully resisted by the World Bank, with the assistance of the Carter Administration. The power of final decision rests not in the institution itself, which lacks a vote, but in the member states. Similarly, the IMF is "prisoner" of its voting membership, with voting weight proportional to contributions to the fund. Such basic decisions as liquidity creation (through Special Drawing Rights) and loan terms result from decisions reached by member states voting their "shares." When agreement exists, both the World Bank and the IMF exercise considerable power, especially over financially and economically weak countries. Loans and assistance can be made conditional on the adoption of specific economic policies by the recipient state. But this leverage has no equivalent to force chronic surplus states to adjust either their exchange rates or basic economic strategies. Indeed, this very inability of the IMF to control national economic policies (particularly the monetary supply of the United States) and force surplus countries (notably Japan and West Germany) to accept revaluation contributed to the crisis of the international monetary system that was envisioned at Bretton Woods.

The ability of states to fashion the monetary environment is limited less by any institution (for example, the IMF) than by the nature of the system itself. In two areas, money markets are partially independent of states—as a source of liquidity outside natural jurisdictions and as the venue where the relative value of currencies, or exchange rates, is established. This latter role, however, was the conscious, if unavoidable, creation of states that abandoned fixed exchange rates. Moreover, the abandonment was never total, as central bank intervention and "dirty floats" persist, while recent arrangements (such as the European Monetary System) indicate a desire to increase the stability and predictability of rates. In all these cases, however, the functioning of the various money markets or exchanges is not immune to the policies of states, either directly or indirectly. Besides being affected by direct central bank intervention, the value of any currency will reflect relative national economic performance, inflation rates, and balances for the public sector, trade, and payments. Gold markets, in part independent, are affected directly by government policy toward the value of its currency, all of which affect the demand for, and hence the price of, gold. Other commodities are increasingly the object of efforts to augment predictability of price and supply through stockpile and stabilization schemes. Oil and a few other items provide another special case in that price and availability are determined by the policies of key states rather than by market forces alone. On balance, it appears that although states cannot control markets in most circumstances, state policy remains a key influence on market behavior.

Despite the efforts of the ongoing Multilateral Trade Negotiations, trade is moving into an era of greater state involvement. Imports and exports are affected by tariff and nontariff barriers, subsidies, tax credits, preferential access commitments, government procurement policies, and a number of additional inducements and restrictions, all muddying the waters of free trade. With "orderly marketing agreements" becoming increasingly common, trends toward protectionism and "managed trade" are gaining momentum. This is not necessarily all to the bad. "It is the power and the politics of states that create order where there would otherwise be chaos or at least a Lockean state of nature."[27] Ironically, some state intervention is required if massive state intervention is to be averted; in either case, trade follows the flag rather than the other way around. In this, trade is simply conforming to the larger pattern of the politicization of economic relations. As Geoffrey Barraclough writes, "The one thing that is clear at the moment—perhaps the only thing that is clear—is that the liberal world economy, as it existed for a quarter of a century after 1945, is on the way out."[28] Just as the "New Information Order" of UNESCO promises to be a challenge, if not a threat, by a majority of states to influence the flow of information, so the New International Economic Order is an attempt by states to structure the flow of market forces to redistribute the world's wealth. The outlook is not auspicious for the devotees of laissez faire, nonstate actors, or even the small, weak state. Indeed, the politicization of the economic order will bring states and collections of states into play as never before.

IV

Stanley Hoffmann recently raised the question, "Is the state-centered concept of international politics, with its focus on the diplomatic-strategic chessboard and its obsession with the use of force, still relevant to the age of interdependence?"[29] As I indicated at the outset, there is no consensus as to whether the traditionalist state-centric or the modernist transnational paradigm should be the norm. The range of opinion is considerable, from Hedley Bull, who asserts that "it is sovereign states which command most of the armed force in the world, which are the objects of the most powerful human loyalties, and whose conflict and co-operation determine the political structure of the world,"[30] to Joseph Nye and Robert Keohane, who argue that not only is the state-centric view inadequate, but also that "it is becoming progressively more inadequate as changes in transnational relations take place."[31] Attempts to reconcile these and similar views are not altogether convincing. To claim, as Hoffmann does, that nonstate actors are not simply processes operating within a state system but form part of the structure of the system itself,[32] or to accept Seyom Brown's "polyarchy" of nation-states, subnational groups, and transnational interests and forces[33] is to avoid the central matter of their autonomy. That nonstate actors exist proves neither their importance nor their independence. Equally, Samuel Huntington's effort to demonstrate that the relationship between the two views is not "zero-sum" —"The conflict between national governments and transnational organizations is clearly complementary rather than duplicative"[34] —fails to coincide with a reality in which states have at time viewed these organizations and forces as threatening and have acted when possible to limit their freedom and power.

The modernist school has made some major contributions in highlighting the shortcomings of literature that overemphasizes the military dimension of international relations, and in drawing attention to the new forces and actors within the system. Perhaps most important, however, the modernist critique has stimulated and broadened the debate about the contemporary world. Yet, the modernist perspective is in need of a corrective; as is often the case, the revisionists require revision. The modernists have exaggerated the long-term importance of nonstate actors, projecting their initial impact into the future without anticipating sufficiently the countervailing reactions from states. The inherent bias against the likelihood and utility of force requires a fresh look. What is more serious is the tendency to allow subjective analysis of the adequacy of the state to replace an objective assessment of its primacy, for example, in Seyom Brown's comment that "the existing territorial bases of political community are becoming increasingly incongruent with the physical and ecological interdependencies brought about by contemporary technological developments,"[35] or George Ball's verdict that the state is "still rooted in archaic concepts unsympathetic to the needs of our complex world."[36] In so doing, they move close to the centuries-old tradition of advocating alternative visions of world order[37]—hardly where one would expect to encounter a modernist.

Whether a world in which states held a less central place would be a better one is doubtful: the process of transition would be a messy one, and it is difficult to feel confident that the new order would be any more just or peaceful. In any case, this is properly the subject of another essay. What is interesting for the purpose of this essay, however, is that the modernists tend to underestimate the capacity of the state to cope with internal and external challenges to its authority. If demands on the state have never been greater, the institution has never appeared stronger. By a blend of flexibility and resolve, states, whether in concert or competiton, continue to dominate the international relations of our time. The old boy may not be alone, but vigor and bite he has.

REFERENCES

[1]Arnold Wolfers, "The Actors in International Politics," in Arnold Wolfers (ed.), *Discord and Collaboration: Essays on International Politics* (Baltimore: The Johns Hopkins University Press, 1962), p. 19.

[2]See, among others, Raymond Aron, *Peace and War* (New York: Doubleday, 1966); Kenneth N. Waltz, *Man, The State, and War* (New York: Columbia University Press, 1959); Hans Morgenthau, *Politics Among Nations* (Alfred A. Knopf, New York: 1948); Hedley Bull, *The Anarchical Society* (London: Macmillan, 1977).

[3]Stanley Hoffmann, *Primacy or World Order* (New York: McGraw-Hill, 1978), p. 110.

[4]The best single collection of modernist writings is to be found in Robert O. Keohane and Joseph S. Nye, Jr. (eds), "Transnational Relations and World Politics," *International Organization*, 25(3), (Summer 1971).

[5]Stanley Hoffmann, *Gulliver's Troubles, or the Setting of American Foreign Policy* (New York: McGraw-Hill, 1968), p. 42.

[6]Keohane and Nye, "Transnational Relations," p. 331.

[7]Stanley Hoffmann, *Primacy or World Order*, p. 112.

[8]See "New Technology and Deterrence" in *Strategic Survey 1977* (London: IISS, 1978).

[9]For a sense of the evolution of this debate, see John Herz, *International Politics in the Atomic Age* (New York: Columbia University Press, 1959); Klaus Knorr, *On the Uses of Military Power in the Nuclear Age* (Princeton: Princeton University Press, 1966), "Is International Coercion Waning or Rising?" *International Security*, Spring 1977, and "On the International Uses of Military Force in the Contemporary World," *Orbis*, Spring 1977.

[10]James Mayall, "International Society and International Theory," in Michael Donelan (ed.), *The Reason of States* (London: George Allen & Unwin, 1966), p. 210.

[11]Michael Howard, "Problems of a Disarmed World," in Herbert Butterfield and Martin Wight (eds.), *Diplomatic Investigations* (London: George Allen & Unwin, 1966) p. 210.

[12]Seyom Brown, *New Forces in World Politics* (Washington, D.C.: The Brookings Institution, 1974), especially chap. 9.

[13]Joseph Frankel, *International Politics* (London: Pelican Books, 1973), p. 100; see also Hugh Seton-Watson, *Nations and States* (London: Methuen, 1977).

[14]The International Bill of Human Rights includes the "Universal Declaration of Human Rights," the "International Covenant on Economic, Social and Cultural Rights," and the "International Covenant on Civil and Political Rights and Optional Protocol." (Texts can be found in *The International Bill of Human Rights*, document 36494-OPI/598, published by the UN in June, 1978). The most complete statement of U.S. policy can be found in an address delivered by Secretary of State Cyrus Vance, "Human Rights and Foreign Policy," at Athens, Georgia, on April 30, 1977.

[15]For one assessment of the condition of human rights, see *The Amnesty Report 1978* (London: Amnesty International, 1979).

[16]See Rosemary Righter, *Whose News: Politics, the Press and the Third World* (London: Burnett Books, 1978).

[17]For a more generous view of the role of international law in the determination of international developments, see Abram Chayes, *The Cuban Missile Crisis* (London: Oxford University Press, 1974); Robert R. Bowie, *Suez 1956* (London: Oxford University Press, 1974); and D. P. O'Connell, *The Influence of Law on Sea Power* (Manchester: Manchester University Press, 1975). More general studies of the role of law include Milton Katz, *The Relevance of International Adjudication* (Cambridge: Harvard University Press, 1968) and J. E. S. Fawcett and Rosalyn Higgins (eds.), *International Organization: Law in Movement* (London: Oxford University Press, 1974). Also see the related study by David P. Forsythe, "The Red Cross as a Transnational Movement: Conserving and Changing the Nation-state System," *International Organization* (Autumn 1976), 30(4).

[18]Bull, *The Anarchical Society*, p. 265.

[19]Quoted in Robert O. Keohane and Joseph S. Nye, *Power and Interdependence* (Boston: Little, Brown, 1977), p. 3.

[20]See Gerhard Mally, *Interdependence* (Lexington, Mass.: D. C. Heath-Lexington Books, 1976) and Klaus Knorr, *The Power of Nations* (New York: Basic Books, 1975), especially chap. 8.

[21]Raymond Vernon, *Sovereignty at Bay* (New York: Basic Books, 1971), p. 15. See also John Diebold, "Multinational Corporations: Why Be Scared of Them" in Richard N. Cooper (ed.), *A Reordered World* (Washington, D.C.: Potomac Associates, 1973).

[22]Growth rates of MNCs traditionally have been greater than those of states. In 1971 sales of MNC foreign affiliates were greater than the exports of market countries, and the "value added" of MNCs that year, some U.S. $500 billion, equalled approximately one-fifth the total world GNP of noncentrally planned economies. At the same time, the stock of global direct foreign investment increased from U.S. $105 billion in 1967 to U.S. $287 billion in 1976. Even allowing for inflation, the growth is considerable. Additional qualifications notwithstanding, including the fact that MNCs affect certain countries and certain economic sectors more than others, it is impossible to dismiss the notion that the multinational corporation has transformed the productivity of the international economy. See, in general, Jack N. Behrman, *National Interests and the Multinational Enterprise* (Englewood Cliffs, N.J.: Prentice-Hall, 1970); *Multinational Corporations in World Development* (Document ST/ECA/190, United Nations, Department of Economics and Social Affairs, 1973); and *Transnational Corporations in World Development: A Re-examination* (Document E/C. 10/38, United Nations, Economic and Social Council, 1978).

[23]Besides the two UN studies of MNCs cited above, see Centre on Transnational Corporations, *National Legislation and Regulations Relating to Transnational Corporations* (Document ST/CTC/6, United Nations, 1978); Charles P. Kindleberger, *Power and Money* (New York: Basic Books, 1970); Paul A. Tharp, Jr., "Transnational Enterprises and International Regulation: A Survey of Various Approaches in International Organizations," *International Organization* (Winter 1976), 30(1); Robert O. Keohane and Van Doorn Ooms, "The Multinational Firm and International Regulation," *International Organization* (Winter 1975), 29(1); and *National Treatment for Foreign-Controlled Enterprises Established in OECD Countries, 1978* (Paris: OECD, October 1978).

[24]*Transnational Corporations in World Development: A Re-examination*, p. 132.

[25]Samuel P. Huntington, "Transnational Organizations in World Politics," *World Politics*, 3 (April 1973): 355.

[26]Ibid., pp. 366-367. See also Robert Gilpin, "Three Models of the Future," in C. Fred Bergsten and Lawrence B. Krause (eds.) *World Politics and International Economics, International Organization*, 29(1) (Winter 1975). Gilpin proposes three possible future environments: a "Sovereignty at Bay" world of powerful MNCs, weak nation-states, interdependence, and low utility of force; a *dependencia* model similar to the above, but with MNCs seen as agents of neo-imperialism; and a "mercantilist" world dominated by the interaction of states in an increasingly competitive and politicized manner.

[27]Stephen D. Krasner, "State Power and the Structure of International Trade," *World Politics*, 3 (April 1976): 343.

[28]Geoffrey Barraclough, "The Struggle for the Third World" *The New York Review of Books*, November 9, 1978, p. 56. See also Mary Kaldor, *The Disintegrating West* (London: Allen Lane, 1978).

[29]Stanley Hoffmann, "An American Social Science: International Relations," *Daedalus*, 106(3) (Summer 1975): 53.

[30]Bull, *The Anarchical Society*, p. 272.

[31]Keohane and Nye, *Transnational Relations and World Politics*, p. 345.

[32]Stanley Hoffmann, *Primacy or World Order*, pp. 111-112.

[33]Seyom Brown, *New Forces in World Politics*, p. 186.

[34]Samuel Huntington, "Transnational Organizations," p. 366.

[35]Brown, *New Forces in World Politics*, p. 125.

[36]Quoted in Huntington, "Transnational Organizations," p. 363; See also Daniel Bell, "The Future World Disorder: The Structural Context of Crisis," *Foreign Policy*, 27 (Summer 1977): 132 and Edward L. Morse, *Modernization and the Transformation of International Relations* (The Free Press, New York: 1976). Also of interest are views found in Stanley Hoffmann (ed.), *Conditions of World Order* (Houghton Mifflin, Boston: 1968).

[37]See, for example, F. H. Hinsley, *Power and the Pursuit of Peace* (Cambridge: Cambridge University Press, 1967) and Michael Howard, *War and the Liberal Conscience* (London: Temple Smith, 1978). Also note Richard Falk, *A Study of Future Worlds* (Amsterdam: North-Holland Publishing Company, 1975) and Barbara Ward, *Nationalism and Ideology* (London: Hamish Hamilton, 1967). For criticisms of a world not based on nation-states, see Michael Howard "War and the Nation State" (Oxford: Clarendon Press, 1978) and J. W. Burton, *International Relations* (New York: Cambridge University Press, 1967).

ANNIE KRIEGEL

The Nature of the Communist System:
Notes on State, Party, and Society

The Communist Cycle: From Liberation to Oppression[1]

SINCE ITS REAL BEGINNING IN 1914 with the First World War—the war that in so many ways cut history in two, defining a before and an after—the twentieth century has, with distressing regularity, under the most diverse circumstances, and with infinite variation in concrete detail, presented us with a repetition of the same cycle.

It starts with a *revolutionary rupture*, that is, a collapse of the society and the State. To those who would use it is the starting point for their revolutionary enterprise, this collapse will result from a defeat in external war or from an economic crisis that degenerates into a general depression—the type of crisis that Lenin foresaw "when the lower class no longer want[s] and the upper class can no longer sustain the old regime." In truth, however, such a revolutionary rupture can today occur by chance, like a wrench thrown into a sophisticated machine. A series of unfavorable circumstances may set it off; or it can result from the power of social imitation, for the revolutionary rupture has become one model among others available in contemporary history.

There then follows a formidable, if relatively brief (a few months to a few years), *explosion* of fervent hopes, enthusiasms, new ideas, and fantastic projects—some, pure extravagance; others, more reasonable visions, rich in intuition and portent. Yet, this second period is more than mere frivolity or insouciance, the joy one finds in a liberation that joins freedom to every form of liberty. For hidden amid this carnival of joy is the anguish of nonbelievers, already fearful of speaking, already aware of the humiliation of prudent silence and of the unhappiness (expropriations, trials, punishments ranging from exile to death) that awaits those who have become the "excluded" in this vicious dialectic of masters forced to become slaves. There already is a terror, but it is the classic terror of the beginnings of revolution, a still-innocent terror whose net is still wide-meshed.

The third period is a dreary, interminable, and, most often, hideously bloody relapse into generalized oppression—one no different from other oppressions—that affects all areas of personal and social life and that fixes authoritatively the unbreachable limits of their autonomy.

This analysis of the three stages in the cycle of communist experience affords a rough schema that can accommodate very different experiences—those of large and small peoples; of ancient, immense empires and tiny countries hitherto outside the stream of history; of relatively advanced and traditional societies; of Christian countries and those that hold other religious beliefs; of centralized states and peoples who know scarcely anything of states and constitutions. This schema encompasses a history of communist experience that the oldest among us remember and the younger can learn, usually badly, from textbooks that deal with the last half century.

My purpose here is not to display distaste or revulsion, but rather to ask whether this schema denotes some fatal inevitability, and whether it is a ponderous curse on humanity, denying us a better, wiser, happier, and more equitable life. Or rather, is it the regrettable, if absolutely necessary, price we must pay for a future of power and glory? Or, is there here some faulty conception that spoils and wastes, in a tragic irony of history, the best of intentions? This last is indeed the healthy conclusion, for by choosing it, we can escape the sterile despair that invariably follows a dream turned sour. And it is a fruitful conclusion, too, for it allows a growth of knowledge about fundamental social mechanisms. A careful and painstaking analysis, supported by the study of a significant number of cases (at least of social experimentation), leads us to believe that this faulty conception is an inherent part of the communist system itself, so much so that there is no remedy. Yet, it is no longer realistic to anticipate the self-destruction of the communist system in the short run, for despite its faults, it shows great stability and persistence.

This faulty conception rests on the essential fact that between society and state—or, in Leninist language, between the masses and the state apparatus—Lenin introduced a force that is not merely a mediator but an actor; an actor, moreover, that aspires to be, and in fact becomes, after the revolutionary rupture, the leading player in a three-character play. As conceived and promised by Lenin, this new actor is a political party of a new type, the Communist party.

How did social thought develop to a point that made the emergence of Leninism possible? The eighteenth century *philosophes*, in a major doctrinal innovation that altered society's conception of itself, suggested that the emancipation of individuals would thenceforth be the measure of modernity; in other words, the social contract is a pact between individuals who are free and legally equal. In the nineteenth century the early theorists of industrial society changed the emphasis: they altered the meaning of emancipation by reducing it to a mere profession of faith in an abstract or, at best, partial emancipation. Individuals could only be free through a collective freedom that preserved the dimension of individual identity compatible with group membership. For the socialists, and for Marx particularly, the individual would be able to enjoy his full human rights and humanity, to become free, only when the emancipation of the working class *as* a class, as the Messiah-class, as the mediating class, had entered the phase of realization. Lenin turned this schema to his own purposes. The emancipation of the working class as the prior condition and as the basis for the emancipation of mankind, both universally and as individuals, demands the forging of the instrument indispensable to this goal. Lenin called that instrument "the party of the working class," the Communist party.

This central role of the Communist party as "the party of the working class" is at the heart of Leninist logic and underlies every variation based on it. How the party operates at each stage in relation to the other two fixed elements of the game—the masses (or what sociologists call civil society) and the state—distinguishes the different phases of Leninist strategy. After the revolution, for example, the Communist party will encourage release of the energy stored up in the masses, and in the most savage and destructive form possible—libertarian anarchism. The old state, already beaten but not yet eradicated, will be utterly destroyed. This second phase is one of triumphant and exalted liberation. The new state, erected on the ruins of the old, is but another face of the Party, for the Party cannot tolerate separation of this new state from itself. It does not become merely a Party-state; rather, the Party has, in a sense, absorbed the state into itself and reduced it to a bureaucracy, a necessary by-product, a valueless residue. The Party then turns against the masses, against the civil society, serving as the instrument of repression. In the Communist world, oppression begins precisely when the Party-state becomes the only locus of historical action. Though civil society is not entirely moribund, it is a mere shadow of itself, living in quiet, desperate obscurity, emerging periodically for short, brutal gasps of air—spiritual protest, uprisings of misery, workers' revolts, and nationalist upheavals.

As the Party evolves toward the absolute power of the Party-state, how does the latter's omnipotence develop with regard to economic matters? Recall Lenin's famous formula: "Communism equals soviets plus electrification." Its meaning is, of course, uncertain, and it has been the object of interminable exegeses. The inclusion of "soviets" is obvious, but it is worth reflecting on the symbolic significance of "electrification." Electricity was at that time the most modern form of energy and served as an ambiguous common ground between civil and military concerns, as does nuclear power today; in other terms, between the economic and the political, when extrapolated to their wartime forms. The confusion in all this arises from the fact that, before the revolutionary rupture and while still contained within capitalist societies, the Communist parties presented themselves as heralds of increased production, a necessary obeisance to the working-class tradition that was part of their point of departure.

But the whole history of communist experience demonstrates that, after the revolution, the economy becomes the natural arena in which the fusion of Party and state is worked out. Here we must distinguish what properly can be called the "economy" from those elements of an economic nature inherent in the construction of military strength. Military power is essential to the logic of expansion that underlies the whole communist enterprise. From the outset the goal of communism has been to operate on a worldwide scale and to take over the entire planet.

Thus the economy under communism, when not directed to military goals, loses all autonomy; it is no longer asked to provide more than the barest minimum necessary for the survival of civil society, a fixed minimum set as low as possible by the omnipotent Party-state.

One can now understand how Leninism is a political "ism," how every communist experiment, even if undertaken in an economically advanced country, implies an inescapable economic regression destined to destroy the autonomy of economic forces. One can also understand how, even though endowed with considerable industrial capacity, the Soviet Union has never been a properly industrial, let alone post-industrial, society.

One can also finally understand how nationalization could have served as the rock on which, in France, the Union of the Left was smashed. For the Socialists, nationalization is but one tool among others for administering the economy; for the Communists, it is an essential instrument for the destruction of at least part of the autonomous economy for the benefit of powers properly political.

*   *   *

In France we no longer read the "good" authors. More than eighty years ago Durkheim, to whom we occasionally render homage as the father of academic sociology and as a friend of Jaurès, had already said, in comparing socialism and communism:

> Communism is only secondarily concerned with what are properly called econom-
> ic matters; it proceeds to modify them only with a view to pursuit of its main goal,
> the abolition of individual property. Socialism, conversely, only affects private
> property indirectly, that is, to the extent necessary to place it in harmony with its
> own major goal, an economic rearrangement.

Who has said it better?

From this analysis we can extract three brief points that I believe allow us to escape from the communist morass. It is necessary to protect the state against any attempted takeover by a single party that, while preserving the appearance of political pluralism, functions in practice as a ponderous, hegemonic party even before it has attained a monopoly of power. This is why I oppose all attempts, Right or Left, tending to anarchism, for they afford the most effective way to weaken the state decisively. Yet, it is equally necessary to protect civil society by defending the free exercise of its capacity for autonomous initiative. But if all is not to be lost, we must bear in mind that we have need of a state *and* a civil society; we must emphasize the delicate, sophisticated interrelationships between them, so that no force, internal or external, can exploit the frustrations of civil society, aggravated by the encroachments of the state or the weakening of the state, that intensify the imbalances and injustices of civil society

Translated by J. Braun

Party, State, And Society: The Soviet Arrangement

Most historical, political, and theoretical works dedicated to the Soviet Union rest on assumptions of the sixties that have not only been belied by events but have revealed themselves to be a source of mealymouthed and, insofar as they are a substitute for prior Stalinist orthodoxy, self-seeking illusions. As Alexandre Zinoviev stresses in *L'Avenir Radieux* (*L'Age d'Homme*, 1978), "We liberals really only differ from obscurantists in that we do the same thing a little better, with slightly different methods and with a greater sense of modesty, or, what amounts to the same thing, of cynicism"—in short, "of watered-down Stalinism."

These are the assumptions that perhaps had, for a short time, infused their spirit into the short-lived experience of Malenkov; assumptions that unquestionably had spasmodically supported some of the intuitions and intentions, however confused or ambiguous, of Krushchev; assumptions that can be summed up in our contemporary term, "liberalization." The idea was this: Stalin had, by atrociously brutal methods, spawned out of Russia and socialism the evolving nucleus of a dynamic, systemic, and universalist complex of states, parties, and movements; this done, it was permissible to revert internally to a norm not so different from that of the West. Such a view strengthens the presumption that East and West will ineluctably converge. This loosening of constraints, this appeal to the initiative of the masses, this bet on the efficacy of liberalization was supposed to allow the Soviet Union to reach a new and decisive stage—advanced socialism. This development had supposedly nothing in common with the brief, tactical episodes of the Stalinist period that periodically restored life to the desperate people of the Soviet Union, episodes that caused a hundred flowers to blossom for a brief, uncertain spring.

Such a "liberal" perspective rests on a purely historical and circumstantial interpretation of the Soviet drama. At the core of this interpretation one finds the concept of backwardness, whether the backwardness of Russia relative to the victorious imperialism of the Allies in 1917 or the backwardness of the conventional Soviet army in 1947 compared with American nuclear power. The concept has served both to justify the past and to plan the future. According to the theory based on it, the Soviet Union "catches up," that is, comes to function more or less in the same way as Western political systems. It experiences *tensions;* it has to deal with a *ruling class* whose ambition is to develop its own *participation* in power, and that proceeds, through alliances and compromises between sectional institutions, to the redistribution of power among these diverse segments. Inevitably an *opposition* emerges that, as everywhere, is not unified or homogeneous in its *perspectives* but divided into factions that aim at more or less radical or more or less reformist *transformations*. Considered together, these terms—tension, ruling class, participation, redistribution, opposition, transformation—constitute a system that argues against the persistent belief (naive or not) that Soviet socialism is founded on a logic radically foreign and unassimilable to Western democracy.

Several of Krushchev's initiatives would seem to bolster this generous "liberal" interpretation and to some extent justify the error. There is the famous "Secret Report." Many pertinent and just analyses have placed the drafting and presentation in Congress of these irretractable confessions within the context of "successional struggles" (a euphemism for the bizarre interludes in which no law or custom holds, not even the law of silence). Yet the fact remains that the deepest roots of this report lie in the recesses of the soul of this strange, crude man. Somehow through the layers of lies that perforce encased him, the burning truth burst forth irrepressibly.

In any case, the thaw, to use another metaphor of the period, was not all ruse and *trompe-l'oeil*. The return of the deported, at least those who had survived the unspeakable material and spiritual torments of hunger, cold, and general inhumanity, was not just a dream. Similarly, Krushchev was truly tempted to find a way to lead the peasantry out of its condition of "plantation slavery." It is also true that Krushchev and those around him often inveighed against the misfortunes of the "little man" and proposed to comfort him by granting greater priority to consumption.

Can we still accept such an interpretation today? Can we still believe that for the past quarter of a century the Soviet peoples have been on a civilian Long March toward the double goal of abundance and liberty? The answer is No. This vision of things is not innocent. It did not spring spontaneously from the minds of men of good will, of honest liberals belonging to all continents who only erred in being too optimistic and in underestimating the time required for the accomplishment of such a project. When the old Stalinist theme of the "socialist paradise" came to be judged no longer tenable, this conception was suggested, adopted, and propagated in order to salvage whatever possible. It was constructed piece by piece to perpetuate the convenient and useful misunderstanding of the communist phenomenon. Predictably, it has been systematized by Communists distinguished for their transcendental fidelity to the Party. It is a Party conception, a Party position no less valuable and obligatory than the prior conception that invoked the heroic record of the "perfect society." It, too, is founded on the idea of "catching up," but in this case it is only a question of verbal "catching up." And it is worth noting the ease with which one wins certification as a bona fide enlightened man of good will, by recognizing once and for all that things did not happen exactly as we had imprudently maintained, that there have been deficiencies, blotches—many blotches, even unacceptable blotches—but that everything is now on the right track and all that is needed is hard work.

Ironically, for reasons peculiar to the internal evolution of the international communist movement, first the Italian, then the French, and, in even more striking fashion, the Spanish Communist parties have come to reject the subtle, soothing conception of a socialist society with blotches. By admitting that, for the time being, anti-Sovietism should not be the touchstone of anticommunism, these parties have in principle freed us from the delicate task of choosing a critical stance that simultaneously satisfies our own consciences and yet does not excessively offend them. It is now high time that, rather than weigh the pros and cons of the Soviet system with reference to our own society as the ideal type, and rather than calculate whether we should be pro- or anti-Soviet and up to what point, we begin to analyze the socialist system for what it is in itself, as a "total" system wholly different from our own, not in degree but in kind.

By a total system I mean a system whose advantages and (formidable) disadvantages can be compared element for element with the advantages and disadvantages of liberal democracies, though this would be a meaningless exercise. It is much more interesting to understand that the advantages and disadvantages of the Soviet system can eventually be reduced or maximized, but that they are produced by modalities of functioning that at least succeed in doing one thing common to all functioning, i.e., perpetuate themselves.

Although it has often been said that the Soviet system depends entirely on "one man" (Number One), time has shown it to have a remarkable capacity to

function quite adequately, and even well, when the Number One spot is occupied but apparently only nominally, as during the current period. Each cog-
wheel is so well-adapted to its function that the system works without needing
more than intermittent adjustment or coaxing from above. Brezhnev is the first
of Soviet Number Ones whose age and illness have become the butt of Moscow
humor (even Krushchev did not tolerate such verbal liberties outside a very
restricted circle). This is not to say that Brezhnev serves no purpose. When that
period of general disruption throughout the length and breadth of the Socialist
world dubbed the "period of succession" begins anew, we shall see that it will
be less painful because of him.

If the personal decline of the current Number One is so easily endured, this
is surely due to the particular talents of Brezhnev himself. After the uncertainties of the Krushchev era, Brezhnev knew how to restore an internal equilibrium, whose secret is the secret of every kind of equilibrium—the machine is
perfectly adapted to its ends. The Soviet system is exceptionally balanced because it does not try to settle questions that fall outside its sphere of competence
or jurisdiction—for instance, the welfare of the people or the respect for values
such as dignity, justice, and freedom. Its equilibrium is based on the principle
that it never stray from its one appointed task—to maximize the chances of
attaining what it was conceived for, power on the global scale.

Here let me correct another common misconception concerning the Soviet
system as a whole, namely, its presumed obscurantist immobility. This would
only have meaning if the Soviet system maintained that it *ought* to change, that
it *had* to change to face certain challenges or threats that would compromise its
future—for example, the persistent nationalisms of the peoples' republics or the
non-Russian Soviet republics. The Soviet system asserts nothing of the sort. It
is happy to perfect the tried-and-true methods and techniques that aim precisely
to permit it *not to change*—in other words, not to lose time and energy, or better
yet, not to run the risks that any transformation implies.

This attitude is based on two powerful ideas. The first is "living with" what
one is not equipped to deal with, whether these are popular aspirations, the
desire to live better, a growing cultural and national identity, the iconoclastic
temptations of intellectuals, or whatever. One must not commit the insane error
of imagining that one can completely extirpate all "negative" aspirations and
desires. One must learn to live with them, *controlling* them at the appropriate
time and with appropriate force.

The second is that blocking a reform impulse in areas irrelevant to socialist
logic does not necessarily result in routine, immobility, and impotence. If, for
example, the commercialization of consumer durables is a permanent failure
throughout the Socialist world, should routine be indicted? No. The case of
South Vietnam is instructive in this regard. Why was such high priority given
to the rapid destruction of the old and sophisticated Chinese commercial apparatus? As in other cases, this was not done to crush the unassimilable social class
of Chinese tradesmen, nor with the (hardly realistic) hope that Vietnam would
be able to avoid the habitual failure of socialist commercialization. Rather, this
was done because in a socialist system the aleatory scarcity of consumer goods is
as natural as abundance is in the West. It is a feature as integral and all-pervasive
as the market in traditional rural society. Equally endemic to socialist systems is

the fantastic gap between the public exaltation of the virtues of work and the frantic scramble for parasitic occupations (now a mass-participation sport from East Berlin to Vladivostock). A related trait is the universal taste for poor workmanship. These are all fundamental characteristics of a "whole" that has its pluses as well as its minuses. The standard of living of the nonprivileged is very low indeed, but at least they are not forced to submit to the demanding discipline of manual work (except in the case of forced labor or such watered-down substitutes as "communist Saturdays" or apple-picking campaigns of city workers that are resorted to now that the forced-labor camp is no longer an effective solution for all sorts of indispensable but unsavory tasks).

The Soviet system, then, is superior to the Western system of liberal democracy in that it need not value change or the capacity for change. Imagination, invention, the "new," and the "never-seen-before" do not interest it. Let others make the expensive scientific or technological "firsts." If they prove usable, it is easy enough, and certainly cheaper, to send over an official, or secret team, to bring back the applicable formulae, plans, models, or prototypes.

The fundamental stability of a system that aims only at identical reproduction in all areas save that of power demands a regulatory mechanism. This job is filled by the Party. The relation between society and the state that in the West defines the variety of regimes is in the socialist world entirely irrelevant. There the state is merely the administrative arm of the Party, which absorbs within itself all political life. Society itself is merely the largely undifferentiated place, kept as unstructured as possible, where the Party recruits the phalanx of those who agree to belong to the ranks of the privileged, that is, to benefit throughout their lives from enormous material and moral advantages (compared to the ordinary man), but who also agree to assume a host of obligations and risks. Party cohesion consists largely in this ambiguous consciousness of belonging in a half-voluntary, insecure fashion to the co-opted cohort of the privileged. "Ideology" is not the set of beliefs embraced as the only alternative to cynicism and immoralism, but rather this consciousness, this understanding of the Party. The Party is quite simply the most propitious place to engage in what comprises the essence of socialist society: "the general, desperate struggle for the attainment of privileges." (Zinoviev)

Clearly, the concept of opposition is meaningless, and therefore the opposition, since it does not exist, cannot have perspectives. What is christened "opposition," by an abusive borrowing from Western political vocabulary, is really two distinct phenomena.

Within the well-defined context of the Party, there is, on the one hand, a complex game of service trade-offs, a "general and bitter" struggle of groups and influences that structures the pyramid of internal fiefs, of which, as in all feudal systems, some are on the decline, others in the ascendant. Protection is the supreme value and the object of all maneuvers. For one cannot afford to fall asleep under the shadow of a protector who, if one has miscalculated his weaknesses, could suddenly leave you helplessly exposed. Naturally, this game feeds on the thousand and one opportunities provided by the necessity of arriving at immediate solutions to general as well as specific problems posed in the course of everyday collective life. However, these disagreements, divergences, collisions, compromises, breaks—in short, this permanent state of confused local wars—should not be taken literally and analyzed in depth, but instead considered in their instrumentality, that is, as the very texture of the decision-making procedures in this type of hierarchy.

On the other hand, there is in the Party, the state, and society a network of men and women who have lost the taste for playing that game, or who, never having had it, cannot tolerate that its exclusive use should be imposed upon them. These men and women do not form an opposition in any strict sense, as they are unable to oppose anything at all. They are dissidents, and, as Zinoviev emphasized, the very opposite of liberals. Gropingly, these dissidents, with all dissidence implies in terms of spiritual strength and resistance to fear, have learned how to place themselves outside the game. Outsider status is not without its benefits. The service of truth can be its own reward, but it carries with it horrible dangers (labor camp, exile, and psychiatric prison). Perhaps the supreme advantage of dissidence is that it breaks the radical isolation of individuals, who, divested for the interim of any nonaleatory personal destiny, are the sole authorized units of the socialist system. Vis-à-vis the Party, and outside the Party, there exist in the Soviet Union only atomized individuals. Dissidence, whether of intellectuals, radical democrats or liberals, nationalists or Jews, has the effect of reorganizing nuclei, of articulating networks, of reestablishing collectivities that are not communist collectivities. Why, then, has this dissidence, which is not an opposition, acquired such extraordinary freedom, even as the dissidents remain individually subjected to arbitrary authority? This is probably the cost of the transition from a sanguinary Stalinism to a dreary but tranquil Brezhnevism. Stalin had criminal initiative; the dissidents have the initiative of protest. In each instance, an economy of means is observed and a peaceful image of socialism projected. Nevertheless, with an irony that history often exhibits, socialism's credit has collapsed just at the moment when it least merits such a fate.

The fact that there is dissidence rather than opposition, in the Western sense of the term, leads to a result that should not be overlooked. To claim that socialist power is continuously threatened from within and that it could crumble any day, undermined as it is by the persistent incapacity to impose its legitimacy on the masses, would be far-fetched. Certainly, anything can happen, but, like the possibility of the sun not rising tomorrow morning, this, too, is scarcely plausible. All the flaws, all the imperfections that one can complacently list—the disorder of the Russian (or anti-Russian) economic machine; the demographic stagnation of a semiurban population; the restiveness of the intelligentsia, even when corrupted; the crude face of a society that even industrialized, is not an industrial society and even less a postindustrial society—are organic, integral parts of the total system. The motor tirelessly selects the number of careerists and *arrivistes* needed in each sphere to keep the machine running continuously, a rule that applies equally to the peoples' republics, where latent indigenous resistance impedes even the beginnings of structural readjustment.

The core of the Soviet system remains to be analyzed. If the socialist system has the ability to ignore "models of transformation" that well-wishers ingenuously propose, it is not only because its heart, the Party, directs its identical reproduction, but also because it functions positively, with a view to producing what by its very nature it is designed to produce: ever-expanding power.

Just as it is a mistake not to put the Party at the center of any analysis of the workings of the Soviet system, so, too, is it wrong not to put Soviet foreign policy (with its material foundation: military policy) at the center of the analysis of the system's goals. The socialist system does not function in a void; if it is in a state of internal equilibrium, it is because this equilibrium is not mere repetition, but because the system is implacably bent on external conquest, and that by the most classic of methods—force.

Here again we must take care to avoid misunderstanding and define our terms. Take, for example, the word *peace*. The idea that the socialist camp is the peace camp only means that war made by socialists is by definition "just" and the necessary prerequisite of peace, whereas war made by nonsocialists is necessarily "unjust" and the antithesis of peace.

The quest for expansion is not to be confused with the quest for adventure. Concretely, the Soviets no more pride themselves on waging revolutionary war on their own initiative than communists vaunt themselves when they "make revolution"—it is the revolution that makes itself. The Soviets merely exploit conjunctures and circumstances furnished by a propitious terrain and indigenous opportunities. They usually act with tremendous prudence and in a manner as indirect as possible. Moreover, they do not always win on every front. Indeed, they can err and fail. Nevertheless, one cannot leave unrecorded four remarkable developments that have blessed the Brezhnev era. First—at the level of objectives—the build-up of gigantic conventional and unconventional fire power made possible by transference and concentration of formerly civilian resources to the military sphere—this at the obvious costs of a low standard of living and strain on the institutions responsible for its control and maintenance. Second—at the level of means—the setting up of a mechanism for pumping resources from the West, based on the rational exploitation of the "contradictions of capitalism." Third—at the level of the utilization of means—a very astute redistribution of powers, a division of labor between the Soviet state and the diverse components of the international communist movement, particularly in regard to the specialization of functions that relate to the art of conquest (information, logistics, and the formation of expeditionary forces). Fourth—at the level of results—the solid establishment of the foundations for socialist expansion in Asia and Africa. The Western economic crisis and the ongoing American political crisis (from Watergate to the present)—the latter much more than the former—provided opportunities that were exploited, with a rare determination, to effect the necessary breakthroughs, no matter how high the cost in human lives. Ethiopia comes to mind.

Translated by John Muresianu

The Future Of State Collectivism: The Reinforcement Of State Power

The title of this essay has been chosen to illustrate a misinterpretation that underlies almost all analyses of the way communist regimes function. These analyses generally rely on the concept of state collectivism and are intended

primarily as grave denunciations of the malevolence of a state that became totalitarian by means of a generalized collectivization.

It is easy to see how this misinterpretation has prospered. Solzhenitsyn has
shown us that concentration camps are one consequence of all communist experiments, and in France we have recently seen that the notion of a common
practicable program between Socialists and Communists is an illusion. The error resulted from construction of several artificial symmetries: Auschwitz/
Gulag; state monopoly capitalism/state collectivism. Liberalism and collectivism are thus both seen as becoming part of the state—this monstrous, barren
state that aims always and only at oppression and exploitation in all its forms. It
is as if the state could exist only in the form of an unchangeable Moloch; as if
one could still, after four millennia of Empire-states, City-states, Kingdoms,
Nation-states, State-nations, and now even Party-states, repeat such monotonous
denunciations of the unvarying, universal "state." Such denunciations assume
the existence of an improbable society that, shorn of its state, would be nothing
more than a collection of local fiefdoms whose quarrelling lords are more or less
at the mercy of the hegemonic pretensions of any candidate for the role of arbiter—as, for example, the Church. In short, we must begin with a comparative
consideration of the diverse historic *models* of the state.[3]

In examining the communist regimes, to focus on the present and the future
of the state is to utilize something that is not a window or a mirror, but a
deception, something that does not exist. I have elsewhere[4] explained why the
eschatological expectation that the socialist state will disappear at the millenium
is vain, for this Messiah has already come. The Soviet state has not withered
away as was prophesied, because it had already disappeared—at the very moment when Lenin and his companions conquered the old apparatus of the Russian state and proceeded to dismantle it.

The best proof of this is that the core—the Rule of Law, the rational center
of the modern state's reality—was damaged beyond repair in the flood of the
revolution. This explains how the apparatus of a justice that was forsaken and
parodied could, in the Soviet Union of the 1930s and in the people's democracies of the 1950s, serve as the basis for the production of vast, mysterious spec-
tacles, the famous Trials, that aimed primarily at educating the masses and
internalizing the new faith.[5] Nothing could better demonstrate that law had
given way to faith—and a perverse faith at that.[6]

Certainly it could well be that the communist state remained a state even
after having forsaken the rule of law, in that Bolshevik "science" could condemn
the rule of law only because in its eyes that rule was but a travesty concocted by
the class state. This perspective allowed casting off, in the name of "truth," all
the trappings of bourgeois law—justice, judicial institutions, magistrates, lawyers, and even law itself. Similarly, most Third World states with "socialist"
pretensions have remained "states" of the tyrannical type. Although they sel-
dom conform entirely to the communist model, they have adopted the single-
party system and therefore, of necessity, many communist methods. Here the
state apparatus becomes the focus of all thought, decisions, and political action.

It might also be that the communist state, even after discarding the rule of
law, remained a state in a more limited sense, and particularly in the high visi-
bility area of international relations between states. Within the international

community of states, the Soviet Union does count as one, or even three states, for, as a federation of republics each having a potential right to sovereignty, the USSR managed to wrangle three votes at the United Nations at the end of the Second World War. Similarly, within the international community, the communist states are no longer seen as a militantly unified "socialist camp," yet have remained a socialist community that is properly a collection of states, even if now more loosely and informally united than previously.

Under these circumstances, one should concede that the Communist world, at least as seen by the outside world, has its own form of state. Yet, this outward image is but a mask. Hélène Carrère d'Encausse in her recent book[7] presents a detailed demonstration of the hollowness of Soviet federalism. Even more decisive, while the historical experience of Western Europe points to a natural affinity between state and nation—the Nation-state—d'Encausse stresses the ongoing procedures by which the nation/state cleavages within the Soviet Union have been radically shorn of significance (dévitalisés), admittedly, though, to different degrees. For the operating principle throughout is a partisan centralism, a principle entirely foreign to these nation/state cleavages. And partisan centralism, as has been frequently asserted, is nothing more than a disguise for the exercise of a Great Russian monopoly. It shows no concern, except in the short run and for instrumental reasons, for any sort of equitable distribution, any sort of quantum between the diverse nations and nationalities. It is satisfied with insuring its hold over the vast territory it owns, mobilizing as best it can the available resources, still mostly Great Russian, but increasingly also non-Russian to the extent that the parties of the republics take root.

Similarly, in the socialist community, the cooperation of Communist parties in power entails a general procedure of integration, such that the apparent sovereignty of the states is nothing more than the residue of a momentary necessity, a convenient and provisional window-dressing. Also, the international socialist community is marked by a less advanced degree of evolution than the Soviet community—the internal partisan logic of the former is still contaminated by an external state logic—that requires, less for administrative convenience than for reasons of security and control, both the maintenance of intersocialist frontiers and local peculiarities and the maintenance of a still fiercely explosive Soviet hegemony.

It is thus not at the level of the state that the capacities for persistence and resistance of a collectivist system of the communist type are to be observed; rather, we must look to the Party, the only center of power that counts, and whose administrative arm the state now is.[8] The Party serves as the untiring mechanism of suppression of social requirements and a no less untiring mechanism of absorption of the administrative functions of the state. It is only ignorance of these party roles that gives rise to the periodic speculations about the eventuality of the army or the police gaining the upper hand over, or arriving at a compromise with, the Party. Bonapartist, Thermidor, or police state—all the prophecies have been falsified. Even if the general secretaries of the party would have liked to assume the titles of general or marshal; even if they associated freely with the Ieyovs and the Berias on occasion; the Party was nevertheless the immutable source of their power. And if some day soon, for example, the present director of the KGB becomes Brezhnev's successor (quite possible, for he is well enough placed in the current constellation of the Soviet *Politburo*), it would still be wrong to assume that the USSR is a mere police state.

A similar false deduction, though one that now meets with considerable skepticism in the West, is evident in the idea that excessive nationalization can give birth to a communist system. The mistake lies in the failure to see that the collectivist element of such nationalizations is, in itself, of no great importance: as a technique of economic administration, nationalization has advantages and disadvantages. If Communists are in favor of the maximum amount of nationalization, this is only because this contributes to weakening the autonomy of the economic sector to the profit of the political, for the latter will be the setting for the final conflict of Party against (liberal or collectivist) state. From this point of view, it is highly symbolic that ten of the fourteen members of the Soviet *Politburo* are engineers by profession.

Finally, to the extent that Eurocommunism is groping toward a model of socialism that, while within the realm of communist ideas, is nevertheless differentiated from the Soviet model of socialism (the "existing socialism" as installed wherever there is a Bolshevik regime, thus including China), it must face the question whether the state must be restored. But, as articulated within the framework of the Eurocommunist variant, this restoration is so adventurous that the Eurocommunist parties, for the moment at least, avoid the issue in two ways. Instead of speaking explicitly about restoration, they talk of a renovation and a perfection of democracy. The escape clause is evident. Exactly what is it that needs to be "democratized"? And rather than develop a project for restoring the state, they prefer the restoration of something less inclusive than the state — "society" is both looser and more diffuse. Therein lies the basis for their voluntary conversion to self-determination, a conversion that demonstrates their conviction of the relative malleability and the ultimate insubstantiality of *soviets*. In practice, the Communist parties in power have shown that, while no compromise is possible with any force situated within the sphere of the state, it is perfectly possible to arrange relatively durable compromises even with substantial forces, provided, as in the case of the Catholic Church in Poland, they pertain only to civil society.

Translated by J. Braun

From The International To Comecon

Officially founded on January 25, 1949, Comecon, or CEAM (Council for Mutual Economic Assistance), as the Soviets prefer to translate the Russian expression, is now thirty years old. Under the transparent veil of a project of economic cooperation, it was at the outset merely the expression of a tightening of the bonds between the seven new "people's republics" of Eastern Europe (Bulgaria, Hungary, Poland, Romania, Czechoslovakia, joined in the months immediately following by Albania and East Germany) and the metropolis, that is, the Soviet Union. This tightening was aimed primarily at combating the temptation to return to the West expressed in the Czech hesitations in the spring of 1947, at the moment of the American offer of the Marshall Plan. It was further intended to combat the centrifugal tendencies that the dissent of Tito and Yugoslavia could have provoked. Comecon was the counterpart, within the category of socialist states, of the Cominform, which since September 1947 had been the gathering place for Communist parties. The Cominform is doubly superior to Comecon: it is not only older, but also includes two kinds of parties, counting among its members the two most important Communist parties of nonsocialist Western Europe, the French and the Italian, and the parties in power in socialist states. But for almost ten years Comecon and Cominform showed few signs of life: Stalin always preferred to have expeditious, direct relations with his agents and proconsuls in conquered or missionary territory rather than vast conferences where unwieldly multilateral relations could form. Besides, the struggle against Titoism, which soon became the central objective, was only partially successful. It undoubtedly accelerated Stalinization of the Communist parties and the drawings of "people's republics" as satellites into the Soviet orbit, but it did not bring Tito or Yugoslavia to heel. For the lack of a new mission, the Cominform wasted away and died in 1956.

The signing of the Treaty of Rome in 1957 saved Comecon from a similar fate. It testified to the vitality of the European Economic Community (EEC) and gave the lie to the sarcastic predictions of socialist augurs who staunchly adhered to the Leninist theses on the "contradictions of imperialism" and the Kautskian utopia of "superimperialism." As the Common Market revealed itself to be tougher than expected, Comecon was revitalized to become the socialist counterpart; such, at least, is the gist of the Moscow charter of December 14, 1959. The differences between the model and the copy, or, rather, between the rivals, are surely more striking than the similarities. To begin with, Comecon does not have a strictly European vocation, as its mainspring, the Soviet Union, is only partially a European country. In addition, Comecon brings together a group of countries whose inequalities in terms of resources and development are so enormous (e.g., Hungary: 93,000 square kilometers; USSR: 22,402,000) that the system is entirely dependent on the dominant partner, the Soviet Union (in 1967 Bulgaria had a GNP of $2.1 billion; Russia, $70.7 billion). Above all, socialist economic integration is not conceived as an integration of national markets in the Western manner, but rather as an integration of productive systems. The idea of a regional common market with free circulation of goods for members and a common tariff for all nonmembers is completely alien to Comecon. Its principal aim is to act on the structures of production, to coordinate plans and production itself in the various industrial and agricultural sectors; in short, to change the international division of labor. This orientation, sanctioned by the adoption in 1962 of the resolution "Fundamental Principles of the International Socialist Division," was reconfirmed nine years later in 1971 when the Twenty-fifth Session of the Council adopted the "Complex Program" that tended "to deepen and perfect cooperation and to develop economic socialist integration." Thus, during the sixties Comecon became the decisive instrument of dependence binding member states to the Soviet Union, a mission that continues and that assures the Soviet Union, through the offices of the general secretariat of the organization, overall control of the economic dimension of the system of socialist states.

Meanwhile, Comecon received a second, more ambitious, and, this time, strictly political mission. The entry of Mongolia in 1962 accentuated the non-European perspective of Comecon, without deeply changing its objective. Even the adherence of Cuba in 1972 could conceivably be interpreted as having only a symbolic significance, that is, to show that Comecon did not want to be a club of rich-nations-to-be. On the other hand, the invitations successively proffered to Korea, Angola (1976), Laos (1976), and Ethiopia (1978) to participate as observers in the working sessions of the Councils, and the full incorporation of Vietnam (1978), go far beyond the simple accords of economic cooperation such as those signed with Finland (1973), Iraq, and Mexico, or the agreements that, since 1976, Comecon would like to make with the EEC.

We have, in fact, been watching the formation of an international system of an interstate and intercontinental character that is coterminous with the area considered to be definitively won over to Soviet-style socialism. Briefly: since, contrary to the initial Leninist conception, history has made the Soviet Union, inasmuch as it is a multinational state, merely the framework for the union of the republican heirs of the ancient czarist empire (Bessarabia and the Baltic states could fit the definition, but not Korea), another cadre had to be found to represent and to rule the functioning and extension of the entire community of socialist states. The Warsaw Pact has been ruled out, because its military function is too technical and too visible. For the moment, this role will be played by the Comecon.

Translated by John Muresianu

REFERENCES
    [1]Paper presented to the colloquium "Economie et Libertés," September 1977.
    [2]November 1, 1978.
    [3]Cf. Blandine Barret-Kriegel, *Réflexion sur l'histoire de l'État* (à paraître, Calmann-Lévy).
    [4]In my contribution to the special number on the Soviet Union of *Pouvoirs*, 1978, pp. 121-130.
    [5]In 1972 I attempted to analyze these Trials in *Grands Procès dans les systèmes communistes. La pédagogie infernale* (Paris: Gallimard, "Idées"). But we now have an important document on the topic: Karel Kaplan, *Dans les archives du Comité Central. Trente ans de secret du Bloc sovietique* (Paris: A. Michel, 1978) (trans. from Czech).
    [6]See Alain Besançon, *Les origines intellectuelles du léninisme* (Paris: Calmann-Lévy, 1977). See also, Besançon, *La confusion des langues*, 1978.
    [7]Hélène Carrère d'Encausse, *L'Empire éclaté* (Paris: Flammarion, 1978). The author's thesis, contrary to what her title conveys, is precisely that the shattering of the Empire is hypothetical only.
    [8]Citizens (in the USSR) are those who are "administered," an excellent observation by Leon Robel in *L'U.R.S.S. et nous*, E.S., 1978, p. 137.

DAVID E. APTER

Notes on the Underground: Left Violence and the National State[1]

As a spectacular phenomenon, terrorism is declining, even if the number of violent acts is not. From a tactical point of view, terrorism has lost—so much so, that one wonders why it was so frightening. The term itself has lost its implacability: the state, its target, has been restored to its previous dignity. Moreover, terrorism has been eclipsed by the oil crisis, inflation, the condition of the dollar, and many other serious matters. All these put terrorism in proportion as the desperate acts of desperate men and women who, pathological or egomaniacal or perhaps as romantic children who never grew up, prefer terrorism to more constructive pursuits.

Terrorism is just one more thing the state may have to contend with. But it will pass, and the state will live on. Yet, there is a difference between crisis as such and terrorism, for terrorism aims not only to overthrow the state as it is, but to convert ordinary problems into something larger. Terrorists seek to demonstrate that the ordinary business of coping, the capacity of government to conduct the business of the day, is done so at the expense of some large, disadvantaged section of society—a class, an ethnic group, a religious body. By doing so, terrorism has as its aim the accomplishment of some practical end by extraordinary means. It is not an interest group gone wild. Rather, it seeks to raise matters of principle so fundamental that they will discredit the moral basis of the state as constituted. To do that, ordinary crises need to be converted from wearisome tribulations into convergent contradictions in which the state is rendered impotent. If this occurs, or better, such a convergence of predicaments can be made into what we will call a "disjunctive moment," terrorism will increase, spread, and get of hand, and even the most strongly armed state, if it loses its legitimacy, will fail. (Iran is a case in point.)

Normalcy must be transformed into heightened danger. The more visible the police guards, strong points, checkpoints, watchtowers, and armored cars, the better. They are signs of the weakness of the state rather than its strength, testimonials to the success of terrorists.

Terrorists, of course, differ in purpose, object, and tactics, but they share a common aim—to make the state morally bankrupt and to generate a disjunctive moment. After that the picture blurs. Some terrorists seek to abolish the state, such as modern anarchists or anarcho-syndicalists. Others want to reconstitute it, to make it into an instrument of revolution from above, like modern neo-

Leninists who favor government by the dictatorship of the proletariat (and emphasize the former term over the latter). Still others seek to create new ethnically or linguistically based territorial units carved out of old ones.

Whatever their purposes, the common target of terrorism is the legitimacy of the state as given, its moral credibility. Hence, the means, no matter how repugnant, represent judgments. Their outrageousness is a measure of moral seriousness. The more outrageous they are, the more they paralyze public activity, forcing suspension of the public's judgment, atrophying normal support, and turning citizens into bystanders rather than participants. The first act in the social drama of terrorism is a psychological battle of the good against the evil, the oldest human story of all. But the second act is to create a disjunctive moment in which crises seem to converge. It is the second stage that terrorism rarely accomplishes.

However, if there are chronic difficulties that the state as we know it cannot resolve, if disjunctive moments are more likely than we believed possible, if, indeed, the state is no longer able to cope as well as in the past, we may be facing a new condition, one in which it is not terrorism that produces a crisis in the state, but rather the crisis of the state that produces terrorism. That possibility must be confronted. But before doing so, let us examine terrorism itself, and particularly terrorism on the left.

Terrorism and its Explanations

Perhaps no topic has been subjected to as many *ad hoc* explanations as terrorism. Certain facts are well known. The incidence of violent acts against the state has been escalating steadily since 1968, although unevenly, in bursts, and in different forms. Hijacking is out of favor; murder is in.[2] Killing selected individual targets or maiming (society maims, therefore maim the maimers) have become more favored tactics.

There is also a consensus, indeed it is almost dogma, that, especially in Germany and Japan, terrorists tend to come from middle-class families. A high proportion are the sons and daughters of professionals, teachers, and other respected representatives of the bourgeoisie. Women are prominent among them. In Italy, militant terrorists include in their ranks the educated children of working-class Southerners who moved north to work in industry (educational reforms having made it possible for almost anyone who completes secondary school to go on to university). In general, modern terrorists have intellectual interests, are employed in jobs that are bureaucratic, and when they live underground, it is on monies gathered by a variety of means, from bank robbery to ransom.[3]

A few more commonplace characteristics of specifically Left terrorism generally: elite terrorists from better educated and intellectually sophisticated families tend to stand apart from, and distrust the inconstancy of, their radical militant peers, especially at universities; at the same time they use the universities as their main recruiting ground. The most violent terrorists in Germany and Japan are among the "best" products of the democratic state but hate its meritocratic aspects with an abiding passion. Liberal scholars, who considered democracy as the solution, not the cause, of such behavior, find terrorism of this sort so revolting that they prefer to put it down to individual causes and personal pathologies. There is the great desire to normalize violence by making terrorism plausible, the rational explaining the real.

In general, most of us believe that terrorism breaks out in rashes or erupts like boils on the body politic; while there are many reasons for each outbreak and many explanations, most make sense but none are crucial. The few general characteristics that can be described do not stand up well under close inspection, such as the notion that violence is a function of rising expectations. It may, in fact, also be a function of declining expectations. But so far there has been little discussion of how the meaning of terrorism changes with circumstances, or of the effects of different types: for example, *primordial*—racial, ethnic, linguistic, or religious movements; or *radical*—Marxist, anarchist, and other Left extremist movements or their equivalents on the Right.

Even less examined is what one can speak of as a "dialectic" of terrorism, especially of the Left-Right variety. For example, in Argentina, Brazil, and elsewhere in Latin America, and in Italy as well, left-wing and right-wing terrorism have literally fed off each other, and in the first two instances, terrorists have divided between antistate versus pro-state forces, the right wing being in part sponsored by the police. Left terrorists also try to create a military dialectic by transforming terrorism into civil war and provoking the government into using military forces, a situation that not only dignifies the struggle but gives terrorists the status of soldiers. Finally, such a dialectic recaptures symbolically all previous "just" wars on behalf of the oppressed, making heroes of terrorists, justifying their acts, and ensuring that they will become the text of history rather than merely a footnote to it.

These are only a few of the considerations appropriate to an understanding of the phenomenon. Here, however, I want to make a more selective argument, namely that terrorism and the state are reciprocals of each other. The state is the target of terrorists. Terrorism defines the limits of the state. This suggests that those defending the state are normal citizens while those seeking to destroy it are not. But what is surprising is the extent to which those on each side are "normal." Indeed, if terrorism is in some part an aberration, it is one to which many quite ordinary people are prone. (One of the more remarkable findings of interviews with terrorists is how normal they seem to be, at least to outward appearances.)

What makes a difference is, first, the particular events that embroil individuals in terrorism, and second, once involvement has occurred, the discipline, the militancy, indeed, the life of the cell that nurtures terrorism by creating a singular network. Then, the terrorist discovers how to transform ordinariness into an "event" in one explosive moment. He lives on sudden action—the "coiled snake syndrome."

This leaves open the question of when terrorism is effective apart from the short-lived publicity. (The public can adjust to terrorism as just another form of "natural" catastrophe.) What is required is a "disjunctive moment," a multiple crisis in society that reveals to a significant segment of the population that the society can delegitimize the state, with violent acts exposing the government as a losing proposition—its control, its grip, and its rationality all withering away.

Jürgen Habermas describes the components of such a disjunctive moment as a composite set of crisis tendencies as follows:

Crisis Tendencies	Proposed Explanations
Economic	a) The state apparatus acts as unconscious naturelike executive organ of the law of value
	b) The state apparatus acts as planning agent of united "monopoly capital"
Rationality	c) Destruction of administrative rationality occurs through opposed interests of individual capitalists
	d) The production (necessary for continued existence) of structures foreign to the system
Legitimation	e) Systematic limits
	f) Unintended side effects (politicization) of administrative interventions in the cultural tradition
Motivation	g) Erosion of traditions important for continued existence
	h) Overloading through universalistic value-systems ("new" needs)[4]

When these conditions are present, terrorism can be effective. It is not necessary to agree specifically with Habermas's formulation. The point is that, if terrorist acts can combine these crises into a single disjunctive moment, government can only fail. Fortunately, such moments are rare, and few terrorist movements have the leadership and organization to produce such crises. Indeed, where the crisis potential is high, as in Italy, the state is preserved not because of its power, but because of the weakness of terrorism as a political method.

Origins and Leaders

If leaders of terrorist movements are as diverse a lot as political rulers, pious, foolish, and presumptuous, the issues they fasten on are deadly serious. What distinguishes terrorists is their special ability to identify crisis issues and to use them against the state. Some are would-be "cosmocrats," theorists out to remake the world (with themselves at the center of it). Some are "phallocrats" whose power comes from the barrel of a gun. Some are "aristocrats" but have been redeemed.

Such terrorists are not without antecedents. The most interesting trace their pedigree to the French Revolution, particularly its Left, late-Jacobin phase;

their putative ancestor Rousseau had numerous followers in France and elsewhere, especially those who upgraded the romantic spirit and made it into a
solidaristic bond, like Fichte with his *Bund der frein Manner*.[5]

Farther back we find the Anabaptists, led by the redoubtable Thomas
Muntzer and his teacher Niklas Storch, whose millenarian visions were embodied in the League of the Elect that was to bring the New Jerusalem.[6] The antecedents of terrorism even include social banditry, the Mafia, and mob action,
with leaders striking heroic poses, Robin Hood adventurers who favored the
poor for personal gain.[7] All these used violence instrumentally. But in terrorism, violence is a modern Archimedes lever, not only enabling a small group to
effect vast changes in government, but the terrorism of means becomes intrinsic
to the terrorism of ends. The millenium, redemption, and the New Jerusalem
become essential parts of an unfulfilled mission of historical necessity.

To understand this more fully, it will be helpful to consider the lives of the
prototypes of Left terrorism, Filippo Michele Buonarroti (1761-1837), the "first
professional revolutionist" as Elizabeth Eisenstein calls him, and Francois-Noel
Babeuf (1760-1797), the first radical victim of the Thermidor. Babeuf was the
premier communist. He differed from his fellow Jacobins over the issue of property. He regarded the abolition of private property as essential to the abolition
of classes that divided people into the exploited and the exploiting. He formed a
radical society that included Buonarroti among its members, the *club du Pantheon*, whose purpose was open agitation. It had a journal, the *Tribun du Peuple*.
The society was driven undergound by the government in 1798, and a secret
directorate was established that included Babeuf, Buonarroti, Sylvain Mare-
chal, Felix Le Peletier, and A. A. Darthe. Its aim was to rally the people of
Paris to bring about the overthrow of the established government. Babeuf, leader of the peasantry, became an organizer of the sansculottes.[8]

Babeuf not only founded Jacobin communism, he claimed it as the only
proper legacy of the revolution of 1793.[9] (As such, it endures as a form of
romantic realism, retrieved, or rather resurrected, as in the Commune of 1848,
1870, or even the October Revolution.) By challenging the state's claim to a
monopoly of violence he gave violence itself a revolutionary meaning. "When a
nation takes the path of revolution it does so because the . . . masses realize that
their situation is intolerable, they feel impelled to change it, and they are drawn
into motion for that end."[10] His slogan "The aim of the society is the welfare of
its members" became an inspiration for Lenin.

> Every step in the development of the revolution rouses the masses and attracts
> them with uncontrollable force precisely to the side of the revolutionary pro-
> gramme as the only programme that consistently and logically expresses their *real,
> vital interests* . . . the destructive force of the revolution is to a considerable extent
> dependent on how . . . deep [was] the contradiction between the antediluvian
> "superstructure" and the living forces of the present epoch.[11]

Here we begin to see the relevance of Habermas's crises. For Babeuf, when
the "superstructures" of the French state became not only obsolete but oppressive, terror became its equal and opposite force. Then, no matter how weak and
halting in the first instance, terror was decisive. Thus terrorism came to have
meaning as history and as revolution, one that finally smashes the bourgeoisie.

This still remains the hallmark of Left terrorism, indeed, the militant Left generally. As Lenin added, one cannot ally with the bourgeoisie; to ally with it will produce "an abortion, a half-baked mongrel revolution." Of course, Leninism is not simply Babeuvism upgraded. "We shall . . . have, if we live to see a real victory of the revolution, new methods of action, corresponding to the character and aims of the working-class party that is striving for a complete socialist revolution."[12] But there is a sense in which for neo-Leninists, like the Red Brigades, the real ancestor is Babeuf.

If Babeuf is the original communist terrorist, Buonarroti is the prototypical anarchist. He regarded the French Revolution as a new beginning, a disjunctive moment, a new phase in human history, with terror a kind of essential human energy, a force for the good. He was a patrician of a distinguished family; skilled in mathematics; an urbane and talented literary scholar; and a musician, a role he used to disguise a career punctuated by "arrests, expulsions, deportations and imprisonments."[13] For him, the underground life consisted of lodges, circles, and codes, a life of permanent danger. There he organized cells and was a follower of the *Illuminati*, a radical freemasonry, and the *Sublimes Maitres Parfaits* (whose supreme command was called the Grand Firmament). His closest friends were the Babeuvists. The French Committee of Public Safety was his model of the state.

Buonarroti represented the revolutionary in romantic guise; his bravado was often carried to the point of foolhardiness, and he was no doubt a bit mad. He had a mania for rules, statutes, ciphers, and certificates, and thought "that in order to form an efficient and permanent political association, men need to be tied to each other by signs, by mysteries that flatter their sense of self-importance" (p. 53). Nor is this different today, for the terrorist cell has its own "legalism," rituals, and texts.

Buonarroti's own text was an unoriginal combination of the writings of Rousseau and Robespierre. It specified the enemies and manipulated friends, and created a myth out of Babeuf's conspiracy. He venerated Jacobins for causing.

> the Constitution of 1793 to be replaced (until the peace) by a form of authority which preserved to those who had commenced the great work, the power of completing it and substituted at once, for the hazards of an open war against the intestine foes of liberty, prompt and legal means of reducing them to impotence. This form was called the *revolutionary Government* and had for its object complete redemption, had not subsequent events destroyed all (p. 71).

He thus legitimized violence and made hortatory vision into a romantic accomplishment. The revolutionary government changed the vast population, once the sport of voluptuousness, cupidity, levity, and presumption, from hedonists to zealots content with "demanding for their all, bread, steel, equality" (p. 70).

For the first time terror forced people to be free, a necessary purge to save them from themselves. The public could not be expected to govern until it was free of all corruptions of the old regime. So Buonarroti exploited the idea of being linked to a select and secret company that "set in motion the Great Revolution, and bequeathed to surviving colleagues the task of bringing it to its ultimate conclusion" (p. 44).

He saw the significance of the cell as the revolutionary nucleus. Whatever its impact at the time, the *Sublimes Maitres Parfaits* was an institution which set a pattern for the future, especially in the strict authority which characterized its relations with similar societies outside its auspices, in the techniques of infiltration and creation of "fronts," and in its cosmopolitan composition. Like the secret societies formed later by Blanqui and Bakunin, it might be described as the private army of the professional revolutionist who created it, who wielded it, and whose life span set a term to its existence. As a product of romantic individualism, it set a vogue that would pass with the Romantic generation itself, but traces of Buonarroti's fine Italian hand would remain in the tactics adopted by the more impersonal conspiratorial organizations that followed (p. 49).

The Cell as Revolutionary Nucleus

Modern terrorists retrieve Babeuf and Buonarroti both as leaders or organizers when they act out in their own lives equivalent metaphors of an underground and violent struggle. Both countenanced terror as the way to freedom, and bequeathed to Left revolutionaries their legacy of legitimate violence. Both believed in the cell as a unique organism, an autonomous life-giving, life-sustaining unit whose violence punishes those living aboveground in their crimes.

In opposition to the cell is the society. Against the revolution is the state. Against the conspiratorial movement is the aboveground cell of the prison and the classroom, both opposite to the clandestine life, both weights of the institutional apparatus applied to the limbs and minds of a citizenry captive and without rights. The life of the revolutionary thus depends on the death of society. Revolutionary punishment is reserved for the crime of the state. The purpose of violent and clandestine acts is to separate society from state and to redeem the former by destroying the latter.

While life "below" is very different from that "above," not much is known about it. Do recruits have feelings of impotence or intellectual inadequacy for which violence compensates (as Stalin supposedly felt when he went underground as a party terrorist, compared to Trotsky, who went abroad)?[14] Does a high degree of personal guilt, transmuted into passionate hatred, distinguish such people? Do they act out early social betrayal after previous attempts to "act" fail? Do some make a fetish of violence and its instruments?[15] Are violent acts proof of authenticity? Does the willingness to engage in outrageous attack serve as a ritual transposition of previous shames? Do terrorists engage in competition with one another to take on the most visible dangers and risks? These questions have particular relevance to the xenophobic life of the cell when it has achieved total affiliation.

Moreover, with total affiliation comes the paradox of complete devotion and extreme wariness. Available evidence shows that even in the most disciplined cells there is much wavering between loyalty and suspicion. Everyone is potentially unreliable; thus members are continually tested for proof of loyalty or renewal as new initiatives inspire more terror-prone activities, which in turn reinforce or renew commitment. Although leaders operate within intensely personal networks of relationships, they are haunted by the possibility of informers and *agents provocateurs*. Meanings become peculiarly joined. Political acts of devotion reappear as shared sexuality. Self-accusation and vindications add to the internal torture. The occasional outrageous crime is both a demonstration of purity and commitment and a necessary catharsis. There is also a curiously abstract quality to such personalism that has long-range effects on the personality.

These and other factors are common to Left terrorism in particular. Connections between intimacy and discipline are crucial in each group. Freedom of action requires intimacy, obligation to a leader. But the leader is metonymic for the doctrine. If the cell is to be sufficiently tough to survive under any and all conditions, the individual must be entirely controlled. And the cell is everything. A biological metaphor that not only extends outward to society, it operates inwardly as well. Males and females not only manipulate weapons, but each other. The cell is subject to the same pressures and tensions that all bio-relationships generate.

One can extend the metaphor. The cell is produced in a "culture" that provides virtually no initial warmth, moisture, or protection. It grows in dark places underground, shielded from the sun. Yet no matter how vulnerable and primitive a form of life, it must become the foundation of renewal. This simplest form of existence, capable of infinite growth and permutation, requires intimacy without a corrosive dependency. The cell is as independent as its members, for once they have been controlled by abstract personalism, the cell itself is as free as its members are collectively to act, depending on the quality of its leadership.

Finally, the power of abstract personalism is that of infinite regeneration. Thus this most primitive form of existence, cell *life*, becomes important, not as any particular cell, but as life itself. And if any member is destroyed, it does not matter much. Another will take his place.

The cell is the metaphor of the minimal life, the microunit of "deconstruction." Its aim is to reduce to impotence all remedial solutions and all *democratic* responses. Its tactics are to force liberals and Marxists to reveal their détente, to expose their common repressiveness.[16] From this standpoint it matters little whether the enemy is the social welfare state or a state-capitalist bureaucracy.[17] The terrorist cell as a nucleus for the new society lives on the anticipation of the death of society.

The symbolism is cell versus superstructure. It is not individuals, who might indeed be quite likable fellows, who are destroyed, but roles—father, king, philosopher, scientist—all those who are part of an institutionalized network that controls, dominates, organizes, and mediates.

Destroying those who represent death in order to liberate life brings us face to face with chaos, the original condition of primitive myth. Transcending it is the necessary starting point for a new order, a new sequence of creation and redemption. Terrorism in its widest sense not only aims to destroy the state, but the place the state occupies as a rational center of modern life as well. Hence, terrorists can attach themselves to virtually any cause, giving voice to any nonsense, plausible or implausible, if it helps to contrast the wordlessness of violent death—which itself becomes a "language"—with the wordiness of a despised legalism. And the cell rejects the failures of previous revolutions; it carries no failures in its genes—only potentiality—despite its pedigree, and repudiates weariness of the kind that beset the radicals of 1968. Such terrorism also universalizes class war as war. (The Japanese Red Army proclaimed this when it announced the third world war had begun.) Hence, too, the cell as army or brigade. It uses such military labels to emphasize *class* war against a generalized middle class, and to radicalize the young to prevent their joining its ranks or becoming part of a technocratic elite. Most Left terrorists seek to mobilize workers and "marginals"—the unemployed and the unemployable—against the social welfare state to bring down liberal-democracy with all its attendant evils, like the "culture of commodities," the "embourgeoisment" of the poor, the co-optation of radicals. But for hierarchy and hegemony to disappear there is need for extreme confrontation and the cooperation of terrorist forces—PLO, the Japanese Red Army, Baader-Meinhof. Such radical and primordial combinations use appropriate tactics to randomize the structure of the most highly organized industrial states, and relies on a moral, universalizing, "expropriated" class (the marginals, the functionally superfluous, the proletariat) and a radical intelligentsia (teachers, lawyers, psychiatrists, and others) to intervene between society and the radical underground, the cell creating its own clientele and its diaspora.

Types of Terrorism

Having speculated about its diverse origins and some of the characteristics of its cellular life, I want now to distinguish between different kinds of terrorism, emphasizing not only their differences, but also what they have in common. It should also be clear that by terrorism I mean the use of illegal violence to gain political ends.[18] Violent tactics alone do not define terrorism. These have always been available, and in one form or another have been used throughout history. Terrorism begins with acts of violence designed to "violate" the legal basis of the state and to injure permanently the instruments on which it depends for order. Left terrorism is against the democratic state, root and branch, and not in favor of rectifying its errors. It has no specific target save the bourgeois state itself. Its definable aims are general—to promote fear, to demoralize, and to randomize social life—but its means are specific—attacking selective targets, real and symbolic. Its purpose is to discredit the state in the eyes of a large sector of society, to cause people to lose faith in the efficacy of democratic solutions, and to become so frightened, they will be a pushover for a militant takeover.

By restricting terrorism to violent acts directed against the state, we not only identify it as a specific phenomenon, but also emphasize the acts of individuals or small groups as opposed to the mass mobilization of cadres or armies, as in a revolutionary war. This definition also implies that acts of terrorism are in some way a retaliation for some presumed violation to a pariah class or other wronged or exploited population. Terrorism thus by its very existence serves as its own explanation for what is wrong with the state, a self-evident morality that legitimizes violence.

This also distinguishes between terrorism and the use of terror by the state. The state can be only metaphorically terrorist, although the terror it uses may be real enough. In modern society, even where the state itself is hated, it is widely accepted that implicit in the very definition of "state" is its legitimate monopoly of violence. This explains why terrorism against the democratic state is so explicitly against it *as a state*, for it can be said only of a democratic state that the use of its coercive power is a truly legitimate way to exercise force. Hence, acts of violence against the democratic state must discredit the state while validating violence. And violence must be restricted in form: it does not include looting or mob action that break out during blackouts or in race riots, because these not only lack specificity but also political ends.

Ends, then, are important. (Robbery, assault and other violent acts, or random murders are more characteristic of right-wing than left-wing terrorism.) To deserve punishment the victim must in some recognized way represent a hegemonic class or an organ of state power. Distinctions must be made between the goals and tactics of the kidnappers of Hans Martin Schleyer or the executioners of Aldo Moro, on the one hand, and fascist bands like *Ordine Nuovo*, *Avanguardia Nazionale*, and other such extreme right-wing groups, on the other.[19]

But there is a second kind of terrorism that may not be directed against the state per se, what we can call primordial terrorism, that is based on ethnicity, religion, race, language, or nationality—a kind associated with nationalism, independent states, revolutions, or civil wars—including terrorism that seeks to break up the domination of a large state over a particular religious, ethnic, linguistic, or racial minority. Among these are Basque, IRA, PLO, and other primordial terrorist organizations whose successes have brought on virtual civil war.[20]

Radical terrorism can easily join with primordial terrorism, so much so that it may be difficult to separate one from the other. Nor can a clear line be drawn between Left or Right primordial or radical terrorism. For a time it was not at all clear whether the Italian Red Brigades were fascist or Leninist (especially where radical Left extremists were anti-Semitic in the classic sense of the term and took pains to ally themselves with the PLO). In turn, primordialism can be Left and Right at the same time. Arafat, for example, despite his "moderate" position among the Palestinians, is a primordial terrorist seeking a national state. He virtually venerates violent means in terms redolent of fascism while supporting Left programs in the name of Arab socialism. Such affinities make possible many alliances and frangible coalitions that defy ordinary detection or control.

	PREDOMINANTLY LEFT	PREDOMINANTLY RIGHT
PRIMORDIAL TERRORISM	Fanonism	IRA
	Basque nationalism	Kurdish nationalism
RADICAL TERRORISM	Japanese Red Army	Neo-Nazism
	Red Brigades	Neo-fascism
	Baader-Meinhof	Third World equivalents like the Chilean FNPL (*Frente Nacionalista Patria y Libertad*).

Figure 1—A Typology of Terrorism

Of the various types of terrorism, Fanonism was perhaps the most explicit about the need for violence as a creative and cathartic transformation (that is, the act of violence itself is the emotional transformation). The purpose of violence is to create a revolutionary consciousness to enable the damned and the wretched by the same acts to become the redeemers of themselves and their colonial masters.[21] Other movements of a primordial kind may employ specific radical goals, such as the Popular Front for the Liberation of Palestine (in contrast to *Al Fatah*).

Under the general heading of Left forms of radical terrorism are the various Leninist, anarchist, and anarcho-syndicalist groups, including those that have roots in Cheism, Maoism, and Left Trotskyism.[22]

Finally, under the general heading of right-wing radical terrorism are neo-Nazism and neo-fascism and their counterparts in Argentina, Spain, and Italy, where they attack the state *and* the Left, as, for example, the bombing of Communist headquarters by *Anno Zero*, *Fenice*, and *Avanguardia Nazionale*.[23]

For all groups the use of terror is both instrumental and consummatory. Instrumental terror is used tactically against carefully selected targets; consummatory violence is an end in itself, an expression of fundamental commitment, a form of discipline where outrageous action is counterposed to the outrageousness of the state. Each act is a metaphorical opposite of the other, with terrorists and police engaged in a ballet of action and counteraction, a ritual killing on both sides.

Terror on the Left

A special characteristic of Left terrorism is that it requires a theory: the closer terrorism is to Marxism, the more theory becomes crucial; the more one moves away from Marxism toward anarchism, the more the act speaks for itself. Thus there is a spectrum of Left radical terrorism with neo-Leninism at one pole and anarcho-syndicalism at the other. (The Italian Red Brigades represent the neo-Leninist; the various "autonomia" groups, the more anarchist.) The more neo-Leninist the group, the more important the text, and the greater the tendency to split or break up over dogma. In contrast, the more anarchic groups are more personalistic. Leadership, money, and love affairs all play more important roles.

For neo-Leninists, discipline is crucial. As individuals they reject the world in order to rise above it. Their conduct should be exemplary, their lives inspiring a new standard of revolutionary conduct. A disciplined radical consciousness is essential to extend proletarian class war. But the proletariat remains the universalizing class. (For anarchists, the lumpens occupy the place of honor.) The purpose of a Marxist theory is to show when terror can and cannot be used: if it cannot serve the interests of the working class, it cannot universalize its gains; it should not be used indiscriminately; and its final acts must be politically self-liquidating. The particular arguments take off from the debates of Kautsky, Lenin, Trotsky, and Luxemburg, all of who linked terrorism to the state under capitalism.

Kautsky ruled out terrorism in all forms as antithetical to both socialism and democracy.[24] Lenin maintained that Kautsky, by using a classic liberal definition of democracy and in its nineteenth century individualistic form, had "deliberately" misinterpreted the distinctions Marx had made between the state and forms of society and argued for state terror, but not for terrorism as such. It is permissible, indeed necessary, for the dictatorship of the proletariat to engage in violence against the hegemonic power of the bourgeoisie in a society in which the laws of governments are instruments of that power. Parliamentary democracy or bourgeois democracy only serves the interests of the bourgeoisie.[25] However, violence against the exploiter is a precondition of the successful revolutionary transition to socialism. In theory, there is appropriate terror and inappropriate terror. Trotsky believed that "terror can be very efficient against a reactionary class which does not want to leave the scene of operations," but he reserves its use until after a successful revolution.[26]

The original debates centered on whether the revolutionary state *should* apply terror. Neo-Leninists today argue that, if the world of the clandestine cell is the mirror image of the aboveground cell, it is, in effect, an underground government, an incipient revolutionary dictatorship of the proletariat; thus violence is appropriate before the revolution has been realized. Terrorism applies, then, before and after the revolution. This is Curcio's answer to the Communist party and to Euro-Communism. Terror alone, and of the most directed kind, will enable the revolutionary neo-Leninist party to go aboveground.[27] This expanded use of terror is an amendment to classic Leninist theory, one in accord with history, an instrument to be used as a substitute for revolution itself.[28] And if it should prove to be the case that the revolutionary dictatorship of the proletariat is rejected by Communist parties, they become part of the state and thus legitimate objects of neo-Leninist violence.

Left terrorism employs a theory that suits its purposes and justifies the necessity for acts by persons against persons, supremely situational acts that violate the essential space, the privacy, and the "property" that mark the individual off from his neighbor. Each act serves as a lesson, an instruction, and thus every nuance must be exploited. Hence, the exceptional importance attached to a captive's voice heard pleading or the public distribution of his photograph, taken as in a police photo. The "prisoner of war" must look broken, his eyes showing fear and vulnerability, his expression passive and defeated, his hair disheveled. But it should also show the face as guilty and villainous, so that the captive is no longer perceived as a real person but merely an impotent representative of his class. All his other characteristics must disappear, and the record made to show he is guilty of crimes, regardless of his virtues, private or public. The prisoner as "filler of the role" is killer of the dream of the bourgeoisie. Hence, too, the impersonality of his murder, the body dumped out of a car or left in a hotel room or a gutter, whatever represents the ultimate gesture of contempt.

But contempt alone is dangerous, "Rightist"—what is required is a durable ethic embodied in a class ally. A good theory provides both, and provides as well a basis for connections—to a proletariat, to primordial movements like the PLO. (The Palestinians, displaced from their land, are the new pariahs, the new marginals of the world, the objects of a new racism, of religious discrimination. In their redemption lies the mutual acceptance of all by all.)

By applying theory to violence in this way, the most rationalistic and primordial affiliations can be combined. Behind the theory is drama and myth.

Terrorist acts enable individuals to figure in events like legendary heroes. Metaphors penetrate the "theory," giving it symbolic density. The job of the leader is to wound the social body, to make it "bleed," to interrupt all those preferred reciprocities of role and class that compose the interstices of power—technical, political, and bureaucratic. Each event—kidnapping an individual, murdering a child, capturing a jet plane loaded with "successful" tourists ("oppressors" condemned to death by the price of a ticket)—is carried out alone or with one or two others, using a relatively primitive technology of grenades, pistols, or rifles against heavily armed gendarmes and tanks); using, in effect, their own bodies, their youth and vitality, to confront the great sagging, tired bulk, the bureaucratic weight of organized society. Monteneros, Red Brigades, Red Army factions, armed Proletarian Nuclei, the Baader-Meinhof—whatever their names, each implies militant collective action. Each offers a theory plus itself as the unit of social restructuring (such as the Italian Worker's Autonomy) or the agent of permanent revolution (such as the Italian *Lotta Continua*). All oppose Euro-Communism as too bourgeois, the USSR as too state-capitalist, and bureaucratic and social democracy as corrupt and exploitative. All have elements of fascism in their "vitalism."[29]

The Disjunctive Moment

If any or all of these different kinds of terrorism are to be regarded as significant, it cannot be because terrorism, owing to its appeal to those profoundly opposed to the status quo, creates more terrorism, although this may be important. In the final analysis, it is the state that creates the conditions for its own downfall; terrorism can only be an efficient cause. Learning to live with terrorism will make it as ordinary as crime or poverty or undisposed garbage. Analysis of terrorism is its own form of social restorative. Sufficiently studied, nothing is shocking. Indeed, examining terrorism has become a growth industry. Psychologists, police chiefs, specialists on violence, deviant behavior, counterintelligence professionals—all are busy helping to repair the damage and restore "rationality" by determining causes. When terrorism becomes commonplace it can be accepted. Accommodating to terrorism is certainly one solution.

But such solutions do not always work. A historical parallel might be useful. Compare the "revolutions" of 1848 and 1968. Both failed. The failure of the first stimulated anarchist and other terrorist movements in Europe, particularly in Russia. The failure of 1968 left a smaller but powerful residue of intensely passionate political doctrinaires and exalted revolutionaries.

In Tsarist Russia, where there was no possibility of liberal political reform, the most totalistic solutions seemed plausible. A sophisticated elite, unable to mobilize a backward peasant society, and subject to the most rigorous terror, turned to romantic populism and the extreme response. Acts of violence were interpreted as proof of personal strength, of purity of emotion, and of inner liberation from political fear. One remained a Hegelian, albeit a tormented one, to preserve transcendence as the only possible solution. One knew what to be against with all one's might, not only the despotic state, or the depraved state of society, but weak-kneed liberals,

especially those who begin revolutions and then try to extinguish their consequences, who at the same time undermine the older order and cling to it, light the fuse and try to stop the explosion, who are frightened by the emergence of that mythical creature, their "unfortunate brother, cheated of his inheritance," the worker, the proletarian who demands his rights, who does not realize that while he has nothing to lose, the intellectual may lose everything.[30]

Transpose to 1968. Replace the despotic state with the corrupt bourgeoisie, the peasantry with the lower middle class. Add a new Hegelianism, revive Gramsci, Lukacs, and an overdetermined Althusser. Once again the enemy is the despised liberals and their democracy. Nor are orthodox Socialists or Communists immune, for they, like liberals, have betrayed the workers. One is against the social welfare state or the totalitarian Stalinist. It is all the same. And just as the liberals in Russia betrayed the working class by fleeing abroad, erstwhile militants of 1968 voted with their feet into the ranks of the bourgeoisie, the administrative service, or the Communist party. Like old soldiers reveling in chic nostalgia, they live off radical capital, the "coupon-clippers" of the Left. Terrorists, looking back in anger on the generation of 1968, see it as all self-indulgence and no self-discipline. Its revolutionary "production" consisted of nothing but theater and text, books attacking books, pamphlets attacking pamphlets, a battle that only mystifies as its revolutionary rhetoric exhausts. Radical terrorism is the hard core left after the meltdown of a proto-revolutionary generation.

But such parallels do not really work. More structured explanations of terrorism, more linked to development and its discontents, are required. Indeed, we live in a world that promises more and delivers less all the time. And if ours no longer is an age of development, a decline in belief in it prejudices normal solutions. Add to this the doubt that science in the service of mankind will live up to its promise. Accept that poor states will continue to be plundered by rich ones; that the prospects for man will worsen rather than improve, that the golden age of man's intelligence is gone, turning our patrimony into a wasteland; and that perversity rules through a privileged caste, reducing most of the world's population to a condition of marginality—and we confront the disjunctive moment, the specter of superfluous man, an insight so Gothic as to make terror seem like a natural outcome.

Indeed, if "curvilinear growth", with its booms and busts, is associated with crisis and the modern state, this, then, is the general predicament to address. If under these economic conditions the state appears powerless to prevent a new class struggle between the functionally superfluous (the unemployed and unemployable) and the functionally significant, (those whose skills are essential to the economy); and if functional polarization and expanding marginality—overwhelming numbers on the dole—increase the social overhead costs of society while productivity declines, one can expect, in due course, new opportunities for modern versions of Babeuf and Buonarroti. How easy it is to revive the radical Jacobin tradition is the basic lesson of the sixties. Whether or not the state will become vulnerable to the assaults of terrorism may be the lesson of the seventies. What may save us is the gap between the disjunctive moment, in which all crises are blended into one grand overdetermined condition, and how well terrorism has prospered; for to seize the moment, terrorism requires an appropriately cosmocratic leadership, an effectively organized cell structure, the support of a more general radical elite, and a significant degree of identification with a class, either proletariat or marginal. If all are in place, terrorism will have a chance in precisely those liberal and democratic states that fail to cope with the negative consequences of curvilinear growth, the inequities that result from it, and the deepening of public uncertainty to the point where primal chaos looms large as the common personal predicament. Then the primitive solution, the mythic one, becomes plausible as a substitute for more realistic solutions. Then terrorism can grind bureaucratic institutional facilities to a halt, invade the psychic space of individuals, explode the natural meeting grounds of people, and ensure that the conventional mediating institutions work at cross-purposes.

The success of terrorism thus needs to be measured by the impotence of government, but also in the degree that people withdraw from society, retreat from civility, and avoid public space, to live instead with alarm systems, dogs, and guns, all instruments of a society where every man is for himself, the hermetic society, a society without trust or obligation—a condition under which cell life prospers. Under such circumstances, too, a wider clientele makes itself available to terrorists. Those more sympathetic to violence place themselves in the service of moral or redemptive ends, and liberal solutions and democratic means become so discredited, they appear as part of the problem, not the solution. The whole distance between 1848 and 1968, and between the French Revolution and the Russian, is the idea that the pluralist state cannot transcend its developmental predicaments, and in the act of trying, will only make matters worse.

Terrorism and the State

This brings us to the relationship between terrorism and the state itself. Braudel in his massive work on the Mediterranean showed how, at the moment of their apotheosis at the end of the 16th century, the city-states of Europe— Venice, Genoa, Ragusa, and Florence—had already passed their prime. For a brief moment the Spanish Empire replaced them as an instrument of world commerce, trade, and political power. But the latter, unable to extricate itself from an oppressive mercantilism and an excessive political centralization, became vulnerable to the twin forces of capitalism and the territorial state that replaced both the city-state and the mercantilist empire.[31]

Today we question whether the nation-state is not similarly endangered. Increasingly fragile, overextended, and unable to handle the major problems and predicaments of curvilinear growth, the fundamental question is whether old forms of political jurisdictions are becoming outmoded and new responses to functional needs required. Although it seems unwise and premature to prophesy the death of the nation-state or to suggest that it is likely to wither away now or in the near future, it is an open question whether it can endure intact in the face of chronic difficulties. If violence remains endemic, some new forms, new jurisdictions, indeed new solutions will be necessary. These are matters we have barely begun to confront.

Moreover, we are theoretically and politically unprepared for the uncertainties and contradictions of modern social life. The alliance between growth and government that has prevailed within a context of nationalism, the connection between territoriality and democracy, and the notion of government as a system of public rationalities and choices can no longer be taken for granted. In this sense, development generates not only economic crises, but the crisis of rationality and legitimation suggested by Habermas as well. If these lead, in addition, to a crisis of motivation, the decline of the nation-state and terrorism may easily become mutually precipitating. Only a small number of violent people are necessary for terrorism to become effective. Not surprising, it is in Italy—where the effects of curvilinearity are already visible, and government falters—that terrorism is having its greatest success, so much so that even bands of twenty-five or fifty terrorists, if they are sufficiently determined and shrewd, can give the impression that society is falling apart.[32] When curvilinear growth helps stimulate terrorism, terrorism itself creates additional terrorism and the support of an outside clientele, a body of sympathizers who share the aims and purposes, if not the method, of the terrorists. Add a diaspora, an external population more "terrorist than the terrorists," as in the case of the Provisional IRA or the PLO or the FALN, and a given terrorist movement can depend not only on its own internal activities, but on the support of groups abroad as well, a worldwide collaboration, a clandestine "pluralism," an underground of coalitions that can share any occasion and use one another's facilities and good offices.

If, on the other hand, governments can prevent functional polarization and a decline in productivity, and the social overhead can be paid for by the general population without too much sacrifice, opportunities for terrorism will remain episodic and irregular.

This suggests that if we are to avoid disjunctive moments and over-determined crises, neither the liberal social welfare state nor its Marxist alternative will do. Each is a better critique of the other than a solution. It may be that we need to think in terms of multiple jurisdictions and to reconsider whole constructions of territory and new concepts of governing them.

> Freedom, wherever it existed as a tangible reality, has always been spatially limited. This is especially clear for the greatest and most elementary of all negative liberties, the freedom of movement; the borders of national territory or the walls of the city-state comprehended and protected a space in which men could move freely.[33]

It was the job of the liberal territorial state to add more positive liberties, and for this purpose it enlarged its territories and jurisdictions. It may be that the lesson of both development and terrorism is that such jurisdictions and the forms that go with them now need more substantial modification than we think. And if we resist the kind of projective consideration these require and cling to more modest solutions, it might be useful to recall Marx's comment that

> the more powerful a state and hence the *more political* a nation, the less inclined it is to explain the *general* principle governing *social* ills and to seek out their causes by looking at the *principle of the state*, i.e., at the *actual organization* of society of which the state is the active, self-conscious and official expression. *Political* understanding is just *political* understanding because its thought does not transcend the limits of politics. The sharper and livelier it is the more incapable is it of comprehending social problems.[34]

The large question posed by terrorism is whether the state as we know it is becoming obsolete.

REFERENCES

[1]The research on which this paper was based was made possible through a grant from the Concilium on International and Area Studies at Yale University.

[2]For example, the Japanese Red Army has apparently rejected hijacking as a tactic. A Japanese Red Army terrorist wrote in an open letter to his mother from Beirut in 1978, (published in a radical but ephemeral journal) that, after the Dacca incident, his faction had decided such tactics were wrong. Too many innocent people were endangered, taking away from the seriousness of the Red Army's purpose, i.e., to show that terrorism was a necessary response to the "official" terrorism of the state.

[3]Michael Baumann, "The Mind of a German Terrorist," Encounter, April 1978, 61 (3).

[4]Jürgen Habermas, Legitimation Crisis (Boston: Beacon Press, 1975), p. 50.

[5]Peter C. Ludz, "Ideology, Intellectuals and Organization: The Question of Their Interrelation in Early 19th Century Society," Social Research, Summer 1977, 44 (2): 260-307.

[6]Norman Cohn, The Pursuit of the Millennium (New York: Harper, 1961).

[7]E. J. Hobsbawm, Primitive Rebels (Manchester: Manchester University Press, 1959). See also Anton Blok, The Mafia of a Sicilian Village 1860-1960 (New York: Harper, 1975).

[8]John Anthony Scott, The Defense of Gracchus Babeuf (Amherst, Mass.: University of Massachusetts Press, 1967), p. 7. The sansculottes were "men who possess, as it were, no means of livelihood other than the work of their hands."

[9]J. L. Talmon. The Origins of Totalitarian Democracy (London: Seeker and Warburg, 1955).

[10]p. 44.

[11]V. I. Lenin, Two Tactics of Social-Democracy in the Democratic Revolution (New York: International Publishers, 1935), p. 47. (Italics added) This pamphlet was written in July 1905, after the split with the Mensheviks.

[12]Ibid., p. 48.

[13]Elizabeth L. Eisenstein, The First Professional Revolutionist: Filippe Michele Buonarroti (1761-1837) (Cambridge: Harvard University Press, 1959), p. 19. All subsequent quotations in this section are from Eisenstein.

[14]Robert C. Tucker, Stalin as Revolutionary (New York: W. W. Norton, 1973), pp. 91-143.

[15]Baumann, "The Mind of a German Terrorist," "Baader was a weapons maniac and later had almost a sexual relationship with pistols . . ." p. 82.

[16]From an interview with Renato Curcio's lawyer, February 16, 1978, Turin, Italy.

[17]In the French election of March 1978, the extreme Left lumped centerist Prime Minister Raymond Burke, Jacques Chirac of neo-Gaullist right, Francois Mitterand of the Socialists and Georges Marchais of the Communists all together, calling them "the gang of four." The New York Times, March 17, 1978.

[18]See Walter Laqueur, Terrorism, (Boston: Little, Brown, 1977).

[19]In the case of Moro, the "main aim was to eliminate the central figure of the system of mediation on which the delicate balance of Italian politics, including the shaky accords negotiated between Christian Democrats and Communists, depended. They intended to bring the hostage to trial as the symbol of their concept of an 'objective enemy,' and of themselves as agents duly appointed by history and invested with powers of life and death." Albert Ronchey, "Guns and Gray Matter: Terrorism in Italy," Foreign Affairs, Spring 1979, 57 (4): 826.

[20]Conor Cruise O'Brien, Herod, Reflections on Political Violence (London: Hutchinson, 1978), pp. 57-81.

[21]G. C. Grohs, "Frantz Fanon and the African Revolution," The Journal of Modern African Studies, December 1968, 6 (4): 543-556.

[22]Daniel and Gabriel Cohn-Bendit, Obsolete Communism, the Left Wing Alternative (New York: McGraw-Hill, 1968).

[23]Ronchey, "Guns and Gray Matter," p. 928.

[24]Karl Kautsky, The Dictatorship of the Proletariat (Ann Arbor: University of Michigan Press, 1964), p. 4.

[25]V. I. Lenin, The Proletarian Revolution and the Renegade Kautsky (Moscow: Foreign Languages Publishing House, 1952), p. 48. "There can be no real actual equality until all possibility of the exploitation of one class by another has been totally destroyed."

[26]Leon Trotsky, Terrorism and Communism (Ann Arbor: University of Michigan Press, 1961), pp. 58-59.

[27]Ibid., p. 179.

[28]A sophisticated attack against this view was made by Rosa Luxemburg. See *The Russian Revolution and Leninism or Marxism?* (Ann Arbor: University of Michigan Press, 1970), pp. 90-108.

[29]G. P. Maximoff, *Bakunin* (Glencoe: The Free Press, 1953), Sam Dolgoff, *Bakunin on Anarchy* (New York: Alfred A. Knopf, 1973), and D. E. Apter, "The New Anarchism and the Old" in D. E. Apter and James Joll, (eds.) *Anarchism Today* (New York: Doubleday Anchor Press, 1973).

[30]Isaiah Berlin, "Herzen and Bakunin on Liberty" in *Russian Thinkers* (New York: Viking Press, 1978), p. 99.

[31]Fernand Braudel, *The Mediterraneans* (New York: Harper & Row, 1972).

[32]"A January 17, 1978 Italian Communist Party (PCO) survey put the number of underground guerrillas at 700 to 800 and the extremists living on the fringe of legality—and often armed—at about 10,000. According to an autobiographical account by the member of the Prima Linea faction published in the Italian weekly *Panorama*, the "combatants" number about 3,000, or about the same as the number of Italian partisans who were active between September 1943 and March 1944." See Ronchey, "Guns and Gray Matter," p. 924. This says nothing of the large numbers of student and ex-student sympathizers and a wider circle of intellectuals, some of whom might be deeply involved on a sporadic or temporary basis, such as Professor Antonio Negri, a professor of political science at Padua University, or some of the sociology professors at Trento University who were teachers of Curcio and other Red Brigade leaders.

[33]Hannah Arendt, *On Revolution* (New York: Viking Press, 1963), p. 279.

[34]Karl Marx, "Critical Notes on the King of Prussia and Social Reform, in *Early Writings* (New York: Random House, 1975), pp. 412-413.

Notes on Contributors

CLARK C. ABT, born in 1929 in Cologne, is president of Abt Associates, Inc., a social research organization in Cambridge, Massachusetts. He is the author of *Serious Games* (1970), *The Social Audit for Management* (1977), and *The Evaluation of Social Programs* (1977), and numerous articles in the field of social research.

DAVID E. APTER, born in 1924 in New York City, is Henry J. Heinz Professor of Comparative Political and Social Development and director of the Division of the Social Sciences, Yale University. He is the author of *Choice and the Politics of Allocation* (1972), *Introduction to Political Analysis* (1977), and "The Mythic Factor in Development Ideology" (forthcoming), and co-author of *Anarchism Today* (1972), *Contemporary Analytical Theory* (1972), and *The Multinational Corporation and Social Change* (1976).

HEDLEY BULL, born in 1932 in Sydney, is Montague Burton Professor of International Relations at Oxford University. He is the author of *The Control of the Arms Race* (1961) and *The Anarchical Society* (1977).

HARRY ECKSTEIN, born in 1924 in Schotten, Germany, is IBM Professor of International Studies at Princeton University. He is the author of *Division and Cohesion in Democracy* (1965) and *Political Performance* (1971) and co-author of *Patterns of Authority* (1965). He is co-editor of *World Politics* and former editor and founder of *Professional Papers in Comparative Politics*.

JAMES FISHKIN, born in 1948 in Washington, D.C., is associate professor of political science at Yale University. He is co-editor of *Philosophy, Politics and Society, Volume 5* (1979) and author of "Tyranny and Legitimacy: A Critique of Political Theories" (forthcoming). He is associate editor of *Ethics* and was a 1979 Mellon Fellow at the Aspen Institute.

RICHARD HAASS, born in 1951 in New York City, has recently joined the Policy Bureau of the U.S. Department of Defense. For the past two years he has been research associate at the International Institute for Strategic Studies. He is the author of *Congressional Power: Implications for American Security Policy* (1979) and is at present completing a study of the Indian Ocean and post-Vietnam dilemmas of U.S. foreign policy.

MICHAEL HOWARD, born in 1922, is Chichele Professor of the History of War at All Souls College, Oxford University. Among his many books are *Studies in War and Peace* (1970), *Grand Strategy* (volume 4 of the UK History of the Second World War [1971]), *The Continental Commitment* (1972), *War in European History* (1976), and *War and the Liberal Conscience* (1978).

GEORGE ARMSTRONG KELLY, born in 1932 in Pittsburgh, is a member of the Institute for Advanced Studies at Princeton University. He is the author of *Lost Soldiers: The French Army and Empire in Crisis, 1947-1962* (1965), *Idealism, Politics and History* (1969), and *Hegel's Retreat from Eleusis: Studies in Political Thought* (1978).

ANNIE KRIEGEL, born in 1926 in Paris, is professor of political sociology and director of the Department of Social Sciences at the University of Paris, Nanterre. Among her many books on working-class and minority affairs are *Aux Origines du communisme français* (1964), *Les Juifs et le monde moderne* (1977), *Un autre communisme?* (1977), and *Le Communisme au jour le jour: chroniques du Figaro 1976-1979* (1979).

JOHN LOGUE, born in 1947 in Denton, Texas, is assistant professor of political science at Kent State University. He is the author of a variety of articles on Scandinavian politics, on trade unions in politics and vice versa, and on industrial democracy. His book "Socialism and Abundance: The Appeal of Radical Socialism in the Welfare State" is forthcoming.

DOUGLAS RAE, born in 1939 in Indianapolis, is professor of political science and a member of the Institution for Social and Policy Studies, Yale University. He is the author of *Political Consequences of Electoral Laws* (1967) and numerous articles on political theory. He is a consultant to the Spanish government on laws governing elections.

Index

Abt, Clark C., xi–xii, 89–100
affirmative action, 37, 38, 44
Albania, 151
Al Fatah, 165
Almond, Gabriel, 28, 33
Amin Dada, Idi, 57, 59
Anabaptists, 159
anarchism, 157, 160–61, 165
anarcho-syndicalism, 165
Angola, 153
Anno Zero, 165
anomie (normlessness), 14, 15, 16
Anti-socialist Laws (1880s; Germany), 70
Apter, David E., xviii, 155–72
Aquinas, Thomas, 117
Arafat, Yasser, 164
Arendt, Hannah, 24
Aristotle, 9
Aron, Raymond, 125
Austria, 77
    Social Democrats and welfare state in, 72, 73–74
Avanguardia Nazionale, 164, 165
Avenir Radieux, L' (Zinoviev), 142–43
Avineri, Shlomo, 23

Baader-Meinhof, 163, 164, 167
Babeuf, François-Noel, 159–60, 161, 168
Bakke v. University of California at Davis, 38, 51
Bakunin, Mikhail Aleksandrovich, 161
Ball, George, 136
Barraclough, Geoffrey, 135
Basque nationalism, 164
Berlin, Isaiah, 28, 39, 55
Beveridge, William, Committee on Social Insurance and Allied Services, 70, 73
Bevin, Ernest, 72–73
Bismarck, Otto von, 70
Blanqui, Jérôme Adolphe, 161
Bluntschli, Johann Kaspar, 9
Bodin, Jean, 21
Bosanquet, Bernard, 21
Braudel, Fernand, 169
Brezhnev, Leonid Ilyich, xviii, 145, 147, 148
Brown, Seyom, 135, 136
Brüning, Heinrich, 73
Bulgaria, 151, 152
Bull, Hedley, xiv–xvi, 111–23, 125, 131, 135
Buonarroti, Filippo Michele, 159, 160–61, 168
Burdeau, Georges, 23, 25–26, 29

bureaucracies, 8
    citizens as clients of, ix, 30, 32
    as "nuclei" of modern states, 7
    uniform solutions vs. interpersonal comparisons of utility in, 48–49

capitalist institutions, egalitarianism in, 37, 46
Carrère d'Encausse, Hélène, 150
Cato, Marcus Porcius, 28
CEAM, *see* Comecon
Childs, Marquis, 69
Chile, CIA intervention in, 106
Churchill, Winston, 73
CIA, as symbol of evil, xiii, 106
citizenship, viii–ix, 21–36
    defined, 27
    legitimacy of state and, viii–ix, 24, 34–35
    limited capacities of, 32–33
    models for, 28–35
    pluralist, 33–34
    rights and responsibilities of, 24, 27, 30–32
    in sociopolitical realm, 31, 33
    "theory of," ix, 35
civic, 27–28
    defined, 27
Civic Culture, The (Almond and Verba), 33
Civic I, 28–29
    defined, 28
Civic II, 28, 30
    defined, 29
civil, 27–28
    defined, 27
Civil I, 28, 30–31, 32, 34
    defined, 29
Civil II, ix, 28, 31, 32, 33, 34–35
    defined, 29–30
club du Pantheon, 159
cold war, 105
Comecon (Council for Mutual Economic Assistance; CEAM), 151–53
    as fully international system, 153
    production coordinated by, 152
Cominform, 152
Common Market (EEC), 152, 153
communism, communist system, xvii–xviii, 103, 104, 122, 130–31, 139–53, 168
    of Babeuf and Jacobins, 159–60
    belief in sovereign state in, xv, 109–10, 120–21
    cycle of, 139–40
    economy under, 141–42, 151
    Euro-, 151, 166, 167
    future of state collectivism in, 148–51
    global expansion as goal of, xvii–xviii, 141, 145, 147–48

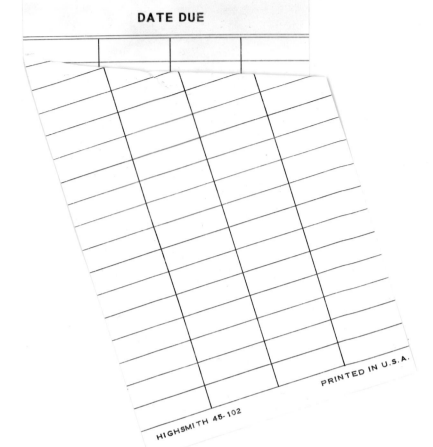

DATE DUE

HIGHSMITH 45-102

PRINTED IN U.S.A.